MW01488626

FRIGHTEN THE HORSES

FRIGHTEN THE HORSES

A
Rusty Coulter
mystery

by
Kurth Sprague

Writers Club Press
New York Lincoln Shanghai

Frighten the Horses

A Rusty Coulter mystery

All Rights Reserved © 2003 by Kurth Sprague

No part of this book may be reproduced or transmitted in any form or by any means, graphic, electronic, or mechanical, including photocopying, recording, taping, or by any information storage retrieval system, without the written permission of the publisher.

Writers Club Press
an imprint of iUniverse, Inc.

For information address:
iUniverse, Inc.
2021 Pine Lake Road, Suite 100
Lincoln, NE 68512
www.iuniverse.com

ISBN: 0-595-26455-7 (pbk)
ISBN: 0-595-74476-1 (cloth)

Printed in the United States of America

For

Bushie, Quin, David, and Charlotte

&

The Bengal Lancers

I don't mind where people make love,
so long as they don't do it in the street
and frighten the horses.

—Mrs Patrick Campbell

Acknowledgments

Souls that have toil'd, and wrought, and thought with me,—
That ever with a frolic welcome took
The thunder and the sunshine...

Warner Barnes, Tom Beckett, Lee Biggart, Robert Blake, Ron Brown, Tom Cable, Jean-Pierre Cauvin, John Chalmers, Ramiro Chavez, Nancy Critchfield-Jones, Paddy Dillon, Herbert du Plessis, Terry Todd, John and Betty Hettinger, Glenn Johnson, Henry Dietz, Rollin Donelson, David Evans, Ellen Fuchs, Sue Fuller, the late Goldia Hester, Rolando Hinojosasmith, Bill Hobby, Martha Hyder, Bill Kibler, Bob King, Linda Kirk, Mrs Masika Lancaster, David Lindh, David Lindsey, Bill Livingston, Roger Louis, the late Bob Lowe, Walter Melnick, Bob Mettlen, Frank Morris, Marlyn Robinson, Tom Shippey, Bill and Sis Steinkraus, George Willeford, the late Charles Alan Wright, and Custis Wright.

＊　　＊　　＊　　＊

I am grateful to the Estate of Sir John Betjeman for permission to quote from "Oxford: Sudden Illness at the Bus Stop."

CHAPTER I

▼

The air in the English department mailroom was chill and dead, with an illusory top note scent of burnt wiring—what you sense more than smell in the aftermath of violence. You find it in lawyers' offices after unforgivable things have been blurted out, or even under the lights in a show ring where somebody's gotten thrown into a jump while you're waiting for the ambulance and Michael Carney's gearing up to play "New York, New York."

By the tree-filtered sunlight through the window I saw Sebastian Roylett lying crumpled on the floor, blood leaking from his ears.

A scream of pure terror shattered the silence.

It all started the Sunday morning before Labor Day, the same day I first met Tom Sturtevant and the girl with the surplice-tied shirt.

I remember waking up a few minutes before four, surprised not so much by the earliness of the hour—I was, after all, an old hand at waking early tangled in the sheets, full of wild regrets and bloody sweats—but by the unexpected reappearance of what had been, actually, a fairly familiar sensation in my life—the letdown aftermath of a successful horse show.

Not that I'd been given a hell of a lot of opportunity to enjoy the modest pleasure I'd derived from coaching plump little Audrey Simmons to a brace of fourth-place ribbons in limit equitation out on a simmering rocky pasture west of town.

Along with a gin-and-tonic reluctantly tendered me by Arthur Simmons at his impromptu tailgate party after the class, I also got the benefit of a lecture on what Art's intentions were, for, as he put it, his daughter's riding career.

As I listened to him, it became clear to me—and, thanks to the volume of Simmons's voice, to the assortment of people standing nearby: one of these, a stocky, sunburnt man in his forties, was smiling broadly—that Stephen Coulter had no place in these plans.

"Nothing against you, Steve, you know what I mean—"

Nobody who knew me called me Steve. At school, college, and in the service, I'd been known as Coulter. The few USW faculty I'd become acquainted with were likely to address me as Stephen, save, alas, for the beautiful Sarah Jane Collins who rarely condescended to use my first name. In keeping a cool, professional distance she took advantage, intuitively, of what I tried to make clear to my students any time they used the "Doctor"—that I didn't come with a stethoscope around my neck, and Mister Coulter was just fine by me. Years ago on the hard-riding, hard-drinking Eastern show circuit I'd answered to Rusty—a nickname that no one in my present world was likely to be aware of.

"It's just that Terri and I"—Simmons bored on—"we've been thinking, and it seems like to us that Audrey would be all things considered happier over at Bobby Robberson's."

I tried not to look at Audrey, slumped on a nearby hay bale against the horse trailer, her face pinched with misery.

"The thing is, we've got to decide on the basis of what's good for the *child*," Terri Simmons, a slender blonde woman in her early thirties, chimed in. I noticed irrelevantly that she was getting fine lines around her carefully lipsticked mouth.

"We've already talked it over with K.C."—K.C. Gordon was the owner of the barn where I worked on weekends and taught free-lance—"and she sees where we're coming from." Terri looked at me earnestly. "It isn't that you haven't done a good job, and we appreciate that, we really do, but with the horses Bobby's got over at Hickory Creek and the chance Audrey'd have there to meet more kids her own age…"

Art, a small real estate developer riding a local building miniboom, weighed in with a self-deprecating smile that didn't quite reach his eyes. "Business the way it is, Steve, we can find her a nice young horse of her own. Bobby just got in a green prospect he wants us to take a look at, and that way they can learn together—"

Pretty soon, I was sure, he would say something about investment. Art was cast from the same mold as university regents who expressed their views on higher education in bottom line terms as the ed biz.

I winced. Better, quicker, and cheaper to hand a child a loaded gun to play around with than a green horse: without an experienced rider to instill confidence, the horse was almost certain to find himself in trouble and hurt himself or his rider. Conversely, an experienced old stager could baby-sit a novice rider and was worth every penny of the price a made horse brought over a green one. Linebacker, K.C. Gordon's wise old gray school horse Audrey'd been riding, may not have been much in the looks or natural athleticism departments, but he did have a powerful sense of self-preservation, which is not a bad thing when you've got a beginner rider up.

Somebody's got to take care of the combination.

I lost track of what Simmons was saying. There was no point in trying to reason with him. He had his mind made up. Nothing I could say would change his mind. Audrey's welfare had little to do with it, really. Once they'd seen the BMWs, Mercedeses, and Range Rovers pulled up outside Bobby's tackroom, Art and Terri would appreciate immediately the networking possibilities presented by a move to Bobby's very social stable.

Bobby was a hardworking young pro with his eye fixed firmly on the main chance. His impressive natural ability, fresh good looks, considerable good-ol'-boy charm, and shrewd business sense far outweighed his frequently abrasive manner and volatile temper. He'd gotten his start, so I'd heard, riding for a respected old professional in Houston who'd rescued him from a childhood of real poverty, a circumstance Bobby was not about to let anyone forget. Then Bobby, so the story went, having learned everything he could, picked up sticks and leased a place east of town, where he was fast doing a thriving boarding business. Some of the really rich of Bobby's youthful and generally affluent clientele had been persuaded to come in as partners in setting him up with a new operation north of town.

Bobby's serious income came from sales, and if he was sometimes a bit quick off the mark matching up customers with appropriate horses, it was well known that he always stood ready to take the first one back and find you another—inevitably, of course, for a bit more money. Naturally, new boarders flocking to Bobby's were soon put on notice—sometimes by various ingenious methods—that the horses they brought with them were really not suited for competition in the kind of company Bobby had in mind for them. But not to worry, Bobby always had lots of prospects coming in from the East. If some of the new acquisitions, so relaxed and exquisitely mannered in their first few days at Bobby's, suddenly underwent a startling transformation into iron-jawed orangutans with eyes rolling around like chromium balls in a pinball machine, a circumstance that I privately attributed to sudden withdrawal from generous doses of acepromazine, why, for a training fee plus about a hundred bucks a round, Bobby would prep your new horse for you till it was ready for you to take into the ring. Maybe. That was where the investment notion was so seductive. All you had to in the meantime do was go get your picture taken for the cup and the cooler and pop the cork on another bottle of Dom Perignon and stand around the shows talking to your friends about investment possibilities, and you might never have to climb on.

There is the school of thought that holds that a good horse is far too valuable a commodity to entrust to its owner, and Bobby was one of its principal exponents. Some of Bobby's owners had the gall to go out to the stable to ride their expensive new horses a couple of times a week; a few of them of them even insisted upon showing them. But after a couple of times of splurging for a whole weekend—motel, steak dinners, baby-sitters, the works—and turning up for a class and learning that the class had already been held or canceled, or the horse had colic, or it had grabbed a new handmade aluminum shoe and torn up a hoof—disasters that never seemed to occur when Bobby handled the riding chores—most owners learned to indulge their pride of ownership by taking their nags out to graze on the end of a halter shank twice a week and feeding the odd carrot.

Bobby had his ways.

If Audrey didn't work out with the horse and Art Simmons decided he'd had enough and wanted to get out from under his investment, I suspected he'd be in for a not very pleasant surprise. By the usual terms of his agreement with his boarders, Bobby collected commissions on every horse bought or sold out of the barn. This meant that if Art Simmons went through on his intention to buy a horse from Bobby, the price he paid, perhaps $15,000 for a decent novice horse, had included in that price not only what the previous owner was getting, but Bobby's commission as well—anywhere from 20% to 40%—the seller's agent's commission—another hefty whack—and, a grace note to the art, a third commission going to the dealer who'd put seller and buyer together. That's why amateur owners hardly ever get what they pay for their horses when it comes time to sell them. Of the $15,000 Art was going to pay Bobby, the previous owner, probably another little girl like Audrey, would be lucky to receive $2500 to $3500.

When I remained silent, I could tell that Art was feeling cheated. Done out of the argument for which he'd clearly prepared himself and had apparently been looking forward to, Art wasn't about to be deprived of blood.

"I mean, let's be honest, shall we, it isn't as if you were doing a lot of showing yourself—" This was a point well-taken even if it did make me uncomfortable, since Bobby commonly rode four or five horses a class and, I reminded myself, taking his lumps, while I hadn't shown over fences for years. Not that I hadn't wanted to.

"—or making any big effort to expand K.C.'s operation and get to the big shows. In fact, you seem just as happy to stay right where you are. With Bobby, Audrey'll have the opportunity to be with kids her own age, meet people—"

Important people, Art Simmons meant to say, not someone like Stephen Coulter who did something over at The University and gave riding lessons at a rundown barn south of town in his spare time.

*   *   *   *

Later, I bumped into Bobby Robberson on the way to the concession stand. Excusing himself from a knot of adoring teenage girls and their equally rapt mothers, he signaled me to hold up for him. "Simmons get a chance to talk to you?"

"Yes. He said they were going to start Audrey riding over at your place."

"Yeah. Well." He bestowed on me his famous boyish grin. "They told me they wanted to get involved more, buy a horse, make the big shows."

"You'll like the kid, she's got some talent."

"Screw the talent," Bobby said cheerfully. "Question is, her daddy got bucks? But what I saw of her, I got to admit she ain't bad. Get her a decent horse, make her lose about ten pounds, stick out her tits—you got to admit she don't show a lot in the lungs department—fix up her hair, she'll knock 'em dead in junior."

The extremely competitive junior hunter division was notorious for inducing in its riders anorexia, bulimia, temper tantrums, and plain nervous breakdowns. Horses showing in that division commonly went for six figures. If Bobby's well-known Pygmalion tendencies didn't do a number on Audrey, the pressure from the precocious nymphets in his barn surely would. The pressure, and the necessity for owning a very expensive horse in order to compete on anything like even terms: Art wouldn't be the first parent to be seen moping around the shows looking poleaxed and leaden-eyed. For his sake I hoped the local building boom continued unabated.

"No hard feelings?" Bobby looked anxious and then reassuring himself that I wasn't going to make a fuss, and because he was Bobby and couldn't help himself, in derision of the effete Eastern tones he appeared to detect in my speech or in scorn for middle age, added, "old man. And, say, Coulter," he went on, "understand this is a done deal. I don't want you giving me any shit over this, you hear?"

*   *   *   *

"I mean, what else could you expect?" K.C. asked me later, her homely face creased with concern. "The Simmonses weren't going to stay around forever with what we've got in the way of horses for Audrey to ride. They wanted to go on to better things."

I had tried to explain that Linebacker was a good horse for Audrey. K.C. looked doubtful. "They said you only put her over two fences before the class, was that a good idea? I don't know much about it, but it seems to me the other trainers, they put their kids over, I don't know how many jumps before a class. More than two, anyway." Yes, I nodded in agrement, tactfully refraining from pointing out to her that horses taken over a great many jumps before a class often tended not to do so well when they at last went in front of the judge: in horsemen's jargon they were said to "leave their best rounds in the warm-up ring."

"Did you see her smile today?"

K.C. nodded hesitantly.

"She was having fun," I said. "Do you think she's going to have fun over at Bobby's?"

K.C. looked at me wonderingly. "I never thought of it that way." She considered, and then added slowly, "I never thought of you thinking that way, either."

I smiled.

"You want to watch out for Bobby, you know," she said. "He is a bad man." Her old-fashioned choice of words impressed me. I would have done well to have heeded her advice.

*   *   *   *

Besides losing the Simmonses as customers I had other reasons for feeling depressed when I awakened at four on Sunday morning. The rent on my efficiency apartment was four days overdue, I owed on my credit card, and the nice lady at the bank had been leaving messages on my answering machine almost daily during the past week.

In addition, the check from The University for my summer's teaching was two days late.

But today was the day, I encouraged myself as I got out of bed, when I'd at least know for certain if the department wanted me back to teach in the fall—the fall semester beginning, naturally enough, the day after tomorrow.

Uneasily, I reflected that the flaming row I'd had with Roylett on Friday afternoon was hardly likely to put my name at the top of his list when it came time for the chairman to choose who among the lecturers would be invited back to teach.

I drank a cup of instant coffee standing at the sink. Then I put on my running clothes and left the apartment and made my way down the stairs in the dark and went out past the pool and out the gate.

I picked up a jog through the streets, silent save for the slapping of my feet against the asphalt. I made my way east on Twenty-Sixth Street, turned south on Seton two long blocks to Twenty-Fourth, gained speed heading west down the long hill past the lawn-surrounded tennis courts and across Lamar and over Shoal Creek bridge.

As I started to pump up the steep incline of Windsor Road, I broke a sweat and my breath began to rasp in my chest. Breasting the top of the hill I bore north along Harris Boulevard, then I followed Wooldridge, neighborhood of doctors, lawyers, bankers, investment counselors, and others who slept o' nights—no youthful harlot's curse would blast these magnolia-scented streets—domestic disturbances of the sort that got on the police blotter were rare, though I had early one morning seen a woman no longer young, blonde hair disheveled, standing on her blue lawn, barefoot in her wet nightdress suffused by the mist from the sprinklers. She was holding a glass and I thought she could be crying. From the shadows behind her, I heard a man's voice, low, urgent, entreating. I had kept on running.

I turned sharp west, then ran south on Hartford Lane; crossed Windsor, and headed up Niles Road, with more lawyers, doctors, insurance men, more of the few remaining gentlemen and ladies with private means, and I extended my stride, freewheeling down the hill back to Shoal Creek and Lamar, where, digging deep within myself, I began a final sprint up Twenty-Fourth.

Winded, I dropped to a walk for the last hundred yards to the Circle K at Rio Grande where I bought a newspaper with the silver I'd held clenched in my fist.

"Damn paper, they don't deliver till six." It was a lean gray man I sometimes saw running in the early morning. He smiled ruefully, exasperated by this latest confirmation of moral decay in the national character as evidenced by the fact that paperboys no longer felt under any pressure to deliver newspapers to subscribers before six in the morning. It was true. I hadn't seen the paper being delivered anywhere on my run, though there were piles of today's newspapers already piled up in the store.

Back in my apartment I went over to the stove and put the water on to boil for the Medaglia d'Oro espresso. Then I stripped off my running clothes and stood under a tepid shower. I was toweling off when the kettle started whistling. I poured the boiling water into the top part of the coffee pot and went back to shave and fight the morning gag reflex as I brushed my teeth. Booze, cigarettes, and black coffee: *I treat my body like a temple*, an aerobics instructor who'd provided a pleasant if temporary interruption to my celibacy once told me: *you treat yours like an amusement park.* I regarded myself without enthusiasm in the mirror. Wide-set, deep-sunk, spit-gray eyes. Unruly auburn hair—what horsemen call singed chestnut: hence my nickname. High cheekbones, narrow face. A chronically peeling beak of a nose, saved from a too-close resemblance of one of those high-bridged numbers bestowed by painters like Raeburn or Reynolds on their aristocratic patrons by twice having been broken in falls. An even six feet tall, I weighed just shy of 165 pounds.

I sat down at the kitchen table with my coffee and a cigarette and read the paper. Afterward I started in on my daily stint with Sir Jonah Barrington's *Historic Memoirs of Ireland.* Twenty minutes later I got up from the table and washed out the coffeepot and put the cup back on the drainboard. I turned out the lights and left the apartment and went down the stairs and out to the street where my car was parked.

Dew pearled the windshield despite the heat, and as I allowed the engine to warm up I worked the wipers. Then I switched on the headlights, pulled the brake release, put the car in gear, and turned south on San Gabriel, driving in the predawn darkness through the sleeping west university neighborhood to the Circle K over on Fifteenth Street where I bought a pack of cigarettes and a twenty-ounce Daybreaker coffee refill and headed over to the interregional and turned south, enjoying my cigarette and taking cautious sips of the scalding tasteless coffee. At six, just as I passed St Anselm's, the local classical music station came on the air with Fauré's *Requiem.*

Five miles south of the river I left the expressway and headed east where the country opened up. Around the edges of the big air base clustered fast food outlets, convenience stores, pawn shops, and trailer parks. A mile past the air base I turned right on a county road, drove past a complex of Little League baseball fields and the Del Valle Independent School District Opportunity Center and the Travis County Correctional Complex where I'd read that, under court order, they'd built two sweat lodges for the recreation and religious practice of the Native American prison inmates. Four miles later I turned left at a restaurant called Little Vietnam. On my right were large oak and pecan trees, a pond, and rotting post-and-rail fencing.

Sempiterna…Requiem.

A gravel drive wound through the trees. Up ahead, behind the small house that served as the stable office with tack room added on, was the long, low stable, built of cinder block and cedar siding. Next to the stable was a concrete pad and picket line that served as a place to groom and wash the horses, a seldom-used stocks made out of three-inch pipe where a vet could deal with the odd dangerous patient, and an ancient six-horse gooseneck trailer. There were often several two-horse trailers in various stages of decrepitude parked helter-skelter; some customers trailered in for lessons on the weekends and stabled with us for shows.

I pulled up in front of the stalls and got out and stood contentedly in the dimness, listening to the last of the Fauré before switching off the ignition and taking pleasure in the smell of parched summer grass and horses. Momentarily there seemed to me to be a poignant oneness to the multitudinousness of life: my running shoes on the nighttime streets, the arrogance of young Barrington toward the Irish patriots, the grandeur of Fauré's music, and the grace of horses.

CHAPTER 2

▼

When I flipped on the lights from the breaker box next to the feed room, horses popped their heads out inquisitively over the stall doors, ears alert.

For conformation the six horses weren't exactly what you'd pick to lead into the ring at Upperville, but they did have their distinct personalities. As I grained them according to the amounts scrawled on the small Dri-write bulletin boards in front of each stall, I glanced at the nameplates on the stall doors and marveled anew at the difference between their brave show names and what they were known by in the stable. A seal-brown four-year-old thoroughbred just off the track, Classy Minx was known in-house as The Mare—and by me, in private moments, as Bitch Kitty. She was owned by Janice and Rick Damon, a pair of pale, lean young orthopedic surgeons.

They resembled each other unnervingly, even to similar unisex haircuts, and were generally attired in scrub suits or expensive and rather ostentatiously shabby running clothes.

They enjoyed a flourishing practice—when, that is, they were home and available. They concentrated their medical practices into bursts of two or three months in order to afford the expensive and time-devouring enthusiasms to which they were susceptible: whitewater kayaking in Nepal, African safari photoshoots, a brief fling with bungee jumping, skydiving, wind surfing, and modern pentathlon. The riding phase of the last led to an interest in horses that resulted in their purchase of The Mare from a colleague in Lexington whom they met at a medical convention. The idea was that they'd come out to ride on the weekends. Possessed of limitless self-confidence—no bad thing if you're a doctor—they apparently didn't worry about the effect of a horse being kept up in a stall and fed grain during the rest of the week. The truth of the matter was that neither one of them had much time to ride, so the thing was doomed to failure even if they'd known what they were doing, which they didn't. There'd been ego mixed up in it as well: I'd had a pissy little scene with Janice of this-is-our-horse-and-we'll-do-whatever-we-wish-with-her, and I of-course-you-must-do-whatever-you-think best, I-was-just-trying-to, etc. Result: a bloody shambles. Janice took a bad spill and Rick, all manly and protective, climbed on and got run away with. When I (calling in early evening, warbling in lowest key) offered to ride The Mare a couple of times a week and work the kinks out, no expense to them, they'd seemed relieved, but made it clear they were doing me a favor. Which in a way, they were: I liked her.

Subtext—plain Harry in the barn—was owned by a colleague of mine from the English department, who listed her name unselfconsciously on the nameplate as Professor Joan Strossner-Boynton. She schooled the immense, glossy-coated Dutch Warmblood with the same intensity that she brought to bear in deconstructing texts in the classroom. The other four horses were K.C.'s: Evening Shade—Kevin in the stable—was a tall gent with doubtful ankles who reminded me of Walter Pidgeon in one of those grand old flicks—I always half expected him to come out with a scarf and a cigarette holder. The others were equally venerable stagers—George, Warren, and Murray—or, to give them the names they enjoyed during their brief and undistinguished show careers, Linebacker—Audrey's mount from the day before—Far West, and Intrepid, the last, despite his name, a notorious quitter at anything over eighteen inches high.

I finished topping off their water buckets and as I coiled the hose and hung it on its bracket I glanced over toward the indoor dressage ring nestled back in the trees. Some of K.C.'s boarders liked to use the ring at odd hours and had a habit of leaving the lights on after they got through, thus adding another expense to an already foundering-with-debt enterprise.

It's a sad fact that all but the most successful stables are run on the ragged edge of financial disaster, woefully undercapitalized but typically possessing a zany overabundance of optimism and wholly unrealistic love of horses. Many stable owners—and K.C. Gordon was a case in point—were not infrequently canny business people in the real world, but when it came to horses threw their common sense out the window. As a matter of fact, if you can scrape enough money together to open a barn and already possess or pick up along the way a modicum of charm, you needn't suffer from not knowing anything about horses. The average guy just getting into the sport by way of buying a horse for his kid doesn't know zilch about his trainer's credentials and more often doesn't give a damn, just so the kid, usually a daughter, gets through the half dozen years from teddy bears to football studs without turning into a druggie or a dropout or both and so long as the stable's located somewhere close to home, preferably not too far off the beaten track from school to supermarket to orthodontist.

I needn't have worried about a careless boarder running up the electric bill—the ring was dark.

Settling myself at the battered desk in the stable office, I began to sort through the pile of mail that had accumulated during the week and that K.C. had left for me to deal with. Earlier in the week I'd worked at the monthly customers' bills and these I put in a folder for her to look over before sending out.

There were a couple of premium lists from local shows that I noticed with a pang of regret were offering classes that would have been ideal for the little Simmons girl to compete in without being overfaced. The Christmas Show was announcing that it would be held

Saturday and Sunday, the twenty-first and twenty-second of December. It was our largest show of the year, held out at the county exposition center, and everybody liked to go to it.

There were also bills: vet bills, farrier bills, bills for the hay and shavings we used for bedding. And the federal withholding tax and social security invoices for Joe Chavez, the weekend stable help, which had been due the end of July but which K.C. had only recently gotten brave enough to take out of her handbag and leave out on the table for me to deal with.

I went over to the filing cabinet and found Joe Chavez's folder, thumbing through the various bits and pieces till I came across his W-4 which I noted with misgiving was three years out of date.

I glanced down the page: Joseph Jesus Chavez, social security number 455-86-1021, home address 1106 Forest Glade, down south of the river two blocks off Ben White, where I remembered I'd once dropped off a pay check for Joe. Most of the houses in the neighborhood had been built, I guessed, sometime in the 1930s. The houses were mostly frame with asbestos or clapboard siding. To the side a short driveway led back to a one-car garage. Vines and weeds grew lushly along the wire fencing between the houses. The original owners, I guessed, had been bookkeepers and clerks and salesmen who were happy to have jobs in the Depression, and they planted trees and tended their tiny lawns and kept their houses painted and in the still evenings sat on their front porches watching the their kids chasing fireflies. They counted their blessings. Now most of the original owners had died or their kids had sold out and moved away. The paint had blistered off on many of the houses, the wood on the windows, doors, and porches was split and cracking, and the roofs were sagging. Both sides of the street were lined nonstop with pickup trucks and cars in various stages of disrepair. But for Joe Chavez and for his wife Estella, who had a good job with the state, Forest Glade was a step up the social ladder from the treeless inhospitable plains of Montopolis east of town where for generations the city's Hispanic population lived and sweltered and were occasionally flooded out.

I looked at my watch. A few minutes before eight. I really couldn't figure the stable's liability until I had an up-to-date-W-4 from Joe, who should be arriving shortly to hay and muck out and clean the water buckets. With that excuse for doing no more, I rose from the desk and went back over to the barn.

After grooming The Mare on the picket line, I led her out to work on the longe line in one of the empty paddocks. When she'd bucked and played the kinks out, she settled down into a low, easy canter, and I leaned against her weight as she circled me on the long rein, clipping the strides off rhythmically against a backdrop of oak trees and bright morning sky. It was easy for me to forget Simmons, debts, the unpleasantness with Roylett and the uncertainty of my future with the English department.

As I led the mare back to the wash rack, letting her put her head down to snatch a couple of bites of grass on the way, I noticed the two visitors, a man and a woman, who'd pulled up in an old blue station wagon sporting state official plates. They'd apparently been watching me while I'd been longeing the mare. The man looked somehow familiar to me. It took me a moment to place him as one of those who'd been standing nearby when Simmons had fired me the day before out at the show. I recalled he'd been smiling, deriving some kind of amusement from the awkward situation. He was stocky, his sandy hair cut short, and dressed in faded red polo shirt and jeans much like the ones I had on. The woman was a good deal younger, and taller than the man, and gave the impression of being athletic. She wore her brown hair carelessly loose, and in the bright sunlight I could see a few strands of silver. She was dressed in a deep watermelon pink surplice-wrapped silk blouse and beautifully-cut, lime green linen Gurkha shorts. On her feet she wore dark rose espadrilles. Flawless skin, pale lipstick accentuating a deep tan, long legs, heavy gold bracelet. When she took off the dark glasses I could see humor lurking in her brown eyes, in the tiny lines fanning out from those eyes. She favored me with a look in which amusement, distraction, and challenge were nicely mixed.

I asked if I could help them.

"This your place?"

"No, I'm afraid not." The man looked to be in his early forties, maybe a couple of years older than I am. "I just work here, give lessons, keep the books."

"I'm Tom Sturtevant," the man said. "This is Mary Linscomb. Saw you out at the show yesterday, thought we'd stop by."

"Stephen Coulter. Are you a friend of the Simmonses? I'm afraid that wasn't my brightest moment, getting my walking papers from Art."

Sturtevant smiled and shrugged and sidestepped saying how well he knew the Simmonses. "We'd been watching you school Audrey before the class. That was one of your lesson horses she was riding, Art said. Do you board horses?"

"Yes, we board a few, mainly dressage prospects or amateur hunters. Audrey Simmons was really about the only junior rider we had. But the person you should talk to is Mrs Gordon, she's the owner. She ought to be here any minute if you'd care to wait. Make yourself at home." Sturtevant thanked me, and I gave them an impersonal smile, awarded points to myself for not staring too obviously at Mary Linscomb's bosom, and turned my attention to sponging off the mare's head. Tire kickers.

I heard the story one hot day when I'd been holding a horse for the talkative farrier, who filled me in on the details. Katrina Christina Gordon had been a successful hairdresser who'd worked her way up to owning her own shop when she'd gotten swept off her feet by a high-rolling wildcatter from Odessa named Vince Gordon. Gordon had a taste for Willie Nelson, Wild Turkey, and, I was guessing, tall girls with serious blond hair from small Czech farming communities who liked to laugh a lot and listen to John Denver's 'Thank God I'm a Country Boy.' For about ten years there was a lot of Willie Nelson and

John Denver, a lot of Wild Turkey, and a lot of laughs. When the bottom dropped out of the oil business in the mid-eighties, Vince's company was one of many that went belly up. At the point of signing bankruptcy papers in his lawyer's office, Vince obligingly keeled over dead of a massive coronary. Creditors took the plane, the seven-thousand-square-foot cottage in Aspen—K.C.'d shown me the spread that had appeared in *Architectural Digest*—they even took Vince's Presidential Rolex and the customized Bang & Olufson hi-fi set-up. They took a big chunk of K.C. as well. She went back to cutting hair, but now she was humming Whitney Houston's 'How Will I Know' with no question mark at the end of the title, and she tuned the Panasonic to another station whenever they started playing 'Whiskey River.' She said it made her cry. One day a Dallas lawyer with a manicure and wearing a white-on-white shirt dropped by and told her she was beneficiary of a half-million dollar insurance policy that Vince had been able to squirrel away out of the reach of the IRS. Now in her late thirties, K.C. was, like a good many people, frustrated in her dealings with other people—she wanted to make for herself some small warm place where she wouldn't get hurt. Helplessly sentimental, blessed naturally with a kind disposition, she bought an old place south of town and, at the time I'd come on the scene about a year ago, had arrived at a weird and uneasy truce with the horses she loved but knew little about. K.C. was two-stepping and Cotton-Eye Joeing it gently into that good Texas sunset, her safe world circumscribed by the shop, the stable, and her small frame house, with weekly Saturday evening forays to the Broken Spoke with a girlfriend, and Sunday mornings at her Sunday school. You can have the rest, she'd told me. I've seen it and once was enough.

I had finished doing the mare off and was setting her up when Joe Chavez arrived. He was a spare, flat-backed man of about forty, black hair combed straight back. We grunted companionably at each other. He watched me rub the mare's legs with liniment and sniffed appreciatively at the juniper and pine oils, thymol, and menthol that helped make up its expensive bouquet. He, too, was a connoisseur of enthusiasms, though drag-racing cars, not horses, were Joe's obsession: the car-buretor intake valve of his gutted 1983 Pontiac was fitted with a special tank supplying nitrous oxide. When he'd reached fourth and popped the release button on the shifter, Joe told me, there was nothing like it. Nothing. *Whoosh.*

Afterward, satisfying myself the mare was cool, I put her up and swept off the picket line and put back the hose. Then I went over to the office and found Joe's W-4 and tracked him down at the hay shed where he was loading the flatbed with bales of coastal bermuda.

"Hey, Joe, K.C. needs to get another W-4 for you, the last one you filed was three years ago."

Joe bounced a bale off his raised knee onto the bed.

"Still married to Estella, right? You still living on Forest Glade? Any kids?"

Joe spared me a faintly ironic glance. Joe and Estella weren't about to get caught in the family trap, especially now that they'd made the jump from the east side of town: he was one of eight, Estella one of ten.

"Any brothers, sisters, parents and so on living with you?"

Joe shook his head in a hard negative.

"Okay, sign right here." I watched Joe sign the form, as always tak-ing pleasure from his confident, well-formed handwriting. Assholes, and I used to be one of them, kept waiting for the cloud of Tres Flores brilliantine and omnipresent salsa blaring out of a jambox. Joe usually tuned his Walkman to the classical music station; he occasionally made delicate, impressionistic sketches of horses, and he possessed a photo-graphic memory, a real advantage in his job at the autoparts store where he'd worked his way up to assistant manager. Most nights he took courses at the community college; his weekend work supported the drag racing. This gave a chance for K.C.'s week-day help, green card exchange students, a chance to head south and see their families for a day or two.

"We on for Wednesday night?" Wednesdays were bingo.

He nodded. "Over at the place on Ed Bluestein? What time?"

"Seven." The bingo place over on Ed Bluestein was the state fire-men's and state fire marshals', I recalled, sanctioned by the Mental Health Association of Texas and something called Parents Anony-mous.

"They got that Double Postage Stamp?"

"Yeah, and the Crazy T, too."

"I guess I'll see you there." He nodded, and I took the paper back to the office, filed it, locked the office and left. Over the summer I had played bingo almost every week. There were a nice group of people there, a lot of them dressed up for the occasion. It was all very quiet and laid-back, except when somebody was shy a number. I didn't see anybody from The University there.

*   *   *   *

Back home I opened the fridge and took out of the freezer from its place next to the ice trays the bottle of José Cuervo Centenario Extra and poured four fingers into a jelly glass and half-filled another glass with Sangrita Viuda de Sanchez—Blood of the Widow Sanchez—a spicy, sweet mixture of tomato juice and orange juice. I knocked back the tequila, and followed it with a mouthful of Sangrita. Then I poured another glass of tequila and took it in with me to the bathroom and put it down on the sink while I took my second shower of the day. Then I polished off the second glass of tequila and what was left of the Sangrita, brushed my teeth, put on clean clothes and took a tuna steak out of the freezer compartment to thaw and marinate with key lime juice and olive oil. Then I drove over to The University to see if my check had come in.

*   *   *   *

The third-largest single-campus university in the nation and one of the top ten research universities worldwide, The University of the Southwest (over 50,000 students, plus another 6000 or so staff and faculty), occupies close to 400 acres situated just north of the complex of state office buildings and the capitol, huge, sprawling, yet possessing a rough beauty of jumbled architectural styles.

The Department of English is in MacFarland Hall, a vaguely Mediterranean, white limestone and red-tile-roofed building on the tree shaded west side of the campus. Across the main drag separating town from gown were the usual university-area cottage industries. There were three churches—Baptist, Catholic, and Methodist—quiet during the week except for the odd funeral and each running its own day care center for harried university parents' children; now, midmorning on a Sunday, halfway through their busiest day, having commenced with early morning mass at St Michael's. There were a bookshop, a record store, a small restaurant run by a Vietnamese family, and a European-style coffee shop which sold battery-acid espresso and fey prints, and rented mailboxes. I drove onto the campus on Twenty-Fourth and wound around the inner campus drive until I found a parking space near MacFarland Hall.

The main door was locked and I had to let myself in with my key. Inside the building, although the air was, as usual for the summertime, dead and chill, I was aware of that crackle of ozone that tells you something's gone seriously wrong. It's the residual stench of danger, of undissipated tension. I've noticed it in lawyers' offices where unforgivable things have just been said; in houses where couples have broken off bitter arguments as you enter the room; and out on a windy hunt course while you're waiting for the ambulance to arrive and everyone is very quiet. Not quite the stink of burning insulation, but a hint of it. Just a whiff.

Spray-painted graffiti smeared the walls and bulletin boards. Papers were strewn across the floors. The work of rage and fury. I made my way down the hall to the mailroom and jiggled my key and opened the door. Triggering recollection, smell bypassed sight and overrode reason: mud and sun and swollen bodies; then, my mother's hospital deathbed.

By the subaqueous light from the window across from the door I saw Sebastian Roylett lying crumpled on the floor, his scalp showing pinkly through his wavy silver hair. Blood had leaked in rivulets from his ears pooling onto the floor. He was lying across the width of the mailroom from left to right, resting more or less on his right side, his face away from me, his right arm and shoulder drawn up underneath and slightly behind him, his torso twisted so that his chest was almost square to the floor, his left arm stretched out toward the far right corner of the room. His blue-gray raw silk jacket was rucked up in back. I could see where his roughly-woven madras checked shirt was tucked into his gray slacks, now soiled with the final humiliation of incontinence. He was wearing soft Italian-style burgundy loafers. On the periphery of my vision I was aware of the bank of mailboxes filling the wall to my right, most of them stuffed with papers, while on the floor beneath were stacked a number of book cartons. Near the chairman's body in the far corner was what appeared to be a very large, thick book. On the left wall was a corkboard with the usual notices pinned up above a table. Past Roylett's body to the left of the window was a small desk and rolling typist's stool and wastebasket.

I looked at him for a moment, lying there, and then, as I'd been taught to do, knelt to feel for the pulse in the juncture below his ear. I heard the door behind me being unlocked, and, an instant later there was a ululation of genuine terror.

CHAPTER 3

▼

I turned my head to see the English department's senior secretary, Amanda Vennible, standing in the doorway, keys dangling from suddenly nerveless fingers, while just behind her pressed assistant professor Sarah Jane Collins.

"Why, Stephen...what on earth are you doing?" Then, squeezing her way past Amanda Vennible, she caught sight of the body on the floor. "My God!"

Chastened by the aftermath of violent death and overwhelmed by sensory overload, I yet noted wryly that Sarah Jane Collins's cool blond beauty had no trouble in claiming my attention. She was dressed in a crisp white blouse, gray skirt, and pale hose. Her usual dazzling smile looked slightly fixed but I was encouraged that the tone in which she had addressed me had been marginally less disdainful than usual: she wasn't one to waste her time on forty-year-old lecturers on the fast track to nowhere.

I moved my hand away from the chairman's head. "It's Roylett," I said. "He's dead." I rose to my feet. There was a little blood on my hand which I wiped off with my handkerchief.

"One of us ought to stay here," I told them. "Use the main office phone and call emergency. They'll send someone."

Sarah Jane looked at me consideringly for a moment as if I were a stranger, and turned and left the room. Amanda Vennible and I faced each other in awkward silence, not altogether attributable to the discomforting presence of the chairman's body lying on the floor behind me.

The last time we had seen each other had been on Friday afternoon as I stalked out of Roylett's office following the quarrel I'd had with the chairman.

"Someone will have to call Mrs Roylett," I told her gently. The chairman's Jamaican wife was never far from anyone's thoughts.

"She's away at a conference," Amanda said. "She isn't due back until tonight."

"Well, then," I began. "Do you have any idea…?"

She tore her horrified gaze from the chairman's body. "It's those damned lecturers. Beddington and that lot. Did you see what they did to the halls?"

I had forgotten the chaos of the graffiti and the strewn papers. The English department and its denizens—including, I recalled, Amos Beddington, an almost incredibly tall, thin, and intense contract teacher once prominent in departmental politics and now fired from his job for getting in a fight with some unlikely person—comprised the world of Amanda Vennible and anything that threatened the sometimes precarious equilibrium of that world Amanda took as a personal affront.

"Miss Vennible, I don't really think—"

"It is, I know it is. That's why we came down. They called me at home from security, and I called Professor Collins. One of their night people reported it. Somebody had been in here over the weekend. Look at the place. Disgraceful."

I was spared having to respond by the sight of the department's associate chairman, Huw Rhys-Davies, appearing in the doorway. Crowding in behind him were an elderly and very plump professor called Ed Vere and the department's lissome undergraduate work-study person, Melody Harker.

Black Welsh, burly, and with a bald head sun-burnished like a mahogany newel-post, deprived during the summer of his usual physical outlet of playing a bruising game of rugby, Huw was obviously ripe for distraction. He, like the others, had been summoned from his upstairs office by Amanda Vennible's screams.

"What in bloody hell's going on here?" He glanced at Roylett's body, then at me, and something he saw in my face must have provided him the answer.

Melody Harker's eyes widened and her hand went up to her mouth. Abruptly she turned, brushed by the gaping Ed Vere standing in the doorway, and fled down the hall, narrowly missing Sarah Jane Collins on her way back from the main office.

"I made the call," reported Sarah Jane, ignoring what I was sure she privately thought of as Melody's inappropriately missish behavior. "I called the emergency number and they said someone will be right here."

"I don't suppose anyone's had a chance to call *la veuve* Roylett?"

"She's at a conference, Huw," I said. "At least that's what Miss Vennible—"

"Professor du Plessis-Roylett's in Chicago," said Sarah Jane definitively.

"I was just saying to Dr Coulter, she's due back tonight," Amanda offered.

"I expect we ought to try to reach her at her hotel. Does anyone know where she's staying?" Huw looked around.

"One of those big hotels near O'Hare, I think she said," Sarah Jane said. "Was it the Marriott?"

"Coulter, see if you can get through to her, will you? Here, take my key."

I went down the hall to the main office and spent a hectic ten minutes dealing with university access codes, and finally losing my patience and charging the call to my telephone card. Eventually I got through to Chicago information and a helpful hotel operator.

Outside the main office I was met by Amanda Vennible, Sarah Jane Collins, and the plump, bespectacled Ed Vere.

"Where's Huw?"

"Professor Rhys-Davies went off to find Melody," said Amanda.

"Really, I must say, Huw does take a lot on himself," Vere huffed. "Turned us out of the mailroom, as if we didn't know enough to leave things undisturbed."

"What about you, Stephen?" asked Sarah Jane. "Were you able to get in touch with Carlotta?"

No, I wasn't, I admitted. They said she'd already checked out.

*   *   *   *

"Do I understand that you were the one who arranged for Carlotta's tickets, Amanda?" Sarah Jane Collins asked. Amanda nodded tightly. "When is she due to return?"

By common consent we had adjourned to the graduate students' lounge to await the arrival of the police.

Keeping my eyes studiously occupied with announcements given prominence on the bulletin board, I reflected that, given the circumstances and the people concerned, the conversation was apt to be depressingly predictable. I just knew two things were going to happen. First, that within, say, five minutes, somebody was going to find it necessary to say something like *Who would have thought the old man to have had so much blood in him?*

The second thing was that, not long afterward, the conversation was inevitably going to be worked around to *Conquistador of the Caribbean.* And, if Huw managed to find Melody and bring her back with him, how long would it take before all of us were tiptoeing ponderously around the late chairman's rumored infatuation with her?

"Ordinarily, faculty are responsible for making their own reservations," commenced Amanda tranquilly in response to Sarah Jane's question. "But in this case Professor Roylett himself asked me to make Mrs Roylett's reservations."

Sarah Jane favored Amanda with a sharp look.

"He asked me to call her that," Amanda said defensively. "He said it saved time. So that's why I know. She is due to return on the six-fifteen American flight this evening."

As she spoke she glanced at me. I reminded myself that to Amanda the department was her whole world. She might have been recalling that earlier in the week, when I'd been at the reception counter to turn in a change of grade sheet, there'd been loud voices from the behind the doors of the chairman's office; equally, if *I* remembered that, she might have been saying, *she* remembered no less clearly the argument I'd had with Roylett on Friday afternoon. (In truth, there was nothing very unusual about loud voices from Roylett's office: that was simply his managerial style, demonstrated with impartiality, like the sign on his desk which said "Words to Live By: Age & Treachery Will Overcome Youth and Innocence.") The message was clear: let the department launder its own dirty linen. I took the hint and remained silent.

"I wonder who will take over as…chair," said Amanda with a sidelong look at Sarah Jane, seeking to make up lost ground for using "Mrs Roylett" instead of the academically correct "Professor du Plessis-Roylett."

"Huw's the associate chairman: I suppose it may be a matter of 'the king is dead, long live the king'." Sarah Jane broke off an uncertain laugh as Huw and Melody appeared in the doorway. "Isn't that right, Huw, you'll be taking over as chair?"

"For the nonce, I daresay, at least till our masters on the executive committee and that mad mullah in the dean's office have had a chance to pass on it. Coulter, did you contrive to speak with Carlotta?"

"The hotel said she'd already checked out."

"Well, she's in for a surprise, isn't she? Back from a conference to find her husband's…dead. I expect one of us needs to go meet her at the airport. Where in the bloody hell are the gendarmes?"

"On the way, Huw," said Sarah Jane. "But surely you ought to be the one to go meet Carlotta; after all, you've known her the longest."

Not long now, I reckoned, till *Conquistador of the Caribbean* got mentioned.

Huw flushed darkly but was spared having to reply by Ed Vere who with surprising tact deflected the potentially embarrassing direction of the conversation by addressing a question to Melody. "Miss Harker, weren't you also attending a conference? With Professor Strossner-Boynton? Was this the same conference as the one Professor du Plessis-Roylett was attending?"

"Why, yes, I did," said Melody, obviously grateful to turn her mind away from Roylett's body on the cold, cold linoleum. "But the one I went to with Joan was up in Pittsburgh, Professor du Plessis-Roylett's was being held in Chicago."

"Oh, I see," Ed Vere said politely.

"Basically, the conference Joan and I attended was on the Canon and Essentialism, from a feminist perspective," said Melody, giving her audience perhaps more information than it needed. "Joan delivered her paper on the first day. It was very well-received. And Ruth Stepnovic from Stanford really addressed some important issues at the round table discussion Friday evening on Identity Politics. When I visited with her afterwards, she said she'd sign my copy of her book, you know, the one called *Icepick and Inner Tube: Studies in Gender Analysis and Transformation in Master Narratives.*" Melody paused slightly, perhaps embarrassed at having to own up to wanting to obtain the academic equivalent of Emmitt Smith's signature on a game ball, but then she plowed ahead resolutely. "There was the dinner scheduled for last night where Susan Faludi was going to be the keynote speaker; originally, of course, Joan and I were coming back together this afternoon—"

"The fact of the matter is," said Huw, "that when I got a good look at the freshmen enrollment figures as of the end of last week, I called Melody first thing Saturday morning and yelled for help. She very kindly offered to cut her trip short to come back and pitch in with the class assignment schedules."

Arranging fall semester teaching schedules was nothing to be taken lightly.

"It wasn't really that big of a deal, Huw. To tell the truth, I was getting the teeniest bit…bored, you know, all that talk about sexist imperialism. I mean, after you've listened for three hours to a panel talk about the hegemony of the penis, what's there left to say?"

Her audience, myself included, sat enthralled.

"Even Joan seemed like she was getting tired of it all," Melody continued, "but of course as one of the organizers of the conference, she had to stay for the final session and sit up at the head table for dinner. At least I was able to set her mind at rest by telling her I'd look in on her cat."

Not for the first time I warned myself not to find Melody's appeal quite so irresistible, but the fact was I was cheered by her youth, her clear eyes, her gentle humor, and her genuine enthusiasm for literature not yet blunted by the grinding necessity of finding a fashionable academic topic to do to death in order to get hired somewhere. In her filmy highnecked, long-sleeved minidress, and her long dark hair, Melody was as much an icon of romantic poetic inspiration as Sarah Jane was the epitome of the fearless, independent woman administrator/teacher; and I really had no business thinking of either one in quite such personal, unprofessional ways. Not an easy task, particularly with Melody, as we had developed over the past year a ridiculous private badinage bordering on the risqué. Even in the present circumstances, I half expected her to interrupt her earnest narrative with a wink in my direction.

Looking back on it, I suppose that by now all of us had realized that our plans for yet another safe, relatively uneventful semester full of the predictable busy work of teaching had suddenly jumped the track. From the moment I had all unawares chanced upon Roylett's body, our lives had begun to veer from their safe and charted courses and

gone off the rails, careening in new directions with unforeseeable con-
sequences.

"Professor Collins?"

Authority had finally arrived in the slender capable person of a
blonde, blue-eyed campus policewoman smartly turned out in starched
white uniform shirt and dark blue trousers. Slung about her narrow
hips was a heavy leather belt from which depended an assortment of
patrolman's impedimenta. Her nameplate proclaimed her to be Officer
Maginnis.

"I'm Professor Collins," Sarah Jane volunteered. "I'm the one who
called. We found—that is, Dr Coulter"—she nodded in my direction
and I briefly felt the impact of Officer Maginnis's azure gaze—"was the
one who actually found the body."

Officer Maginnis glanced around the lounge, her neat ponytail
swinging pleasantly.

"No, not here, in the mailroom."

"Could you show me the mailroom, Professor Collins? In the meantime," said Officer Maginnis, "would the rest of you remain here till I
get back? And please refrain from speaking to one another about…the
incident?" As she followed Sarah Jane from the lounge, she was unhol-
stering her walky-talky.

"Very impressive," murmured Huw.

Although it was in fact only a matter of twenty minutes or so until
we were escorted in separate cars to the university police building back
behind the stadium near the expressway, it seemed to me we were left
meditating on our sins in the graduate student lounge for hours, while
an assortment of intent men and women, some in uniforms, others in
plain clothes, carrying tapes, radios, cameras, and various small cases,
began to potter about at arcane tasks.

Among the six of us—Sarah Jane was absent only a few moments
which, judging from the expression on her face when she returned
from showing Officer Maginnis the body in the mailroom, was quite
long enough—there ensued a desultory conversation as we waited for

whomever Officer Maginnis had called to come and decide what to do with us.

"The *university* police? In-bloody-credible!" Huw snorted derisively and bestowed upon us a brilliant smile. Departmental rumor had it that the opportunity to acquire a new set of gleaming white American teeth—the old ones long since blasted out by some Aberystwyth loose-head's elbow in a legendarily gory rugby match in Swansea and replaced until recently with stainless steel incisors, courtesy of the National Health Service—had played no small part in Huw's accepting an appointment at The University.

His teeth, and Carlotta.

"When that student stole that Schweitzer manuscript last year," I reminded him, "it was the university police who took charge of the case. If you remember, the papers at the time seemed to make rather a lot of the fact that the state has invested the campus police with absolute authority in criminal matters taking place on university property."

Huw and the others digested this information in silence, Sarah Jane favoring me with the same kind of frowning glance she'd given me in the mailroom, as if she were seeing me for the first time. They weren't used to me speaking up, and I made a mental note to watch myself. I'd invested too much of myself for too many years now to risk attracting attention. That wasn't in my game plan, which was to keep a low profile.

I reckoned it was a blow to their egos to face up to the fact that the death of our chairman—head of possibly the largest English department in the galaxy—hell, the universe!—was going to be investigated by some representative of the campus police, known for the most part to faculty members for their maddeningly imperturbable courtesy while issuing traffic tickets for minor parking violations. At the very least, they probably felt, Roylett's passing ought to be something for the city police if not for the state Department of Public Safety, or, for that matter, the FBI or CIA.

"That blood…it looked like it was coming from his ears," offered Amanda.

"From the 'porches of his ears'," Vere mused. Close now, very close.

"It was," I said. "Or it had been. I think you can rest assured that whatever it was that Professor Roylett died from it wasn't just your basic cardiac infarct." I shifted ground a bit. "There was a book there, I seem to recall. A rather large book."

"On the floor?" Vere queried, squinting through glasses with clear plastic frames. A round and rumpled man, he had the anxious look of an enthusiastic bat-boy, off to the side of the action. Looking at Ed, I mused uncharitably that few teachers dressed with the same flair as Sebastian Roylett—the raw silk coat he'd been wearing put me in mind of one of my old man's Dunhill numbers. Even so, with his frayed blue oxford button-down shirt, ancient madder tie, and seersucker suit, Ed provided a change from those of our colleagues given to sports shirts and slacks in earth hues, and in summer shod in Birkenstocks. Ed was the department's specialist in vision poetry of the fourteenth century. Perhaps the late fourteenth century.

"Fucking fascist pigs!"

"Ah, methinks I hear the dulcet tones of young Fishbach, the life force out of the seventies," Huw drawled. "Come no doubt to rescue his lady from the Castle of Oppression." He glanced slyly at Melody.

Melody's cheeks mantled with color, but she managed to respond evenly to Huw's gibe. "Come to take me down to the river, more like it," she said. "Rowing practice: Head of the Neches is next weekend, you know, and we're rowing a double in the mixed." One windy afternoon the past spring I'd seen Melody double-sculling on the river, the dark cloud of her hair skinned back, all sweep and grace and sweat-starting skin under her thin nylon singlet.

"I hope Henry's scholarship's more up to date than his diction," observed Sarah Jane tartly. "Incidentally, what happens when somebody's dissertation director…dies?"

"What happens is that the student petitions for a new director—ball's back in Fishbach's court," Huw said succinctly. "As a practical matter, it's usually someone who's already serving on the student's committee, read into the scene. Anybody know who's on Fishbach's committee? What's the man writing on, anyway?" Huw gave the "bach" in "Fishbach" full guttural Teutonic—or was it Welsh?—value, and I noticed that the "man" provided a nice irony with the ruckus in the hall in which Fishbach's reedy tenor came across all-too-stridently compared to the rumbling bass of whatever sturdy minion of the law was preventing him from entering the room.

"Lang/ling," said Melody. "Lexicography, really, but with a focus on the politics of cultural genocide as practiced by Jacksonian democracy. Something to do with Cherokee dictionaries in the nineteenth century. Seb—Professor Roylett was his director, Joan was second reader, and then there was somebody from Anthropology and Edmond Altschul from Linguistics."

"As second reader, Joan's senior and can step in and take over," said Huw. "It's a bloody awful thing to say, but I must admit that Roylett picked as good time as any to hop the perch, start of the semester like this. If it were in late May, say, beginning of the summer vacation, there's no telling where that lot would've been scattered to." We were spared Huw's speculation about the ultimate estival destinations of somebody from Anthropology and Edmond Altschul from Linguistics by the reappearance of Officer Maginnis, who informed us authoritatively that we were wanted at headquarters to have our statements taken.

On the way out of the building, vouchsafed not even a glimpse of the ardent Fishbach, Huw walked beside me. "Coulter, a moment of your time. It has come to my ears that you had words with our late chairman on Friday." I said nothing. "It might not come amiss were you to drop by the office tomorrow before doing anything rash."

Then Huw paused, and spoke with a fearful joviality. "'The wild regrets, and the bloody sweats,/None knew so well as I—'"

"'For he who lives more lives than one,'" I filled in, always the team player, "'More deaths than one must die.'" Huw smiled as though pleased that I'd passed some private test, but the question lay there between us, unanswered: Who did Huw think had been living more lives than one, Roylett, or me? Or was he speaking of himself? Or of all of us?

And yes, I had been thinking of doing something rash, cutting my losses and making a run for it. When I'd stalked out of Roylett's office Friday, so far as I could tell, I had been dead meat, designer road kill.

CHAPTER 4

▼

The campus police station was behind the stadium, a nondescript white stucco building on a nondescript lot bounded on the front by a paved road leading to the interregional north-south expressway, and on its sides by hardtop that played out in a large graveled parking lot in the rear of the building.

The taciturn young patrolman who drove me parked the car in front of the building and showed me up some shallow steps, through heavy glass doors to a light and airy main room the focal point of which was a white Formica-topped desk presided over by three uniformed officers. We walked down a long, sunny hall to a small windowless office. There I spent two hours reading an article in a two-month-old copy of the *FBI Bulletin* about highway patrolmen incurring cancer by running radar checks and trying not to think of how much I wanted a smoke and a drink and a quiet dinner.

I was interviewed by a slim dark-haired man about my own age. He wore a white shirt and navy blue trousers, and his plain toed shoes were highly polished. He was carrying a small notebook and a microcassette recorder. "Doctor Coulter? I'm Lieutenant Melnick, the officer in charge of this…case." He had regular features and a disarming smile.

Docta. Colta.

Something in Melnick's voice reminded me of Queens or Brooklyn, and put me in mind of the tough, competent racehorse trainers I'd known around the New York tracks.

He sat down opposite me and smiled ironically. Wince marks etched the skin around the outer corners of his black eyes. "Before we get started, let me say that some of the other faculty members we've spoken to have had questions about who is going to handle the investigation into Professor Roylett's...death. The fact of the matter is that under state law, the USW police department has jurisdiction; we are the law keeping unit that will take total charge of this case. Now if we find there are any tests we need to run that we can't do here—identification of serums, fluids, and liquids, for example—we will make use of other facilities such as those of the Department of Public Safety or the FBI." He paused, and then spoke with deliberation. "But we are the ones you deal with."

"I see," I told him. "At least I guess I see. You're not saying anything about whether Professor Roylett's...death"—his eyes hardened at my unconscious mimicry of his own hesitation—"was accidental or murder." I paused to give him time to reply, but he was silent. "I can see where The University's taking charge of the case may have come as a surprise to some of my colleagues, but I take your point. How can I help?"

He relaxed fractionally. "I'd like you to give me a statement."

Fair enough, I told him.

He turned on the recorder and made sure it was functioning properly, ran it back, then started recording. "This is Lieutenant Walter Melnick of The University of the Southwest Campus Police, on Sunday, one September—" he glanced at his watch "—at 1313 hours, at Police Headquarters."

"With me—" Lieutenant Melnick fumbled a pair of old-fashioned horn-rimmed glasses out of his shirt pocket, placed them carefully on the bridge of his nose, and referred to his notes "—is Doctor Stephen Coulter—"

I nodded, and he jabbed a finger in the direction of the recorder.
Yes, I said.

"Would you please state your name, address, and connection with The University."

I told him.

"How long have you been employed at USW?"

"Last year was my first year."

"I understand you were the one who found Doctor Roylett's body this morning?"

"Yes, that's right."

"What time would that have been? Approximately."

"Approximately a few minutes before ten."

"Where was this, please? For the record."

"I found Professor Roylett's body in the mailroom on the ground floor of the English department in MacFarland Hall."

"Would you describe what you saw when you entered the mailroom? Was the door to the mailroom open?"

"No, the door was locked and I had to use my key to get in." I paused and Melnick nodded for me to go on. "Professor Roylett was lying on the floor at the rear of the room—"

"What direction is that?"

"Direction? East, I suppose. With his feet stretched out toward the left-hand wall—the north wall—and his head pointing south where the mailboxes are. The back of his head was facing me with his right cheek resting against the floor and I could see blood leaking from his ears—there was a little pool of blood on the floor below his right ear and, because I was looking at him from above, I could see where the blood had run down from his left ear into the hollow of his jawbone and trickled out of sight away from me."

"You say you could see the blood leaking from his ears: are you absolutely certain it was flowing?"

I thought for a moment. "No, I'm not absolutely certain. I remember it was shiny and it looked wet. It *felt* wet. But it might not have been running down."

I was wondering if we'd crossed over into the liquid-serum-fluid area yet where the campus cops were going to call in the FBI, but Melnick gave me no time to ponder the question. "If the back of his head was facing you when you came in, how did you know it was Professor Roylett and not somebody else lying there on the floor?"

"I recognized the silver hair, and I'd seen him wearing that jacket and shoes before."

"What did you do after you saw him lying there?"

"I knelt down and felt below his left ear to see if he had a pulse."

"And?"

"I couldn't find a pulse and I got a little blood on my hand."

"Do you recall noticing anything else out of the ordinary besides the blood?"

Melnick's expressionless gaze restrained me from observing that even if you judged it by the high standards the English department sometimes set for itself in matters of strangeness, finding the chairman's body laid out in the mailroom was pretty damned extraordinary. And certainly I'd found the conversation in the graduate students' lounge to be bizarre and unsettling, with its predictable concerns, musty allusions, and preoccupation with departmental procedure, while our chairman's body lay bleeding not a hundred paces distant. Perhaps, though, I reflected, that was the nature of actual tragedy: to cause those within its ambit to avert their gaze in safe contemplation of the commonplace.

I tried to recreate the scene in my mind: the cold, rather featureless institutional room, the scuffed linoleum floor and white walls, the narrow oak table along the left-hand wall and above it a corkboard with various departmental notices pinned to it. The desk about midway of the facing wall with a telephone and scattered sheets of paper on it. The rolling desk chair crammed against the wall in the space between the table and the desk. The casement window slightly to the right of the desk on the facing wall through which the summer's brutal sun filtered palely green through the trees. The wall to my right almost completely taken up by mailboxes which, having seen little use over the summer, were—most of them anyway, if their owners on leave over the summer hadn't come by to sort through the contents—stuffed full of the bureaucratic bumf that arrives with the beginning of the fall semester: nine or ten vertical rows, eleven to the row running in alphabetical order—Adams, Alteck, Ashton, Barber, Bernstein, Brown—with one shelf all the way across the top saved for cardboard boxes with the names of teachers on leave or retired. On the floor below, cartons of books sent on by new faculty members from their last university. And on the floor in the far right corner of the room, beyond Roylett's body, a very large thick book.

"It all looked pretty much as usual for the beginning of the school year," I told Melnick. "Boxes of books piled up. Except for the one book, lying there in the corner."

If Melnick was disappointed he didn't show it. "Would you describe for me your actions from the time you got up this morning until the time you opened the mailroom door and saw Professor Roylett's body?"

"Well, let's see." I considered. "I got up about four..."

"Four?"

"I go to bed pretty early," I said. "After I got up I went for a run. I left for the stable a little before six."

Melnick raised his eyebrows quizzically.

"That's right. I do part-time work out at Gordonwood stable south of town giving lessons and helping out with the bookkeeping chores."

"Go on."

"Well, let's see. I remember KMFA came on just as I was passing St Anselm's on the expressway. That made it just on six, so that put me at the stable at about six-twenty or six-thirty."

"Did you see anyone when you got there?"

"No, not then, but that's not surprising. A lot of times in the summer, boarders like to ride before it gets hot, but yesterday we'd gone to a show which meant that today the horses were off and most of the boarders wouldn't be coming out to ride. When I got to the stable I grained the horses and topped up their water buckets. By that time it was getting light, maybe a few minutes after seven. Then I remember I went over to the office and fixed some coffee and started in on the paperwork. After she'd had a chance to digest her morning feed, I did off a mare I've been working with and took her out on the longe line." I thought some more. "Somewhere in there Joe Chavez, the weekend help, showed up to muck out and hay."

"Is Mr Chavez likely to remember seeing you?"

"I should damn well think so. We talked about his W-4 and agreed to meet at a bingo game Wednesday night. And there were a couple of visitors, wanted to know about boarding, turned up."

"Then what?"

"Then I went home, took another shower, got a bite to eat, and read the paper." I didn't see any reason to mention knocking back a half pint of tequila with Widow Sanchez's blood, something I could have used right about now, judging from the threadlike nerve beginning to jump under my right eye.

"What happened when you arrived on campus? Did you notice anything unusual about the building when you got there?"

"Yes, I guess you could say that. As soon as I let myself in, I saw the place had been…vandalized. Graffiti spray painted all over the walls and hell's own amount of papers scattered around."

"Do you have any idea who was responsible?"

"For Professor Roylett's death?"

"No. For the vandalism in the building."

"Not really." I shrugged. "Early betting seems to be that it was the work of some discontented element in the department."

"Such as?"

"Well, I suppose the folk wisdom is that it's the work of the usual suspects—lecturers, TAs, and graduate students, the last two groups not mutually exclusive—all TAs being graduate students but not all graduate students being teaching assistants."

"You don't agree with this?"

"No, as a matter of fact, I don't. For one thing, what is supposed to have precipitated the lecturers' resentment took place months ago and most of those affected have long since left town…"

"Many, but not all?"

"Not all of them, no." On my way back to the john at Mañuela's last week I'd caught sight of Joella Cremona, who'd written her dissertation on George Herbert and the metaphysical poets, in the kitchen, filling dishwasher racks with dirty china; I supposed that Andy Finch with two articles accepted by *JEGP* on Anglo-Saxon riddle poetry was still tuning up Porsches at that place down on South Congress. And of course there was Beddington himself, now oddly caught sight of working on the grounds crew replanting the flower beds on the mall and around the main building, longhaired, sticklike, attired in black, casting a cold and somehow sinister shadow across a sunlit scene.

"But most of them. Now if you're talking about the TAs and graduate students, why that's something else."

Melnick nodded, inviting me to go on.

"Miss Vennible and Professor Collins," I said carefully, "have got two suspects, one a lecturer, one a grad student, whom they rather fancy…"

"Beddington and Fishbach." He looked at me inquiringly.

"That's their opinion. I don't happen to share it."

"Right," Melnick said. "Getting back to this morning. Do you need a key to unlock the outside doors?"

"Yes. Faculty members, teaching assistants, graduate students with cubicles in the basement, and I suppose work study people—students holding jobs—they all get keys. People with a need, vouched for by someone in the department, key authorizations signed by Miss Vennible."

"The building's kept locked on the weekends?"

"So far as I know, the building's supposed to be kept locked at nights and on the weekends." I thought a moment. "There are some nighttime classes, of course—once-a-week seminars meeting, say, seven-to-ten, or review sessions and the like—and for these, as for regular classes, students have to be able to get into the buildings just as at other times. I expect the custodial staff are the ones who lock up after those classes at night. But on weekends the building should be locked. I know that when I've come on campus early in the morning sometimes I've met one of the custodial people—janitors—with a bunch of keys unlocking the doors. And occasionally when I've come on campus at night or over the weekend to grade papers or get something out of the mailroom, there'll be somebody coming up behind you wanting to get in just as you're turning the key in the lock. Most of the time it's another teacher or departmental staff person, but sometimes a student needs to slip a late paper under the door of his teacher's office. And you don't like to just slam the door in his face—"

"So you let them in without always knowing who they are or what their business is. I see. When had you last been in the mailroom?"

"Friday afternoon."

"Is there usually a Saturday mail delivery?"

"Not usually, no; or, rather, not a mail delivery in the ordinary sense of the term. But occasionally mail does get delivered to the department on Saturday and if someone's in the office and feeling public spirited he brings it down to the mailroom and lays it on the table along with whatever may have arrived too late Friday to be sorted out and put in the boxes. Then if you come in over the weekend you can look through the stuff on the table before it gets distributed on Monday."

"But Saturday deliveries don't in fact happen very consistently?"

"No, not often."

"You had a special reason for coming in to campus check the mail."

"I had two reasons for coming in to campus, actually, Lieutenant. One was, I've been teaching during this summer and it was possible that my August paycheck had arrived. Two, I wanted to see whether there was anything in my mailbox about if I was going to teach in the fall."

"In the fall?" He leaned back in his chair and stared at me from under his lowered eyelids. "Correct me if I'm wrong, Dr Coulter, but doesn't the fall semester start the day after tomorrow? Isn't that cutting things a little fine?"

"Regrettably, it's a not unusual state of affairs, believe me, Lieutenant. With a student enrollment of more than fifty thousand—give or take a thousand or two—I'm sure you know those figures—The University never knows how many kids are going to show up the first day of classes."

"That sounds like a real mess."

"It is a real mess. The department's not only got to staff its regularly scheduled undergraduate and graduate classes as announced in the course catalogue, it's also got to provide for the freshmen—and the legislature has decreed that there shall be no more than twenty-five students in freshman classes." I was warming to my subject; it wasn't often I got a chance to snare an appreciative audience.

"Complicating matters is that a lot of the schools and colleges in The University won't admit students as majors in their programs until they've gotten their English requirements out of the way, so you can't just stagger those freshman offerings over, say, four years.

"And the administration won't increase the English department's budget to hire more teaching assistants and assistant instructors—traditionally, graduate students and hence cheap, consequently very attractive to the administration—until it's known how many freshmen there are going to be. Not that the graduate students are likely to scream, poor devils: they're desperate for any job that'll help pay the rent."

"You say it's graduate students who mainly teach freshman classes?"

"Yes, mainly graduate students, although all junior faculty teach freshman classes and a number of senior faculty, too, as well as some of the lecturers."

"Most of whom I understand got fired in the spring."

"Well, you don't really fire lecturers, Lieutenant," I corrected him. "You just don't renew their contracts." Lecturers always reminded me a bit of the goliards of the Middle Ages, the roaming scholars who begged and sang their way from town to town. They were the true *gyrovagi*—the ancient Latin term meaning wandering vagabonds—of the academic caste system: PhDs who were non-tenure track, temporary help, hired year-to-year to help teach freshman or sophomore classes, some of them extraordinarily competent in certain areas, but not perceived as desirable enough or settled enough for a department to recruit actively. They hired on wherever they could, part of the unique freemasonry of the academic life, and they brought to the mix a prickly individualism. "You'll never hear anybody talking about brilliant young lecturers, lieutenant," I said, "the two adjectives always seem to go together: brilliant, young. On the other hand, all assistant professors are talked about as brilliant, until, of course, they get booted out at the end of the seventh year. Then they're said never to have fulfilled their promise."

"That may answer my next question," Melnick said placidly. "Aren't you a bit senior to be a lecturer?" He consulted his notes. "What are you, anyway, forty?"

I shrugged. "'When regrets take the place of dreams a man is growing old'. John Barrymore."

"Barrymore? Really?" Momentarily he looked skeptical, then got back to business. "So if you don't fire them, how do they find out they're being let go, besides not getting a contract in the mail?"

"Talk in the halls, bush telegraph; word gets around. The ones you're remembering were the seventy-odd who rated a write-up locally and got picked up on the wire services for a mention in *Time* and

Newsweek. Actually, Roylett called them in to his office and gave it to them up front and personal over two months ago."

"Why such a large number?"

"You'd find it a long and rather tedious story I'm afraid, Lieutenant," I began tentatively, but since Melnick gave no sign that he was daunted, I proceeded to tell him how the whole sorry mess had evolved.

CHAPTER 5

▼

"First thing you've got to keep in mind is that English departments wear two hats. One, they're trying to get their graduate programs nationally ranked, the only widely accepted method of determining how good the department really is. National ranking depends on a number of things, all of them more or less having to do with how many faculty the department has who have distinguished themselves as scholars and how widely respected their publications are.

"Second, they're in the service business, taking care of the rest of The University—all the colleges and schools, like natural sciences, engineering, communications, fine arts, and so on, all of which have English requirements for their undergraduate majors.

"About ten years ago The University finally figured out that some of its graduates couldn't write very well. They were found 'not to possess the necessary minimal written communications and verbal skills.'

"What had occurred, apparently, was that university alumni who had distinguished themselves in business finally got pissed off at having to stay in their offices forty minutes a day longer than they had twenty years before because they didn't dare send out the illiterate memos and reports being generated by their new and very expensive MBAs.

"It was time, they told The University, to stop fucking around with 'meaningful' courses putting a premium on sensitivity, and get busy teaching their kids how to read and write. Particularly write. And skip the horse shit about how the real problem was in the high schools and with too much t.v.

"As a matter of fact, some students graduating had never had to write an essay their entire time at college, a predictable state of affairs when you consider that, in order to save money, lower-division classes commonly run upwards of fifty students. These are numbers that discourage all but the most dedicated teachers. Reading and grading large numbers of undergraduate papers take a hell of a lot of time, and few teachers are committed to teaching composition. Sure there are still some conscientious senior faculty who year in and year out teach sections of freshmen and sophomores. But younger scholars, particularly those with an eye on promotion—which depends to a great extent on their publications—tend to shun teaching of writing courses.

"With its customarily high-minded disregard for the realities and comfortable in the knowledge that they were offending no important constituency, the legislature then decreed three years ago that all undergraduates should henceforth be required to pass three semesters of post-freshman college English with a substantial writing component, taught not just by graduate students, but by full-time faculty with advanced degrees.

"Never slow to take a hint from the Legislature, The University's administration embarked upon a well-publicized 'initiative' that would require all USW undergraduates to take during their freshman and sophomore years six hours of courses containing a minimum of 40 pages of written work. Teaching these courses would be, The University administration stressed in a convulsion of conscience, a university-wide faculty responsibility.

"Laudable in intent—who the hell would vote against it?—the legislation proved difficult to implement. Anybody could see that there'd be a problem in getting Professor Sniddley who was working his balls off teaching chemistry to three hundred sophomores to somehow come up with a way of shoehorning into the semester's syllabus four carefully-graded writing exercises totaling in excess of ten thousand words. And on chemistry? What you're telling Sniddley is, in effect, 'Say, Professor, in addition to whatever it is you're doing now to keep the kids off the streets three hours a week in class and, say, another thirty minutes or so correcting homework, we want you to do a bit of old-fashioned grading which shouldn't take you much longer than, let's say thirty minutes a paper times four papers for each student, that's two hours per student times your three hundred students, why that's only asking you to put in 600 extra hours during the semester…for the satisfaction of knowing you've done a good job, for we sure as hell can't pay you any more than you're getting. A return to olden traditional values, Sniddley, that's the thing. And, oh, by the way, we can't give you any extra help. And don't forget that two-and-a-half percent merit raise based on new publications. Questions? Sorry, Sniddley, old man, but I've got a date out at the golf course. I'll see you later, around commencement time.'

"What's Sniddley to do? He's going to tell them to fuck off, that's what. Let somebody else carry the can, count him out.

"Somebody else turned out to be, surprise, surprise, the perennially luckless Department of English, which suddenly found itself faced with the prospect of having to teach X hundred sections of USW courses to an influx of Y thousand students, because at the same time as all this was going on, the student population was rising dramatically, thus exacerbating the problem.

"Naturally, the English faculty, always on the defensive, always feeling put-upon, passed pious resolutions denouncing what they saw as the demotion of the department to service status. Research and scholarship, they argued, were obviously going to be put on the back burner. The department would never be able to recruit good people in a situation where three out of the four courses new people taught were, in effect, lower-division courses. The Faculty Senate was primly silent; the administration stood firm.

"The totally predictable result was that ultimate responsibility for teaching substantial writing component courses once more sloshed back to the English department—which gave a collective howl of outrage. The same old arguments about its being a university-wide responsibility were trotted out and dusted off. Recognizing the handwriting on the wall, the mad mullah dean of the college of liberal arts made a desperate and impassioned pitch to the administration and succeeded in obtaining some money to hire lecturers—the most economically feasible way to patch up the problem since each lecturer received minimum wages and taught four sections of writing classes.

"Even so, thoughts of breaking into the top twenty English programs in the country dissipated. Senior faculty mumbled impotently about resignation. Bright junior faculty burned up the telephone to solicit bids from other institutions. Morale descended to an all-time low, if such a thing were possible.

"The only ones for whom this sudden increase in classes signified anything of a windfall were out-of-work PhDs who were hired, in Roylett's delighted grind-their-faces-in-the-muck phrase, as 'temporary, one-year, non-tenure-track, non-renewable contract' lecturers, the *gyrovagi*, the goliards of the Academy. It goes without saying that Roylett made a practice of hiring lecturers at the last possible moment, at maximum inconvenience, frequently after the first week of classes had begun.

"By the end of the spring semester the regular faculty were feeling threatened. Lecturers presented a real problem for which a final solution was desperately needed: faculty found them brash, disrespectful, politically off-the-wall—and, though no one actually used the word, unattractive."

"They were qualified, I take it?"

"Oh, hell, yes, they all had degrees; some from very good places. In fact, if you look at the exit polls and teaching evaluations, you'll see that some of the best teaching that has been done around here in living memory has been done by lecturers. And, Jesus, it isn't as though there isn't a real crying need for the courses they were teaching.

"But I digress. During the two weeks after commencement when The University's pulse had as usual flatlined, the Substantial Writing Component courses by administrative fiat ceased to become an English Department responsibility. Henceforth, it was decreed that the SWC was to be spread out over four years which would bloody well get the whole university faculty involved whether they wanted to or not.

"That ruling neatly made the lecturers, as they say, redundant.

"Following time-hallowed tradition, the administration waited to announce its new plans for the dead days of June and July when there were few of the student and faculty hotheads buzzing about to oppose them...and the English department, with no funding for the courses, had to let them go, just when they'd developed a taste for this particular kind of Lotus land: Sunbelt paradise, with the country music and the lake and the cookouts and fresh veggies at Whole Foods and a relatively low cost of living, and had allowed themselves the stupidity of counting on actually teaching what they loved and, God forbid, inculcating a few ideas into those lovely young heads at the same time.

"This news precipitated (again, to anyone knowledgeable about The University, predictably) a media holiday—letters in the press, television interviews with soon-to-be ex-lecturers, harassed administrators, notices in *The New York Times*, *The Chronicle of Higher Education*, and *Time* magazine.

"Now Roylett had his chance to demonstrate why, at least from the administration's point of view, he had been an excellent choice as chairman. The prospect of telling 74 lecturers that their contracts weren't going to be renewed when classes started in the fall didn't seem to faze him in the slightest." In fact, when I'd come in to see him on Friday, he'd seemed still jubilant and glowing from the kick of his Kristallnacht back in May. There remained no question in my mind about it: Roylett was one of those fortunately rare people who took joy in visiting pain on others.

"The upshot of the matter was that as a result of Roylett's Memorial Day Massacre a bunch of the ousted lecturers got pissed off. And as the realities of eking out an existence on food stamps and standing in unemployment lines sank in, they got really pissed off. One of the most vocal of the lot was or is a man named Amos Beddington—"

"Yes, I've heard of Beddington."

"A bitter man, so I hear. Put one of The University's prize javelin throwers, an import from Iceland, if you can believe it, right out of commission for the whole season a year or so ago. They say the lad suffered severe neurological damage. I never did get the whole story. That little fuss got him suspended from teaching even before the lay-off. For Beddington the lay-off was just lagniappe, the icing on the cake, so to speak. But from what I hear—I've met him I guess only once or twice—Beddington wields a certain malign charm. With that tall, gaunt look of his, and the long hair, and the black outfits he fancies, he's a quite romantic figure to others of the disenfranchised—at least that's the way they see themselves and I'm not sure they're wrong— and it's quite within his powers to have assembled a strike force of other disaffected and militant types to vandalize MacFarland Hall. Which happened this morning, possibly quite close to the time that Professor Roylett met his end. God knows the whole bunch of them had keys."

"It was while they were inspecting the damage that Miss Vennible and Professor Collins discovered you kneeling over Professor Roylett's body—is that correct?" Melnick asked.

"They told me they were called by one of the night security people."

Melnick settled himself more comfortably in his chair.

"You went to see Professor Roylett on Friday. Did he invite you to drop by, or what?"

"No, I made an appointment to see him. And I may as well tell you if you don't already know, that anyone who was standing within, say, fifty feet of his office will swear to it they heard us having words."

"Oh?" He looked politely interested.

"Time's run out for applying to teach anywhere else locally, like St Anselm's or the community college, and though I haven't been let go, I still haven't heard a damned word about the fall." I paused. "That wasn't fair. So I wanted to get the air cleared, and"—I added reluctantly—"see for myself if what I'd heard was true."

"What's that?"

"That he was the kind of real thorough-going son of a bitch that absolutely reveled in the humiliation he was able to inflict on the lecturers—"

"And was it true, that Roylett was a real thorough-going son of a bitch?"

"Yeah, pretty much."

"What did you ask him?"

"Well, I told him that. I told him I really wanted to know if he was that kind of a son of a bitch."

"You did? And what did he say?"

"He laughed. I think I amused him. And then he went on to say I was fucking presumptuous, and that the lecturers that were fired were bloody well going to stay fired. Then he seemed to cool off a bit and told me I had no reason not to suppose I'd be hired—"

"Double negatives?" Melnick shook his head.

"That's right. He didn't seem to harbor any rancor, though, of course we were both screaming there for a while. The thing was, and you might as well know this, Lieutenant, I'd made my mind up to—I don't know, complain, get him to make an apology—"

"Apologize? To whom?" Melnick was frankly skeptical.

"To the people he'd treated like dirt. I was, I don't know, ready to go to the dean about it, or the president. It simply wasn't fair."

"'Fair'?" Melnick scoffed. "It seems to me like you've got some very dangerous do-gooder tendencies."

He was right. The only good causes that interested me were lost causes.

"Up until this time were your relations with Professor Roylett cordial?"

*   *   *   *

"Well, that's been a lot of help," Melnick said without apparent irony after I'd gotten through telling him what I knew. He closed his notebook and shut off his recorder. "Where can I get in touch with you?"

I gave him my home number and the number at the stable. I started to get up from the table.

"Oh, by the way, Dr Coulter, did you find your check in the mailbox?"

"No."

"Was your teaching assignment there?"

"No."

Melnick leaned back. "It was Fauré's *Requiem*, I think."

"What?"

"This morning, on KMFA. What you heard when you were driving past St Anselm's on the way to the stable." He hummed the first majestic, melancholy bars. "You remember: *Sempiterna...requiem.*" He gave me a dazzling, apologetic smile. "I get up early, too."

*   *   *   *

In front of the police station I lit a cigarette and looked around but didn't see Huw or any of the others. I supposed I must have been the last to have been interviewed, and the rest of them—in various degrees of shock, I reckoned—had probably waited not upon the order of their going, but had gone directly about their business, eager, if how I felt was any yardstick to go by, to put behind them at least temporarily the tumult and emotional abrasion of the day. For Roylett's death raised, as they were fond of saying over in the Faculty Senate, a number of issues that needed to be addressed. It was not going to be at all a business of Sebastian Roylett simply ceasing upon the midnight with no pain, passed away poor devil in his sleep; what it was shaping up to be, in fact, was a real fucking mess.

A headquarters officer who followed me out of the building asked me if I didn't want a ride to my car and I thanked him but explained it wasn't really necessary, I'd make my way back across campus on foot.

I walked like one of those old time FAO Schwartz toy divers you used to submerge by means of a rubber bulb and tube and cause to trudge solitarily across the bottom of a bathtub. I was drenched in sweat by the time I got to my car. I rolled the windows down and turned the radio off and just sat there, looking around at the statues of chivalric dead white males, the wide, grassy, oak-bordered mall sloping down to the fountain, and the few people walking down to the library. Bright blood on raw silk on a summer's morning: but nothing was changed, life went on, apace. I thought of Auden's "Musée des Beaux Arts" with Breughel's stolid plowman's gaze fixed on the furrow before him, all unaware of Icarus plunging into the sea.

After a while I started up the car and headed out to the stable. Sunday evenings I liked to fix a hot bran mash for whatever horse I'd been schooling. Besides, I wanted to check the mare's legs. I'd enjoyed watching her buck and frolic and get the kinks out of her system, but I needed to make sure she hadn't strained anything. Young horses working in a small circle on a longe throw a lot of weight on their joints.

There was nobody around the stable when I got there—par for late on a Sunday afternoon in summer. Joe had left the mare's scrubbed-clean feed tub in the aisleway and I opened a couple of packages of grocery-store bran and dumped them in the bucket and then took the bucket into the tackroom and ran some hot water in on top and stirred the gruel with the end of a sweat scraper. While the mixture cooled I slipped a halter on the mare and led her out of her stall over to a patch of grass near the picket line. While she grazed contentedly I ran a hand over her legs. They were cool and the fluted tendons smooth and tight. During the heat of the day she'd started to sweat again and I brushed out some of the damp whorls on her neck and over her loins, and then put her up. When I hooked the bucket in her stall, she plunged her head into the mash and started chomping away with absorbed concentration. The emotionally constricting coils of the day dropped away from me and I relaxed listening to the homely reassuring sound.

On the way home I stopped by the laundromat out on the highway and did two loads of laundry I didn't get done on Saturday because I'd been out at the show. There was a bar next to the laundromat called the Busted Spur where I often dropped in for a drink or ten on my way back home from the stable and to see Rhonda, the part owner and full-time bartender. Today I gave the Busted Spur a miss and just sat on the rickety pastel plastic chairs laundromats seem to get from some laundromat supply place and I stared at the swirling shirts.

I was becoming involved in something. For a long time I had made a habit of not getting involved in anything and I didn't care for the feeling.

When I got back home the apartment was seething with trapped heat. Rather than turn on the air conditioner I opened all the windows and switched on the two K-Mart floor fans. Equally unwilling to light the oven, I went down to the patio next to the pool where I fired up the communal outdoor grill and seared the thick tuna steak I'd left marinating. There were a bunch of kids in swimming and flirting with each other. They were beautiful.

✳   ✳   ✳   ✳

At home I served myself the tuna steak with cold asparagus vinaigrette and a cold bottle of Chilean Riesling. As usual I was conning myself: this gourmet put-off-the-blahs ritual didn't do me a bit of good, and I wound up the evening watching Ronald Coleman as Sidney Carton and making a large dent in my dwindling supply of Bush-mill's.

I wondered why I frequently thought of it as "home" and not sim-ply, as most people would, "my apartment." I looked around at the scarred desk with peeling veneer, the plastic and chromium kitchenette table and chairs, some blue-and-white china and stainless steel table sil-ver in the sink, the partially eviscerated easy chair and sofa; and, in the bedroom, the hook rug, camp bed and oak bedside table—everything bought at garage sales over a single weekend, all without a trace of indi-viduality—and saw little to recommend my apartment as a home. Yet I did think of it as home and I supposed its anonymity was what appealed to me. Personality was safely tucked away out of sight on the top shelf of the bedroom closet: the few photographs in greening silver frames of old hunt race meetings and point-to-points in the cold Vir-ginia spring sunshine, and trophy presentations at big shows, and one of my ex-wife and one of my mother and her English friend Lisa as they smiled at each other in the idyllic sunshine of a Greek isle, and a picture of the old man that had appeared on the cover of *Time* a few years ago when he was called to Washington to testify in front of a Sen-ate committee about one of his big insurance company takeovers.

My father rejoices in the English-sounding name of Warwick Coulter. "Wick" Coulter is large and red, similar to if not indistin-guishable from men whose pictures you often see in glossy magazines, sweaty and triumphant, clutching some ornately-chased silver polo tro-phy in the sunlight of Palm Beach or Jackson Hole or Oak Brook. He is descended from Presbyterian Scottish stock from the north of Ire-land who came to the Boston area about the middle of the last century and started a small produce market catering to hotels and restaurants. Later the family became associated with United Fruit and branched out into the commodities market. They flourished and my father in a kind of natural progression founded an immensely successful insurance company. From what my father has let drop from time to time, I gather that there was in his family besides a deeply ingrained work ethic a good deal of silence and secrecy and heavy drinking and an innate belief in sin and the inevitable retribution exacted by an austere and vengeful God.

An Irish connection existed, too, on my mother's side of the family, but Catholic not Protestant, and exhibiting altogether a more joyous cast of mind. Anne Villiers Coulter, my mother, came from an illustrious and splendidly impractical Tidewater family, descended from a long-established Anglo-Irish Ascendancy family from Meath. The present-day Villiers males, mainly lawyers in the Charlottesville area, potter about with codicils, do the honors in closing on the odd bit of real estate, grow roses, and breed Thoroughbreds remarkable for their utter lack of a turn of speed. (You could time the buggers with a sun dial, I once overheard my father mutter uncharitably.) My mother's father, a gentle soul, had spent his declining years in his library setting out to write a family history. His one essay in breeding bloodstock—a timber horse named Homestead—proved a notorious exception to the family rule of consistent failure by winning the Gold Cup.

I grew up on a horse farm near Wenham that my father bought from the cash-poor heirs of one of the last of the New England railway-banking robber barons. It featured a lot of split-rail chestnut and locust fencing, random ashlar stone work, slate roofs and copper gutters: Solid Olde English. Piecing it together years later, I came to the conclusion that what the old man wanted to do, really, was to create for himself an appropriate background and the robber baron's demesne was right up his alley. Perhaps he derived amusement also from the knowledge that his patterning himself along the lines of Squire Western would cause his Presbyterian forebears to whirl in their graves. Certainly I was touched by the unaffected pleasure he took in seeing his mares and foals becomingly grazing in their paddocks. Not that he had much time for looking, for his rapidly expanding empire of insurance companies demanded his energizing presence almost weekly in places such as Denver, Spokane, Omaha, Salt Lake City, Cincinnati, Atlanta, Phoenix, and Dallas. In any case the Presbyterian forebears had their revenge. It was clear to me that my father was embued with and driven by their same relentless work ethic.

When my mother was at home—which became progressively more seldom as she developed a taste for travel—she drank an impressive amount of brandy while staying up late at night listening to Puccini booming out over the snow-mantled paddocks. When I went through her things after she died, I saw that as a girl she used to keep a commonplace book, write poetry, and draw pictures of horses.

CHAPTER 6

▼

I was a frankly acknowledged mistake. My arrival on the scene and the consequent demands of parenthood left them aghast. With relief my good-natured, fun-loving parents surrendered me to the ministrations of, first, a Scottish nurse and, as I grew older, a black groom. I saw no reason to think this course of action was unusual and far from holding it against them learned to relish the hours I spent with Nanny Beaton and Hilbert Washington.

The result was that I grew up with a run of the library many of whose books had made their way north from Grandfather Villiers' and without much thought or effort I developed a small reputation for being a useful hand with mettlesome horses, particularly mares. These advantages I took for granted, too.

With a sigh of relief my parents shipped me off at the first possible moment to prep school in New Hampshire. I remember that by the end of my first term I had committed to memory—why, I have no idea, except that I was, oddly enough, homesick—the better part of two books: the first, Kipling's short stories in *The Day's Work*, and the second, most of the poems in an anthology of golden oldies called *Magic Casements*. I received a modest pleasure from having some of my writing published in the school literary magazine. And I played hockey, occasionally surprising myself by exhibiting a gift for violence that I tried with varying degrees of success to conceal.

I graduated from college with a degree in English, a taste for scotch, an inclination toward romantic involvement with tall blonde girls, and the determination that I was not going to go back again to Wenham and face my ferociously genial father asking me what I was going to do with my life, son. Degrees in English, even summa cum laude, really didn't impress him.

Like a lot of other young men, I joined the army, but unlike most during those strange dark years, I found I liked it. Besides, for someone who'd survived four years of the rigors of the cold New Hampshire pile I'd been sent off to, military discipline held no terrors. There, a taste for action and a thirst for whisky were no drawbacks. Besides, the army afforded me a welcome respite during which I did not need to decide what I was going to do with my life, son, and I extended my service.

Toward the end of my second tour of duty my mother died and I returned to Boston just long enough to claim the money she'd left me in her will. My father treated me with a grave and distant courtesy, hurt showing plain in his eyes. We found we didn't have much to say to each other.

After the medal and the final drunken fiasco back at Devers in the summer of 1976, followed by convalescence amid the dogwood and rhododendrons in Warm Springs, my application for an early release was swiftly approved.

For the next four years I did the horse show and hunt race scene in the East, sinking money into horses, some good, most of them bad, and wound up marrying in a haze of mimosas and orange blossoms the horse-mad heiress of another large red-faced millionaire. Serena had bought one of the good ones from me, and said she was just protecting her investment; she told her friends she counted on my being useful. My father, who was unable to attend the wedding—he was in Paris with my step-mother—I never did meet her—sent a huge silver wine cooler from Tiffany's and a bottle of an obviously expensive champagne of a kind I'd never heard of.

To no one's surprise, least of all mine, my marriage did not pan out. Things undertaken in a haze of mimosas seldom do, and the hard work and killing long hours it took to train and show national high-point hunter champions took their toll. I had become a bore, tiresome, actually, Serena told me, not unkindly, for she liked the winning, and we did plenty of that. But, she complained, I hardly ever wanted to go out at night anymore, and meet new people, exciting people. When a green prospect with more looks than talent fell with me in the warm-up ring at Harrisburg and did a number on my ankle and the ligaments in my lower leg, the center could not, and did not, hold. After she'd seen the doctor, Serena put in a call to Jerry Fahey, a fresh-faced Irish kid we'd met the year before when we were out in California. Fahey had come over with a load of horses from Tipperary. With his gap-toothed Huck Finn charm he'd settled comfortably into the relaxed California lifestyle and had made a name for himself showing hunters on the West Coast. Fahey took on my riding duties for the remainder of the circuit at Washington, New York, and Toronto. He took on Serena, too. From the telephone calls to my room at the hospital where I could look out at a gray river and skeletal trees and small figures on an island, I learned that Fahey was proving a great success with both. The horses never went better, I was assured, and Serena was flourishing. One bright cold morning in December after I'd returned to Virginia, I received a certified letter from the American Horse Shows Federation telling me that our champion hunter, whose entry blanks for the National Horse Show in New York I had signed as agent (S. Cameron Coulter: Serena rather liked the sound of it, more upscale, somehow, than Rusty), had been tooling decorously around the Garden's courses with his system awash with an industrial-strength tranquilizer. I didn't bother to attend the hearing committee meeting and found myself fined and set down indefinitely from showing at any AHSF-recognized show. At that point, and with my own system awash with Glenlivet, I decorously tooled off down the crushed gravel driveway bordered by the espaliered chestnut-and-locust fences with a change of clothes and my Hermès saddle and my copy of the Great Hoggarty Diamond edition of *Vanity Fair* in the back of the farm pickup. My wife and the people around the barn seemed sad to see me go and there was some talk of throwing a party out at the Red Fox before I left but nothing ever came of it. We were separated, but not—yet—divorced, though we had been moving toward that melancholy end in a rather desultory but glacially slow fashion, since, when the fancy took her—usually after she'd been on a trip and met an interesting man—Serena gathered up the legal papers and went in to Middleburg to talk to her lawyers. My father found the whole thing appalling and the truth is I did, too. I sent Serena money when and how I was able, invariably from my paycheck. A misplaced sense of something or other forced me in a spectacularly stupid move to churlishly turn down my father's offer to help defray my expenses at school once he saw I'd mended (his word) my ways and, as he put it, "do the decent thing by the girl"—the girl herself the beneficiary of a seven-figure trust fund. Seven figures to her credit or not, she'd never forgive me for spurning the old man's money.

*   *   *   *

That winter I spent in Bay Head, New Jersey, in a cottage on the ocean, stoking a driftwood fire in the fireplace to keep warm, reading, and taking stock of myself. I decided to apply for and was accepted at graduate school. The last of my mother's money saw me finish my degree in English, surrounded by bright twenty-five-year-olds. I wrote what was generally admitted to be the dullest dissertation within anybody's memory, on a late eighteenth- and early nineteenth-century lawyer and author named Sir Jonah Barrington. Barrington was just right for me.

When the time came I made the pilgrimage to the MLA meat market in New York but had no luck in finding a tenure-track position. I finally responded to an ad placed by The University of the Southwest in *The Chronicle of Higher Education* looking for lecturers on a one-year appointment and was hired. Since then I'd been one of the *gyrovagi*. Starting the previous spring I began to get involved again with horses in a mild kind of way, doing the odd bit of teaching and keeping the books for Kay; the show on Saturday—unrecognized by AHSF—was the first show I'd appeared at in over five years, and I still hadn't gone into the ring.

I haven't seen my father in quite a few years, but manage to get off a card to him at Christmas and on his birthday. The farm near Wenham is gone now, but there's a new apartment on Park Avenue which my father's third wife has written to say I am always welcome to stay at when I come to New York. The old man's taking it a bit easier now, she tells me: they have a summer place in Wyoming, and usually spend a month or two in Saint Croix during the winter. With sincerest regards, Wendy.

Wendy writes in the same kind of earnest round hand in which I used to get letters from Farmington.

She sounds nice. I'd like to meet her sometime.

There was nothing on the ten o'clock news about Sebastian Roylett's death.

*   *   *   *

As usual, I woke up several times during the night soaked with sweat, which meant that by morning I had already made a good start on my next batch of laundry. At six, I got up, brushed my teeth and shaved, pulled on a pair of khakis and a polo shirt and walked down to the Circle K and bought a paper. Roylett's demise ("USW Chairman Succumbs") merited only scant attention, buried on the second page of the "City & State" section. According to the article, Roylett had been found dead of a possible heart attack. Funeral arrangements were pending. The paper went on to speak in glowing terms of Roylett's chairmanship, alluding approvingly to his Final Solution to the lecturer problem ("Chairman Roylett was not afraid of making the tough decisions," stoutly declared The University's provost), his academic achievements, and his significant contributions to the cultural life of the community.

I reflected on what I knew of Roylett, based on what I'd heard and observed during my few meetings with the man on campus and on the single occasion when I'd been a guest in his home at a party he'd thrown to welcome newly-hired faculty.

First of all, Sebastian Roylett had money, which is something few teachers have and those who do are apt to be slightly hangdog and shamefaced about it, tending to give themselves away only by making the odd quite extraordinary donation, indulging their habit for expensive books and travel, putting a better type of wine out for their guests than do their less fortunate colleagues, or sending their children to private schools.

But with Roylett it had all been up front and in your face. He had been attractive, in a brutal kind of Anglo-Saxon way—he was what used to be called in women's books "masterful"—with, it was rumored, a penchant for young girls, brandy, and Cuban cigars. Physically, he was a Type A De Luxe, ripe for cardiac infarct. Tall, about six one or so; robust—close to 200 pounds; of florid complexion; rather too much wavy silver hair worn long.

I'd thought of him as a magnifico, a grandee. He was partial to boldly striped shirts, bespoke suits, and suede ankle boots. He drove a Jaguar. He lived overlooking the lake in a huge airy ranchstyle house on Cat Mountain, whose walls were hung with a stunning collection of contemporary French and Mexican art. If there had been a cocktail party thrown by anyone in the past year that he and his wife hadn't attended, no one had heard of it. And he had the credentials to back up his swagger: It had been said even by people who had no cause to like

Sebastian Roylett that he was brilliant, the department's leading scholar.

All of which should have pretty well guaranteed that Roylett would never in a million years have been considered as a serious candidate for the department's chairmanship, which came up for grabs the year before I arrived on the scene. Except for two things: he was an ardent and very generous supporter of trendy causes, and he was married to a woman of color. In fact, Carlotta Irenée du Plessis-Roylett had a marvelously translucent tan skin; she was a Jamaican, a poet and critic in her own right, an academic jetsetter. I had seen her in the mailroom from time to time returned from long voyages with bruised and puddled eyes, wearing one of the gold-threaded saris she affected, speaking in a Gitane-husky voice, and carrying the scent of Tigre. Crisp raven curls lay feathered athwart the ivory nape of her neck. In the gym where I worked out a couple of times a week I'd admired her taut sleek grace as she did step conditioning in a class with Joan Strossner-Boynton, managing to infuse the frenetic heavy metal on the boom box with a languor redolent of palm trees and ocean breezes.

The central fact of Roylett's interracial marriage threw everything heretofore held against him out the window: he became, from all reports, an immensely popular candidate for chairman.

I supposed that after the soft voiced, courteous, and self-effacing Southerner who'd been pointed out to me as Sebastian Roylett's predecessor as chairman, Roylett recommended himself to the executive committee and to the dean as a man who could get things done, and under whose leadership the department would go places and not so incidentally distinguish itself nationally in the rankings. Certainly he himself occupied a nationally recognized position of prominence.

Nevertheless he'd had his critics—not many and frightened of him, I sensed—who regarded him as unpredictable and, at times, gratuitously cruel. In response to comments that he too enthusiastically fulfilled the legislatively mandated change in the curriculum which required him to dismiss 74 of the department's 80 lecturers and teaching assistants, he was said to have murmured unapologetically, "Nits make lice." Withal, Roylett had been clever and tough; at times whimsical and wickedly amusing, almost always at someone else's expense.

I had not liked the man.

* * * *

After I finished my coffee, I checked in with Kay.

"Oh, hullo, Stephen," she said dully.

"Kay, I called to tell you we need to get caught up on the second quarter withholding and social security taxes for Joe that were due the end of July, and I'm not at all sure that we weren't supposed to have made deposits on account of the third quarter in the meantime. And we need to get squared away on the state employment commission stuff that was due. I looked up Joe's W-4 that we had on file and it's three years old, but fortunately he tells me there haven't been any changes that would result in a different number of exemptions.... Kay?"

"Yeah."

"Is there something the matter, Kay? I mean, besides this tax stuff?"

"It's just," she quavered, "it's just that Bobby Robberson's sent a man over to pick up Audrey's tack trunk..."

"Oh, Christ. Look, Kay, I left the monthly board bills and hauling charges and board bills out in a folder on top of your desk. Are you calling from the stable? Do you see the folder? Don't let the tack trunk go till you get the money for the Simmonses' August board and charges."

"It's too late," she wailed. "He's already gone."

I suppressed a sigh of frustration, and found I didn't have the heart to tell her I'd paid the entries on Audrey, who'd been sent to the show with no money by her parents. Fat chance I'd ever get reimbursed. Another black mark for Bobby and the Simmonses.

"Stephen," Kay said, defiantly. "Linebacker's gone, too."

"What?" I was aghast. "That horse is yours."

"Not any more, Stephen. Bobby sent me a check and said take it or leave it. When you get here, you'll see—"

"Jesus, K.C. I hope he paid you what that horse was worth."

"He paid me five thousand dollars."

I bit my tongue. Competent baby-sitters like Linebacker were pretty rare, and five thousand was a fraction of what he would bring in the East.

"Last I heard," I said. "Art Simmons was all set to buy Audrey a green horse from Bobby. I don't suppose Bobby offered you a commission on the sale of Linebacker?"

A long silence, and then she said rather doubtfully, "It's not as though we'll never see him again. Bobby'll look after him."

"Sure," I said, trying to salvage the best of what was clearly a bad situation. "Bobby'll look after him."

*   *   *   *

I turned my attention to the Barrington project and managed to lose myself for a few productive hours going over his highly personal account of the Rise and Fall of the Irish Nation. I was now up to his entering the Irish parliament in 1790, where he cannily insulted a number of patriots held in scorn by the British. The British rewarded Barrington with a cushy job in the Dublin Customhouse that brought in £1000 a year. Afterward I rustled up a sandwich and walked over to the campus about one.

Even though it was Labor Day with most businesses and state agencies closed, the department was invested with a kind of Mad Dogs-and-Englishmen delirium. Someone had come in to clean off the walls. The main office was humming with activity. The only notice taken of Roylett's death that I could see was that the mailroom had been fitted with a new lock of a different sort and a hand-lettered sign on the door said that faculty could pick up their mail in the graduate student lounge.

The energy in the building was contagious.

Against all odds, I felt my spirits rise even before I found my check for the summer and a mimeographed notice from "Acting Chair" in my new mailbox informing me that I'd be teaching four classes for the fall semester "on a temporary non-renewable one-year-only appointment, please sign here to show that you understand and acknowledge that you are temporary only at a nine-month salary of $18,500.00." In a spiky scholar's hand in black ink across the bottom was written, "Delighted you're on board—I've assigned you Roger Isaacs' office. HRD." Isaacs was spending the year doing research in Galway and thanks to Huw with any luck I wouldn't have to share office space.

On Mondays, Wednesdays, and Fridays I saw I'd been assigned sections of Freshman English at nine and ten and expository writing at one. On Tuesdays and Thursdays I had a section of sophomore literature at three. My office hours would be on Wednesday afternoons from two to five.

The remainder of my mail was the usual hodge-podge. Bob Talbot, a colleague from history, had sent me an announcement from Commonwealth Studies listing its offerings for the fall: inevitably, there were scheduled meetings on Virginia Woolf and D H Lawrence—these two throw-offs from the powerful Woolf and Lawrence multinational scholars' consortium trawling The University's rare books and manuscript archives—one on the Art of the Raj in the Nineteenth Century which looked promising, and one in late October by a visitor from All Souls on "Sources for the History of British Secret Operations during World War II." While I was perusing a flyer for an English Department guest speaker from Zimbabwe on Olive Schreiner's *Women and Labour*, Melody Harker appeared.

CHAPTER 7

▼

If I had supposed that she would be chastened by yesterday's tragedy, my expectations were immediately dispelled.

"Hullo, lover." Her voice was husky.

"Darling. What took you so long?" I tried to assume an expression of amused sophistication, as if the graduate student lounge were a Noël Coward drawing room and I, in evening clothes, were about to mix her a shaker of Orange Blossoms. One of these days somebody would happen in on us when we were going through what had become by now an almost ritualistic routine borrowed from old movies, and there would be hell to pay. But it was a game we both enjoyed, and so far we hadn't been caught.

"You like?" She was bare-legged, wearing sandals, her only concessions to makeup a slash of pale lip gloss and mauve eyeshadow. Her dark brown hair swung free, just touching her shoulders. She was wearing a gauzy print long-sleeved dress, and apparently nothing else except, clearly discernible, a pair of flowered panties and a wispy matching bra.

"Yes, indeed. Very, er, natural." With considerable effort I lifted my glance to her face and caught her looking at me with a sweet and forgiving mockery. "Did you have a pleasant weekend on the Côte d'Azure?"

"Never got that far, actually. Went to Biarritz—filthy weather and Freddy was in a foul mood: last night at chemmy was an absolute disaster." She made a moue of unutterable world-weariness, and crammed a publishing company catalogue into Jerry Bernstein's mail box.

"Maugham?"

"Mmm. Might be, I haven't read all his stories. Possibly the one they made the movie of, about the tennis player—"

"'The Facts of Life'?"

"That's the one. But actually I was thinking of Capote. The movie he did. You know: *Beat the Devil*." I suspected this was a side of Melody she showed to few, and I valued her confidence. Probably because she thought I was safe. I was a stodge, she'd told me. A stick-in-the-mud. Besides, she said, even though I was a stodge, I was mysterious. There was lots more to me than met the eye.

"Oh, right. That's one of the all-time greats. Have you gotten caught up yet?"

"Caught up, what a laugh. As a matter of fact I've been here almost ever since I got off the water last evening. I helped Huw until practically midnight—seventy-five new sections, can you believe it?—and we started in again this morning at eight. I guess you found your notice of appointment?"

"Right. It was a great relief. Many thanks. I was getting kind of nervous."

She made a face. "Four classes. You and Professor Vere."

"Vere? But he's senior faculty—he should only be teaching two, with committee work."

She referred to a printout. "It says four here, look." She was right, Vere was down to teach four classes.

"How did that happen?"

"I don't know, you'd have to ask Miss Vennible."

"Where did you disappear to yesterday? We all got worried."

"I had to get away from that body in the mailroom." She blushed. "It was simply too much. I couldn't handle it. I got sick to my stomach. Did you see the paper this morning?"

"Yes. It said he died of an apparent heart attack."

"But that's bullshit, you know it is. You saw the blood. Who do you think did it?"

I shook my head. I didn't know.

"It would be so nice if it turned out to be Carlotta," she said with disarming candor. "She's such a bitch. Really, that's the only word I can think of to describe her. You should have heard the way she talked to poor Miss Vennible when she went to get her tickets. I mean, that's not Amanda's job, is it? To run around picking up tickets for faculty? If she wasn't, hadn't, been the chairman's wife…

"Joan didn't get that treatment. God knows I didn't, either. We had to make our own arrangements and pay for our tickets, up front…"

I reflected that Melody had had a rather rotten week. The department hadn't wanted to let her go up to the conference in Pittsburgh in the first place. Then she'd had to come back early to help Rhys-Davies with the fall class scheduling on Saturday morning. In the event she hadn't been given much of a chance to enjoy the conference.

"Surely," I said slowly, "if there was…foul play, I really don't think Carlotta could have been the one responsible. For one thing, she was out of town—"

"No, of course not, Stephen, don't be silly. It's just the way I'd like it to be. Not the way it was. The story of my life. Impossibilities." She looked at me intently. "Amanda and Sarah Jane and Walter had to go out to the airport to meet her—"

"Walter?"

"You know, Lieutenant Melnick, the one with the nice smile and the sad eyes."

Oh, yes, I said. Lieutenant Melnick. "I guess he spoke to you?"

"As if I had anything of interest to tell him."

I said I supposed that the police had to be very thorough and question everybody about where they'd been and what they'd been doing when Professor Roylett...died.

"Well, I told them," Melody said, challengingly. "I was at home. All evening. With Henry." Henry Fishbach's temperamental presence in Melody's life as what he termed unselfconsciously her 'significant other,' was something she knew instinctively bothered me and she usually managed to keep Henry to the background in our badinage.

I tried to change the subject. "I guess there'll be some kind of a service."

"Will there?" She didn't seem interested.

"You're not planning to go? I thought you...liked Roylett."

"You mean you thought I was sleeping with him."

"Melody," I remonstrated helplessly.

"Well," she said, "I suppose a lot of people did. Oh, for a while I guess I found him pretty attractive—I've always had a soft spot for older men—" a glint of mischief here "—and he seemed to find me...attractive. But I never did. Sleep with him. Besides, he was *such* an asshole." She mused. "And to think she could have had Huw."

"*Conquistador of the Caribbean?*"

She nodded.

"But it must have been years ago that Huw wrote that."

She shrugged. "Roylett must've known about Huw and her; God knows he kept Huw under his thumb. Besides, it was something he could always use if he wanted to divorce her, which he was—"

She waited for my reaction.

I counted to five, slowly.

"Everybody knows they weren't getting along, even if they did manage to put a good face on it when they went to parties. With her husband out of the way, Carlotta will be sitting pretty. Think of all that money and those paintings. And that house. The truth is, Dr Coulter," Melody said over her shoulder as she walked down the row of boxes, favoring me with a view of her trim rear end, "that if Roylett hadn't been, hadn't died, Carlotta was going to be left out in the cold. Like subfuckingzero."

And Melody—she didn't need to spell it out for me—could have been the next Mrs Roylett: Melody Roylett—it had a nice old-fashioned ring to it. I wondered how many times she had said it to herself, and seen herself in a large, airy house full of chintz and teak and vast pots of spring flowers.

Now she was angry with me for drawing her out, angry with herself for saying too much. "'Bye, lover. Menton next weekend?" I asked tentatively.

She was a good-humored girl, and forgave me. "Um, Menton's past hope," she said. "Wogs begin at Calais. Juan-les-Pins 's a better bet. 'Bye, darling."

*   *   *   *

The late afternoon sun tinged the oak trees apricot as I rode on a borrowed saddle. When I'd gotten out to the stable I'd learned that, in addition to Audrey's tack trunk and Linebacker, Bobby Robberson's minions had walked off with my saddle, too.

Out of the corner of my eye I could see, leaning against the fence, the slim dark figure of Lieutenant Melnick waiting for me to finish working the mare. From the indoor ring I could hear K.C. giving her afternoon kid lesson.

The Mare had come out of her stall in top form. Naturally a bit light in the front end department, she'd decided to try me by cake-walking delicately on her hind legs the whole way down to the gently sloping front field. I'd no sooner gotten her to settle down and walk on all four feet than she got on the muscle, boring in on the bit. A creature of extremes. I'd finally coaxed her into trotting on a long rein, making gradual turns around the big oak trees without losing impulsion, making her think it was her idea. I was trying to teach her to learn to balance herself, rather than relying on me and leaning on my hands each time she stumbled. That's the trouble with a lot of race horses and horses kept in stalls generally: they've never been worked over natural terrain. The problem is not just that they have to learn to balance themselves, to establish and maintain their own equilibrium, they have to learn to compensate for a rider's weight on their back, too: the moment you climb into the saddle you're changing their natural center of gravity. They'll take care of you if they can, if you let them. It was a big change for the mare, but she was showing herself up to the challenge.

I didn't know how long Melnick had been watching; there'd been no one around when we'd cakewalked down the hill. When I had finished, I rode over to him and dismounted. Though not many people observe the old-fashioned courtesy these days, I had had it drummed into me that you never carry on a conversation with someone on foot without first dismounting.

"Lieutenant Melnick."

"Dr Coulter," he said, acknowledging my greeting with equal formality.

"Lieutenant, with all respect I've got to tell you I really hate that doctor business. It makes me think somebody's waiting around for me to pull a stethoscope out of my pocket and write out a scrip."

"Sorry," he said mildly. "I thought that's what…academics like to be called."

"Not this one, I'm afraid."

"Look, I want to apologize for coming out here to bother you, but I need to talk with you. Besides, to be honest, I wanted to see something more than just the cement and asphalt around the university area."

We looked at each other for a moment, and he stretched out his hand. I shook it. That handshake marked the beginning of a friendship.

"I know what you mean," I told him.

I ran the irons up on the leathers and loosened the girth. "How the hell did you manage to find this place, anyway?" I led the mare through the gate, waited for him to follow me, and then closed it behind us.

"Looked in the book. Only one Gordonwood listed, and with a map…" We walked across the empty stableyard to the washrack. The three or four adult dressage riders were waiting their turn to get in the ring while the kid lesson was winding up, and so our conversation could be carried on in normal tones.

"Is that your regular saddle?" Melnick asked curiously, as I put it down on a bench.

"No, it isn't." I buckled a halter around the mare's neck and took off her bridle and hung it up. "What's on your mind?"

"The truth is, I need your help." He hesitated. "I guess you saw this morning's paper?"

"From what I read, it sounds like Roylett died of something like a heart attack."

I started to sponge the mare off, nose and ears first—I hate these clowns who spray water in a horse's face—then the tail. Doing a horse off after a hard work is a very special time for me, a kind of holy communion between me and whatever horse has been kind enough to share some good moments with me. I hated to have somebody around at such a time talking or hurrying me or spoiling it.

"That's the way the paper made it sound, all right. Of course we won't be sure until we receive the medical examiner's report and the test results have come back from the DPS lab."

Melnick took a new pack of unfiltered Luckies out of his shirt pocket and began stripping off the cellophane. "You're sure you saw blood leaking from his ears."

"Damn right, I'm sure. Anybody who wasn't legally blind could see it."

"Could everyone coming into the room see the blood?"

"I guess so. I noticed it from the doorway, when I opened the door. You could see the back of his head the way he was sprawled out on the floor."

"And you say you immediately knew it was Professor Roylett."

"Yes, that's right. Because of the clothes and the hair." I winced. "That silver hair and the pink scalp and the blood—"

"Scalp? You didn't say anything yesterday about his scalp."

"Didn't I? I guess I was trying to recall too many things at once, like what kind of clothes he was wearing. But now that I think about it, I can remember being surprised at seeing that pink scalp shining through his hair. I suppose I had always thought of Roylett's hair as being somehow…luxuriant, you know, and it must have been thin on top."

"And to the best of your knowledge the body wasn't disturbed before the police arrived at the scene?"

"I know I didn't disturb the body. But after I left the room to call—" Somehow, the thought of Sarah Jane Collins or Amanda Vennible prodding old Roylett's corpse seemed pretty ludicrous, although I had no trouble picturing Huw's giving the body a matey nudge with his thick-soled New Balance trainers to determine whether the chairman was going to get up off the floor before the whistle blew for another scrimmage. I shook my head. "No, even though I was out of the room I'm sure the others would have left the body alone. And if one of them had touched him, somebody would have said something."

"Well, they all say they saw the blood," said Melnick. "That's one thing, the blood. The other thing is that book you saw, the one lying on the floor? They all see that, too?"

"If they all say they saw the blood, then I suppose they're all going to say they saw the book, too, whether or not they really did," I observed. "It's only human nature, after all, Lieutenant. One of them, like Miss Vennible or Professor Collins, will say something about how she saw blood, and then the rest of them are going to remember it that way, too. Christ, it seemed like hours we were all sitting around until the police came and separated us for interrogation."

"Where was it, how was it lying when you first caught sight of it?"

I tried to summon up afresh in my mind's eye the scene that had greeted me as I'd opened the door. "'Caught sight of it' I don't know about. Once I'd seen Professor Roylett on the floor, I got a fix on him and then everything else was peripheral—mailboxes, walls, window, book. How big's the room, anyway? About what, fourteen, fifteen feet wide? About twelve deep? Something like that? Well, there was that desk not quite midway along the wall facing me, the chair shoved back and to the left against the table along the left-hand wall. Roylett's body was more or less below the window that takes up the rest of the facing wall. The right-hand wall is full of mailboxes, ceiling to floor. The book was lying on the floor beyond Roylett's left hand stretched out toward the corner made by the mailbox wall and the facing wall."

"The book was just lying there?"

"Just lying there, closed neatly, not like you'd throw a book down, say, and its spine wrenches awry. And don't forget, there were a lot of other books there, too, along the wall with the mailboxes, wrapped up mainly, sent on to new members of the department from God knows where."

"Anything else you remember about the book?"

"Now that I think about it, I couldn't see the book's spine: the long side of the cut pages was facing me. I remember it registering on me that it was a very large book, what they call quarto—most books except coffee-table books, they're octavo. This was a lot bigger, but it was no coffee-table book. It was brown, bound in brown buckram, and it looked familiar, like it was one of a series—not the size, you know, but the color of the binding—one of the scholarly presses puts out from time to time. Well, a good many of those presses or institutes have a certain kind of color they use for the binding, and a special logo or design, often stamped in gold on the spine. There are a lot of them that are blue of various shades: Oxford, Yale, Columbia, and Cambridge, and I recall Oxford always seems to have a logo with three crowns, like Nebraska has a buffalo. But the cover of this one was blank. There wasn't anything on this one that I can remember."

"Which means what, exactly?"

"Not much, probably, except that, since the spine of the book was away from me, the book either had a blank cover or it was lying face down, with the top of the book pointing toward the center of the room."

"Well, there was a book, it wasn't your imagination. I sent it to the lab to be gone over and photographed. When I get the pictures back I'll show them to you."

"Fingerprints?"

"Well, yes, although the chance of finding anything we can use is pretty unlikely, I'm afraid. Especially with library books, where you've got a rough, textured surface. I was thinking more in terms of—"

"Fluids and serums?"

"Signs of compression, anyway, if the book was indeed employed as a weapon; in which case there may be blood, hair, and skin samples…"

"Something else I was going to ask you about," Melnick said. "I got to thinking about how when you found Dr Roylett, you went to check for the pulse in his throat. How come with all that blood around, you didn't just pick up his wrist?" His eyes were steady on me. "All those great minds, the ones just standing around, they would have settled for picking up his wrist…"

"What's your point?"

"The pulse in the throat's surer, somehow."

I shrugged.

"But you didn't seem to mind the mess." He shook his head. "Plunged right in, like you'd done it before. Or trained for it."

He shook his head and watched me as I led The Mare back to her stall and hung up my tack.

"Come on over to my car for a second, will you? Let me show you something."

CHAPTER 8

▼

Lesson kids, chattering, hard hats pushed back on their heads, feet out of their irons, started pouring out of the ring on their way down to the wash rack. In a moment it would be pandemonium.

We made it to Melnick's clean, polished dark blue car, and he unlocked the trunk and searched in the kind of suitcase-sized attaché case that airline pilots carry around the terminals that you always suspect they've got sandwiches and a bottle of Chardonnay in instead of maps.

"I've been doing some checking around, which I might add isn't all that easy these days, with rights to privacy and so on—"

"Fishbach would call you a fucking fascist."

Melnick snorted derisively, and then decided to relax. "Now there's a piece a work: Fishbach. Him and that master a the martial arts, both. Beddington. But what I got in this file, what I want you to look at, this is the best I've been able to come up with so far.

"The fact of the matter is that you and I both know that Roylett may not have just popped off of a heart attack. What's giving me a problem is that the people I need to talk to are right off my screen."

"What you mean is, they're weird."

"Your word, not mine, but, yes, by my standards, anyway, weird. I feel like I'm in one of those dreams where you're walking through mud. I can't find out what these people are really like. That's why I came to see you. I want you to help me, find out something about, say, if Roylett really did get killed, who might've had a reason to do it. What's so funny?"

"Jesus, Lieutenant, who *wouldn't* have wanted Roylett out of the way? He wasn't exactly flavor of the month. Even Miss Vennible or Sarah Jane Collins might have had their reasons for not liking him. But that's a hell of a long way from saying that they might have killed him."

Melnick shrugged. "Yeah, I know that. But I've got to begin somewhere. That's why I want you to take a look through these files and tell me what you think.

"In the meantime I'm going to try to talk to the one got fired, that lecturer, Beddington. He may be able to shed some light on how the English department building got vandalized over the weekend. Even if he wasn't one a the lecturers that actually trashed the offices and did the paint-spraying, he may know who was, or have seen something. Miss Vennible says he hadn't turned his key back in. Not that that means much—from what I've heard there could have been faculty members—remember you told me how you felt?—who thought Roylett gave the lecturers a raw deal and thought they saw a way to even the score without any risk by letting them into the building with their own keys."

"What is it, exactly, that you want me to do?"

"You've seen dossiers before, granted maybe not like these. Don't even ask where some of this material came from. Look them over. Anything that doesn't seem right to you, give me a call. You find you want to talk to some of them, go ahead, it isn't going to do any harm."

"Who all's in here?"

"Except for Miss Vennible and Professor Collins, all the main players. Which brings up a point. I'd appreciate it if you'd keep the information I'm giving you strictly confidential. What's in these files comes from…different sources. Not just from your basic university personnel folders—"

"I see. What about Mrs Roylett?"

"What about her? She's in here."

"Didn't you go out to the airport to meet her plane?"

"That's right, I did. She was on it. Even so, there's a folder on her, too, as well as one on the other lady who was out of town, Professor—"

"Joan Strossner-Boynton?"

"Thanks. Yes, that's the name. There's one in here on her, too."

"How did Mrs Roylett seem to take it when you broke the news?"

"Pretty well, I'd have to say. Went on about her business. Naturally, I'll be talking to her again." He paused. "You know, no one said anything about her."

"About her being, you were going to say, a lady of color?"

"Yes, that. Nobody said anything about that." Melnick had his prim side.

"They probably didn't think it was important."

The look he gave me was frankly skeptical. I wondered how long it would be before Melnick stumbled across Huw's book of poetry, *Conquistador of the Caribbean*.

"Lieutenant Melnick, why are you telling me all this?"

"Call me Walter, all right? You don't remember me, do you? It was a long time ago, back East. It was the year you were riding one of your wife's hunters at the Garden: Rusty Coulter on Lord of the Isles—Jesus wept, you were good."

I shook my head.

"Nah, not that last year, but I was there for that, too. When that Irish boy, what was his name? Jerry somebody, was riding.

"I was with the NYPD Mounted unit put on an exhibition during the show—you know, a couple of matinées and evening performances. I used to stay after to watch you ride. You're a bit thinner now, a little older, but you still sit a horse the same way you used to. I'd have recognized you today, anywhere. You got a real way with the tricky ones.

About how you tranked that horse and got set down? I never believed it, not for a New York minute. You know, thing is, Rusty, *I* got set down once on a bad drug bust. Back to patrol. It was a frame, pure and simple." I said nothing. "I guess nobody around here knows who you are, were, who you were married to. It made all the papers back home."

"That was a long time ago, Walter. This is now. I've got a different life now."

"Bullshit, different life. You can't get away from the horses, I don't care what you do, how many degrees you got. You know that? It's in the fucking blood. What brought you down here anyway, you mind me asking?"

It was time for a change, I told him. "You seem to know a lot about me, Walter. What about you, how did you wind up in Texas?"

"GTT? Gone to Texas, isn't that the old saying? My daughter wants to get me a pair of boots, Manny Gammage hat, the whole thing. Cowboy." He snorted.

"I like those shoes you've got on."

"I take care of them. Tree them, even. People around here, they never heard of trees. I had enough of the Big Apple. My wife died three years ago. I came down here to be with my daughter. Polly. Paulina Eileen. Her mother was part Irish, God rest her. Polly's just finishing up her degree in classics, they got one of the best programs in the country down here apparently. So I took early retirement from the NYPD, sold the house in Queens, decided to see what all the fuss was about, the Sun Belt, came down here. Got a call from New York, old friend, put me in touch with this guy at USW, roar of the greasepaint, smell of the crowd, first thing I know I'm at work again."

"A little different from busting chops in South Vietnam?"

"SoHo? No." He seemed embarrassed. "Silk stocking stuff. Manhattan North. Your old stompin grounds, guy like you: ZIP code 10021.

"You really sit still on a horse, you know that? You leave them alone. I never could do that, always had to take charge, make a big move."

"They all want to go a different way," I said. "They're individuals. I try to see how they like to go best."

Our conversation was interrupted by Kay's strident voice admonishing her twice-weekly dressage ladies to drive their horses up onto the bit.

"No strong arm stuff?"

"Not unless it's absolutely necessary."

"What then?"

I considered. "I guess then I get after them, at once and very hard."

"I'll remember that," said Melnick.

*   *   *   *

It was twilight by the time I found Bobby's place. It was located behind an affluent new subdivision northeast of town, and spread out over several acres. The road leading from the highway up to the complex of low white buildings was neatly asphalted with smoothly-trimmed verge and espaliered fencing on each side. I passed several shedrow barns, outbuildings for trailer, hay, and shavings storage, one large covered ring, at least two outdoor rings, one with lights, some small turnout paddocks, and, close to a boundary fence, a large round Hitchcock pen for schooling prospects over fences.

I pulled up in the parking area near a frame building that had a sign on its covered porch that said "Office." From what I took to be the lounge next to the office came music and bright après-riding chatter, the kind where folks in Harry Hall breeches and sparkling boots talk knowledgeably about big fences and bad falls. It was a sound I knew very well. It seemed to me I could hear the seductive sound of ice tinkling in tall drinks, but that may have been because I was getting very thirsty. The burning-leaves scent of prime cannabis was so strong you couldn't smell the horses.

The vehicles parked around me gave a pretty fair idea of the lines along which Bobby's clientele were divided, part top-dollar show stable, and part high-volume after-school lesson business. Near the office, a BMW, a Mercedes, two Jaguars, and two Range Rovers. I guessed boarders who paid top dollar got box stalls with private turnout runs for their horses, grooming, individual lockers for their tack and equipment, and keys to the paneled customer lounge, with a bar and big screen television set. Smaller box stalls with no turn outs were provided for boarders with less clout. Down near what I judged to be the lesson horse barn—a couple of long shedrows housing a number of straight stalls for lesson horses—there were an Ford Aerostar minivan, an '85 Bronco, three Chevy Suburbans, a Volkswagen Jetta, and a rusty blue Grand Am. While most of the BMW/Mercedes crowd seemed to be in the lounge—though, even as I watched, a gray-suited man got in one of the BMWs, and a thin helmeted figure ran down the steps of the lounge and took off on a big Harley hog—below the salt the Surburban mothers trudged grimly from vehicle to stall to ring, arms filled with bags of carrots, bootjacks, hunt caps, and, rather optimistically, bits of knitting. Hither and yon in the gloaming silent slim dark men mucked stalls and filled wheelbarrows.

In the lighted indoor ring Bobby was giving a jumping lesson to a few of his customers on expensive looking horses. He had a remote microphone and when he wasn't talking somebody was playing Los Del Rio's hot club song "Macarena." In the other ring under lights, outside, a woman with a loud voice was instructing about a dozen kids in self-assured tones, while mothers watched intently and knitted feverishly.

On my way over to the shedrows I had to walk past the Hitchcock pen. It was a professional and obviously well-used setup. The pen consisted of an eight-foot solid board outer wall that a horse couldn't get her head over and a smaller concentric fence set about ten feet inside the outer wall, leaving between them a kind of circular lane where you could drive a horse around and, by placing poles in various configurations in brackets along the outer wall and on regular jump standards on the inner wall, longe them over fences to get an idea of how they balanced themselves. There were a number of chewed-up rails glittering on the ground. Tack rails penalized a clumsy jumper. They were regular jump rails studded with a broad strip of closely-set nails; some pros used them, set—if they had any sense—not in a usual jump cup, but on the lip so that the slightest hit would dislodge them, as a form of passive encouragement: if the horse jumped clean, nothing happened. There was some kind of battery charger device near the small entrance gate and some hopples and a scarred, heavy leather bomber jacket were hanging on one of the jump standards. I reached up and felt the back of the jacket where it was torn. I brought my fingers to my lips. Salt.

I found Audrey's trunk in the shack-like tack room in the middle of the shedrow, its lid thrown back, its contents scattered on the floor. My saddle was dumped in a corner, with the girth still attached to it. For some reason the cantle hadn't gotten skinned and it still had my irons on their Gibson leathers that some good soul had thought to punch a few homemade holes in for some lead-line rider's short legs.

I finally tracked down Linebacker. He was standing uncomfortably on the hard uneven ground in a tie stall at the end of the farthest shedrow. Dried sweat gummed his back, around his barrel, and the bridle path behind his ears. His knees were scabbed and his shins were pockmarked with dry blood. There was a gall on his withers where somebody hadn't taken time to adjust a saddle properly, and sores behind his elbows where he hadn't been groomed. We exchanged looks. It was a tough world, I told him, but urged him to recall the old horseman's saw, "it was a long way from the heart."

I walked back over to the indoor ring, put the saddle down at the ground at my feet, and leaned on the rail, and for a few minutes watched Bobby in action. Parents, including, I noticed, Terri Simmons, were watching as Bobby had his class perform individually over a small course.

"Hey, Coulter," Bobby yelled, catching sight of me and speaking in his normal voice. "You want to see me?"

"Yeah, your guys got my saddle the other day. I came to pick it up."

"No shit? The guys must've taken it by mistake." He sounded amused and unrepentant. "It's probably down in the tackroom in the last shedrow, if it's anywhere. Make yourself at home. I'll be through here after a while and I'll go down there with you.".

"I already found it, thanks."

"Oh yeah? Good."

"And the horse, too. Linebacker."

"Yeah, well, that's cool. You see Audrey?" He handed over the mike to an assistant and started walking over to the rail where I was standing while the lesson continued.

Audrey was riding a nice capable-looking brown gelding with a lot of white on its front ankles and a blaze face. She was wearing a tube top and California tights. When she turned away from me, I could see her knobs of backbone, her collarbones sticking out. Her hair, a different color, was cut in a Nancy Spungen haystack. Her nails were chewed down to the cuticles.

"Yeah," I said. "I see her."

Audrey had a vacant expression. She appeared exhausted and dirty. She exuded a kind of tawdry sexuality. In her made-up mask of a face, with its vacant expression, her eyes looked haunted, sick. She was terribly thin, even emaciated. Her jaw was working at a wad of gum, and she was talking nonstop out of the side of her mouth.

She reminded me of the kind of fourteen-year-old girl you saw in *Vogue* selling thigh creme, and I recalled a model I'd once dated and come across years later, married to a sundried Californian with specialized interests. She looked—I tried to remember the phrase—"turned out."

"What you think of that?" Bobby asked me. "Lookit that little bitch come down that last line! See that horse? She's going to be limit champion in Dallas with that big brown sucker, with me riding him in the green classes. I tell you one thing"—laughing—"how long you been around her, Coulter, not saying anything, keeping it all to yourself"—another yelp of laughter—"I tell you straight when I get through with her she'll be pure-dee stump broke, *and* she'll give head's good as her old lady. Suck the chrome off a trailer hitch, I promise you."

He stopped talking as I squared around to face him.

"Listen, Bobby, I've got to tell you something," I said, keeping my voice flat. "That pen of yours, Bobby, you can practically fucking kill a horse in there really easily, with you standing in the middle with a good long longe whip driving him around and around. Till they drop. I expect you know that. Much less the tack rails, and those electric hopples, try to see some green horse's got any jump in him, sharpen up an old one. Matter of economics, salvage an investment, I understand that. But you want to be careful with those kind of training aids, Bobby. And the rock salt shotgun treatment on a quitter, poor bastard riding the horse takes a real risk…

"Now you know and I know, Bobby, that me calling in a report of animal cruelty to the humane society isn't going to mean jack shit. Before they do anything to you, you've got to be caught doing a lot worse than what you're doing now. Fact, they got to be dead, or damn near, before anybody makes a move. Right?"

He looked at me intently, the beach-boy blond hair and million-dollar smile not hiding the tough Houston slum kid underneath.

"But just take time to think a minute, Bobby, with me down at The University, surrounded by all those bleeding heart activists, shrub-huggers and ethical-treatment-to-pets types and such—every one of them's either an intern down at the paper or with *Texas Today* or with the television stations, or they know a reporter. In this new sensitive culturally-aware environment we're living in, I place a few calls, invite a couple of them to take a field trip, come out here with a photographer. Who knows, maybe I even go down the courthouse, swear out a complaint, so the sheriff has to at least investigate. What this means, is it means publicity, right? Maybe nothing happens, chances are it probably doesn't.

"But the coverage doesn't do you any good, right? Everybody reading the morning paper. Or watching the ten o'clock news with one of those twenty-year-old girls with the big eyes, bosom swelling with righteous indignation how those horses owned by the idle rich are being mistreated. Then daddy or whoever paying your bills, reading the paper, watching the news, says who needs this shit?"

"Is that a threat?"

"Take it any way you want," I told him mildly. "If the shoe fits...From taking a look at some of your customers, a lot of publicity isn't exactly top of their Christmas gift list, if you take my meaning, let alone something to do with cruelty to animals. Or the odd baggieful of marijuana a person might find looking hard enough. Or, for that matter, all a person'd have to do to chase off those exchange students you got working for you'd be to come in one day yelling 'Migra!'"

"You finished, old man?"

"Not quite," I told him evenly. "Last, about that Linebacker horse from K.C. If I were you I'd get a vet out, look him over, especially those cuts on his shins and where his knees are scraped."

I hesitated.

"By the way, Bobby, you want to keep those tack rails of yours—I see you at least had the brains to use aluminum nails—good and dry. They get wet like that, lying on the ground, they tend to swell up and start spitting those nails out and first thing you know you go to use them you wind up with a hell of a bunch of deep cuts. Then you need to pound them in again, clip them off to about an eighth-, quarter-inch. Tack rails are a serious investment, you got to take care of them. Besides, the big boys went a long time ago to those plastic strips you use for carpeting; you can hardly see them. You're behind the times."

Bobby's face showed consternation as if he'd grabbed hold of a rattlesnake and didn't quite know what to do with it.

The truth was there was no substitute for starting with a good clean-minded horse, but the realities of a professional horseman's life sometimes forced him into an acquaintance with things like tack rails and electric gimmicks.

I walked back to the car and was spreading the saddle out flat in the trunk when I heard a voice from behind me. "Mr Coulter?"

"Yes, Audrey?"

"It's good to see you."

"It's nice to see you, too, Audrey. You looked good in there over those fences."

She shrugged and those chickenwing collarbones shifted up and down above the skimpy tube top.

"Well, I just wanted to say hello."

"That's a nice horse you've got there," I said. I didn't have the heart to mention Linebacker. She knew, and I knew she knew and felt bad.

"I'm glad you like him. I—"

"Audrey, what do you think you're doing?" It was Terri, quivering with anger. "You don't have any right to come over here and bother her. Causing trouble."

"I just came over to pick up my saddle, Terri," I said protestingly.

"Well, now you've got what you came for, you can leave. Audrey's just doing fine. We both are—"

"Please give my best to Art," I said. "I'm sorry to have missed him."

"Oh!" Her face turned white with rage.

"Good bye Audrey," I said, and gave her a smile as I got in the car.

Christ, I thought, disgusted, doesn't anyone see this? Had the whole world gone mad?

CHAPTER 9

▼

On the way home I stopped at a farmer's market out on 290 and picked up some fresh tomatoes and sweet onions. When I got home I sliced and sprinkled them with olive oil and balsamic vinegar and put them on a plate with Norwegian sardines for supper.

Afterwards, I brewed some coffee and washed the dishes and put them away. Then I spread the contents of my briefcase out on the kitchen table. For the next several hours I drafted assignment schedules and closed up loopholes in the policy statement I would distribute to my classes—that ironclad contract between teacher and student handed out the first day of class. Policy statements covered such matters as criteria for awarding grades, weighting of written work and tests, class participation, and absences. Often written late at night and under pressure, policy statements have been accorded the weight of Holy Writ in the light of day in courtroom proceedings brought by litigious students (or their parents) against teachers who, it is alleged, have, by awarding a semester grade of a C, deprived the plaintiff of the opportunity of being accepted at Yale Law School or Harvard Medical School (and thus the expectation of earning an income commensurate with that of an F Lee Bailey or a Denton Cooley). Even in an academic discipline as modestly rewarded as college English, professors have been known to avail themselves of liability insurance. Hence, I found myself writing "Is there any reason you can't make the scheduled office hours?" The previous semester I'd had complaints that the time I'd set aside for students' conferences didn't fit their schedules.

The fourth course was a new one for me and I was still waffling about what text to assign. It was a course called Masterworks of Literature, with the inevitable sub-colonic qualifier: either English or American. I'd opted to teach the English. For most of my thirty-five or so students this would be the only exposure they'd have to English literature at the college level, and for most of them it'd be just another course to be gotten out of the way in the earning of a diploma.

I sighed. I could see myself ending the semester barely up to Samuel Johnson. I reflected ruefully that many of my colleagues teaching the course found it congenial to give short shrift to anything before the eighteenth century, spending the majority of their time on Fielding, Dickens, the Romantic poets, and Joyce, Yeats, and Eliot.

How the devil could I be expected, in sixteen weeks, to expose my students to the matchless range and breadth of English literature? To guide them past the temporary but very real barriers that differences in diction and vocabulary of past years imposed. To enable them to appreciate the glories of the language. I knew I'd be lucky if one or two heard, paused, and listened to those voices—Herrick's and Herbert's and Marvell's and Milton's and Keats's—which sang heart-to-heart across the centuries, the gulfs and mountains of an imperfectly-recognized history.

One method was to concentrate on relatively short lyric poems. I thought I'd begin as usual with a bracing dose of old ballads like the "Three Ravens" and "Lord Randal" and "Edward"—ancient, savage, mysterious tales of murder, honor, and family; then serve up a taste of Old English with "Caedmon's Hymn" and Pound's translation of "The Seafarer"—no matter what the serious scholars thought of the liberties the old magician had taken with it—then go on to the sonnets and Marlowe and Webster and Ford and...of course it would be a shame not to expose them to some bawdy Restoration comedy. I noticed in the paper that the university drama school was putting on a production of Wycherly's *The Country Wife* and I could dovetail…I sighed.

*   *   *   *

At eleven-thirty, just as I was putting the final touches on the assignments—the department actually gave us wide latitude in choosing the writers we covered—I was including a bit of Betjeman, Larkin, Heaney, and Hill at the expense of—heresy!—one or two poems by Yeats and Eliot—the telephone rang.

I might have known it would be Serena, calling from Middleburg, with the late-night huskiness and bonhomie that come from cocktails in a paneled room with the french doors open to a doubtless moonlit garden, underdone filet, vintage claret, a slice of Stilton, and an iced sherbet.

Upon being decanted from whatever Rolls or Land Rover she'd been driven home in, I guessed, and being deposited at her door by a safe pinkfaced gent in an ancestral dinner jacket, and facing the prospect of a night alone with her own company, my ex-wife had not unreasonably been seized by blackcord fever.

"Hello."

"Hello," I said. "Serena?"

"Stephen? Are you alone?"

Yes, I told her, I was alone.

"It's a beautiful evening here. Just a hint of fall."

Jesus.

Yes, I said, I could imagine; it must be beautiful. It was hot here.

"In Texas."

Yes, in Texas.

"You don't have to be there, you know."

Yes, I said, I know; I don't have to be in Texas.

"With all those dreary people."

"Serena—" I sighed; we'd been all over this before.

"I had a lovely evening, an absolutely wonderful evening." I could picture Serena's windflushed face, her sparkling hazel eyes, her heavy mass of silver-blond hair caught back in an artlessly simple chignon; the old red gold bracelets and the emerald ring I'd bought her when I sold Epitome to the Italian team.

"I'm glad. Who was there?"

And she told me, reciting the begats of her host and hostess and the other guests. Effortlessly and uncharitably my mind reconstructed the evening: conversations of a predictable and stupefying banality, centering on what local veterinary would make house calls…children…we had none, I thanked God.

"You must miss the horses. It must hurt terribly not to be able to ride in shows. It was the one thing you did well. But I don't suppose there's much in the way of shows there, or horses, either, for that matter, is there?"

Desperately, I lied, knowing it was what she wanted to hear. I told her I'd seen that Montrose had been champion at Devon.

"Yes. And at Upperville, too. The horses never went better."

"Great," I said, in the hearty voice I reserved for speaking with Serena; it went with the petit-point fox-head evening slippers she'd given me one time for my birthday.

"I suppose I ought to thank you for the check you sent. But when I think what you could have had from your father—"

"We've gone all over that—"

"Yes. I know. You and your honor. And I'm the one who's made to suffer for it." Her words dripped with scorn.

Yes, I told her, she was right, I'd made a mess of things.

"As usual." Silence. "I can't think why I'm calling you, I really can't."

"Well," I began.

"No, let me finish. You make me furious, you could have done so much. And you did so very little."

"Serena—"

"I had a perfectly wonderful evening," she said defiantly. "I'm flying over to spend Christmas in Zürs with the Lamberts."

"Well, that's great," I said in my hearty insincere voice, and got to listen about how she was going with Mark and Edie to Jackson Hole after they wound up the spring show circuit at Wellington.

I dropped my gaze to the assignment sheet. I reckoned I could get to Rochester's "To Phyllis" right before Thanksgiving; things always dragged a bit then, and I noticed that A Sensitivity to Words was my week's listed subject for discussion: "swiving" as a verb—and not so incidentally Rochester's skill as a prosodist—ought to attract respectful attention once it was explained that to swive meant to fuck, but I made a note for later to rein in my Ruskin story. Poor Ruskin, whose only knowledge of female nudity as he grew up had apparently been gained from looking at statues and who on his wedding night had been so repelled by the (as he thought) deformity of his wife's pubic hair that he found himself unable to consummate the marriage. The problem, of course, was that the pubic hair story was so wonderfully sensational that it was likely to color and override and shortcircuit whatever else I might try to teach of Ruskin. I shook my head, reflecting guiltily on the hordes of students I was sending out into the world whose sole knowledge of the great Victorian champion of art was limited to a single, quite possibly untrue, discreditable—and, yes, memorable—story—which I expected, unrepentantly, I'd probably go right on making use of as a kind of literary starting fluid. All in all there was a lot I had to answer for.

Serena's next words brought me back with a jolt.

"Stephen. Lordy had to be put down."

"Oh, God." Lord of the Isles under the lights at the Garden with the top hats and evening dresses, in the rain at Devon, or in Upperville's oak-dappled shade, he'd stand at the in-gate so utterly calm. Once in the ring he'd prick his ears, ready for business, and smoothly lengthen his stride out toward the fence, with confidence unchallenged. I remembered his clench and gather, the coiled spring unsprung, the thrust and the fold and the far buoyant landing. That horse never put a foot wrong with me, dropped a toe, even, all those years. I found myself blinking back sudden tears.

"I'm so terribly sorry."

"That's about right for you," she said with satisfaction. "'Sorry' about sums you up."

"I don't know what else to say," I said. "He was a great horse. He was a part of my life—"

"The only thing you're sorry about is that you weren't the one riding him the last time he was champion at the Garden."

"No, that's not true…"

"I haven't even heard from Jerry in I don't know how long; I saw in *The Chronicle of the Horse* where he went back to Ireland"—and then, irrelevantly—"you know, Stephen, you really don't relate to people very well, do you?"

Rather desperately I found myself saying that I supposed she was right, I didn't do well in my relationships with people. And I guessed it was true.

After our conversation had worn itself down among increasingly uncomfortable silences, and we'd said good-bye, I entered the changes I had been making while we talked and printed out a final draft, ready to be taken in to Kinko's for Xeroxing in the morning.

I got up from the table and stretched and made myself a very large drink and opened the door to the apartment and looked out to where the tanned girls and boys frolicked in the aquamarine pool.

Then, because I could put it off no longer, I turned my attention to Melnick's assignment.

I placed the expanding manila wallet on the table, untied the tape, and opened the flap. Within were cobbled-together dossiers from God only knew what sources. First was Sebastian Roylett—pride of place accorded, I guessed, to his being the victim—and then, in no obvious order, files on Carlotta du Plessis-Roylett, Ed Vere, Joan Strossner-

Boynton, Melody Harker, Henry Fishbach, Amos Beddington, Huw Rhys-Davies, and Stephen Coulter.

*   *   *   *

By the time I had finished going through the dossiers it was almost four o'clock and as I got up to make a nightcap I noticed that the pool lights had been turned off, the golden lads and girls gone off to sleep.

From the start I'd figured my chances were about nil to zero of coming across one of these people standing over Roylett's corpse holding the metaphorical smoking gun. Sure, everyone on Melnick's list—I was pleased he didn't consider Sarah Jane or Amanda as suspects—had reason to be better off with Roylett out of the way. There wasn't a one of them—us, I amended—who wasn't provided with sufficient incentive to want to crush the old rip's skull with a big book. But to really do it? Denied tenure, assistant professors might go in for abusive late-night phone calls or even tip the odd pound or two of sugar into the gas tank of the chairman's Jaguar, but actually committing murder struck me as a bit overreactive.

I reflected on what I now knew about these people, piecing it together from what I'd known of them first hand, what I'd heard about them, and what I'd come across in their dossiers.

Sebastian Roylett had been reared in the Midwest. It was talked of in the halls that his money had something to do with patents on tiny and homely and essential auto parts: tire valve stems, I seemed to recall hearing. He received his bachelor's degree from Kenyon, gotten married, and gone on to Columbia for graduate school. The marriage didn't survive the slog of graduate school. Ruthlessly revised with an eye for washing off what publishers like to call the dissertation stink, his thesis on Congreve came out under the imprint of a respectable house the year after he'd earned his doctorate and had gone to teach at Wisconsin. Then, three years later, having expanded the scope of his research, Roylett published a four-volume scholarly blockbuster on Restoration comedy which won him a good bit of critical attention.

Next—finger to the wind, Roylett was quickly proving himself a spotter-of-trends before they got trendy, was how I read it—he turned his considerable energy to mining the then-underdeveloped areas of folklore and ethnic studies. His wildly popular account of the Jackson Whites was awarded a Pulitzer Prize and became the basis for a television miniseries.

Several long articles he'd found time to write on the mystical elements in fiction by and about Native Americans came out as a book at the time of Wounded Knee II. A couple of years later he was memorialized in a photograph appearing in *Time*, wearing a red headband and carrying an upside-down American flag as he protested side-by-side with Russell Means and Oscar Standing Bear at the Custer Centennial at Crow Agency, Montana.

Then, having apparently exhausted his interest in seventeenth- and eighteenth-century English drama, post-Revolutionary War miscegenation, and the genocide practiced on Native Americans, Roylett focused his attention on Ireland. For the best part of a year he taught American literature at the University of Galway, traveling to Dublin on the weekends where, according to *People* magazine—Roylett had now established himself in the public eye as a kind of academic jetsetter—he carried on an affair with a well-known fashion model. He embarked on a translation of the Book of the Dun Cow, and wrote a monograph on Old Irish verse forms that was reviewed approvingly in *Celtica* by Calvert Watkins of Harvard.

In the early 1980s he was teaching in France on a visiting professorship at Paris-Nanterre. Reports about him were glowing: he must have been a charismatic lecturer. From what I could tell he'd taken an apartment in the Rue des Rosiers; it was easy to envision him making himself welcome in the literary world; it was at this time, I reckoned, that he began to buy manuscripts and accumulate paintings at an impressive rate.

From Paris he went to Yale for a semester and then did six months' committee service with the National Endowment for the Humanities. Then came the offer from the University of the Southwest, in those palmy days flush with oil income. Roylett was generally perceived, I expected, as providing the genteely enervated English faculty at USW—at the time coasting along with a few elegant old stagers on the Romantics and Victorians, a superb Chaucerian, and a brace of distinguished Anglo-Saxonists—with a much-needed jumpstart in the newly-popular areas of folklore, linguistics, and ethnic studies; besides, the man had tremendously valuable international contacts, many of them established as he had acquired a very respectable collection of manuscripts and iconography which with luck might make their way into the holdings of the USW library. Another photograph, this one from the archive of the USW news service: wearing a Grateful Dead T-shirt and Armani suit and sporting black wrap-around shades, a three-day growth of golden beard, and a young gorgeous wife by his side, Roylett was his own best advertisement. His multimedia course— The University's first—The World Literature of Sexual Intimacy, proved an instant success, immediately provoking questions raised about it, and him, both in the State Senate and House of Representatives. ("I don't believe that it's in the best interests of the citizens of the Great State of Texas," declaimed a senator from Odessa, "to turn out students who don't know anything about Mark Twain while they spend all their time studying on Eurotrash like that Italian filmmaker Fellatio.") Predictably, Roylett won wholehearted endorsement by The University's student newspaper and achieved, for a while at least, immense personal popularity.

It was acknowledged that he'd been generous with his own money. He financed the publication of a departmental anthology of faculty and student verse and prose. He sponsored the visits of a number of speakers to the campus. He threw memorable parties attended by an admirable mix of administration officials, local businessmen, faculty, lawmakers, and students. He raised endowments for professorships and scholarships. And he proved to be a devastatingly effective recruiter, attracting to USW a number of world-class scholars. He kept up a high local visibility, maintaining memberships in several downtown clubs, and serving on the boards of two theater groups, a light opera company, a museum, and the county animal shelter.

At the time that the courtly Southerner who'd been Roylett's predecessor had announced his intention to retire from the chairmanship, Roylett had recommended himself as an obvious choice to succeed him. And he'd proved a good chairman, if by that you meant that he had a strong enough personality to keep the faculty in line. Heaven knew his political and academic credentials were not in question. His vita listed no fewer than fifteen national organizations of which he was a member, ranging from the ultra-conservative to the flamboyantly radical. I shook my head in silent admiration: Roylett had been a trend-spotter, a weatherman. The man was amazing, he truly was; he was, or, rather, had been, all over the academic landscape like kudzu vine.

Naturally absent from his dossier, I noticed, was any hint that Roylett had gone in for young girls; some regard for the dignity of his position as chairman had apparently prevented him from making too much of an obviously bloody ass out of himself. Not that there hadn't been liaisons: if you could believe the stories, there'd been many. But recently it seemed Roylett's only pleasure had come from the obvious joy he took in the firing the lecturers.

One of the last entries in his file noted briefly that in the past year there'd been two student complaints lodged with the dean's office about his teaching. It didn't say who'd made the complaints. There was also a note calling attention to the fact that at the time of his death he'd been directing fourteen doctoral dissertations.

I went back and studied the photograph taken at the Custer Centennial. A younger Roylett, to be sure, but the same penetrating gaze, the harsh sun striking down on the long locks of hair thinning on top, the tight hell-with-you smile.

The dossier said he'd been sixty when he died.
A dangerous age full of unlucky and inappropriate pursuits.

CHAPTER 10

▼

Putting down Roylett's folder, I turned to his wife's. Carlotta Irenée du Plessis-Roylett had been born in 1956, the younger daughter of a planter family originally from Mauritius whose holdings were located near Port Maria, on Jamaica's North Shore. She graduated at sixteen from a Catholic girls' school near Montego Bay. At twenty she earned her BA in English literature from the Mona campus of the University of the West Indies, in Kingston, and had apparently decided to go on for her doctorate at the same place, writing as her dissertation a social and cultural history of the Maroons. Carlotta took her degree at UWI in 1979 and for the next three years did postdoctoral work in linguistics at the Université de Paris 4 at the Sorbonne. In 1983 she accepted a one-year appointment to teach at Yale, and was recruited by The University of the Southwest in 1984 as an associate professor with tenure. She was well-established as a scholar of Jamaican Creole syntax, as a critic, and as a poet. Besides the beauty of her dark curls on that lovely nape of neck, long eyelashes and the scent of Tigre, she owned the priceless self-assurance of one who knows she has distinguished herself in the intellectually vigorous cut-and-thrust of the academic world and won the respect of the best practitioners of her discipline.

She came through the print like a rich bright girl. With a social conscience, I added as I looked over the list of her publications; no one could have grown up in Jamaica in the sixties and seventies, those decades of turbulent political upheaval and civil violence, without developing a lively social conscience, particularly, I surmised, at UWI.

She must have met Roylett when she was in Paris and then either gone off with him to Yale or followed him there; in any case, when Roylett arrived at USW it was with Carlotta as his wife, hired on as a full professor; it was no hardship for The University to find a place for her as well, for they were gaining a real winner.

*   *   *   *

I'd read somewhere that when there's a murder, the police always look first to the spouse as the primary suspect. Motive? So far as I could tell, Carlotta stood to inherit not only Roylett's money but that dazzling collection of art and the dramatic clifftop house above the lake as well. What she'd gain from her husband's death looked like a very compelling motive to kill him. But why? Had Roylett's legendary roving eye finally proved too much for her? Carlotta was very far from stupid; she was bound to have known of his peccadilloes, she must have known of them for years—and Melody—if the rumors were to be believed—was, after all, simply the newest in a long line of pretty girls.

After envisioning the tall, languid grace of Carlotta, and placing her in my mind's eye standing next to her tall, flamboyant husband, it took me a moment to focus on the subject of the next dossier, Ed Vere. Roly-poly, permanently disheveled, anxious-blue-eyes-behind-spectacles, he was a reach. I always expected Vere to wear a belt with suspenders. His obsessive punctuality was legendary in the department.

His vita said he had been born in Hardin, Montana, in 1922 and, like Carlotta, had graduated from high school at sixteen. Next—oddly, it seemed to me, with my mind now trying to visualize Montana in the 1920s—he was listed as receiving his BA from Oxford in 1942. Ten years later he earned his Ph.D. back in this country, at Pennsylvania, writing his dissertation on Langland's *Piers Plowman*, and joining the faculty of The University of the Southwest as an assistant professor. He had been teaching at USW ever since, rising slowly through the ranks, publishing the odd article on what appeared to me to be very precise and focused points concerned with methodology of research, bibliography, and Langland. At one time or another Vere had served on just about every departmental committee. He had received no prestigious awards, although he had from time to time been given a faculty research grant. I saw that he had married while he was in graduate school. His wife's name was Priscilla, and the Veres had two children, Thomas Newbold, born in 1949, and Jennifer, born in 1952. Vere's address was given as 2901 Clearview, in what I recognized as the quiet, tree-shaded neighborhood west of town toward the lake. On a slip of paper attached to the vita was a handwritten notation that the son was at present a research chemist with Du Pont, and the daughter now a single parent with two children, teaching school in Florida.

I next turned to Joan Strossner-Boynton's file. Because I saw a good bit of her out at the stable and occasionally at the gym, usually with Carlotta, I felt I knew Joan rather better than I did the others. Her vita said that she was originally from Sioux City, Iowa, where she attended a local high school. She'd apparently won a scholarship to Radcliffe, dropped out for a couple of years to serve in the Peace Corps in Central America, and then went on to graduate school at Yale. For her dissertation she translated and provided a commentary on an early work by Derrida. While she was still A.B.D.—"all but dissertation"—at Yale, she'd been recruited as an assistant professor. Closely involved with women's studies, Joan had now finished her seventh year of teaching at USW and was currently, as the saying goes, up—for tenure—or out.

She gave a course entitled Concealment, Lack of Conviction, and Calumny in which, according to the course description, she examined mid-century sentimental explorations of the abuses suffered by both white and African-American women in the patriarchal home and discussed some familiar mid-century male masterpieces in relation to the aesthetics of the closet.

She'd published a book on the aesthetic responses of Victorian women who traveled to the Middle East, "Three Sisters Who Led The Way". Her psychobiography of Isobel Burton was being seriously considered for publication by Princeton University Press. She had been a Mellon Fellow, a visiting professor at the School of Criticism and Theory at Ohio State University, a Mary Ingraham Bunting Institute Fellow at Radcliffe College, and an NEH Fellow.

She was a serious, capable woman and, with her solid publication record, I couldn't see her getting turned down for tenure. I knew her to schedule her time rigorously, paring her life down to the essentials: teaching, office hours, research for her next book, riding whenever she could fit it in, sometimes late at night, a bi-weekly trip to the gym, the quick odd dash for dry cleaning or groceries. Her social life was limited to an early dinner once a week with a couple of the other young women in the department. One evening at the Mexican restaurant on the Drag they'd spotted me dining alone and invited me over to their table, where I'd reciprocated by getting tight. Since then they'd acknowledged me in the halls with somewhat distant nods. I had plenty of time to reflect not for the first time that what passed for a pleasant and unremarkable jocularity in horsemen's circles was judged unspeakable or at least unacceptable conduct in the self-consciously tolerant groves of academe—no matter that many of the masterworks they (and I) taught were replete with instances of less than impeccable behavior.

Out at the barn Joan was a holy terror with a hoofpick. She had a mission to clean out Harry's feet all the way up to the heart, adding as a nice touch a dollop of Kopertox that typically resulted in him walking on eggshells for the next four or five days. When she took him out on the longe, she always put on side reins and bitting rig or a chambon. I don't think I ever saw her let the old horse really stretch out or play to get the bucks out. A good-looking girl—woman—Joan herself rode stiffly, with rigid spine, chin screwed down on her chest, and elbows locked. Riding as expiation, martyrdom. And she could get after a horse, really lose her cool, punish him. I'd been looking for a tactful way to show her some photos I had of Reiner Klimke and Ahlerich, radiant and sparkling, but so far the opportunity had eluded me. Besides, I reminded myself, so far as Joan was concerned, I was just hired help. And it would have been meddling, something I was in danger of forgetting I'd abjured.

The next three files were very slim, their subjects too young to have laid down much in the way of paper trails: Melody Harker, Henry Fishbach, and Amos Beddington.

Melody Harker, she of the filmy springtime dresses, was the daughter of a West Pointer, a retired Air Force brigadier general and his wife who lived up near Marble Falls on one of the highland lakes. Melody had grown up all over the world. It had been in Wiesbaden when she was in seventh grade, she told me, that she'd had a teacher who'd opened her eyes to English literature. When she got to USW she'd augmented her scholarship with work in the department. She began writing poetry of her own and won a prize in the spring departmental writing competition. It was the beauty of the thing that had appealed to her initially, she said, but now she'd gotten interested in what went into a poem to give it beauty: what's called prosody: the meters and rhythms, the rhymes, the techniques of enjambment, assonance, alliteration. The world was so obviously fresh and young for her and out of the modest materials of the department as she knew it I suspected she had constructed a private pantheon, the idealized features of whose gods and goddesses were slowly being eroded by the abrasion of reality. Melody was still in that stage of life where she found most people fascinating. Nevertheless, behind that idealism I thought I detected a kind of basic street smarts that would, I hoped, prevent her from making too many mistakes. Ask me about Miss Harker, Melnick had written in the margin of her dossier in his surprisingly prim handwriting. She was due to graduate in December.

Henry Fishbach had grown up in North Dakota and gone to college at St Olaf's in Minnesota before being accepted at USW as a graduate student in English. He was concentrating in the particular area of English called language and linguistics and was writing his dissertation, under Roylett's supervision, as Melody had said, on the political implications of nineteenth-century Cherokee dictionaries on Jacksonian democracy. I noted that Fishbach had done considerable long distance running in college and recalled that I'd seen him pounding along the jogging path around the lake, face contorted with the requisite look of unutterable agony.

Fishbach was involved actively in the graduate student association. I'd seen and heard him in the halls and in the graduate student lounge where I often went for a cup of coffee. He was a strong, good-looking lad with a carefully tended blond mustache and the kind of unconsciously defensive arrogance that sometimes goes with being a male graduate student in a field full of extremely intelligent women. He talked earnestly of bourgeois values, and examined at length with his companions the linguistic determiners of socioeconomic status—from which I inferred that those who had enjoyed the benefits of private education were apt to express themselves with greater precision than those who hadn't, and were likely as a consequence to land better jobs. Fishbach and his friends made rather a show out of referring to their professors, both male and female, by their surnames. Melnick noted he had no criminal record, unless he'd let his ice-fishing license expire up in Minnesota. On balance, I reflected, while I thought the conversation might run a bit thin if we found ourselves together for a long evening over whiskey, neither did I think Fishbach was likely to go around bashing people over the head. Now a bit of idle pointless vicious vandalism, that I could see him doing; but murder, no. And anyway, why, if Roylett was the supervisor of his dissertation? Roylett had a reputation of going to bat for his own graduate students, writing them letters of recommendation, helping them find jobs afterward, and hunting down publishers for their dissertations. Surely killing the chairman would run counter to Fishbach's best interests and he struck me as a man who kept his own best interests firmly in mind. Unless of course the artless Melody had aroused his jealousy over Roylett's attentions to her. Even so, Fishbach struck me as possessing too strong a selfish, self-protective streak to be spurred into committing murder for the sake of a girl, even a girl as beguiling as Melody. I shook my head. The thoughts of youth were indeed long, long thoughts; who knew what went through that northern mind?

Amos Beddington had been born in China, the son of Methodist missionaries killed in the 1971 riots shortly after he was sent back to the States at the age of five to be reared by his bachelor uncle, a retired professor of piano at USW.

Beddington had received his bachelor's degree from USW, had applied for and been accepted for graduate study in English, earned his master's, and then his doctorate, with the usual teaching assistantships offered and taken up along the way. Facts, bland. Other facts, more interesting: as an undergraduate Beddington concentrated on Shaolin Kung Fu martial arts and placed in the Texas State Full Contact Karate Championships competition. He had written his Plan II honors thesis on meditation and violence in medieval China; in graduate school he'd supplemented his TA-ship by working nights as a night security guard at the state hospital. His work on sadomasochistic and homosexual imagery in Ernest Hemingway was nominated by his adviser and won the prize for the best departmental dissertation of the year; sent on to the dean's office with a small blizzard of encomia commending it for special attention for a college prize. Predictably turned down: the mad dean hated and feared in the department as a notorious homophobe. Nevertheless—one in the eye for the mad dean!—hired by the department as a lecturer. Proved himself to be one of the most vocal and outspoken of that congenitally vocal and outspoken breed. Somewhere around this time, I judged, Beddington had gotten serious about trying to build up muscle mass to enhance his martial arts prowess, for he published a book of poetry called 'Roid Rage which made him the sensation of a semester reading on the local coffeehouse circuit. During spring break while he'd been riding his Harley-Davidson hog along the

Drag he'd gotten into that fracas with the Icelandic javelin thrower. That in turn had led to his associating himself briefly and dramatically with what older members of the department were likely to think of as the dissident element of graduate students, and then—over the protests of his ex-committee chairman—being suspended from teaching. A month or two later, having been found guilty of battery, he was turned down by a now nervous department when the time came up to renew his contract. God, how Roylett must have rejoiced at getting rid of that loose cannon on the deck! But, I reminded myself, Beddington still wasn't really out of sight. He continued to haunt The University like a disreputable relative you can't disown. I'd caught sight of him over the summer, gaunt and red-eyed, raking leaves and cutting grass south of MacFarland Hall. Someone had told me that one of the big university presses in the midwest was going to publish his book on Hemingway.

The department's associate chairman, Huw Rhys-Davies, with his dark face and flashing smile, was a grammar school boy from the Gower peninsula near Swansea, who'd gotten a very nice scholarship to Queens' College, Cambridge, where he'd distinguished himself academically and by playing rugby, first for his college with the celebrated Mike Gibson and then for the university side. Afterward he'd gone on to Oxford for a B Litt. It was really a weird course, Huw'd confided to me one sultry June afternoon over drinks, only done at Oxford: a sort of two-year Master's. C.S. Lewis once said that there were three types of person: the literate, the illiterate, and the B-literate. Huw was B-literate, and probably the reason he never stood a crack at getting taken on at Oxford. Even though universities were at the time expanding, Huw said that he counted himself lucky to get a lectureship at Nottingham where he stayed 1968–1976. While he was at Nottingham he published books on Dylan Thomas and on Thomas Hardy and the Georgian Poets, while poetry of his own was regularly appearing in the Penguin Poets series, as well as in collections of Welsh poetry. Bored out of his skull with Nottingham, so I gathered, Huw took up a three-year assignment to the University of the West Indies, met and fell in love with Carlotta Irenée du Plessis who was doing her thesis on Jamaican Creole Syntax. It was during this time that Huw wrote *Conquistador of the Caribbean*, completing it in the last term of his assignment after being advised that Nottingham had not held his place for him and that the best he could hope for would be a job at University College of Bangor, North Wales (population 13,000; students 2,000). Bangor and environs, he informed me with a straight face, *res ipsa loquitur*, are largely Welsh-speaking.

In Bangor, Huw met and married Bronwen Nicholas, the only daughter of a prominent hotelier from Bettws-y-Coed. The marriage was, Huw explained frankly to me, a fucking disaster, partly through social distance, snobbery of grim local chapel social-climber family ("Did you know Ian Fleming?" "Blacks really are a shiftless lot"), and through unexpected and unshakable frigidity of chapel-trained Bronwen. One child was born to them, and, in 1986, they were divorced.

At that point, Huw confided, relishing the Americanism, he was up Shit Creek without the proverbial paddle. The college and the community were all against him. Even after the divorce was finalized, there was no settlement over the property and Nicholas *père* was obviously quite content to hire lawyers till Doomsday. In the end Bronwen got the matrimonial home, or 75% of it. Under the Deferred Trust arrangement, she could stay in it until the child was 21—and Huw wasn't going to be able to lay a hand on any of his lifetime savings capital until three years into the twenty-first century. Bronwen was also into Huw for £6000 a year maintenance for herself and the child, while, as a Senior Lecturer, his pay was only £22,000 per year before tax. This maintenance requirement, he averred, was subject to review and could be increased at any time. As a rule of thumb, Bronwen could be depended upon to start a new round of litigation about once a year, figuring to get the maintenance raised in line with inflation. While the new increment might only tot up to be another £30 per month, Huw'd be charged with both their legal costs for the review, which usually shoveled on another £2000 or so.

British courts, I'd learned, were very slow to entertain the concept of "vexatious litigation" and remained deeply sexist, in the sense of protecting mothers and punishing fathers. "Marriage, for a middle-aged woman in England," a barrister informed Huw, "is a meal-ticket for life."

Huw had two salvations. The first was that the self-discipline that was so much a part of his personality drove him to write, under a pseudonym, *The Horse Lords Saga*, which proved to be a highly popular series of sword-and-sorcery novels set in a romanticized Other Time. Published in the United States, the first volume brought him £2500. The second volume published the next year brought him £5000, and the third, £10,000. His publisher had told him the fourth volume, now in press, was likely to bring him in £15,000. These earnings he'd squirreled away in a bank account he'd opened for himself in Cornwall. In fact, *The Horse Lords Saga* was now paying off Huw's debts and even allowing him to accumulate a grubstake. That is, he said with a shudder, so long as Bronwen, the Nicholas legal advisers, and the Inland Revenue didn't find out about it! If Bronwen even suspected that Huw was making any money outside his salary, it would be back to the law courts and even higher demands.

Huw's second salvation arrived in the form of the Morgan Visiting Professorship at The University of the Southwest. The terms under which the Morgan Chair was awarded were that it be held for one calendar year, with a possibility of being renewed for one more year only. The Morgan Visiting Professorship had been originally established to bring to Texas an academic with strong Welsh connections. Jim Bob Morgan, the donor of the chair, was an octogenarian Louisiana oil man, now on his fifth wife and second bypass.

Huw's appointment to the Morgan Visiting Professorship had indeed been renewed last January and was due to expire the end of this year, at which point Huw must have snaffled a legitimate job in the United States, or else his visa would expire and it would be back to the abiding furies of Bangor and Bronwen.

The past winter a pal of Huw's at Maryland had come up with an invitation for Huw to give a guest lecture on modern Welsh poetry and it and he were well received. Afterward, there had been some pretty sincere talk about getting Huw aboard at Maryland and in April he had been on the point of clinching a deal with Maryland when he'd gone to see Roylett.

Roylett was in an expansive mood and painted a rosy picture of Huw's future with the English department at USW. He told Huw that he was a certainty to be hired in the fall as a full professor at USW. No question about it, Roylett had been working behind the scenes on Huw's behalf. A little paperwork deftly handled, that was all that remained to be done, and Bob's your uncle. Not to worry. Huw expected and indeed was in effect promised by Roylett that he would be made a full tenured professor in the fall. But as June gave way to July, and July to August, Roylett had become hard to pin down, had taken to sounding evasive about Huw's appointment. It was summer; the executive committee was away; the dean was in Europe; there was a budget crunch; both the provost and the vice president and dean of graduate studies were unforthcoming...no new appointments were being made. It didn't seem likely that there'd be any new recruiting...and the truth was (frank, harried look) that if an opening should develop, the department was in sore need of a senior person in Chaucer. Besides, Roylett told Huw, he had to be able to certify in all good conscience that Huw could do a job that no other United States citizen could do. Now, said Roylett, I ask you as a just and reasonable chap, can I say that truthfully, Huw? After all, there's that man Gareth Jenkins at Illinois; he's been down here a time or two and, as no doubt you heard, he made a very strong positive impression when he spoke on The Wife of Bath."

CHAPTER II

▼

Fuck the Wife of Bath, Huw felt like telling Roylett through his new teeth: I need the bread. It was all a lot different story from the one Roylett told Huw back in April, when Huw had all but clinched the Maryland appointment.

Rhys-Davies was by now desperate, and in his heart of poor-boy-playing the-game-like-a-gentleman hearts, found himself also deeply offended by Roylett's dishonest maneuvering.

I speculated that, in the way of such things, the mice would soon be coming out of the woodwork. Following Roylett's death, it was perfectly possible, nay, probable, that the chairman's perennially cowed executive committee would reveal—and this would turn out to be the received view held by the dean's office as well as by the provost and vice president and dean of graduate studies—that *of course* Huw was all set up to be appointed as a full professor. The truth of the matter was likely to be that Roylett had been more or less idly playing cat-and-mouse with Huw for no other reason than the simple pleasure he derived from watching someone suffer.

I was brought up short when I came across my own file.

Stephen Coulter, Lecturer in English. It was pretty much all there. Even SERE. But nothing about Fort Devers, I was glad to see. I finished my nightcap, set the alarm for five-thirty, and went to bed. As usual, sleep eluded me and I thought inconsequentially of the golden lads and girls and Keats lying in his corner room next to the Spanish Steps, listening to the fountain splashing outside, and making his mind up that he wished no epitaph save for the words "Here lies one whose name was writ in water."

*   *   *   *

In the morning I forced myself to go out for a run. My legs were like pig iron. After I'd breasted that last hill on Twenty-Fourth Street, gagging for air, I stopped at the Circle K and bought a paper and, as I cooled down walking back to the apartment, looked through it to see if there was anything more about Roylett's death. He'd been moved back off page two of City and State into the respectable obscurity of the obituary section: private family graveside services were scheduled for the next morning in Peru, Indiana, the late chairman's hometown; a memorial service would be held for his friends and colleagues (they had that right, anyway: separate categories) on Friday in the Dean's Room of the Old Music Building at 1:30 p.m. In lieu of flowers, donations could be made to the Sebastian Roylett Fund in the College of Liberal Arts or to something called the Sunbeam Society which, after having read Roylett's *vita*, I figured was probably an environmentally sensitive gay rights organization.

I put the water on to boil, and took a shower. About the time I'd finished brushing my teeth and shaving, the water was ready to pour through. While I waited I knocked back a half-tumbler face-stiffener of tequila, smoked a cigarette, rummaged around on my desk for a departmental roster, and went down to my car to retrieve a map from the glove compartment. I dawdled at the kitchen table over coffee and a cigarette.

The thick and disgracefully yellowing Barrington file glowered reproachfully at me, and I wrenched my thoughts away from the Roylett affair and tried to focus on Barrington, whence (I told myself) would come my salvation in the way of publication, quickly followed by universal acclaim, and offers galore of well-paid tenure-track positions...After Barrington had been given his cushy job by the British government in the Dublin Customhouse in return for his public excoriation of the Irish patriots Grattan and Curran, he'd been made King's Counsel, even though he'd only been practicing law for five years. If you took him at his word—always a dicey proposition—Barrington could have been Solicitor-General in 1799—had he taken the party line and supported the proposed Legislative Union of Great Britain and Ireland. But he didn't. Barrington was a flake. He voted against Union. He now became popular. On the strength of his popularity and his publicly-avowed dislike of Lord Chancellor Clare, who was detested by the Liberals, Barrington became a candidate in 1803, for the representation of Dublin in the Imperial Parliament. He was defeated, but the first votes recorded in his favor were those of Grattan and Curran, his erstwhile enemies. The university press editor had written in the margin of my draft, "this bit needs to be made more personal."

I realized I was having trouble remembering what it was exactly about Barrington that had initially drawn me to writing about him.

I went back to the map I'd retrieved from my car and began marking where different people in the department lived.

*   *   *   *

When I arrived on campus after dropping off my policy statements and syllabi to be duplicated at Kinko's, The University was already humming like a giant complex machine—irregular verbs chattering away down in the French department, Kant and Schopenhauer having a dialogue, I guessed, over in Philosophy, weird multi-hued potions frothing up cheerfully in chemistry, the dry insect voices of professors professing, and on the quarter-hour, the brazen-throated tower bells pealing. On the Drag, backed up by Japanese boom boxes, Hare Krishnas stood in their saffron robes chanting next to small, clean-shaven men in white shirts and blue trousers passing out miniature New Testaments. Railing like a madman in the hot sun, a large bearded man in cinctured monk's robe and sandals had reached that point in his diatribe where the campus police, experienced in such matters, were about to close in on him—just as he was lamenting, in what sounded like genuinely despairing tones, the sexual attractions of the women students passing in the street. He had a beatific smile as he was hauled off.

Right on, they were beautiful.

*   *   *   *

The duplicating room brought me down to earth. Ed Vere was in the duplicating room. The copier having been vandalized, Vere had happily resurrected the department's ancient mimeograph machine and was churning out his first day's handouts.

I wished him good morning.

Vere nodded—briefly sparing me a glassy survivor-of-the-Titanic glance—then refocused his attention on his handouts. Four stacks of paper were piling up on the small table next to the mimeograph machine.

I wanted to ask Vere about how he'd gotten from Hardin, Montana, to Oxford, but couldn't think of a way to open the subject without showing a knowledge of his *vita* that would be difficult to explain.

Two assistant professors I knew slightly, Adams and Bernstein, came in, chatting brightly about the previous evening's meeting of what I guessed to be their wine-tasting society.

"I mean, that Margaux he served us was dense—"

"—and the length of it—"

"—pure silk, and the hell of a grip on the finish!"

"Better by far than that microwaved Beef Wellington."

"Better? I'll say. Much better. 'Lo, Ed. Coulter. Who cares about the food, anyway?" They laughed.

"And the bubbly at the end. I never tasted anything like it." Bernstein closed his eyes in rapture and blew a kiss off his fingers.

"And at those prices a taste was all we got—"

"What was it, anyway, Kristeller Imperial?"

"Horse piss," announced Ed Vere, never lifting his eyes from the handouts.

"Say what?"

"I said it tastes like horse piss," Ed reiterated grimly.

"What's your pleasure, Ed?" I asked.

"You want to try something good, try Salon le Mesnil."

"El Salon de...what?" said Adams.

"Not *el* Salon, *Salon*. Salon le Mesnil." Vere shrugged. "It's a small place, down toward Troyes."

"Can't say I've ever come across it," Bernstein said.

They left favoring Ed with sideways, unconvinced, and appraising looks.

Very neat, I told Ed. I liked that.

"Product of a misspent youth," he muttered as if he were sorry for having brought up the subject but, without missing a turn of the crank, gave me an unexpectedly boyish grin.

"You know, Ed, that was the hell of a thing, Sunday."

His face fell into its accustomed anxious folds. "Shocking."

*   *   *   *

I climbed to the top floor and walked down to the classroom I'd be using that afternoon and peered through the small window in the door at some poor sod lecturing earnestly to a group of students no doubt figuring the percentages on whether, if they dropped the course, they could add a different section, held at a more convenient hour, with more possibility of entertainment.

No chair for the teacher's desk, a couple of stubs of chalk and one eraser that I could see along what we were now instructed to call the chalkboard.

I found Amanda Vennible in her private office paused between telephone calls. "Yes, Dr Coulter?"

"Amanda. I got the whip—"

She looked at me.

"And now what I need is a chair. For the lion-taming act this afternoon. I just went up to the classroom I'll be using, and I noticed the desk at the front has no chair—"

"Oh."

"And there's maybe two pieces of chalk and only one eraser."

"I'll take care of it," she promised, and made a note.

On the way out I hesitated at the door. "Amanda, why does Professor Vere teach four classes, I wonder. I thought four was for just us proles."

"It was an arrangement he made with Professor Roylett," Amanda told me. "It was something they agreed on."

*   *   *   *

Later that morning Henry Fishbach tracked me down in my office and asked me to serve on his committee. He was bright and flattering and left me feeling depressed. And I said I'd do it, though I knew damn all about eighteenth-century Cherokee literacy.

*   *   *   *

It was getting on toward noon when I finished my paperwork. I put away my notes on the texts I'd be using and went over to Kinko's and picked up the material I'd dropped off to be duplicated.

Carlotta du Plessis-Roylett was just coming up the steps. I'd seen her numerous times in the halls and over at the gym, often with Joan, doing aerobics, making the circuit of the weight machines, and practicing lunges with a foil. For all her tall, willowy languor, Carlotta was lithe and fit, and I recalled the insouciant gesture with which she lifted her fencing mask away from her brow and smiled at Joan who was offering her a drink of Evian water: a fragile Pallas Athena.

Today she had on dark glasses and was carrying a Louis Vuitton attaché case worn at the corners. She was wearing one of her pastel saris, this one pale blue. Why saris if she was from Jamaica was puzzling, but my God, they became her.

"Professor du Plessis-Roylett, I'm Stephen Coulter. Please accept my condolences."

"You are so kind, Mr Coulter; of course we've met. I remember you from the gym. And I think one time at my house, no?" She took off her glasses and regarded me with grave eyes and smiled.

"I noticed in the paper that there are family services scheduled for tomorrow morning in Indiana—"

"Yes, just so: even as we speak I am on my way to leave off my notes for Joan, who is taking my first day's classes, and then going out to the airport."

"—and a memorial service Friday afternoon?"

"Yes, that's right, a rather odd time, one-thirty, but—" a shrug "—there was apparently something else that had been planned for later that could not be canceled. The dean called, very simpatico, actually, despite what one has heard, and we decided upon Friday afternoon, just after lunch, so that the maximum number of Sebastian's colleagues would find it possible to attend."

"What a dreadful shock this all must be for you."

Indeed it had all proved to have been a very great shock for Carlotta. She had been on an exciting trip, a fulfilling trip, in fact, and she had been encouraged by the enthusiasm with which her newly-formulated views on Pritchard had been recognized as a real breakthrough—And then to return home—*home*, what did that word really signify?—to what? To a senseless tragedy. One had been fulfilling one's destiny and been *elevated* by the exhilaration of the frank exchange of ideas, of the *victory*—triumph—of having had something one had done *really mat-ter* and then to find out that instead of the arrangement of birds of par-adise and anthurium lilies and the Bartok octet with which Sebastian invariably greeted her at home along with a stiffish drink, that dark, droll *flic* informing one that one's husband was no more; *defunct*, as it were, *dead* in fact and then to find…It is all really too much: the *bar-barity*, the waste…Her speech expired in a welter of emphases and ellipses.

"It is, I know, an inappropriate time," I said, falling helplessly into her speech patterns, "and I don't want to hold you up, but do you have any idea—?"

"Who could have done it?" She shrugged. "And perhaps employing an old book. There is no textual point of reference here, no moral con-tract with the author. It is too much to contemplate…Those terrible lecturers—that very strange man Beddington—you hire people that way, there are bound to be some unbalanced types…you know."

"Professor du Plessis-Roylett," I asked diffidently, "was your hus-band in the habit of coming in on Sunday mornings to work in his office?"

She looked at me with those bruised and puddled eyes. "Please, call me Carlotta." She gave no sign that she found my question imperti-nent. "My husband was after all chairman. He has, he had, responsibil-ities."

"No, I meant at that hour, so very early. Did he usually come in so early on a weekend?"

"When I spoke to him Saturday he said something about meeting Huw here on Sunday morning to go over a borderline case that might give them—the department—trouble. You might speak to Huw, he'd know."

And she smiled again, donned her dark glasses, turned from me and lightly ascended the steps into the building, leaving behind a trace of Tigre on the hot still air.

*   *   *   *

I walked over to the cheerful multilingual bazaar that the Drag transformed itself into at noontime: crowded with skateboarders, pavement artists, guitar players, and sidewalk vendors of beads, incense, and silver and turquoise jewelry. I bought an egg roll and a bottle of mineral water from a Vietnamese man working out of a cart adorned with a Martini & Rossi umbrella, and went back to eat under the trees in the expansive courtyard outside the SASAC, the Simon Askew Scholarship Archive Center.

My colleague from History, Bob Talbot, called me over to join him where he was brown bagging it on a stone bench.

Originally from Omaha and a graduate of Nebraska, Bob'd gone on to Yale for his master's, and then won a Rhodes Scholarship. While at Oxford he'd read history under A J P Taylor, writing on the last years of Rhodesia and the emergence of Zimbabwe. Back in the United States, he'd earned his doctorate at Harvard where I'd bumped into him a time or two. Bob had been recruited on the tenure track at USW two years before I'd arrived there, and was now well on his way to being recognized internationally as a formidable scholar of commonwealth history. His enthusiasm for the multitudinous subject had inspired him to establish a weekly seminar well attended by both town and gown, at which speakers of widely divergent views and from widely varying backgrounds discussed some facet of the British sphere of influence. Bob liked to sign his books Rob't Sam'l Talbot and oddly resembled a streamlined version of a very young Winston Churchill.

I sat beside him on the bench munching my eggroll as we watched the pigeons strutting over the cobblestones near the fountain at the courtyard's center.

Bob told me he had just returned from England after a financially disastrous trip getting materials photocopied at the Public Records

Office while he did research for the third volume in his account of the Fall of the British Empire.

"Another big fat book, eh, Mr. Talbot? Just scribble, scribble, scribble."

"Oh, piss off," Bob told me without rancor. "Oh, hello, Alex."

"Bob…and Coulter, is it?" We'd seen each other in the halls, he a tall, spare man in what I judged to be his late sixties who walked with the aid of a blackthorn stick. "I wish you two gentlemen of leisure a pleasant afternoon." He nodded and walked on through the plaza on his way to MacFarland Hall.

"I take it you've met Alexander Ashton before?"

"More or less. Seen him in the halls. Friendly enough. Wintry smile."

Bob looked at me with some amazement. "Far be it from me to tell you about your own faculty, Stephen, but among a good many people Alexander Ashton is considered to be the most distinguished member of the English department. Bibliographer, as you know. Professor Dry-as-dust? Perhaps not. That handsome stick he affects is to help him with a war wound sustained in June of 1944 on Omaha Beach. Oh, yes: a genuine war hero. There are a few of them around. Tolerated—after all the few that remain are old now—even in this nursery of the intellectually sensitive." He paused. "That he knows you by name I would take as a compliment, Stephen." He looked serious.

I allowed my glance to linger on a passing scene. It was a lovely day. I couldn't wait to get out to the stable. "You were telling me about your troubles with the PRO."

Pounce on the kill momentarily abandoned. Of necessity, Bob explained, he had to be johnny-on-the-spot when the cabinet papers touching on his concerns became declassified and made available for study. Very tricky stuff, what gets through, sometimes. Or what slips through. Besides, the All Souls-St Antony's old boy network was really out in full force, circling like a bunch of goddamned vultures, really, and he had to be there, right on the scene.

"It wouldn't be so bad if I had a chair," he continued dreamily, "a named professorship, where I could get reimbursed for at least some of my expenses. As it is every goddamned cent I have goes toward photo-copying while the place I put up at, you wouldn't believe, is a stifling bed-sitter in Earls Court, where I share the loo with three Sikh families.

"But, to change the subject, are you going to favor us with your presence this fall at Commonwealth Studies? I think we've got a very good program."

Yes, I noticed, I told him. The offerings had looked exciting.

During the last year I'd managed to attend a number of the Friday afternoon meetings, and had been impressed by the wide range of top-ics and credentials of the speakers. Sherry was served, a custom that both made the seminar lively and a very agreeable way to finish off the week.

"That one on art in India looked interesting," I told him. "I'd like to try and make that if I can. Also that man from All Souls speaking on the sources for writing a history of secret operations during the war."

"Oh, he's a *very* sound man. Don't suppose you saw Max Beloff's review of his book in last week's *TLS*? Glowing, absolutely glowing. Not at all like the usual Beloff."

He waited for me to say something, but since I didn't know what Lord Beloff's usual was, I kept quiet.

"Can I put you down to give a talk on Barrington some time in November, Stephen?" During the past year we'd talked in a more or less desultory way about my gearing up a talk on Sir Jonah but until now Bob had not pressed me.

"Umn."

"It really is about time," said Bob, as usual providing a jolt to my conscience. "How far are you along with him?"

"Not so far as I'd like," I admitted. "The truth is, I don't know when I'll be ready. It's not coming along as well as I'd like. In fact, it's not coming along at all."

"Well, you haven't finished with your research. You're still trying to do research and make your mind up at the same time, and you ought to know that doesn't work, Stephen; you don't have the knowledge *and* the distance to see things for what they are. But where are you precisely?"

"Precisely, I'm trying to work out if the British government was really so nervous about Barrington revealing their conduct in regard to Union that they actually bought him off. They could have. At least the fact seems to be that in order to escape being socked into jail for debt in Ireland, he fled to France…but nevertheless by hiring a deputy he appears to have continued to serve at least on paper as Admiralty Judge in Dublin"

"While lounging about Calais."

"Yes. While lounging about Calais, eating oysters and swilling muscadet."

Bob rose to his feet, folded his paper napkin in neat quarters, put the napkin in the sandwich bag, closed the sandwich bag, and deposited the whole tidy bundle in the trash bin. "That's good. You need to keep after it, you know, Stephen. Barrington's important; *ideas* are important—and time flies." He smiled and turned away. I watched him as he navigated across campus apparently on some kind of sonar, frowning over the contents of the file folder he'd been carrying, pencil poised, mouth pursed impishly, neatly combed blond hair glistening in the sunlight.

CHAPTER 12

▼

I went to see Huw Rhys-Davies about becoming second reader for Fishbach's dissertation.

"No problem at all with you serving as second reader that I can see. Do you a bit of good, I daresay, though I think it might not come amiss were you to touch base with Ed Vere. He's on a kind of rota, and from time to time he drops in to the graduate office, look you, to do some advising for whatever poor luckless sod's time has come, which in this case was the ineffable Fishbach. In the course of reading through the lad's academic record, it has come to Ed's attention—no small thing shall go unpunished—that young Fishbach is deficient in one of his required areas of study: probably the history of grammar, or something equally exciting. You might check with Ed on this and of course you'll need to check with Joan, since you'll be replacing her as second reader, now she's taking over directing."

Huw favored me with a glance through narrowed eyes. "By all means give young Fishbach's dissertation your eagle-eyed scrutiny. We all know you'll do well. Indeed, I may say that before our late lamented chairman hopped the perch"—this without a trace of irony—"he specifically instructed me to keep an eye out for young Coulter. You are obviously a man of many talents. Do I detect astonishment writ large on the Coulterian phiz?"

I admitted I was somewhat taken aback. "On Friday…"

"That was on Friday," Rhys-Davies told me, gracing me with a glimpse of his perfectly even teeth. "I gather there was quite a row. Evidently the Sun King thought better of it afterward."

"I don't know that I'd call it a row," I told him. "But yes, I was angry. It was about the lecturers and what was being done with them."

He looked skeptical. "But surely you knew you were going to be asked to return."

"No, actually, I didn't. If anything, I'd been given to believe that I'd be let go."

Huw nodded vigorously, and gathered some papers on his desk in sign of dismissal. "Our late chairman was, how shall I put it, inclined at times to be a bit on the unpredictable end. Like the Lord, Sebastian Roylett sometimes moved in mysterious ways his wonders to perform. When he called me at home Saturday morning he gave me to understand that this was—you were—one of those matters he was going to discuss with me."

"Really, Huw? I didn't know I figured so prominently in his thoughts. Along, I suppose, with the borderline case?"

"He knew who you were, all right, just as he knew everyone in the department," said Huw urbanely, resigned now to the continuation of our conversation. "And there are always borderline cases to discuss."

"I gather you didn't have a chance to meet with him on Sunday, before…"

"Before, exactly. Oh, I got here in time to meet him as agreed at nine-thirty. But as I arrived at the building, there was Ed Vere pacing about, full of that very curious kind of righteous zeal that one derives I suppose from attending early mass, wanting to discuss Fishbach's alleged dereliction. I don't mind admitting my heart sank: I'd told him when he called Saturday evening wanting to discuss the matter that I'd be tied up with the chairman. Nevertheless, we repaired to my office to discuss the matter, and so I was already running late for my appointment when Amanda burst into song."

"Huw—" I was casting around for a way to ask him without being too obvious what he'd been up to the night before, but Huw was there ahead of me.

"Coulter proves a bit more than meets the eye, no? Two colleagues have already found it congenial to confide to me that Stephen Coulter—heretofore simply one of the great unwashed horde of lecturers—the mere scum of the earth, as Wellington put it—is now acting out of character, taking charge, justifying somewhat his native lean and hungry look, and calling attention to himself by—" He fixed me with an ironic glance. "—asking questions. Our colleagues were somewhat, ah, perturbed if not indeed exercised at your involvement, but I told them that I had no intention of meddling in what I gather is an official if non-publicized association with the gendarmes."

"Thank you."

"So, to sum up: the club enjoyed a modest scrum Saturday afternoon in the park followed by a very restrained booze-up at Maggie May's from which I tore myself away early in order to return to my garret for a frugal repast, and pen by candlelight a few words of scintillating critical insights. I fell into the arms of Morpheus about ten. 'Struth. Word of a gentleman." He paused. "Tell me, do you know anything about Cherokee linguistics?"

"Not a thing."

"Ah, well, not to worry. You have much to look forward to."

About an hour later I ran a comb through my hair, checked my fly, and stepped into the semester's first class.

*   *   *   *

"Right," I said, "This is E316K, Masterworks of Literature, the English variant."

The truth of the matter was that most students didn't really give much of a damn which variant of E316K they got—American, English, or World; it was a required course, one of the many hoops through which they had to jump on the way to a degree, and the crucial thing was when it met.

"My name's Coulter, I'm a lecturer in the department of English, my office hours are on Wednesdays from two to five, location, phone numbers, and so on in the policy statement, along with other information about attendance, participation, and weighting of marks."

As I passed out the policy statement and assignment schedule, I was aware of the first-day jumble of superficial impressions: guileless, suspicious, saturnine, bland faces; T-shirts—some rudely sloganed—and tank tops—some disturbingly well-filled; I always seemed to find time for that kind of reflection—and jeans and shorts and gimme caps, ubiquitous tennis shoes and the odd pierced nose. We were about to embark on a four-month voyage, and the point of no return arrived at on the tenth class day when they had their last chance to drop the course.

Over the next sixteen weeks they'd find themselves gauging the poems they read against their own knowledge of life.

Teachers were arrogant and foolish to suppose that, callow and culture-shy as many of them were, students lacked experience of life, of the "real world." Their very presence in a USW classroom argued survival skills of no mean sort; the sacrifices that many of them had made to attend college were impressive. In fact, most of them held regular jobs, some of them full time, their daily timetables time-and-distance miracles of meticulous planning.

Always I found myself humbled by the realization that within my small classroom was crammed a vast and often bitter experience of life. Chances were good they'd had their love despised, seen innocence punished, endured the ongoing terror of a warped family relationship; stopped thoughtlessly to admire a sunset, a river, a grove of autumn trees against a skyline; been bereft through catastrophe and lingering illness; had hard work scorned; partaken, some of them, in the selfless joys of comradeship under conditions of physical hardship; found themselves oddly and bewilderingly aroused by the hypercharged eroticism invested in a piece of clothing; in conversation in the halls they commonly exulted in hyperbole, in wild conceit. If not already, soon, soon.

Not that they gave the slightest indication that they thought what they brought to the class was in any way unique or even remarkable.

For all that I was allowed to see, life to them appeared to have no connection with what they studied in class.

My more deliberately provocative comments—"the rhetoric of seduction appears to have changed little over the past five centuries"— were likely to be met by blank stares and not a few yawns. But as we discussed the poetry in the hothouse intimacy of the classroom, unpromising stock sometimes produced exotic blooms. Some more than others of them proved willing to imperil their vulnerability, to risk appearing foolish to their peers.

We would grow to know each other. They would memorize my mannerisms, my unconsciously repeated phrases, even as they grew to know my clothes, my frayed button-downs, faded khakis, desert boots. And I would learn to recognize their shorts and shirts and well-worn jeans; grow to know them, too, individually, as Wednesday office hours went by and the leaves turned sere outside my office window.

I always seemed to fall in love a bit, and it was well a semester lasted only as long as it did.

"It will not escape your notice that this class not only confines itself to English literature, but that we read mostly poetry which includes the work not only of English poets but that of all those desperately talented Irish, Scots, and Welsh odds and sods writhing under the intolerable yoke of perfidious Albion." I could hear myself, the out-of-date diction, the legacy of irony-besmitten masters from the New Hampshire pile of stones inexpungably imprinted in my memory and influencing my teaching style. From time to time, when I thought about it, I tried to fight against it.

Then I turned and faced the class.

"All right, let's see what we know about understanding poetry and poets. The first thing is, poems are hard to understand, right?"

Heads nodded.

"They're hard to understand because they've got *hidden meanings*.

"Understanding poems takes special knowledge. People who can really understand poetry are like a kind of, ah, *priesthood*, if you know what I mean. Only those with special God-given talents can really get to the hidden meanings of poetry. And poems have a lot of hidden meanings. Are you all with me so far?"

I looked around.

Most students took notes furiously. A few looked at me bemusedly. One or two smiled broadly.

"One of the reasons—there are many—that poems have hidden meanings and are so terribly difficult to understand is that poets are— to put it most charitably—if not certifiably insane at least mentally unbalanced; almost without exception they led, lead, disordered lives. They are disastrously incapable of managing their finances, commonly sponge off friends and acquaintances, contract undesirable liaisons with clearly unsuitable mates, indiscriminately beget large and very untidy families, drink far too much than is good for them, ingest bizarre substances, and invariably die young and without exception destitute.

"In fact, poets write the way they do because they are very strange people and simply can't write any better.

"And *that's* the reason they make use of hidden meanings."

I paused.

"Got that?"

"Sir?"

"Yes?"

"You don't really mean that, do you? About all of them leading 'disordered lives'? Surely they *all* couldn't have led…'disordered lives'?"

"No," I said. "Of course not, not really—though those are the ones we seem to hear the most about. I was simply trying to make a point...ironically."

A boy in the front row threw down his pencil in exasperation.

"It's a failing of mine, admittedly, 'minding true things by what their mockeries be'.

"The truth is that poets weren't all unbalanced. And, yes, I do believe that, as the saying goes, poets are professional fanatics about words. Even if you get nothing else from this course, I hope you'll take with you an increased appreciation for the richness of the language, an awareness of nuance and sensitivity to connotation. Poets, good ones, make you look at the world a different way, often by focusing on specific images. Sometimes they make their readers work; in the language of the trade, they are not so easily accessible as others—but they don't—the ones we read, at least—deliberately try to hide what they mean. And so far as 'disordered lives' is concerned—there are others, too, always have been, I expect—who were motivated by what used rather quaintly to be called the highest principles, what they perceived as honor. Let's look at Sir Walter Scott, for example: The financial collapse of the bookselling and printing business in which he was a partner threw Scott into debt. But bankruptcy was simply not an acceptable option for Scott, who personally shouldered the burden of the partnership and wrote incessantly at a furious rate to the extent of permanently ruining his health—but succeeded in publishing an immense body of work that earned him enough money to clear his name. Or take Andrew Marvell. Chronically hard up, Marvell found it within him to very gracefully turn down the gift of a thousand guineas—somewhere around ten thousand dollars in today's money—from King Charles the Second—a man, incidentally, with an almost fatal weakness for wit—rather than owe a favor to the king. So the story goes, as soon as Lord Danby, Charles's emissary, had left his modest apartment, Marvell hit up his bookseller for the loan of a single guinea for walking-around money."

"But Scott was basically a novelist, wasn't he, sir?"

"Point well taken, though the letter killeth, the letter killeth."

"I mean, after Byron's success—And, let's face it, sir, they weren't all the…uh, greatest novels ever written, were they?"

"Very true, although I'd have to say that *Ivanhoe*—an early novel—before the business with Ballantyne—has turned out to be possibly the most influential English novel in the history of American literature, certainly Southern American literature. And yes, you're dead on target about Byron; Scott saw the handwriting on the wall—but some of Scott's poems like *Lady of the Lake* are pretty damned good stuff, if you value an exciting story, enjoy a bit of colorful history, and are susceptible to the charms of rhythm and rhyme."

Wise ass, the kind you really grew to appreciate over the semester. I'd have to be on my guard.

The ship was casting off.

From their averted eyes as they sidled by me on their way out of the room after the bell, I could expect some to jump the rail before we cleared port. But, ah! The others…to share the thunder and the sunshine.

CHAPTER 13

▼

Outside under the trees on the mall, I noticed that I was breathing hard, my fingers were trembling, and my shirt was stuck damply to my body: all the symptoms of riding a cracking point-to-point early in the season before you'd gotten really fit. Then I recalled that this was the way I always felt after the first day of classes: surprised that teaching drained off so much energy.

I went back home and sluiced off the school grime and changed into jeans. Before I set off for the stable I took a few moments to go over the map I'd prepared that morning, working from the spring's English Department roster. I wanted to see for myself where some of the people I'd been reading about in the dossiers lived.

Carlotta was no problem; I could cross her off, for I'd a vivid recollection of the parties I'd attended at the Royletts' hilltop eyrie on Cat Mountain. Ditto Huw: he was putting up at the Sherwood Arms, a small and slightly down-at-heels residential hotel just south of campus that catered to the visiting lecturers and adjunct professors who descended on USW each semester, within easy walking distance of the library and the department.

Melody—and Fishbach—were, I surmised from the address, in one of the '60s duplexes just west of IH 35 south of the airport; Joan was on a short street atop the steep hill west of Lamar at about Twelfth

Street; and Vere lived due west of The University past Exposition on Clearview, in Tarrytown. I could drive by Vere's first, I decided, then swing back east on Enfield and duck south to Joan's on my way out to the stable.

The house turned out to be a freshly-painted one-story white clapboard bungalow with a small overhang front porch, and a driveway running back alongside to a detached garage in the rear; somebody had been putting in some serious time in the front yard. I pulled over to the curb and parked in the shade of a large pecan tree.

The front parlor probably opened up onto a kind of living room or family room or, taking into account the time when it was built, a dining room, with the kitchen at the back of the house looking over a back yard; and on the right-hand side of the small central hallway there was probably a study or bedroom and probably another one in the rear even with the kitchen. Dark wood and precisely measured bookshelves lovingly constructed and white ceilings: a hint of William Morris. More meet for civilized Sunday afternoon readings of Campion and Clare than late-night whisky-spurred bellowings from Marlowe or Webster. But what did I know? Perhaps there were tales of love and death lying quiescent in the leaky faucet in the well-worn kitchen sink, the brittle scraps of paper adorning the refrigerator. It all powerfully reminded me of a John Betjeman poem I'd looked at recently, about a don's aged wife in Oxford, thinking about her home:

> From that wide bedroom with its two branched lighting
>   Over her looking glass, up or down,
> When sugar was short and the world was fighting
>   She first appeared in that velvet gown.
>
> What forks since then have been slammed in places?
>   What peas turned out from how many a tin?
> From plate-glass windows how many faces
>   Have watched professors come hobbling in?

A minivan turned off the street into the driveway and a slim brown-haired girl—young woman, really, I reminded myself—got out and went into the house, carrying a small child. I had just turned the ignition on and was about to put the car in gear when she reappeared, sans child, on the porch.

"May I help you?"

So much for any thoughts I'd had of not attracting attention.

There were, touchingly, a few pimples around her soft mouth. Innocent she was, I thought, to come outside to talk to a stranger.

"I was looking for Professor Vere, I'm a colleague of his."

Crashingly improbable excuse: if a colleague, why not meet up with him at The University?

I realized I hadn't got the foggiest notion of what to say if Vere suddenly appeared, roly-poly and sweating, wiping his glasses on his ancient madder tie. The girl was too young to be Vere's daughter; could she be a granddaughter, I wondered?

The girl's next words dispelled that thought.

"Oh, yes, the Veres." She hesitated. "They were the previous owners; we bought the house from them. I'm afraid we never saw them, not even at the closing; but I gather they were older, and I seem to remember the agent saying she's not in very good health."

I murmured something encouraging about the house.

"Yes, isn't it? Of course it needs fixing, open up all those little rooms, strip the wood—you know, brighten the place up a bit. There's this spar varnish we saw in Key West comes in different colors we're using for the floor—

"Wait a minute, I've just thought of something," the girl said and went inside, reappearing almost instantly with a slip of paper in her hand. "Here, it's something the post office sent us, a forwarding address if something comes here for them, not that anything has. 1208 Forest Glade, it says, and the ZIP. We didn't really know them, I'm afraid..."

I thanked her and left, swinging east on Enfield and ducking south past the sunny corner lot where Joan's tile-roofed, cut limestone duplex was sited. As I had at what I'd thought was Vere's house, I parked and tried to get a feel for the place. Pots of late moss roses hung from the eaves along the front and children were playing in the next yard. A sturdy gray-haired lady in blue bermuda shorts came around the corner of the house lugging a garden hose. She seemed to me to exhibit that indefinable sense of proprietorship that distinguishes the owner from the renter. I drove on out to the barn.

*   *   *   *

I'd hoped I'd find the mare in a good mood after our session the day before, but with some horses it's a bright new world every morning, and Classy Minx showed no signs of affectionate recollection of our yesterday's outing. She didn't want to go in a straight line and fell away from my leg like a piece of wet vermicelli, squirming around, either sulking behind the bit or on the muscle in front of it with her hind legs paddling out behind. I played along with her so that she got a lot of lateral flexion work. Eventually, in the course of making one of her loopy circles, she found herself confronted by a log jump and before she had time to think about it had set herself right and arced quite creditably over it and—more to the point—cantered on after she'd landed without indulging herself with her signature buck. Afterward she relaxed and snuggled up against my leg.

They all want to go a different way.

When I returned to the picket line Joan was bent over picking out the massive Harry's off forefoot.

Joan was of medium height—about five five or so—supple and compact. She had dark hair cut off at jaw level, bangs above an aquiline nose, and huge lustrous dark blue eyes. Her wide, generous mouth was dark with lipstick. When she smiled, which she did often, she showed even, very white teeth. Her hands were capable and square and her short fingernails were painted to match the lipstick. Around campus she was given to wearing knit polo shirts and khaki skirts and moccasins. Today she was wearing sleek California riding tights and a tank top with neon accent stripes. She smelled of healthy sweat. Festoons of her usual S/M gear—chambons, bizarre and wonderful martingales, and figure-eight nosebands—hung from a nearby tack hook.

I rather admired Joan, her bracing forthrightness, but she did at times exhibit a naturally tart disposition that could tail off into real rudeness. She had a rough edge, all right—but with nothing so far as I could see to be defensive about. There is the school of thought among some feminists that a woman alone dares display no softer side, and I think Joan subscribed to it. At any rate, I had long ago decided—before, in fact, the disastrous evening when, half-tight, I managed to offend her and her friends at dinner—that it was just her way.

"Hullo, Joan."

"Hullo, Stephen." She didn't look up. "That was quite a display you put on."

I said something conciliatory about not having intended providing so much entertainment, but Joan had her tongue over the bit and was on a real tear.

"For the stable's *resident pro*—" her voice dripped scorn "—you really made a fool out of yourself, letting that mare get away with absolute murder, weaving all over the place like that—For a moment I wondered if you were drunk.

"Heaven knows I've never understood what those doctors see in her, but no matter what I think, that mare really doesn't deserve what you did to her today. The way you got left behind at that fence I don't know how you managed to stay on—you never seem to spend any time on the basics, like driving her up onto the bit. Otto says—".

Otto, tall, lean, twinkling—an Austrian ex-noncom serial fanny-patter from the *hofreitschul* in Vienna—made the swing through Texas about once every sixteen months or so doing a nice little trade in Warmbloods.

"Look, if you're through raking me over the coals, can I ask you a question?"

"Depends what it is, I suppose."

"Fishbach has asked me to serve on his committee. Do you have a problem with that? I wouldn't ordinarily bring the matter up out here, but things are so hectic down at The University this week—"

"Don't be silly—"

Harry flinched as she dug in the hoofpick.

"You might try working from the point back, sometimes that helps."

She looked at me slightly nettled.

"You want to take a look, Stephen?"

"All right."

Tiny discolored bits of cloth were packed in the cleft next to the frog.

"What are these?"

"Pledgets. I soaked them in iodine."

"I see."

"Well, it seemed like the infection was so deep."

"Yes, of course." I hesitated. "You know, it takes a while for something like that to close up. It's pretty sensitive in there, and that stuff you're using is damn strong."

"I got it from the vet," she said defensively.

"Yes," I said. "Well, you might try flushing it out with hydrogen peroxide, or something like Clorox. As they say around the backstretch, sometimes you pick 'em and they never heal."

She watched me as I picked up a rub rag and dried off the patch of skin just below the mare's fetlocks.

"Why do you do that?"

"Well when you clip the fetlock so it looks neat for the ring, that's where nature wanted water to drip down. It doesn't, and then the skin gets cracked."

"Oh," she said, filing the tip away. "No, Stephen, I have no objection whatever. In fact, it would be a blessing. When I was in Pittsburgh at the conference I began to have this terrible feeling of being overwhelmed, do you know what I mean? There's just so much to do, and the term's already started."

I came up with an all-purpose hunting sound designed to convey my appreciation and sympathy for her plight.

"I gather you had a good time. Melody was saying that she was sorry to leave—"

"Huw made her come back—"

"And she said that woman from Stanford was brilliant."

A slight frown crossed her face. "Very adequate; scintillating, I suppose, if you hadn't heard it before."

Melody must have liked her, I observed. She got her to sign her book.

"Yes, well. The child is still at that impressionable age where an author's inscription of a text possesses a kind of totemic value. I must be getting on. Oh, Harry, you lummox, will you for pity's sake stand up?" The incorrigible Harry had imperceptibly shifted almost his entire weight onto the foot held by Joan, whose face was darkening with effort. She threw down the hoofpick, let the foot go, and watched Harry clamber nimbly upright and square. "Oh, damnit," she said, her face flushing unbecomingly. "It's so frustrating—"

"The book?"

"Yes, Joan's famous book. Michigan just turned it down, after leading me on at the MLA." Her eyes were hot with tears.

As I said, I rather liked Joan.

*   *   *   *

On the way back home I detoured north on the interstate and then cut off east near the airport to take a look at where Melody and Fishbach lived. They were tucked away on a winding street with some lovely big trees and the odd flourishing crape myrtle bush scarlet against their limestone veneer, asbestos-roofed bungalow with peeling pastel trim and lots of wrought iron twining the porch. Cars and pickups lined the street and choked the narrow driveways.

In the gathering twilight I followed the winding street past playing children and, suddenly emerging from the old neighborhood, found myself confronting a full-fledged shopping mall and an overabundance of fast-food places.

I headed west toward The University area; in the distance, beyond the lake, was the Balcones Escarpment, and I could just discern the violet crown of hills smudged by the copper afterglow of sunset.

*   *   *   *

Melnick dropped by that evening about eight, accepted a Shiner Bock and sank down into the frayed sofa. "Mind if I smoke?"

"Hell, no, Walter." We both lit up, the socially indefensible act cementing what I was coming to feel was a kind of unlikely friendship. "What's going on?"

"Couple things, actually. First is, we got back a preliminary report from the medical examiner. We also got back some a the results of those tests we sent off to DPS."

I shrugged.

"You're not surprised."

"I figured something like that must've happened, if the body was released in time for the funeral service up in the Midwest. Pretty fast work to get that business squared away and in the paper by this morning."

"Yeah." He shook his head. "Well, Roylett was an important man. People want to make sure everything is done...right. You know?

"Now listen to this. According to the ME, the cause of death is due to an already existing condition—" He settled back, took a long swallow and a drag from his cigarette, clearly enjoying my look of blank amazement. "—which may or may not have been potentiated by a blow to the head.

"'Potentiated.' That's the word. You recall, you mentioned Roylett's scalp looking pink? No wonder: he suffered from something called Sturge-Weber Syndrome. Same thing that Russian Gorbachev had, but hidden under all that long wavy silver hair Roylett had." He shook his head. "God knows how long he must've known about it. If he did. If anyone did, although I can't see it going undetected in, say, a physical. We're checking with his doctors now.

"Thing is, blood from his ears, all that could a come from this syndrome kicking in. All by itself. Roylett keels over, hits his head on the edge of the table, whatever…" His voice trailed off; his eyes were very bright. "Nothing is ever what it seems, right?"

Right, I agreed. "Does Mrs Roylett know about this?"

"No. All any of them know is we got what we needed to do the tests and released his body."

"Jesus Christ, Walter." I was skeptical and told him so. "It's sounding like a cover-up. This information gets out, you'll never find out anything. Nobody'll talk."

Melnick was unruffled. "Far as anybody knows, we're still pursuing…our inquiries. Nevertheless, the truth is, the book there on the floor could a been just a coincidence. Like I told you I thought might happen, textured surface like it had, they didn't come up with any prints clear enough to try to identify.

"Ditto with the business of compression: they say they just can't tell if that book got thrown down or used on his head. Big book like that after a number of years in a library, I guess it takes its licks. They didn't find any, you know, matching indentations, hairs off his head, traces of hair oil, stuff like that. Nothing to identify it as a murder weapon."

"It could have been wiped clean."

"It could a been wiped clean. Right. But so far impossible to prove."

"What about your handy table corner?"

"Well, no, nothing there, either, I got to admit."

"And as you said, Roylett was an important man."

"Yeah." We looked at each other.

"And that's the end of it just like that, Walter? He died of natural causes? Happy ending, nice and tidy, drop the shadows out of sight?"

"Lacking any direct evidence to the contrary, that's what it's looking like."

"But you don't believe he just had a spell of that disease and keeled over, do you?"

"I can't see that what I believe or don't believe matters a rat's ass, frankly, can you?"

"But for instance? Come on, goddamnit."

"Okay, let's play for instance, and while you're pacing around how about another beer if you got one? For instance let's talk about the book itself—"

"The book we cannot connect with the murder? What about the book?"

"The book we can't get anything off of, right. You remember you said you couldn't see the cover of that book next to Roylett's body but that it looked like one of a series put out by some press? You were right. It was a book put out by some outfit called The Early English Text Society. They've got kind of a harp-shaped device they stamp in gold on all their books. This one had that device just below the title: *The Winchester Malory*." Melnick looked at me quizzically. "Know anything about it?"

I tried to recall what I'd learned in graduate school.

"Sir Thomas Malory, knight, of Newbold Revel in Warwickshire, wrote what's widely known as *Le Morte Darthur*, the definitive anthology of King Arthur stories, published in the late fifteenth century. Some scholars still find it difficult to accept that this Sir Thomas—a jailbird, cattle thief, very possibly a rapist—could have written such an idealistic and romantic book.

"Only a couple of printed copies exist. *The Winchester Malory*, if memory serves me, is a one-of-a-kind handwritten version, pre-dating by some years the first published edition. What we've got here is what's called a facsimile copy put out by EETS."

"Whatever, it's a big, heavy sonofabitch. But let's say yes, somebody meaning to kill him hit him over the head. Whether or not they knew about Roylett's small Sturge's Syndrome problem, let's say that blow was made with intent to kill."

"A 'crime passionel'."

"Heat of the moment? Somebody got carried away?" He snickered. "You see any a those people getting carried away? And who the hell sets out to kill somebody with a book, that's what I'd like to know."

"Maybe what it was, was it was just lying around, and it seemed like a good idea. At the time. But it's a heavy book to pick up in the first place, and a person would have to be pretty strong to crush somebody's skull with a book—"

"That's what you'd think, right. But we're talking efficiency here, Rusty, not just force. Doctors will tell you, it doesn't take much, a blow to just the right spot, and"—he snapped his fingers—"you're dead. If you know the spot, or get lucky. Besides, there's nothing says you can't hit somebody on the top of the head and crush not the skull but the cervical vertebra and they die just the same but from a broken neck. But the truth is, most of the time, as I was going to say, the perpetrator of your 'crime passionel' gets carried away, keeps on hitting…"

"That's a lot of rage," I observed. "That's not what happened to Roylett."

"No, that's not what happened to Dr Roylett. With him, let's say— forgetting the Sturge's Syndrome—somebody took one good shot."

"And got lucky."

"And—potentiating the Sturge's Syndrome which they may or may not have known about—got lucky. That point you raise about its being a heavy book? You found anything in those dossiers I gave you?"

"Yeah, I've looked at them. You still want me to poke around?"

"Yes, I do. As I say, nobody on the outside knows about this Sturge's syndrome thing. Far as I can tell, drink, smoke, and hell around like he did, he was healthy as a horse. The primary care physician named on his insurance forms is actually Mrs Roylett's internist; we haven't even been able to find out when Roylett had his last physical. Looks like a dead end, maybe you can come up with something."

"This afternoon I drove by a couple of places where they live—"

"Anything interesting?"

"No. One of them had moved—Ed Vere—but, Christ, I felt like some kind of criminal, lurking around. The houses didn't hold any surprises, but like you say some of the people are weird—"

"Like you said, not me. What I said was the people were off my screen. Those dossiers." He started laughing. "Jesus, I'd a liked to've been there at Fort Devers on the Fourth of July—"

"Come on Melnick…how the hell did you find out about Devers? That wasn't even in the dossier."

CHAPTER 14

▼

"Let me tell you about cops," Melnick said musingly, exhaling smoke. "There's a...camaraderie. Irrespective of where you're from, national boundaries, who you work for, all that sort of thing. You take that course at Quantico, the one that girl, Jodie Foster, took in the movie. That's like Carlisle, the War College, or Leavenworth, Command and General Staff. Not bragging or anything, but I can pick up the telephone, call Sydney or the Seychelles or excuse me fucking Lourenço Marques, find out damn near anything I want. Friend's always got a friend, know what I mean? Nothing admissible, but..." He made a tipping motion with his hand. "So, with you I already knew about you and the horses, right? A couple a calls, I find out, Stephen Coulter, Dink Stover at Yale—"

"Dink Stover went to Princeton."

Melnick shrugged. "Whatever. Frank Merriwell, same difference. OCS. Airborne Ranger. Then something called SERE, in, Christ, Brunswick, Maine. Thailand for six months with a Mobile Training Team. Soldier's Medal: I suppose you'll tell me you got that for showing one of those hot-sauce-loving Thais how to field-strip a forty-five."

"Jesus, Walter, that's years ago."

"*And* Devers. I wonder, will I ever get to hear about Devers? It didn't say, what they sent me. Just someone writing across the bottom, 'This officer was right.'"

I couldn't help myself, I started to smile. "Sometime, maybe."

"After that business at the National went sour," Melnick asked idly, "what'd you do, anyway, drop out a sight for a while? Then graduate school?"

"That's about right."

He turned his attention back to the case. "Okay, back to playing for instance. Let's take a look at the rest of these literary luminaries. You take that Dr Beddington. Now there's another real piece a work. He gets in a fuss with a, what, some kind a Icelandic spear-chucker, short-circuits his synapses so's he can't lift a finger for six months, jury of his peers nails Beddington on battery—judge suspends his sentence—end result is Roylett fires his ass. Now he's being rehabbed on custodial staff or grounds crew, whatever, raking leaves and ogling the co-eds. Guy like that, all fucked up on steroids, he could get pretty disaffected, right?

"Then we've got Professor Rhys-Davies. Reading between the lines there, looks to me like Roylett may've been yanking his chain—"

"There are some things about Rhys-Davies," I told Melnick, and explained about the divorce from Bronwen.

"What about Mrs Roylett? The way I hear it, she had a thing going with Rhys-Davies, and anyway her old man played around on her. She does aerobics and fencing, getting back to that strength issue, like with the Welshman playing rugby and Beddington sporting black pajamas and registering his hands as deadly weapons. The Strossner-Boynton woman rides a lot—no clear motive right now—and you see her working out up in the gym, right? The girl, Harker, she was sweet on Roylett, or maybe the other way round. She rows—"

"You had a note about her, said to see you."

"Oh, yeah." He chuckled. "You'd a never known it but she's got a real temper. When she was in high school she beat up on a classmate for stealing something out a her locker."

"Big deal."

He shrugged. "And the boy, Fishbach, he's a runner. Except for Vere—" he looked at me quizzically.

"I really don't know Ed Vere very well," I said. "But he doesn't seem a very athletic type." I smiled to myself, thinking of his comment about horse piss.

"And, like with Strossner-Boynton, we got no motive." He paused. "Truth is, far as strength goes, they've all got the physical equipment to have taken a swing at Professor Roylett, and the way I see it, all but the two a them got a clear reason for wanting to see him dead.

"Getting back to Mrs Roylett for a second. I lifted it off the Sabre Computer before they wiped it, why, guess what, they had her down flying into Austin Sunday morning on her own ticket."

I stared at him. "I thought you met her at the airport, in the evening, went out there with Sarah Jane and Amanda to break the news to her about her husband."

"That's right. I did. And she did get off that flight from Dallas, a little after six. But that wasn't the first time she'd flown into town that day."

"What made you come to that conclusion?"

"Simple, really. Nothing more than a hunch." I could see Melnick was pleased with himself. "On the way out to the airport Miss Vennible and Professor Collins, they were talking about that conference Mrs Roylett'd been attending up there in Chicago, fancy reception and dinner to wind things up Saturday night, all right?"

"Yeah, so what?"

"So what it is, is when we met her at the airport all she had with her was like a little Gucci carry-on. Now I don't make her for one a your basic academic women, don't care what they wear, you know? Stylish lady like Mrs Roylett, I took one look, even if she wore silk, no way she was going to be up there for four days and take only one a those carry-ons, where you pack at the most two, three dresses." He shook his head and I wondered if he was thinking about his dead wife. I had a feeling that the late Mrs Melnick might have been no stranger to silk dresses and Gucci bags. "After that it was easy. I checked the airline. She came in early in the morning, could a got money out of the ATM machine there in the lobby—"

"So she could have killed her husband, and then turned around and gone straight back to Dallas, waited around till it was time to catch the flight she was supposed to come in on?"

"It's a possibility." We looked at each other. "Be honest: the computer got wiped before I thought to check on a return to Dallas, see if there was something in her name.

"But like I said, this is all for instance. The case is, as you guessed I'm sure, headed fast to being shut down. Tight. Closed: death due to natural causes. No fuss, no muss. Announcement to that effect in a day or two: the media ghouls never did get involved, so there shouldn't be any fuss. But, as you know, there's no statute a limitations on murder. A case like this can *always* get opened up again, new evidence is discovered." He drained his glass. "What was this SERE shit anyway, twenty-seven ways to kill a man with your bare hands?"

"Something like that."

"What's it mean, anyway?"

"Survival, Evasion, Resistance, and Escape."

Melnick thought about that for a while. "I've got to hear about Devers."

*   *   *   *

Melnick stayed talking about New York and the horse show until about eleven-thirty. After he left I thought of going out and then said to hell with it. I ended up re-reading John Le Carré's *The Honourable Schoolboy* and putting an appreciable dent in a bottle of bourbon.

While I was thrashing around before falling into a fitful sleep about four I must have switched off the alarm button on the clock, for I woke up too late to have the streets to myself for a run, and too unfocused to put in time on Barrington.

As I shaved in the shower I spared a thought for Barrington. I envisioned the wily Irishman sitting on a sunlit quai in Calais sipping hot chocolate, lifting his eyes from perusal of his newspaper, and casting a calm eye at the choppy Channel that separated him from his infuriated and frustrated creditors.

There was just time for me to grab a cup of black instant coffee and a slice of toast before dashing off for my back-to-back freshman classes. The hour off before expository writing at eleven would allow me to sort through the already vast heap of paper accumulating at an alarming rate. Then there was a break for lunch and office hours from two to five.

*   *   *   *

After class I decided to skip lunch and went down to the library, where I put in a request for a couple of books to be placed on reserve.

Then I looked up Huw's book of poetry, *Conquistador of the Caribbean*, in the online catalogue.

Conquistador of the Caribbean was unselfconsciously old-fashioned, narrative poetry, what used to be called an epic poem, and it was obvious to me as I skimmed through the first few pages that Huw had the hell of an ear for assonance and rhyme that Celts seem to come born with. Its protagonist was a black-bearded, seventeenth-century Welsh buccaneer, gold-lusting and God-struck, shipwrecked and cast ashore in a tropical island paradise, armed with a steel cuirass and cutlass and silver crucifix, inevitably to perform miracles of coition while under the spell of a native princess. It was full of white sand and waterfalls and bright-plumaged birds and tanned flesh and rosy nipples, and the bitter awareness of love but lately won and all-too-soon to be lost.

It was based, very loosely I guessed, on Sir Henry Morgan, the pirate. The image flashed across my mind's eye of a small boy in a movie theatre on a rainy Saturday afternoon in Swansea, held rapt by Errol Flynn up there on the screen in *The Sea Hawk*, and thrilling to Erich Korngold's exciting score. Huw's poetry took me aback. It so obviously came from the heart. Academic though he may have been, as a poet Huw wasted no time in self-consciousness, exhibited no taste nor patience for academic posing and the current standard-issue professional ennui.

Amos Beddington's book of poetry, *'Roid Rage*, when I tracked it down in one of the library's special collections, was, like Huw's, well named, but I was hard-pressed to find any other point the two books shared. Rhyme and meter were rigorously avoided. Imagery had abdicated in favor of concept; noun or rather acronym served as poetic shorthand to communicate deep spiritual truth; beauty was resolutely eschewed. Christ, there wasn't anything pretty *anywhere*, much less waterfalls or rosy nipples. Sweaty leather and chrome studs were closer to the mark. Its motivating force was rage—inchoate, indiscriminate, over-the-top rage, fueled by equal parts of Human Growth Hormone, Dianabol, Bolasterone, and Quinolone. No wonder he had been a popular draw reading on the local coffee house circuit, glowering and red-eyed.

It was a simple matter to check if The University did indeed own a copy of the book found next to Roylett's corpse, the Early English Text Society's facsimile edition of Malory's Winchester manuscript. Calling it up on the online catalogue screen showed me that The University owned two copies, one retained at the Simon Askew Scholarship Archive Center, and the other available for general circulation in the main library. The Winchester MS. measured ten by twelve-and-a-half inches and was three inches thick. It weighed, I noted with interest, ten pounds. It was indeed a big, heavy sonofabitch.

This second one was due to be returned the middle of December—the end of the semester—which meant that it had been checked out to one of the six thousand-odd staff or faculty members.

The young man at the circulation desk told me that it was against library policy to release the name of a borrower.

I told him he had to be kidding.

"Yeah, right," he said, rapidly running books under some sort of electronic scanning device. "You know Miss Silver?"

I nodded.

"Ask her, you think I'm kidding. I mean, you get a court order for The University to make this information public, you'll like see Miss Silver go handcuffed down to the joint at high noon before she tells you." He snorted, momentarily intrigued by the idea, but then thought better of it. "Let me tell you what," he said, shaking his head admiringly, "she's one tough lady."

It is wise to be wary and very respectful of anyone commonly referred to as "Miss" on a college campus. Almost invariably such women are charged with more responsibility than ninety percent of faculty members and retain the confidence of department chairmen, heads of programs, and mad mullah deans. Besides, I'd seen Miss Silver in action. ("I expect you've already looked through *Little British Magazines 1938–1946*, Dr Coulter...") No question about it, she enjoyed a gift for cutting faculty members down to size—a talent the possession of which, judging by the innate kindliness of her deep brown eyes, afforded her little pleasure.

First with the young matron at the Veres' old house, then with the gray-haired lady with the garden hose, now here, faced by the possibility of Miss Silver, I knew when I was outgunned, and I beat an unceremonious retreat before the young man's amused glance.

I salvaged a bit of self-esteem by putting in a fast quarter-hour before class flipping through The University's map collection down in the library basement.

On the way to office hours I stopped by the mailroom and found my box crammed full of paper. Enough to make one scream.

*   *   *   *

Conventional wisdom holds that office hours are apt to be light for the first few weeks of the semester and you could count on getting in some solid prep time for your next class. This was bullshit. Supplicants and almoners palely loitered in the halls, desperately needing to add classes, almost always because of scheduling. ("I've *got* to have morning classes—I work afternoons in a real estate office and my wife is hostess at the Red Lobster ten to two and six to ten weekdays and four to midnight on the weekends; we split taking the kids and picking them up from day-care.")

Not that there were likely to be any jobs waiting for them when they got out of school, I reflected glumly.

Head popped around door.

"Sir? Mr Coulter?" A boy from this morning.

"Yes? What can I do for you?"

"Nothing, really. Just had a few minutes free, knew it was your office hours. You seem like a very interesting person. I thought I'd come by and get acquainted—"

"Sure," I said. "Sit down." I started to close my papers.

Sinking into Isaacs' overstuffed wingchair: exercise of territorial imperative, spreading of possessions on floor roundabout: backpack, library books, coffee cup.

Another head around door, fair sparse mustache.

"Oh, Dr Coulter?" It was Henry Fishbach. "I got your message—"

"Oh, right. Good of you to stop by. I'll be with you in a moment. Just wait in the hall, will you?"

"I'm sorry, sir, I didn't realize it was necessary to make an appointment." A tendency toward pique; potential flounce.

"Well, it really isn't, normally. It's just that..."

Gathering of belongings, getting to feet.

"Well, I'll come back later." Then, ominously: "There are a few questions I have about tomorrow's reading...oh by the way, you don't have an extra copy of the Norton I could borrow for the semester, do you, sir?"

*   *   *   *

Fishbach sat down and crossed his legs. At once, his body language communicating clearly his resentment at having to answer, however briefly, to authority, Fishbach began to bounce one foot in time to some melody audible only to himself.

I went on to business.

"Henry, I'm pleased to tell you that neither Professor Rhys-Davies nor Professor Strossner-Boynton has any objection to my serving on your committee—"

"Yeah, that's what Huw said," Fishbach told me.

I found myself fascinated by his bouncing toe.

"Sort of like a *formality* is *umhhhhh* what he inferred." The humming sound he uttered was, like the bouncing foot, a graduate student affectation, this one copied from Eastern academics as an Oxbridge import, a curious buzzing the apparent purpose of which is to prevent anyone else from saying anything while the speaker's searching for a word.

"Implied is what I think you mean to say but I've got to tell you that I don't look at serving on your committee as merely a formality."

Chastened perhaps by the possibility that he had unintentionally offended me, Fishbach knurled down the motion of his toe to a barely detectable vibration. Barely.

"Henry, I tell you what, let's go over to the Corral and grab a cup of coffee; I'll just put a sign on the door."

*   *   *   *

· Walking across campus:

"I take it you've made some arrangement to remedy the deficiency in your reading?"

"Yeah. It was nothing."

I waited.

"Professor Vere said I hadn't taken any courses in the seventeenth century. I mean, so what? I read Donne and Milton in college, you know? Take a look at the *Chronicle of Higher Education*, it's not as if a specialty in the Metaphysical Poets is much in demand, got you a decent job teaching in the top fifty programs. Linguistics is where the action is…"

And by the time the curve's perceived, it's already too late, I refrained from saying: when you get your degree linguistics will be grossly oversupplied with pain-in-the-ass MIT types ready to kill for one of the few tenure-track positions open for grabs. I sighed, thinking of the rewards of gluttonous indiscriminate reading in Herrick, Herbert—let alone Marvell or Jonson—or dramatists like Webster. "'One met the duke 'bout midnight in a lane,'" I intoned. "'Behind Saint Mark's Church, with the leg of a man/Upon his shoulder; and he howled fearfully…'"

Fishbach stared at me and his toe was still. "Weird shit." He shook his head uncomprehendingly. "Speaking of which, Dr Coulter, I hear you've been asking a lot of questions about like what people were doing when Roylett got himself killed—"

"When Professor Roylett died—"

"Yeah, died, whatever—You were the one came across his body, right? And that was the morning there was all this mess in the halls—"

"Vandalization, pure and simple—"

He shrugged dismissively. "But you know those lecturers got fired." He looked at me accusingly as if I were somehow suspect. "They got screwed, you know that—"

"Welcome to the NFL, Fishbach: no condition in life is perfect. Those lecturers had been on one-year contracts, and theirs didn't get renewed. Mine did. If you expect me to go around in a hairshirt, beating myself with thorns, guess again. Incidentally, where were you the night before Professor Roylett's body was found?"

I could sense a part of him wanted nothing better than to tell me to take a flying fuck, but for better or worse I was now occupying a slightly superior position in an academic enterprise whose outcome was crucial to his future. He decided to be responsive.

"Saturday night?"

I nodded.

"I was home Saturday night…"

"Just you and…Miss Harker?"

"Right."

"All night? Don't tell me, let me guess: you sent out for pizza and folded your tents after the ten o'clock news? Like that?"

"Yes, that's right. Close enough, anyway."

I must have looked quizzical.

"We fixed hot dogs."

"Ah. Don't tell me, let me guess: no phone calls, either."

"That's right." Then, defiantly: "Only the two of us. Mel was catching up on some reading and I worked on drafting this letter to the president—" he called him by his first name "—about what happened to the lecturers, demanding their reinstatement."

I winced.

"Why, what's the matter?"

"Let me tell you something, Henry: if you're not dealing from a strong position—and I don't think you are—you're not likely to get very far making demands of the administration. Perhaps…"

"With all respect, Dr Coulter, the president ought to represent all the university community not just the regents and the fat-cat industrial-military research cartel, and he puts on his pants same way as anyone else—"

"You're ignoring—"

"—one leg at a time—"

"the realities of the situation—"

"And at the meeting in the afternoon it was decided that all the graduate students and TAs are going to sign it," he concluded triumphantly. "Here, I've got an extra copy." He reached into his backpack.

"Super, Henry, thanks," I said hastily. "I'll stick it in your mailbox in the morning after I've had a chance to read it." I paused. "Just as a matter of curiosity, what time did you get home?"

He thought. "The meeting broke up about seven. Then some of us stopped by Jalisco's for a couple of beers. I got home I guess about nine."

"And Melody was there."

He looked away. "Sure, Melody was there. I fixed dinner."

He was lying. I knew he was lying.

"You didn't happen to run into Beddington, did you, Henry? What do you know about him, anyway?"

"I don't know how well anybody knows Beddington. He's weird. He's like the cat who walks alone, you know what I mean?"

"I know he beat the shit out of some Icelandic field star. And I see him from time to time working on that grounds crew around the Mall."

"Yeah, well," Fishbach said. "fact is, we haven't seen much of him for a long while. He's no longer—"

"No longer 'one of us'?"

"Well, yes, I suppose if you put it that way. I heard he's got a girl friend, though; they're very active with the Demons of the Road, that motorcycle gang. Someone saw them out at the Big Wheel couple of weeks ago."

Henry rearranged his face in the hungry-for-knowledge ingratiating gee-sir graduate student look. "About that Jacksonian democracy thing…"

CHAPTER 15

▼

On my way down to the parking lot, I met Carlotta, evidently returned from her husband's graveside services in Peru, Indiana. I reflected that people who arrive on the campus late in the afternoon are different from those who come to teach in the early mornings—they are sustained by a kind of melancholy satisfaction that as the day draws near its close, the day's mask can soon be dropped. Carlotta was—

My train of thought was interrupted by the sight of Alexander Ashton, limping along the walk. He nodded briskly and I thought favored me with a fractional lift of eyebrow when he saw who I was with. "Professor du Plessis-Roylett. Mr Coulter."

"Alec. Thank you so much for your note. It was very sweet of you. I will acknowledge properly—"

"Such a terribly sad business, the very least I could do." He nodded briskly, and gave a brief wintry smile before continuing on his way.

"*Vieux con,*" she said with sweet contempt.

I rather liked Ashton, at least the little I'd seen of him.

"Well, at least you made it back safely; it's good to see you." Carlotta—I picked up where I'd left off—was an afternoon and evening person. Her appearance created for me—effortlessly on her part, it seemed—a delicate suggestion of unspecified vices.

"It's good to be back," she said and sounded as if she meant it. "Sebastian's parents are really rather sweet, but Indiana is…how shall I put it? 'An embarrassment of riches'?" She smiled, inviting me to share in her irony.

"You must be getting to know that Dallas flight pretty well by now," I observed.

Her eyes were suddenly still.

"Some one saw you," I lied. "Early Sunday morning, at the airport."

"*Le drol flic* doesn't miss a trick," she said with a bitter smirk. "My bags…I knew I should have taken them back with me. But I had already unpacked them. Frankly, Stephen, I became tired of the conference. Bored, in fact, not to put too fine a point on it. I needed some time to myself: can you understand that? I decided to return early. How delicious to have two whole days to oneself, to enjoy one's house—to read, to cook, to listen to music. Immediately I'd gone outside to water the plants, the bloody phone rang. When I came in there was a message for me to call your Lieutenant Melnick. They'd found my husband's…*corpse.*"

"Who was it? Do you know?"

"What?"

"Who left the message? Did you recognize the voice?"

"No…it was just a message. I didn't recognize the voice. I was frightened. I don't know if you can understand what it was like growing up with violence. Machetes, what we called cutlasses. My father and mother had to leave…"

"Well," I said, "They released the body, that's the main thing: they must know he died…naturally. Questions are really academic."

She smiled a small, tender smile.

"Believe me, Carlotta," I said earnestly. "When you talk about wanting time to oneself, I know what you mean, though since I'm single at least I don't have to worry about having to be nice to a spouse sharing living quarters. But you're—were—married: how did you know your husband wasn't going to be lounging around the house when you got home?" Though I had trouble with this notion as soon as I said it: weekend beard, shorts and T-shirt, beer can ring on the side table, chips mashed in the carpet around the recliner in front of the television set happily ablast with Cowboys and Redskins mayhem. Out of the question. Very definitely *not* Sebastian Roylett's style If he'd been at home he would probably have been in his study with the door shut plotting out new and even more bizarre things to do.

"I told you before. It was a stage set, for entertainment. We led separate lives. He was rarely home. Can't you talk about anything else? Really…"

"Well, let's see. Oh, yes. Since I last saw you, I've had the chance to read some poetry."

"Very commendable."

"*Conquistador of the Caribbean.*"

"My God. That was a long time ago. May I have a cigarette? Without a filter? Splendid. What did you think of it?"

I gave her a cigarette and lighted it for her.

"Tremendously moving stuff, I thought."

"Almost like Gitanes, or Gauloises, these Camels," she said picking a shred of tobacco from her lips, paying attention to me for the first time. "You say you found Huw's poetry moving?"

"Yes. Huw must have loved you very much."

Silence; then, "It was very intense. For a while. Definitely for a while. But people change."

"You went to Paris."

"I went to Paris. Where I met Sebastian. And married. And eventually came to this country. Did you know him at all?"

"Who, Sebastian? No, not really."

"*Tu sais*: men have…appetites."

"What's that supposed to mean? All men are beasts? That he liked to fool around?"

"Younger women, scarcely unknown." Gallic shrug. "To be expected, especially in a liberated ménage whose members live full free lives, as we did, so long as no pain is offered. A reasonable discretion asked for and extended, always: understood. But not always, I fear, observed. In grief one takes refuge in safe homely rituals to restore the equilibrium of one's mind, you know? What safer, more quotidian than housecleaning, vacuuming, dusting the crystal—"

"Yes?"

"Yesterday while I was cleaning I found tucked down in the cushions of the sofa an unmentionable, a bit of lingerie—"

I said nothing.

"A flowered tulip bra, to be precise. From sometime over the weekend, I suppose. The housecleaning service comes in on Thursdays, and they are very thorough. It wasn't there then, I am certain."

"And it wasn't yours?"

"No, it wasn't mine," she said with ironic emphasis, her marvelous eyes daring me. "I don't wear a bra, and anyway it was too small."

*   *   *   *

On the way out to the stable it started to rain, huge gouts smacking fatly on the dirty windshield. It was a good day to twist an ankle or throw a shoe and I gave up on the notion of riding. I contented myself with taking the mare out of her stall and walking her up and down the aisle a couple of times and in general making much of her. I wondered what would become of her. If they ran true to form, the doctors Damon would soon be looking for ways to cut expenses or better yet raise some cash to finance their next venture. I fully expected that they'd decide to sell her. They were three months behind on their board bill. They'd never offered to pay me anything for riding their horse, and I'd never asked.

In the office Kay was sorting through some bills with a harassed expression.

"What's the matter, Kay?"

"Oh, I don't know," she wailed. "Everything." Her hands fluttered helplessly among the papers. "All this—And Linebacker—" I saw her eyes were red.

"And then the phone's been ringing. Some Realtor—"

"Oh?"

"Says she's got a client wants to make an offer on this place—"

"Want to talk about it?"

"Oh, Stephen, it all looks so hopeless. You know what I mean?"

"I guess so," I said.

Tentative smile. "She says he's willing to pay—an awful lot of money."

"Maybe you'd better take it. Or at least think about it seriously."

"Oh, I've been doing nothing but think about it since the call came in. But *selling* the stable—What will my customers do, Stephen? What will you do?"

"I'll be fine, Kay," I reassured her. "I'll be okay. So will everyone else. You'll see."

"It's all so sudden. It's *traumatic*. And I have to work on these." She pushed at the pile of bills. "Here's a copy of Joe's W-4 for him. I wonder where I should leave it." She looked at me appealingly.

"Here, I'll take it. I'm supposed to be seeing him tonight at the bingo." I folded the form and put it in my wallet.

"Thanks."

"No problem, K.C." I was idly thumbing through the most recent issue of *Show Times*, the official American Horse Shows Federation monthly magazine I'd found lying on a table: yet another strain of Venezuelan equine encephalomyelitis working its way up into Texas, an account of the annual convention held in Fort Lauderdale, results of the election of new officers and zone vice presidents, and profiles of new directors; all the way in the back were the notices of recent actions taken by the hearing committees and a record of current suspensions. My name was on the list.

I snorted.

"What's the matter, Stephen?"

"Nothing." I said. No one was likely to put S Cameron Coulter, Upperville, Virginia, together with Steve Coulter who worked part time at the stable south of town and took kid riders to local shows at the county exposition center.

Had it been just a point of honor, not paying that fine? Maybe I'd have been better off just paying the fine and forgetting about it. That's what Carson Creswell, the chairman of the AHSF, had wanted me to do. "Just pay the goddamned thing, Rusty, and get it behind you; it's not the end of the world."

*   *   *   *

On the way back home I stopped by the Busted Spur, the bar south of town near the laundromat where I sometimes dropped by after riding. Smoke-stained windows, steel shutters that came down at closing, dark wood, three kinds of beer, and a surprising selection of booze that included Laphroig, Gilbey's Red Breast, and José Cuervo Centenario. Country music and pool cues. Solitary drinkers were left alone to ponder their unfathomable sorrows.

Rhonda, the part-time owner and full-time bartender, seemed glad to see me. Rhonda lived in a re-po'ed double-wide over in Oak Hill and collected first editions of Tony Hillerman. When I'd first come to town I'd woken up a time or two at her place after a late night. Since then the relationship had eased on to something else.

She didn't ask much, and as usual I didn't give much.

By about seven the place had gotten crowded.

"You are Coulter, am I right?" By that time I was working on my fourth or fifth Shiner bock with double shot and I was more or less unsurprised to see that the speaker was the incredibly tall, sticklike Amos Beddington, approaching my table with a dusty-eyed girl by his side who was frowning as if she'd forgotten something monumentally important.

The corded muscles on Beddington's stringy arms squirmed like giant worms in a monster movie. He glowered red-eyed. Beneath the long lank hair I could see his neck was a minefield of angry pustules. His growly voice and swagger: 'roid rage incarnate, juiced to the eyeballs on Dianabol, Bolasterone, Quinolone.

"Yes, that's right. You're Beddington. Funny, I just finished reading—"

"I have heard of you. You are the one that remained after the summer purge. The lackey to the dead chairman. Know that my heart is light now that he is dead. He was an excrescence—"

"Hey, *great* verbalization skills, Amos," I enthused. "I really like your way with words. Short, to the point—"

"A tumor on the organ of the righteous scholars—"

"But sometimes a teensy bit hard to grasp those metaphors all at once—"

One of the girls giggled.

"What did you say?" He spoke in a dead uninflected voice.

"Never mind. Have a drink on me. And your lady friend too."

"Now is not a time for humor, Coulter." He was working himself up to something and unless I tinkered with his script—and soon—this scene was swiftly going to play out in a way I wasn't going to like.

"Oh, hell, Amos," I said in sudden concern, "somebody's gone and spilt salsa on that nice shirt of yours." Standing up I reached across the table and brushed with my left hand against his collar, then waved at somebody standing behind him. While Beddington's head was turning, and his hands were instinctively coming up, fast, my right hand, covered by my dropping left hand, jabbed hard just under his breast bone, with the middle three fingers held rigid in a kind of cup, and Beddington went rigid and silent as if he had just been privy to some cosmic truth.

"Hey, wow," the girl said. Beddington's face was ashen. He was clutching his chest. His knees gave way and he slumped forward into my arms. He reeked of musk.

"Are you okay?" I babbled solicitously. "Here, have a seat. Easy does it." I sat him down in a chair and patted his face while he feebly batted my hands away and made great raling sounds from deep in his chest. "Poor bastard, I think he choked on something; let me get him a glass of water." I made my way to the bar and virtuously tipped one of the wait people to take over a pitcher of water and a couple of glasses to where Beddington was being ministered to by his dusty-eyed girlfriend and a group of friends. Nobody was paying me a bit of attention. I supposed someone who'd been watching *Cops* would wonder why I hadn't tried the Heimlich maneuver. Not likely. He was far too fast and mean to chance it. And I wasn't wild about getting that close to him; musk-based cologne was way down on my list.

I knew I'd dodged the bullet by striking first—and doubly lucky that no one had appeared to notice my part in his fainting spell. I could not expect to be so fortunate another time.

*   *   *   *

Except, I might have known, for Rhonda, who never missed a thing, and had now followed me out into the parking lot. "Coulter," she said with what sounded like genuine regret, "the best thing is you don't come by here for a good long while. That crazy fucker's got friends, believe it."

"Does he come in here often? I never saw him here before."

"From time to time, yes. You just never ran in to him, is all. Don't you have some place to go, Coulter?"

"As a matter of fact, I do," I said, thinking of the bingo game. "Thanks, Rhonda."

"Por nada," she said, and shook her head. "You really are a mess."

I made it out of the parking lot and on to the highway before my stomach started acting up. I pulled off on the shoulder and went around the car and got sick in the ditch.

*   *   *   *

"Estella's mother, Mrs Ramirez."

"Pleased to meet you, Mrs Ramirez."

Nod.

"'N' twenty-three."

"Hot damn," said Joe, plugging down the Day-Glo marker in the middle column. "Gottit."

Mrs Ramirez uttered a short-heartfelt imprecation.

"What was that you were askin'?"

"Nothing," I said. I was never very lucky at bingo. I groped for my wallet. "I brought you a copy of your W-4. Mrs. Gordon would have mailed it to you but she knew I'd be seeing you tonight." I glanced at it as I handed it over to him.

"'O' sixty-one."

"Shucks," muttered Mrs Ramirez sitting across the table.

"Say, that street you live on's not very long, is it?"

"Goes from Alpine down to William Cannon."

"'G' fifty-three."

"Shee," said Mrs Ramirez.

"I think I may know someone who lives across the street from you. Old man, Anglo, a little bit gordo; old woman?"

"Get lucky, I've got a new card for you," a busty little girl said, working between the tables. She had a dimple and a sparkling smile.

"What? Old couple, yeah, that's right."

"'I' twenty-five."

"Sheesh."

"He got an old Hudson. He takes the bus from down the corner. Yeah, they move in, oh, six months ago. I don't see much of them."

Transportation was never far from Joe's mind: no wheels, no work. If he said the Hudson was old, it was bound to be ancient.

"'B' fifteen."

"Chingao, Bingo, Crazy T." Joe waved his card in triumph. The busty little girl dimpled prettily and flashed a smile at him.

"Shee-*it*."

"Oh?"

"She don't leave the house much. My brother Pete's kids, they go by Halloween. They say she's real nice but they don't get a lot of candy. From what they see, house fulla old books. All over. These the people?"

"Yes," I said. "I think maybe they are."

"Three owners," Joe said, "that house have, the last two years, tuna half. The plumbing, electric, something wrong." He shrugged philosophically. "But it quiet, they nice people. No bad things happen there."

"That's good," I said. A quiet place with nice people and no bad things, even with something-wrong plumbing, electric, might not be a such a bad deal. Even without a coat of Key West spar varnish in tuna half years.

"Now we play Double Postage Stamp," announced Mrs Ramirez with happy anticipation.

CHAPTER 16

▼

I got home about ten. The adrenaline from my encounter with Beddington and the high from the boilermakers had drained from my system, leaving me jittery and nauseated. I felt desperately in need of a
couple of good solid face stiffeners. Then I'd heat up a can of chili, stir
in a scattering of fondue chunks, season the mixture with Matouk's
Flambeau Trinidad sauce, and pass a quiet evening preparing the next
day's assignments.

A forlorn bundle was huddled on the steps outside my apartment.

It was Melody. She was wearing cut-off jeans frayed at the knees and
a T-shirt with a Great Dane wearing a halo emblazoned across the
front. Her long hair was tied back with a ribbon. A few strands hung
down over her ears.

"Hello, darling." She summoned up a wan smile.

"Hello, Melody," I said. "Come on in."

I held the door open for her, and then left her looking around as I
went past her into the kitchenette to rummage in the icebox. "Can I fix
you a drink? Something to eat?"

"Nothing, thanks. I had a hamburger."

I poured myself a liberal dose of tequila on the rocks in a short squat
glass and turned to face her.

"Oh, maybe I will have one of those."

I fixed her a drink in a decent glass, light on the tequila, while she walked around and idly looked at my garage sale décor, mostly brown and olive green from the 60s.

"You know, I've never been here before. *Casa Coulter*. It's not what I expected. It's awfully…"

"Anonymous?" I suggested.

"Yes, to be truthful. Perhaps even a tendency toward minimalism. Even bleak." She smiled. "I don't know what I expected. A picturesque cabin on some ranch out in the Hill Country, I suppose." She sat down on the sofa.

"That's nice to think about," I said. "But unfortunately that's not the way it is. The way it is, is shabby but—"

"—without any redeeming aristocratic elegance."

"Yes," I agreed.

We were edging our way into new terrain here, away from the Noël-and-Cole-Young Woodley repartee; away, too, from the limestone buildings where daily the whole glorious jumble of English literature was subjected to such solemn scrutiny. I reflected that Melody was my first guest—no, second, I corrected myself—Melnick had been the first to come to my apartment. First girl, anyway. No visitors at all in my first year, and now two in one week. No doubt about it, Roylett's murder was threatening my lone-wolf status. Even Huw had commented on the change in me.

I sank down in the tripes of the easy chair and kicked off my shoes. "You've got something on your mind. What is it?"

"It's silly, really." She licked her lips. "I lied to you."

"People lie."

"Yes, but I don't like lying to you, Stephen. Even though I don't know you very well, I really like you." She picked up her glass and held it in front of her mouth. "It was about what I told you." She took a quick sip. "About Saturday night." The glass was back covering her mouth.

"Oh, yes. Saturday night." I took a long drink of the tequila. I had the feeling I was about to be confided in. I was beginning to be confided in a lot.

"It was all so predictable, I can see that now. Sebastian made a date with me. That's what he actually called it: a date. 'We've got a date. You're going to come up to the house and tell me about the conference,' he said. 'I want to hear all about it from the point of view of someone young, someone just getting acquainted with the profession'.

"I was so stupid, I can see that now. In a flutter, of course. 'What can I wear to fit in, in that mansion?' I decided to go virginal. I wore that white linen blouse from By George, the kind of 1950s one with the covered buttons that does up the back, and that long silk paisley skirt. Well, it looks like silk, anyway. And heels. I even wore high heels.

"When I arrived there it was...overwhelming. You know, I'd been there for the staff Christmas party and then at the end of the summer, when he and Carlotta welcomed the new faculty. But this time it was different, just the two of us. First he took me out on that beautiful patio, overlooking the river and the hills. The sun was just going down. Then we went inside where he showed me his study and in the living room he had that champagne chilling, you know—that kind with the flowers painted on the bottle."

"I know the kind," I said. "Perrier-Jouet."

"Well, he had that in a silver wine cooler, and the Art Déco glasses, and he had—I asked him what it was—some very romantic stuff on the CD player."

"What was it?" I was honestly curious.

"He said it was César Franck." She looked at me clearly unsure of herself. "It seemed very passionate."

"*César Franck?*" I said. "Jesus."

"'*Le Chasseur Maudit.*'" She pronounced it carefully.

"Right you are. 'The Accursed Huntsman'. Wild piece of music. Fits." All to chase one lone little rabbit through the woods.

"He'd been drinking before I got there, I could see that. He had this expansive glow where you know, you *knew*, that anything is possible, he could make anything happen. All right, he had that brutal streak, but he had a spark, too, to where you couldn't tell what might happen; that was all part of it, too. I guess I found him…exciting.

"We sat on the sofa, drinking the champagne and listening to the music. There were some little boats still out on the water. We watched the sun set over the hills, and behind us the moon was coming up. He kept refilling my glass, and reciting poetry—Shakespeare's 'That time of year' and Marvell's 'Coy Mistress'—"

Vox humana. Pulling out all the stops. Old corny stuff: the time-hallowed argument of seduction—what I referred to in class flippantly as "*carpe diem*—seize the day, seize the dame!" I snorted derisively.

"He said"—she flinched, remembering—"he was about to die." She looked solemn.

Her words sent my train of thought reeling off at a tangent, but I tried not to show my perturbation.

"That's part of the argument," I said gently. "The lover, older, about to die, or go off to war, uses the imminence of his death to persuade the girl to give in to him. Standard emotional blackmail." I leaned forward. "What else do you recall?"

"What I remember best is how terribly expert he was at getting me undressed. First it was just that he brushed up against me in the hall, and touched my hand when he held out my glass to me. A little later when he was showing me the living room with that enormous vase of cut flowers on the piano, I remember he laid his hand on my wrist. Out on the patio he slipped his arm around my shoulders as we watched the sun set. I guess I must've fallen into a kind of trance, not really, of course, but that was the feeling. Then it was the most natural thing in the world for him to be undoing the buttons on the back of my blouse; he slid it down my arms and kissed the back of my neck and then he reached under my arms to undo the front clasp of my bra:

you know that men like that have had a lot of practice, choreographing the moves, but even so—"

"Melody," I started to remonstrate.

"I have to give him credit. He made me feel completely exalted, breathless. He did it all with a kind of—oh, I don't know—ruthless efficiency, like one of those lecherous noblemen with long powdered wigs out of Congreve or Wycherley in Restoration drama."

"I can imagine," I said, truthfully.

"And then, when he was through, he laughed at me." Her lovely eyes welled with tears. She pushed strands of hair out of her face back over her ears. Her cheeks burned red with shame.

"He laughed at you? Why would he laugh at you?"

"I don't know," she said miserably, and then in a voice so low I could hardly hear her, "Perhaps I told him I loved him."

"Yes," I said. "That might just do it." Why, I asked myself, did women never *believe* the Restoration dramatists?

"Please don't think it was just the wine and open french doors and the music; or the sunset or the moon coming up. It was more like the smell of the wood in his study, the soap he used, the scent of the cut flowers—"

"It was the stench of power," I said.

She looked at me with surprise.

"No, I mean it," I insisted, "power is a potent aphrodisiac."

"His clothes, too," she continued somewhat dreamily, "They were gorgeous. The raw silk jacket, the blue linen shirt he wore, those suede ankle boots. And pretty soon I was feeling—I know it's cliché—like I was on a magical cloud."

"And then he laughed," I said.

"That was afterward." Her face hardened, remembering. "I was completely humiliated, in shock. I stumbled around and gathered up my clothes." She closed her eyes. "I even had to scramble around under the couch for one of my shoes. may even have left some of them there. I don't exactly remember how I got home. Heaven knows how I managed to drive with all that champagne inside me without getting stopped."

"What did you do when you got home?"

"First I took a long shower and then got a glass of milk. And a cookie. Then I went straight to bed."

"Does Henry know?"

She looked at me uncomprehendingly. "I didn't see Henry till eight the next morning when the alarm went off and I went into the kitchen to make some coffee."

"You mean he didn't get back till eight?"

"Well, that's when I saw him come in."

Now I was certain that Henry had been lying when he told me Melody had been home when he got back from Jalisco's at nine. Unless, of course, I reminded myself, Melody was lying too, for some purpose I hadn't as yet discovered. But Roylett's laughing at her was pretty rank stuff...

"That's not what you said you told Lieutenant Melnick. You said you told him you were with Henry all evening."

"Yes, I know. That's why I came to see you. You're in touch with Walter, you tell him—*please*."

I promised to pass on to Melnick what she'd told me and, clearly relieved, she finally left. By now I didn't feel like eating.

I poured another slug of tequila and set the bottle by my chair.

Melnick had said that no one "on the outside" knew about Roylett's ticking time bomb, the possibility of potentiation of his Sturge's Syndrome, and I didn't feel I could violate his trust. But what Roylett had said to Melody meant that he could have known, probably did know, that any least thing could kill him. Perhaps he had been telling Melody the truth, masked ironically in the words of others—a strategy of seduction he'd been accustomed to use since puberty. Huntsman, indeed.

I found myself suddenly furious at Melnick. He was the one who'd gotten me entangled in this situation—which had been none of my contrivance, save for the plain bad luck of stumbling across Roylett's corpse. Oddly, I found myself much less incensed by the thought of Roylett so idly and viciously seducing Melody. Taxing Roylett with being a cynical womanizer seemed as stupid as taking to task a force of nature for being impersonal and malevolent. But the truth was I had been jolted out of my safe rut. My hard-won detachment was compromised, my carefully concealed emotions tossed at hazard. And I was exasperated with Melody and her wretched romantic dreams of marriage and becoming the next mistress of that large, airy house full of chintz and teak and vast pots of spring flowers.

With a sigh I reached for the Norton eager to reacquaint myself with the poisoners and parricides who peopled the ballads in the next day's poetry assignment. Before I'd gotten fairly settled down to reading I'd polished off what remained of the tequila. Then, spurred by a now-raging thirst that would not be denied, I ferreted out the bottle heels of Irish and sour mash in the cupboard. I passed out with my head in my hands at the table, but not—I discovered when I woke up—before scrawling in my notebook, self-pityingly, the words to the sonnet by Gérard de Nerval, a poem I hadn't thought of in years: *Je suis le ténébreux,—le veuf,—l'inconsolé//Le Prince d'Aquitaine…à la tour abolie.* I dwell in darkness, deprived of love, the Prince of Aquitaine in his ruined tower.

*   *   *   *

Morning dawned clear; gone from the air was the sultriness of the past few days. I determined to get in a ride before going to The University.

The mare was in an obliging mood and I got an excellent school out of her. She was prompt in her lead changes and snapped crisply over her fences. I thought fleetingly that this was what I could do best. Thanks to her I'd managed to carve out of the day a bright, fleeting moment that no one could take away.

As Joe Chavez once said after having been broadsided in a car race and put out of action for several months, "'*Que me quiten lo bailao*', which he explained to me meant 'Let them try to take away from me what I've already danced.'"

I did the mare off, paying particular attention to her ankle, and left her in her stall happily munching hay, switching her tail in self-satisfaction.

I dropped by the office to hang up my tack. K.C. was working at the desk. I guess my face must have registered surprise.

"What's so funny?" she said, bristling defensively.

"Nothing really," I told her. "It's just that you're sitting right where I left you yesterday afternoon. It doesn't look as if you've stirred from the chair."

"Maybe I haven't."

Looking at her more closely, I could see she was in a deep funk.

"What's the matter, K.C.?"

"It's all so hopeless, Stephen. Just like I told you yesterday—only worse. I keep thinking things will get better, but—"

"'That light at the end of the tunnel is just another train coming toward you'?"

"Something like that." She shrugged disconsolately. "I don't know where to begin."

"Why don't you try starting from the beginning." I pushed over a chair and sat down, assuming an interested expression. If I drove fast I could get back home just in time to grab a shower and change clothes before going off to class. "Tell me what's the matter, and maybe I can help." The truth was I was genuinely very fond of K.C.

"Well, the first thing was, there was this man from the sheriff's office showed up right after I got here this morning." She made a gesture toward some legal documents on the desk; there was a single dollar bill stapled to the sheaf of papers. "Notice of a hearing—the dollar's for a phone call if I can't make it to the courthouse, otherwise, he says, if I don't get in touch and don't show up, they may issue a warrant for my arrest. It's about Linebacker. Apparently he fell over a fence, and now Bobby is saying the x-rays the vet took show he was lame when I sold him. He's suing me not just for the price of the horse but for triple damages for practicing deceptive trade…"

"Is Audrey all right?"

"I didn't hear anything about Audrey—she may not even have been riding."

We were silent for a full minute. If Bobby hadn't sold Linebacker to Art Simmons, he might well come back on K.C. vindictively, perhaps feeling she was an easy mark and not wanting to leave any money on the table. The larger question in my mind was under what conditions the horse had fallen. I was positive that Bobby had tried him out pretty thoroughly before I'd seen him, using his little arsenal of training devices like the tack rails and electronic hopples to see whether he had any real jump in him. Bobby got rid of very few horses that he hadn't tested thoroughly.

"Then," she haltingly resumed, "if you can believe it, some man from the IRS called about the second quarter taxes and asking why there's been no deposit made: He was talking about liens on my property, even my car, for heaven's sake, and freezing my bank account."

In addition, K.C. said, her county and school district property tax statements had arrived and were due, up 30% from last year based on a new appraisal.

"To top it all off, the real estate lady I told you about came by and asked me to make a quick decision on selling this place. She said the person she represented was a horseman who wanted to come in and start up what she called 'a first-class operation.'

"All in all, Stephen, I think I've about had it."

*   *   *   *

On my way home from campus after my three o'clock class, I made a detour by the discount liquor store up on Guadalupe where I bought a pint of bourbon, a pint of vodka, and a six-pack of Shiner Bock.

I just wanted to stop hurting.

I guessed I'd passed out before doing anything really stupid the night before. I hadn't made any late-night phone calls, and I hadn't gone out. When Lethe-wards I'd sunk I'd been wandering around lost in the forest sauvage dreamscape of the ballads and reaching out to the world with the scrawled quote from Nerval. If that was all the damage I'd done I'd count myself lucky.

As usual, the only person I'd hurt was myself.

As an afterthought following the liquor store, I stopped at Central Market and picked up a small packet of boneless chicken breasts, asparagus, fresh sage, oregano, capers, and a bottle of Saint Barbara chablis from The University's extensive West Texas vineyards. When I got home I threw the bag with the chicken breasts into the fridge and washed up.

I placed a call to the Simmonses to find out how Audrey was while I looked at the blinking light on my answering machine. Terri Simmons informed me icily that Audrey was just fine, and not to call again or she would report me; to whom she didn't say.

I shook my head and checked my messages.

Tom Sturtevant's secretary asked me to please call him as soon as possible, and left me both an office and a home number.

Walter Melnick wondered if I were free for drinks and early dinner.

I called both Sturtevant's numbers, but no luck. His office informed me that the senator had left for the day. "Hi, this is Tom," was the calculatedly offhand message at his home number, and I left word I'd called and would try to get in touch with him in the morning.

I reached Melnick over at the university police station and we agreed to meet at The Hofbrau, a steak joint down on Sixth Street.

When I hung up after speaking with Melnick I popped the seal on the bourbon and poured myself four fingers in a jelly glass which I drank down standing at the sink. Then I rinsed the glass, threw in a few ice cubes, and filled it with one of the Shiner bocks which I tossed back as a chaser—standard preparation before going out into society. I threw on clean jeans, a short-sleeved, faded madras shirt and, over it, a favorite old jacket that Serena had told me looked like it had been made out of cast-off oatsacks. Thinking about the relentlessly neat Melnick inspired me to give a swipe to my shoes before I left the apartment.

On my way to the restaurant the bourbon kicked in. I immediately felt better.

Melnick was waiting for me at a table in the back, and got up to greet me. He was wearing a dark blue windbreaker, white shirt, dark blue trousers, and his usual highly-polished black shoes. His black hair was neatly combed. His teeth were very white. We ordered enormous steaks and the salad with the famous dressing the main ingredient of which seemed to be the liquid in which cut olives are bottled. A brief debate about whether to order stuffed jalapenos as well as a serving of fried potatoes was quickly settled in the affirmative. The waitress brought us a frosted pitcher of beer and the world seemed suddenly a better, friendlier place.

I remembered to ask Melnick about his daughter. He smiled broadly. "Polly loves it down here."

"Classics," I said.

"Like I said the other day, they got one a the best departments in the country at The University. Now she's talking about applying to graduate school."

Then he got down to business.

"What you got for me?"

"You said you wanted me to keep poking around. First off, this business with the book: who checked it out is information they tell me they won't release to anyone."

"Yes, I know," said Melnick, sighing. "I found out the same thing."

"Miss Silver?"

He nodded. "Miss Silver. What about Mrs Roylett? Did you have a chance to talk with her?"

"Yes, as it happens, I did. I ran into her in the parking lot. She was cool, very cool. She said she'd gotten fed up with the conference, came back early Sunday morning. She says she was out gardening when the phone rang. She was too late to get the call, but there was a message there about her husband—"

"And, like any devoted wife, she rushed to his side—"

"She says she was scared, frightened to death, couldn't get her thoughts together. Decided to go back to square one. Went back out to the airport, back up to Dallas, taking with her only what you saw: she'd already unpacked her clothes. Knew at once you'd noticed she'd arrived with no luggage to speak of. Called you, incidentally, 'le drol flic'."

Melnick snorted, but I could tell he was amused.

"Since then, she told me, she'd found reason to believe that Roylett had been cheating on her." I wasn't about to get into the tulip bra business with Melnick.

"Incidentally, so far as Fishbach's concerned, I'm not so sure either one of them—Fishbach or Melody—was at home Saturday night."

"Doesn't exactly take me by surprise." Melnick paused. "As I told you, the investigation's about to be shut down. Not that there ever was much of one after those reports started coming in. But that's interesting. You're saying that that studious youth Fishbach wasn't there when the girl got home?"

"That's my understanding. And Melody herself may not have gotten back till late."

"Nothing we can do about it." Melnick appeared philosophical. "Well, one thing, anyway. You'll be happy to know Joan has given you a clean bill of health."

"What do you mean?"

Melnick bestowed a dazzling smile. "Did I forget to tell you that? Jesus, my mind's slipping."

"Joan? What do you mean?" I froze.

"What I mean is Joan said she saw you out at the stable."

"But Joan couldn't have been at the stable on Sunday morning," I said slowly, thinking. "She wasn't due to come back until that afternoon."

"She came back in the morning, early."

"Her too? They *both* came back early, Carlotta *and* Joan?"

Grave nod. "That's the way it looks."

"She lied. She fucking lied."

"Don't take it so serious, Rusty. Everyone lies. Even that little girl, that Melody, remember? She lied. They all lie."

"I got out there at sunup, and her horse hadn't been ridden," I insisted.

"What?"

"I just remembered. When I went to feed, Joan's horse was slick, no sign of sweat. In this weather, if she'd even turned him around in the stall he'd have popped a sweat. And I was there the rest of the morning, and never saw her."

CHAPTER 17

▼

It started to rain on my way back from dinner. Entering the apartment was like walking into a sweat lodge. Taking a tepid shower failed to cool me; neither did standing naked in front of the floor fans afterward dry me off. Finally I flipped on the airconditioner and lowered the thermostat to sixty-eight—a self indulgence I knew I'd regret when I received my next utility bill.

There was a knock on the door.

Melody was leaning up against the doorframe. Her long dark hair swung loose, seed-pearled with moisture; her damp green jersey dress clung to her trim figure like seaweed. Hectic color flushed her pale cheeks. I saw she was slightly tight. "We've got to stop meeting like this," I said lightly.

"Hullo, lover." She didn't meet my gaze. "Yes, I know." Her voice was dull.

"How was the Glorious Twelfth?"

She smiled in appreciation. "It rained every day; not a grouse in sight. Got anything to drink?" She wandered past me into the apartment.

"Of course." I went into the kitchenette and made rather a production out of mixing her what was in fact a very weak spritzer made from the Saint Barbara white and some nearly flat Perrier with the last drops from a desiccated lime.

She made a face. "This tastes awful."

"Sorry; we're running a bit low on the Pouilly-Fuissé." I brought her a towel. "You want to be careful with those Purdeys, and don't let the moisture get into the action."

"Stephen, did you talk to Lieutenant Melnick? Like you said you would? About what I told you last night?"

Indeed I had, I told her—"a suitably edited version, let us say"—and wondered warily what was coming.

"Can I count on you, really count on you?"

"That sounds discouraging."

"It isn't really. It's just that there's…more."

"More?"

"You remember I told you about going out to Professor Roylett's place Saturday night? And how he…. used…me and afterwards laughed at me? Well, I didn't tell you everything. And now it's about to eat me up alive."

"I'm listening."

"I was lying there on the sofa, feeling…discarded…and he'd wrapped this big towel around himself and was walking back and forth, puffing on a cigar, chuckling as he talked. I thought I was going to throw up.

"There were some things he wanted to tell me, for my own good, he said, a kind of critique that he was sure I could profit from. Particularly if thoughts of a serious relationship ever crossed my mind.

"What was it about wanting to fuck young girls, anyway, he asked me? 'Vastly overrated,' he said." She swallowed.

"'Really', he told me, 'having allowed your clothes to be taken off without objection, you gave me the impression that you felt you had honorably discharged your responsibilities, and from that point on your contribution to the proceedings consisted in just lying there on the sofa, several times being stirred to utter small mewing sounds which I am sure you meant me to understand as the wild abandoned expression of your orgasm; once anyway you so far forgot yourself as to signal your enthusiasm by murmuring "O God!" *sotto voce* and *actually moving your hands*. Recall that it was left to me to arrange your limbs, lifting and separating your legs, and so on, not least meeting the challenge of getting my cock into you without being afforded the slightest evidence of enthusiasm on your part.'"

"You've got a hell of a memory."

"How could I forget? I remember every word.

"The whole exercise, he went on to tell me, had proved really quite exhausting and though he was not *au fond* enamored of the Earl of Chesterfield, he had reason, thanks to me, to reflect more favorably on his description of fucking: 'the position is ridiculous, the pleasure momentary, and the price damnably expensive'.

"Until this evening he had been in danger of forgetting just how difficult not to say uncomfortable it is to make love to a young girl. 'Once one is past the novelty of the perky breasts, tiny rosy nipples, and her…tightness', he said, any man would trade all these for some experience and at least the simulacrum of enthusiasm and…a willingness to *experiment*. He told me how he kept thinking (no doubt uncharitably) how very long it would take to train me. And that was just about the sex business, what went on in bed—it had nothing to do with what he called the real business of marriage: entertaining, running the house and so on—

"Then he thanked me for making all this clear to him once more.

"And then he said to me, 'Poor little pathetic slut!'"

*   *   *   *

Thus spurned and humiliated by Roylett, desiring above all else to hurt him, Melody made up the story and threw it in his face that Carlotta and Joan were having an affair, that even now, as she spoke, they were probably in bed together.

"'There are things,'" Melody said she told Roylett venomously, "'that only a woman knows how to do for another woman…'"

She paused, considering.

"I don't know what made me say that to Sebastian. I really don't. Except he was such a pig. I wanted to do something that would really devastate him, shatter that colossal pig ego. I didn't care what I said."

*   *   *   *

When Melody fled from the house on Cat Mountain, she drove home, found it empty, tried unsuccessfully to call Joan at her house, and then went out for a hamburger with fries and a chocolate milk shake.

"I don't remember ever being so hungry," she said. "I sat there at the table and when I had finished eating I wrote a letter to Joan. It was the most difficult thing I have ever written. I tried, really tried, to make a clean breast of what I'd done. I told her the whole thing. That despite myself I got turned on by Roylett, and had like a bitch in heat accepted his invitation to go to his house on Cat Mountain. That he'd surprise, surprise, jumped my bones. And then I told her how afterwards he'd mocked my efforts at…how I, the way I made love. He called it fucking. How he'd ridiculed any thought I might have had that he'd divorce Carlotta and marry me—and how—this was the most painful of all to write to Joan—transported in an ecstasy of fury, I'd lashed out at him by making up a story about how his wife was carrying on an affair with Joan.

"Then I drove to Joan's. I let myself in with the key that Joan had given me so that I could check on her cat when she was away. I left my letter on her desk. Even though there was no red light blinking on the answering machine, I rewound the tape and played it anyway: nothing on it. I finally went home and fell into bed, passing a miserable night.

"As soon as I saw you with Roylett's body on Sunday morning when I'd gone in to work out the scheduling with Huw, I just knew that

Joan had returned home, seen my letter on her desk, read it, gone round the twist, and set out to track down Roylett and kill him.

"That's when I ran from the mail room and raced back to Joan's.

"The first thing I saw was that the envelope I'd left on Joan's desk the night before had been torn open, and the letter was crumpled up next to it.

"No red light blinked on Joan's answering machine. That meant one of two things: either no new messages had come in since I'd checked last night, or that, if there had been, someone had already listened to them. I rewound the tape to the beginning and played it. And, Bingo! there was a message from Roylett—he must have called after I'd left Joan's the night before, and Joan had listened to it when she got back.

"I never heard anything like it. He must have been out of his mind telling Joan the things he did. Except he said it all in this matter-of-fact way he had, so that everything sounded so very reasonable.

"'I'm terribly sorry to bother you, Joan,' he said, 'but your name came up just now and I thought I'd better give you a call.'

"After a good deal of thought, he went on to say—Joan could ask me about this if she had any questions, he suggested—he had decided not to forward Joan's name to the dean for promotion to tenure and associate professorship. He was, as he explained, terribly sorry, but was sure that, given the circumstances, Joan would understand, and, oh, by the way, he would not, regrettably, be able to see his way clear to writing her a reference, etc.

"It was obvious," said Melody, "that Joan got Roylett's message, and my note filled in the details. Can you understand that I was consumed by guilt, Stephen? What mischief had I set in motion, I asked myself, telling Roylett that Joan and Carlotta were having an affair?

"About then Joan showed up, looking rather white about the mouth but very calm. She didn't even seem angry with me.

"I told her Roylett was dead.

"With admirable restraint Joan told me to be somewhat scanter of my maiden virtues and suggested I return at once to the English department, and say nothing about meeting her.

"The thing is, I guess, I really like Joan, and if there's a way to help her, I will.

"I'm so scared, Stephen. It's not like I haven't done things I was ashamed of, either…"

I put my arms around her and walked her back to the bathroom, her nose buried against my chest as she wept. She was shivering with cold.

With my left arm supporting her about her waist, I reached up under her skirt with my right hand and pulled down her panty hose around her knees. I set her clunky shoes together in the hall. Then I sat her down on the closed lid of the toilet and finished pulling the panty hose off her cold feet. I pulled the green knit dress up over her head as she held out her arms like an obedient child. Then I got her out of the rest of her clothes, peeling them away from her trembling body. She had cute toes.

I realized I was digging a grave for myself. What I was doing was, if not strictly illegal—she was after all in her twenties—at the least grounds for my dismissal from The University were she to file a grievance. The truth was that I was aroused by her and disgusted and saddened by myself.

I managed to prop her up in the shower with the warm water running, and left her a large bath towel hanging on the sink, along with a pair of Sulka pajamas Wendy and Wick had sent me on my last birthday and which I'd never worn.

While I was changing the sheets Melody stumbled into the bedroom and I bundled her into bed. She had rolled up the silk cuffs.

I didn't know who she'd been with or where she'd been before she arrived at my place, but it was clear that she had no business out on the street; and frankly I wasn't about to try and take her back to the house she shared with Fishbach. And I think she realized this, too.

"Stephen, I've been so stupid—" She stared up at me from the pillow, her eyes enormous, her face very white, and her damp hair spread out on the tattersall pattern.

"Don't be ridiculous," I told her. "You've had a hell of a time of it. You'll be fit as a fiddle in the morning."

"Sure I will. Tell me, do you hate the way I look?"

"Don't be ridiculous," I repeated.

"No, I mean it, really. Do I...turn you off?"

"Turn me off? Hell, no," I said, laughing. "Why, you..."

"Do you ever think of me that way?"

"What way? I think of you..."

"'Let me count the ways'? No, I mean, do you ever want to fuck me?"

"Constantly," I reassured her. "Though to be fair it's more I want to make love to you than fuck you."

"Really?"

"Really."

She held her hand up to my cheek. "You are a very sweet man."

I had gotten to my feet and was about to go into the kitchenette and fix her a cup of chocolate when she spoke drowsily.

"You know, Stephen," she said, her voice so low I could hardly make out the words, and I paused, my hand on the switch of the bedside lamp. "It was really the strangest thing: as I was driving back home after I told him that story I'd made up—suddenly I just knew, somehow...*that it was all true.*"

"What, about Carlotta and Joan? You just intuited it? Come on, you must've had *something* to go on to come up with a story like that."

"No, not about Carlotta and Joan, or rather—I don't know. But that it could have been Joan. You remember up in the graduate students' lounge on Sunday when you were all asking me about that conference I went to with Joan, and I said that Ruth Stepnovic promised she'd inscribe my copy of her book? Well, when I checked out of the hotel to come back here and help out Huw with the fall scheduling, I managed to remember to leave the book at the desk for her. Joan could pick it up from Ruth and bring it back with her. But in all the rush to get off I forgot to call Joan. So I phoned her at the hotel as soon as I got back—"

"And?" My fingers curled and I pulled my hand away from the lamp.

"And they said she'd already checked out, a day early. That's what made me run to her place after I saw Roylett's body: I thought she might already have come back here.

"Then I began remembering how quiet and…distant…she'd been on the way up—not at all like her. Oh, it wasn't that she was mean or rude or anything, just somehow…*absent*, as if her mind were somewhere else. Like when you're in class and you can't stop thinking about something you want to do. At first I thought it was that she couldn't wait to get there and then, once we got there—before it had even gotten under way—it was like she was bored with the whole idea. But it was like she was getting excited, too, you know what I mean?

"Before, the other thing was, she used to talk about Carlotta all the time, all she'd accomplished in her field. She bragged on her, basically; it even got a bit tiresome. But on our trip she didn't say anything about Carlotta, never mentioned her name. And when I happened to say something about Carlotta's being at that other conference in Chicago the same time as we'd be in Pittsburgh, I remember Joan suddenly…blushed, and changed the subject."

She was silent for a moment.

"Did she say anything about Professor Roylett?"

"She said plenty. Called him a 'skirt-chasing libertine'—"

"'Libertine'," I murmured. "My, my."

Melody opened her eyes briefly and went on in that same low neutral tone. "Oh, it wasn't just a case of personality conflict, or that he was the one calling the shots on her tenure: she really detested the man. How he reeked of cigars and after shave, the way he dressed, the fact he

drank so much, how he spoke down to people, how he treated Carlotta…"

"How did Joan say he treated her?"

"Condescendingly. He had very definite ideas. Trophy wife, first;
beautiful, academic jet-setter; then, act as hostess, help with the running of the department, recruiting, entertaining. You know—" her
hands made a frustrated movement on the covers "—he had these
old-fashioned ideas. The thing is, I'd been *so* looking forward to that
conference, and suddenly there we were, and Joan was…gone somewhere else in her head."

*   *   *   *

I held her hand till she fell asleep, and then picked up her damp
clothes, and hung them up where they had a chance of drying before
morning. Then I reviewed what I needed to do for class and mixed a
nightcap. I regarded the lumpy sofa that was to be my bed for the night
without much enthusiasm. For no particular reason I recalled the careless gesture with which Carlotta lifted her fencing mask and how she'd
smiled at Joan; and then, idly, I thought of the photograph of my
mother and her friend Lisa on that sunlit beach on a Greek isle.

*   *   *   *

I went up to the grocery store early and on my way back stopped at
Texas French Bread and picked up a half-pound of freshly-ground coffee and a couple of croissants. Back in the apartment I cleared the Barrington file off the table and dumped it on a chair, freeing up a space
where I set a place for Melody. I put out the willow-pattern plate, cup,
saucer, and butterplate with three pats of unsalted butter, table silver,
salt and pepper, a small bowl of brown sugar, and an unopened jar of
Rose's lime marmalade. I folded a paper towel for a napkin. Then I
brewed the coffee, set the croissants on a plate in the tiny microwave,

and left a note: "Croissants are in the zotter—fifteen seconds ought to be about right. Juice in fridge, ditto milk. Best, Stephen. PS If you stay over again, I'll lay on kippers and kedgeree."

*   *   *   *

After my ten o'clock class, I used my card to place calls to three airlines. Then I tried to figure out how I could best help Kay.

*   *   *   *

When I got home the bed had clean sheets, and the old ones put in the clothes hamper. The rat's nest on the sofa where I'd slept had been tidied up. All the breakfast things had been put away, and the glasses, plates, and silver washed and put out to dry on the drain board. The bathroom sink was immaculate.

Roylett's behavior had been unconscionable and what he said to Melody unforgivable. It was almost as if he'd lost sight of any accountability he might owe to Carlotta, to the department of which he was chairman, to the college, to The University, and certainly to himself. Had he really had, I wondered, a conviction that his death was imminent?

CHAPTER 18

▼

Fridays I taught freshman English at nine and ten, expository writing at one.

As I walked across campus to my first class, I reflected that the genius who said that virtue was its own reward was possessed of a wicked sense of humor, equaled only by that other ironist who observed that no good deed shall go unpunished.

Here I should have been feeling uncommonly decent, actually righteous, and the truth was I was tired and irritable and generally pissed off. I got to class just as the bell rang and found no chalk, no chair. I excused myself after taking roll, and as I left the room I heard laughter and raised voices behind me.

I went down to the English department office and talked the receptionist/secretary out of three pieces of chalk. I stood patiently as she pointed out how lucky I was that she just happened to have the chalk in her desk, and reminded me primly that the "custodians are the appropriate persons to see for chalk." So far as chairs were concerned, she told me, I could fill in a work request form to be sent to the departmental materials committee for appropriate action at their next meeting scheduled for the first week in October, and, if approved, take the request to the university warehouse north of town for delivery on one of their regularly scheduled once-a-week deliveries.

"What about if I just liberate one from another classroom?"

"Well, I suppose you could do that," she allowed, then added with a simper, "but then whoever teaches in that classroom will be missing a chair."

"Let me observe," I said evenly, "that I am fast reaching a point where what happens in another classroom is of the utmost indifference to me."

Amanda Vennible came into the main office; something in my exasperated voice must have carried down the hall to her office in the back and alerted her that all was not well.

"Good morning, Miss Vennible."

"Good morning. Mr Coulter, don't you have a class you're supposed to be teaching? Is there a problem?"

I explained.

"Oh, my goodness." She actually blushed. "You were in here the other day and I said I'd send an order in. I'm so sorry, I simply forgot. Here, take Cynthia's chair. She won't mind, will you, dear? We've got an extra one around here somewhere. But do remember to bring this one back after class."

I returned the chair to the departmental office after my ten o'clock class. Amanda was behind the counter going over some paperwork with the receptionist. She looked up as I pushed the chair through the swinging door.

"Thanks a lot, Miss Vennible. Thanks, Cynthia. I'm sorry to have bothered you."

"No trouble, Dr Coulter," Cynthia said.

"Large as the department is, these things have a way of happening," said Amanda. "I'll send a note to custodial services reminding them—again—to keep an eye on chalk and the furniture inventory."

She returned her attention to the papers on the counter and then, sensing that I hadn't moved, glanced up again. "Is there something else I can help you with?"

"Well, yes, as a matter of fact, there is. Do you happen to have Professor Vere's home address?"

Amanda looked around and began reaching for the university directory on Cynthia's desk, until my words stopped her.

"The reason I ask, Miss Vennible, is I don't believe he's living at the address on Clearview, the one given in the directory. I...happened to be driving by there yesterday and the people there said the Veres had moved—"

"You could ask Professor Vere, or leave word for him in his mailbox."

"Yes, I suppose I could," I said lightly. "But I thought I'd ask you, Miss Vennible."

Now Amanda Vennible was giving me her complete attention. "Cynthia, would you please hold my calls?" She beckoned me to follow her to her office. "Come in and close the door, Mr Coulter."

We faced each other across her desk. Looking at her, dressed unremarkably in dark paisley, I reminded myself that Miss Vennible was the senior secretary of a large department of English of a very large university. As such, she occupied a unique position of authority, charged with vast responsibility, entrusted with all manner of confidences. She served as the department's resident dragon, the fierce protector and guardian of departmental history, wisdom, and lore. From the frank, appraising look she bestowed on me I could tell that she knew I wasn't seeking answers out of idle curiosity.

"I'm not going to ask you why you need this information, Dr Coulter; but in any case I'm not at all sure that it's any of my concern, or even that I need to know." She favored me with a piercing glance. "I expect it has something to with Professor Roylett's death and what I have heard about you asking a good many questions."

I nodded.

Apparently satisfying herself that I'd passed some kind of test, she wrote out three lines on a yellow pad, tore off the sheet, and held it out to me. Vere's name and address on Forest Glade. No phone number.

We both understood that she wasn't finished with me yet; she had come to some sort of decision when she'd invited me back to her office. "How well do you know Professor Vere?"

"Not well at all, really. Just to say hello to in the halls and mailroom, I suppose, and then of course there was Sunday."

"I don't suppose there are very many people who do know Professor Vere," said Amanda Vennible deliberately. "And even fewer who know him well. Of the ones who do, I suppose Professor Ashton is the closest to him of anybody in the department. I know they go to early church together Sundays over at the Catholic church just east of campus.

"The Veres live a *very* quiet life; she's been in poor health for a long time, and their children grew up and moved away years ago.

"About ten years ago, the Veres refinanced the house on Clearview in order to replace the roof, make repairs to the kitchen, and put in central heating and airconditioning.

"He reached the mandatory retirement age of sixty-five just after Professor Roylett took on the chairmanship of the department.

"Professor Vere went to see Professor Roylett," said Amanda, "and quite routinely sought permission to teach full-time past age sixty-five.

"Professor Roylett brought up his request at the next budget council meeting." She paused again and from what I would later piece together, was trying to choose her words carefully to explain what was a complicated scenario.

"They took a vote. My minutes show that two members voted in favor of Vere's request, one voted against it, and 17 abstained." She smiled thinly. "It was as Professor Ashton said to me later, 'a not untypical vote in an English department budget council.'

"One of the two positive votes then moved for a compromise: force Professor Vere to retire at sixty-five, but allow him to teach one-third time on 'soft' money, the kind of money that arises when somebody's on leave or a position is temporarily unfilled. Everybody seemed relieved.

"Professor Roylett called for another vote, this one passing 16 to one, with three abstentions. I could tell he was absolutely furious, but as things turned out I suppose he could draw some consolation in recollecting the wording of the revised policy, and mentally adding emphasis: '...upon the recommendation of the *chairman and* the budget council...' He then proposed a further codicil to what the budget council had approved, the effect of which would be to force Professor Vere to retire at 65, but allow him to teach one-third time on 'soft' money subject to the approval of the chairman and the budget council year-by-year until age 70, at which time Professor Vere would be compelled to retire 100%.

"That's the way it went up to the dean, Dr Coulter, and that's what the dean, who almost certainly had his mind on other things, approved.

"The net result was to force Professor Vere to live on his very small pension plus one-third of what he had been making. All told he was making less than 75% of what his pre-65 salary had been. I know he must've found it increasingly difficult to make ends meet. I believe there were locked-in mortgage payments which wouldn't be finished until he turned 71, and as far as I know he didn't seem to qualify for any loan. And then of course there were always Priscilla Vere's medical expenses that never seem to be covered by insurance. And on top of it, Dr Coulter, was the galling business insisted upon by Professor Roylett, requiring 'annual approval,' 'annual renewal,' for his continued employment. But you know all about that, don't you?"

I did indeed.

"Actually, during the past few years Professor Vere has been teaching two, three, and sometimes four courses a semester, trying to make full salary.

"He just wasn't able to keep up with the taxes and pay on the second lien, especially with Priscilla's illnesses and the problems with his retirement. That's the reason they sold the house on Clearview and moved to where they are now—"

"I know the street," I told her.

"Yes, well," said Amanda, "as I say, the Veres maintain a reclusive lifestyle. It would surprise me if anyone besides Professor Ashton, you, and I knows that the Veres have moved, or that they are living in…reduced circumstances.

"And with Newbie and Gwen both married and moved away—" She shrugged. I recalled from Vere's dossier that the elder Vere child, Thomas Newbold, was a research chemist with DuPont in North Carolina, and the daughter, Jennifer, divorced with two children, taught school in Florida.

"But why, Miss Vennible, why?"

"Who knows? Professor Roylett was so volatile and unpredictable. It could have been for any number of reasons, starting with the fact that when Professor Vere met with Professor Roylett he was trying to recruit a young eighteenth-century woman that we all thought he…liked."

With his senses pleasantly aflame and focused on this future conquest, Roylett would find himself genuinely shocked at the notion of hard-money lines being taken up with old desiccated farts like Ed Vere.

Amanda was trying hard not to cry. "It was like a game that Dr Roylett played with him. He assigned Professor Vere the worst possible schedule—the most tedious courses scheduled at the most inconvenient times—and, last fall, Professor Roylett somehow contrived to have his classes meet in the farthest reaches of The University's campus…six-student seminars taking place in one of the chemistry building's vast lecture halls at nine in the evening; a tiny counseling room in the nursing school mornings at eight. Throughout, Professor Vere manfully pocketed the insults."

I gave Amanda my handkerchief. My father told me always to carry a clean handkerchief, son. It is one of the few things he has told me to do that I remember to do.

*   *   *   *

"Joan, are you busy?"

I poked my head around her door...

"No, come on in. The only thing I've got on the schedule is Professor Roylett's memorial service at one-thirty..."

"This won't take long," I promised her, and, typically, cavilled at getting to the point. "Your classes settling in all right?"

"I suppose so. Of course there are the usual adds and drops. But my graduate seminar made, I'm happy to say."

"Good. I know that pleases you."

"The only thing is, there never seems time for research or writing." The usual complaint. "I've applied for a grant...But I don't know, since I got funding for that conference, whether they'll even look at my application, money's so tight."

"And from what I gather, you didn't have a lot of fun there, either."

"Ah," she said. "Finally we arrive at the reason for this meeting. Wherever did you get that idea?"

I stepped into her office now and closed the door firmly behind me.

"From the way you talked about it the last time we spoke. I mentioned that Melody found the speaker—"

"Ruth Stepnovic."

"Right, Ruth Stepnovic. Melody said she found her brilliant. And as I recall, you said 'Very adequate; scintillating, I suppose, if you hadn't heard it before.' In my book that qualifies as a less-than-enthusiastic endorsement. Am I wrong?"

Joan shrugged.

"Melody said things were just getting good when she left but that 'even Joan was getting restless'."

"When did she say that?"

"While we were all waiting to be questioned on Sunday afternoon." Pause. "So far as I know, no one else picked up on it.

"But last night she said she tried to get hold of you in Pittsburgh on Saturday afternoon to tell you to be sure to remember to bring back that book of hers that the lady from Stanford was signing. The hotel told her you had already checked out. Where did you go?"

"What do you mean, where did I go? I came back here."

"I don't think so. At least not directly. I think you stopped in Chicago."

"Chicago? Why would I for God's sake stop in Chicago?"

"Not to put too fine a point on it, because you were going to see Carlotta."

She laughed uncertainly. "I see Carlotta all the time." Even so her hawk's face was mantling with color.

"Yes, that's true. But not alone."

"I wanted to be alone—" But her voice was shaky. "Why on earth would you think that?"

"I remembered some things." I was thinking of that photograph in my bedroom. At the same time I was thinking, with a kind of split screen focus, of the looks that had passed between them when Joan handed Carlotta the Evian bottle at the gym that day, their eyebeams twining.

"And then I think something happened. You had a falling out, an argument, probably over Carlotta's not wanting to make the break with Roylett. You stormed back to your room. You decided to leave. And you got back to your house in time to read the letter Melody placed on your desk and to listen to the message Roylett left you on your answering machine.

"Then I think you tried to call Carlotta in Chicago and learnt from the hotel operator that, in fact, Carlotta had already checked out of her Chicago hotel room ages ago, in plenty of time to come back here and kill her husband.

"On Sundays there are six early morning flights coming in to town that someone flying down from Chicago could connect with, either through Dallas or Houston or San Antonio. Not to mention direct flights. Sheer luck, I'll grant you, that you and Carlotta didn't end up on the same flight or bump into each other at DFW or at the airport here. But Carlotta came in at the crack of dawn; my guess is you were an hour or so later.

"There was time for you to drive to The University to kill Roylett. Carlotta had told you he was meeting with Huw. God knows you had reason enough to want him dead. Not only because of what he'd done to that innocent girl—you're still pretty traditional, you know—but because of what he knew about you and Carlotta and, much more important to your academic future, what he would do about opposing you for tenure. And his reasons for doing so which I'm sure he wouldn't be slow in sharing."

"You've thought a lot about this," she said. "You really have."

I looked at her. "Not enough, probably. If I thought enough about it, I'm sure I'd come up with something better. To explain why you told Lieutenant Melnick that cock-and-bull story about having seen me on Sunday out at the stable.

"The fact of the matter is that you didn't come out to the stable and ride early. When I grained the horses and topped their buckets on Sunday morning I checked the lights in the indoor ring. You sometimes forget and leave them on if you ride late at night or very early in the morning. They were off. And Harry's back was perfectly dry, no sweat marks, no places where you'd rubbed him down. These were things I failed to mention to Lieutenant Melnick when he first interviewed me. I have now. I guess the part that's got me interested, Joan, is that you're far too bright to think that story you told was going to hold water. I think you told that story because you knew it *wouldn't* hold up as an alibi. You were bound to be suspected. But it *would* take the pressure off Carlotta. Am I right?"

She was silent for a few moments. "When I heard about Roylett's death, I naturally knew they'd want to talk to me. It wouldn't take them long to figure out I had a motive for wanting him dead. Carlotta..." She groaned the name. "Can you understand?"

I told her I thought so. Then I asked her when she had gotten back. She seemed relieved at that—it was a question, as it turned out, that she could answer honestly without feeling guilty.

"Seven o'clock Sunday morning."

"What did you do then?"

"Just what you envisioned. I went home and saw the note Melody had left and then heard Roylett's message. God, that dreadful man. Then I went out and it sounds so cliché, but I just drove around. I did as it happens go to the stable but of course you had left and there was no one there. And by the time I got back to the house and found Melody beside herself I had pretty well made my mind up to resign and go back to Iowa." She smiled. "I had made such a hash of things. My dreams, and then I thought…with a little luck I could at least spare Carlotta."

*   *   *   *

I dismissed my one o'clock expository writing class early, left my books and papers in my office, and walked under the high-arching oaks down the mall to the Old Music Building where the memorial service was to be held for Professor Sebastian Roylett. Not that I could imagine there was much to memorialize about him, but in the service I'd learned to salute the rank, not the man. Besides, I was honestly curious about who would turn up and what rhetorical contortions some of them would go through in order to find something positive to say about him.

There was a totally spurious hint of fall in the air, the result of a micro blue norther that had blown in at dawn, bringing with it wistful thoughts of red leaves, bright-cheeked girls in plaid skirts. The coolness would not last. September was often the hottest month. The weather didn't really change until the first week in November.

"Rusty."

Walter Melnick fell into step with me.

"You'll be glad to know the investigation into Professor Roylett's death has been changed from an offense report to an incident report," he told me. "In other words, we found evidence of no crime being committed. The tests we got back indicate that Roylett expired as a direct result of acute vascular hemorrhage originating from his congenital Sturge's Syndrome. It could have happened any time. The man was a walking time bomb."

I kept silent.

"I wanted to thank you; I know you put a lot of time and effort into talking to all those people—" here he looked at me narrowly "—when it was something you really didn't want to do." In situations of this kind, he told me, you often have to look at all the possibilities. "All of them, not just some." He paused and there was an uncomfortable silence which I did nothing to break. "I want you to know how much I appreciate what you did and I hope we can meet again, talk about horses. Obviously if something should come up, that incident report could be changed back to an offense report."

"Sure, but the stats look better this way, right?" We both knew I was being ungenerous and he smiled slightly, holding out one of his cards. I took it from him and shook his hand. "Goodbye, Walter." We parted on the steps of the Old Music Building.

I was, naturally enough, more than a little angry with him. Melnick had winkled me out of my safe little shell; figuratively, he'd picked me up, shaken me by the neck, and thrust me into life. Now, after I'd attracted attention to myself, I was being left exposed to twist in the wind. Worse—as I was sure Melnick knew, too, in his heart of hearts—the finding that Roylett's death was accidental felt all wrong, and closing the books on it a miscarriage of justice.

CHAPTER 19

▼

The cypress-lined Dean's Room was located up a flight of marble steps on the second floor.

The memorial service for Sebastian Roylett was surprisingly well attended. And colorful. Representing the local Native American clearing house, a group of portly burghers with silvering hair and wearing blue suits, added a dignified note. Many members of the academy, in respect for the late chairman's well-known enthusiasm for the expression of ethnic identity, came wearing kente cloth dashikis, gold-threaded saris, an antique silk kimono, a variety of guayabera shirts, a long elegant Punjab coat worn with tight trousers and turban; several had on open-necked shirts with collars spread wide, or dark suits; and there was the usual assortment of those in shirts and jeans and earth-toned cotton skirts, and a few who, like myself, were wearing, like the robes of some vaguely updated but not terribly strict mendicant order, jackets, ties, and khakis.

People clustered around a desk near the door waited for Amanda Vennible and Cynthia to help them with their name tags. The Department of English was so large that it was unlikely any one person would know the names of all the departmental staff and faculty and their spouses or significant others.

"Here's yours, Dr Coulter," Amanda said and pressed my name tag on my left lapel.

"I just saw Lieutenant Melnick," I said to her in a low voice, feeling slightly Graham Greene about the whole thing. "He tells me that the official investigation into the death of Professor Roylett has been called off; it's been ruled he died of natural causes."

"Thank the dear Lord," breathed Amanda reverently.

In a corner, someone was earnestly essaying something, I guessed by Bach, on a recorder. I made my way to the rear of the room where, in front of the tall mullioned windows, a table was set with punch and soft drinks and cookies.

All the crowd from Sunday was there: Sarah Jane Collins, Ed Vere, Melody Harker, Henry Fishbach, Huw Rhys-Davies, Joan Strossner-Boynton, and Carlotta. Sarah Jane approached me and held me in earnest conversation until the service began. She held forth brightly on the department's adoption of the next year's graduate studies offerings—a subject evidently dear to her heart, and about which she held strong feelings. Her finely chiseled features were exalted with a kind of Joan-of-Arc higher-purpose nobility.

I managed to catch Melody's eye but she quickly glanced away, embarrassed. Joan privileged me with a look of utter loathing.

"You're not paying attention to what I'm saying, Stephen," Sarah Jane complained.

"I'm sorry," I told her contritely but was spared further self-abasement by a voice speaking my name.

"Mr Coulter?" I turned to see a thin, white-haired woman, smiling at me hesitantly. Her hands moved nervously on the handle hoops of her large tote bag.

"I'm Priscilla Vere." Her eyes shone brilliantly in her sallow face. "My husband has spoken of you. I knew you at once. I thought I would just—"

She fumbled her grasp on the handbag and it fell, spilling its contents on the floor between us. "Oh, dear, *so* clumsy, I'm afraid."

"Not a problem," I reassured Mrs Vere, and knelt down to pick up and put back in her bag a thin checkbook with blue imitation-leather cover, a matching billfold which had flipped open to display a Texas i.d. and library card in the first two pockets of an otherwise empty accordion plastic sleeve, two pairs of glasses in worn cases, an opened pack of honey-and-lemon throat lozenges, a crumpled lace-hemmed handkerchief from which emanated the unmistakable scent of old-lady talcum, some half-dozen small bottles of pills, a plastic rainhat, a compact with compressed powder, lipstick, keys, and a zipper bag with costume jewelry.

"Here, I think that's everything." I got to my feet and handed her the bag.

"Why, thank you so much." And then, with hardly a break, "Did you know the chairman well? Not that I did. I couldn't believe it, I really could not believe it. When Edward came back and told me the news I was stunned, absolutely stunned: I started to think what was I doing when that poor man met his end?

"It was like President Kennedy's assassination, you know? Everybody remembers—*used* to remember, I should say—where they were when Kennedy was assassinated.

"There he was being killed while I was making tea. The older I get, the longer it seems to take me to get organized in the morning. Those homely, stupid Sunday morning rituals: making tea, letting the dog out, watching Dr Gene Scott on television, bringing in the paper.

"Do you know, Dr Coulter, my husband doesn't have one single graduate student now who was even *born* when Jack Kennedy was killed?"

*   *   *   *

Listening to what our colleagues had to say about Roylett made me reflect that they could be describing someone I'd never met. Roylett's ruthlessness, his lechery, his proclivity for the bottle, his talent for self-aggrandizement, his flamboyance, his disastrous attraction to young girls, were transformed in glowing periods into "his appetite for life," "his frank and forthright manner, so sadly rare in academe," "his sincere interest in his fellow man," his "sensitive awareness that there is more to life than what simply goes on in the classroom," and his "caring, feeling, solicitude over his students' welfare."

*   *   *   *

One cool and breezy morning in mid-October—the previous afternoon's blue norther had dropped the temperature forty degrees in half an hour—the mare, feeling full of herself, threw me off in the stable yard.

Sheer carelessness on my part: I'd been up most of the night grading papers and wasn't paying attention to what I was doing. On the off chance the mare was developing a sore back I'd used a new, thicker pad than usual, and I must have misjudged how snugly I needed to do up the girth. As was my custom, after I'd mounted I walked the mare out of the yard on a loose rein, and cocked my right leg up to reach under the panel of the saddle to finish pulling the girth tight on the billet straps. But somewhere early on in this Pony Club scenario the mare'd managed to take in a hell of a lot of air; she had now craftily let her breath out, so that the saddle was far from snug, and with my leaning over even so slightly, it began to slip round her barrel like a loose ring on a thin finger.

Joyfully seizing on this excuse to misbehave, the mare squealed in ecstasy and jumped like a scalded cat, leaving me hanging out in the air like a load of dirty laundry. Even so, I managed to maintain some remnant of contact with her during the first two bucks, but when she planted her front legs and ducked her head, ripping the reins out of my hands, I went headfirst into the rocky roadbed, while she scampered off in the direction of the barn.

Not a soul around, of course. Damage sustained: cracked bone in my wrist, banged-up elbow and shoulder, mild concussion, and a few cuts and bruises around what I surmised would be one beauty of a black eye.

After I'd found a clean rub rag and wiped the blood from my eyes, I limped back to the barn and found the mare, predictably, in her stall decorously munching hay. She noted my presence by favoring me with a coquettish over-the-shoulder glance, then turned her attention once more to the hay. I checked the tack and was relieved to find the reins were unbroken and the saddle undamaged. This time, when it came time to tighten the girth, I unrepentantly kneed her in the belly till she let her breath out, and then climbed on.

For the first fifteen minutes or so butter wouldn't have melted in her mouth. Then, taking fright at the sound of some fearsome animal rustling the tall grass along the fence line—one of the barn cats, I expect—she again lit out bucking. But now I was ready for her and urged her on into a hard gallop around the lower pasture. Gradually it must've occurred to her that while she was lined out galloping she couldn't really do a first-rate job bucking me off, and she began to want to back off my leg and slow down. This I didn't permit, but kept her well up in the bridle at a cracking good pace for about ten minutes.

For the rest of the session she was perfectly well-mannered and bidable. With the weather so uncommonly fresh, I should have worked her on the longe line to get the kinks out before throwing a leg over her and getting down to business.

Work is work and play is play.

Afterward, I untacked her, threw on a cooler and walked her out, stopping every few minutes to let her get a swallow or two of water, and keeping a sharp eye on how she was moving.

It's my conviction that you have to be especially careful with Thoroughbreds, lest they do themselves harm. When they get their blood up, Thoroughbreds often don't exhibit a lot of sense. They'll give you everything they've got: berserkers, some of them—they'll go till they drop or break a bone, theirs or yours. Strong-arm tactics are futile, a lesson many trainers don't seem to understand, and that may have something to do with why you see so many broken down and spoiled Thoroughbreds around the track and the show ring. I was always on the lookout for a good-looking prospect with a well-developed sense of self-preservation—at least enough not to want to hit his fences, and with enough courage to want to take them.

After I'd done off the mare and put her up—in the developing heat of the day it took about an hour for her veins to go down—I stopped by the minor emergency clinic near the airfield for a tetanus booster and an x-ray.

The nurse on duty cleaned out the cuts and abrasions and took an x-ray and I waited a few minutes until a smooth-cheeked young doctor stitched up two of the cuts and fastened a light cast on my right wrist. He shook his head, admonishing me to stay off my feet for a few days, and only reluctantly prescribed some pain pills—three of which, washed down that evening with four inches of tequila following a hot shower, relieved most of the pain and gave me a good night's sleep. No fractures: at least I was spared the humiliation of breaking my collarbone for what would have been the fifth time.

*   *   *   *

Now the semester gained momentum, The University claiming almost every waking moment with inexorably increasing demands. Before the first set of papers was due, I held individual conferences to agree on topics for their second, longer papers. No sooner had I returned the first set of papers than I was faced with midterms. There would be no surcease until the Thanksgiving holiday—traditionally set aside for making a start on the second set of papers, rather optimistically scheduled to be handed in before the students left town. To these demands the Friday afternoon meetings of Commonwealth Studies, with its distinguished speakers, discussion of widely varied topics, cheerful mix of town and gown, and lashings of sherry provided a pleasant if somewhat guilt-ridden respite. Weekends were no longer vast blocks of time to sport with as I wished. With a shocking lack of regret I shoved Barrington to the periphery of my consciousness, along with the necessity for changing the sheets weekly and making trips to the laundromat. I did manage to pay the rent and sent Serena a check. Once I went to a concert the symphony orchestra was giving.

Along its four-month voyage from first day's meeting to final examination, each class had a way of developing its own distinctive rhythm, based in large part on the blood sugar level of teacher and students at the time class met and how much sleep they got the night before. Office hours filled up and overflowed with student conferences that had now to be scheduled for inconvenient times and in sometimes odd places, never mind what the policy statement set out. Departmental and college memos stuffed my mailbox daily, a good many of them requiring immediate action.

After sitting through a lengthy discussion of the candidates' qualifications at a meeting of a scholarship committee to which Huw had appointed me, I half-jokingly suggested a way of awarding each nominee a numerical ranking, based on a number of weighted criteria, similar to the method used by handicappers in assigning speed indexes to race horses. To my amusement and, I must say, gratification, the idea was seriously received and its merits debated, before being—inevitably—tabled.

Then there was the matter of Fishbach's dissertation. The outline we had all picked over—Joan, the Somebody from Anthropology, Edmond Altschul from Linguistics, and myself—was accepted provisionally, and Fishbach started to buckle down to the tough work of writing it—and discovering in the process—if he made the effort to write clearly—what it was he had to say. In my view he was wildly optimistic when he sent out his *curriculum vitae* ABD ("all but dissertation") to a number of colleges and universities, but I had to change my opinion when three of them responded, asking for interviews at the

MLA convention over the Christmas break. At the same time as I was learning about Jacksonian democracy—forget the gallant hero of New Orleans, the man was a raging genocidal maniac—I was also acquiring knowledge about the present-day stock of academic specialties, and finding out that, without having gone on the record with a political or racial slant to their work, teachers of literature could expect short shrift from recruitment committees. It was obvious that, at least among the younger teachers, the stuff itself was not expected nor could it be depended upon to stand on its own merits. Screw the test of time.

Alexander Ashton fell into the pleasant habit of dropping by my office to see if I wanted to join him for coffee or a sandwich at lunch time, invariably rescuing me from a student conference gone on too long over the hour. Cheese and crackers and a bit of fruit shared down by the creek reminded me of the classical Greeks. Come to think of it, Ashton *looked* like one of them, with that carved coin profile and cap of white hair and lean spare body. *Mens sana in corpore sano*, and so on. Once he called me at the last minute to go with him to a concert he had tickets for, the symphony was playing two pieces I was fond of, Delius's 'Walk in the Paradise Gardens' and the Fauré *Requiem* I'd listened to on the radio early on the Sunday morning of Roylett's death as I was driving to the stable.

Awkwardly silent at times, then speaking with evident care for his words, rationing them out grudgingly, he came across as a rather formal old stick, a lifelong bachelor in, I supposed, comfortable circumstances and wed to the profession. I found myself pleasantly at ease in his company, and in the company of some of the other older members of the faculty to whom he from time to time introduced me.

When it occurred to me to get in touch with Tom Sturtevant, it was invariably late at night or too early in the morning, or I thought of it while I was riding, and I finally forgot about calling him back altogether.

Serena, my ex-wife, commenced telephoning me from Virginia, usually late at night, and took me once more on a guided tour over all the old terrain. She was clearly unhappy and bored, but still, she said, had hopes for me when I had served out my exile, as she put it, "in the wilderness." In fact, she wanted me to fly over to Austria and meet up with her and some of her friends skiing in the Tyrol over Christmas. No, I told her, there are things I need to do here.

$$*\qquad*\qquad*\qquad*$$

Being virtuous was easy.

Sarah Jane Collins had invited me for Sunday brunch at the Four Seasons.

I wondered what she wanted.

I didn't have long to wait to find out.

When I met her in the lobby she was resolutely ignoring, chin up, the frankly admiring glances from the line up at the bar. She wore a dark, long-sleeved, high-necked, very fitted dress that came to just above her knees. White, heavy silk stock held with an old gold pin. No other jewelry. She carried a large utilitarian brief case. Clear nail polish on her slim hands; minimal slash of pale lipstick; barest thought of eye-shadow to set off her aquamarine eyes.

What it was, she said, facing me across the blackened redfish and a bottle of cooling Ste Genevieve white, was that the mad dean had put her in charge of coming up with a new freshman interdisciplinary honors course which would be made up, probably, of two to four sections, to be implemented in the fall. She wondered if I would be interested in coming aboard as her deputy director. While she spoke, her face took on that immensely appealing Joan of Arc look I'd noticed at the memorial service: a young Candice Bergen, with a vocation. Responding to her offer didn't take a lot of thought on my part—Sarah Jane was a live-wire in the department and had shown a remarkable ability to commend herself to her superiors: unless I screwed up, or she threw me to the lions—always, I admitted to myself, possibilities (though I considered them to be remote ones)—service on her committee would be a good way to get something on my résumé that might help extend my career at USW.

"Another glass of wine, Stephen?" she asked. "The fact is I owe you an apology." She looked at me candidly. "To be honest, when you first joined the department I didn't pay a lot of attention to you—a dissertation on an eighteenth-century Irish politician didn't look very promising so far as your teaching went. I figured if there was anything worth knowing, we'd learn about it soon enough. But the thing is, you've really slipped into the bosom of the department like Tennyson's lily, and your teaching evaluations have been excellent. You've done a fine job here, and I for one would like to make use of an outstanding lecturer.

"The only thing that bothers me is that, so far as I know, you haven't attended any conferences, delivered any papers, reported any articles accepted for publication, have any book in press, or even put in for a grant—and yes, I realize that as a lecturer you're not under the gun to do any of those things, as you would be if you were on a tenure track, but even so, for the future..." Her voice trailed off. "Stephen, what's the status of your dissertation—no, of course, help yourself, I'm sure the dean won't mind if we order another bottle—have you got a publisher interested?"

I named a university press that hadn't turned it down flat—hadn't had a response from, actually—possibly because its director was on leave.

Time-wasters, those people, Sarah Jane said with confidence; we can talk about it later—she might have some ideas.

What had caused her to select me, she continued, was the way I'd taken charge of matters the day Roylett died, showed her what she suspected—again I was treated to those blue eyes—was the *real* me—that and what she had gotten from Amanda Vennible and one or two others about the way I'd been asking questions after Roylett's death without, it appeared, raising hackles. She assumed, she said, that my efforts had been enlisted by Lieutenant Melnick, and I didn't deny it.

All in all, pretty exciting stuff for me and, I may as well admit it, flattering as well.

*   *   *   *

Silence from Melnick; ditto Melody.

Without late-night confessions from Melody and Melnick's enlisting my help in talking to my colleagues, my life reverted to an old familiar pattern.

I rode the mare almost every afternoon. K.C. could hardly wait to tell me that the prospective buyer of Gordonwood had instructed the agent to reassure K.C. that, after the sale ("and this is what is *so* exciting, Stephen"), she would be welcome to keep her own horses at the stable as long as she wished; the stable operation would continue for the foreseeable future. The lawyer who'd been a customer of K.C.'s in her hairdressing days whom K.C. had asked to help with Bobby's lawsuit on the Linebacker sale had responded to his petition timely, but Bobby's attorneys had never shown up for the hearing, and the case had been dismissed.

I sincerely congratulated K.C. on her good fortune and observed that she looked twenty years younger; or at least how I guessed she looked a score of years ago.

"I didn't look this good, Stephen," she said slowly, "or feel near as good as I the way I feel now." She shook her head. "I just can't believe it."

"You ever hear that old saying, Kay? No? 'He who rides a tiger may never dismount'? That's what you've been doing and now you've been given a chance to bail off: you've got every reason to feel good."

*   *   *   *

After riding, I'd return to the apartment, fix myself a drink, take a shower, fix another couple of drinks, do a bit of reading, and after a while think about getting something to eat.

I found a new place near the Drag where I could drop my laundry off; this allowed me to give the Busted Spur a clear miss, not wanting to face Rhonda's pitying looks.

Most nights I was in bed by ten. The summer's golden lads and girls who played in the pool late at nights had long since abandoned their sport. During my morning runs I watched in vain for the tearful, disheveled blonde standing on her blue lawn with the sprinklers going and a champagne glass in her hand.

I managed to get off what I hoped was a light, cheerful note to Melody, congratulating her on her upcoming graduation, and wishing her well—nothing in it (with a stab under my breastbone) to allude to her confidences and the night she'd spent in my apartment. There was no need for her to feel embarrassed, and it had bothered me when she'd avoided me at Roylett's memorial service. Roylett, of all people, the multicultural arch-lecher!

In the early mornings I contrived to prepare for class and make a stab at the Sisyphus-like task of grading quizzes and papers left over from the weekend. For a few days I surprised myself by forging ahead with that damned Irishman, Barrington.

*   *   *   *

It was amazing how much time you had if you lived alone and kept your dealings with other people to a scant civil minimum.

*   *   *   *

The last public reminder of Roylett's passing was a newspaper article appearing in late October. The university's board of regents passed a resolution in Roylett's memory and presented Carlotta with a splendid vellum scroll at a special ceremony. There was a sidebar photograph accompanying the article which showed Carlotta accepting the award from the board chairman. She thought it appropriate to the occasion to wear a highwayman's broad brimmed black hat with veil, and a very chic little black dress that displayed her spectacular legs and bosom to conspicuous advantage. The chairman looked as if he'd been pole-axed.

*   *   *   *

Little by little the events of early September began to lose their hard-edged clarity and faded into the indeterminate past.

CHAPTER 20

▼

Commonwealth Studies met on Friday afternoons at three in the Evers Rooms, a cypress-paneled suite running along the glass-walled east side of the third floor of the Simon Askew Scholarship Archive Center. The first room was a kind of reception room, furnished like a large drawing room with sofas, low tables, chairs, and a desk. The smaller second room featured glass-fronted, illuminated display cabinets full of the memorabilia of Hedrick Evers, the rancher-oilman entrepreneur in whose name his friends had endowed the suite. A kitchenette opened off the second room. In the third room, where talks were held, there were two tables, the longer running along the length of the room, and the shorter crossing it at its head. Solid comfortable chairs flanked the long table and were set along the far side of the shorter. Cut glass decanters on silver trays gleamed along the mesquite table tops. Hand loomed rugs woven with the Evers ranch brand lay on the random-width loblolly pine flooring. In expectation of an overflow crowd, folding chairs had been brought in for the occasion and were placed along the walls.

Bob Talbot was greeting people at the door.

"You haven't seen Michael, have you, Stephen?" he asked me anxiously. "He said he was going to go over his talk in the director's office down the hall." No, sorry, I shook my head, and walked in.

People were milling around talking.

I caught sight of Tom Sturtevant, being backed into a corner by people waiting to speak with him. In the interstices between their arms and torsos, I could see a triangle of white shirt and a scrap of tie where the points of his vest failed to close the gap with the trousers of his blue suit. He caught sight of me across the room, and motioned for me to join him, but I got sidetracked by Alexander Ashton who made a gesture to sit next to him at the long table. Sturtevant smiled, gave a thumbs up, and pointed at his watch, mouthing the words in dumb show, "Later," and I nodded back at him.

I found a seat, accepted a large glass of sherry from one of Bob's graduate students who was helping with the buttling, and prepared to enjoy myself.

Some people I recognized from other Friday afternoons. It crossed my mind that I didn't see very many familiar faces from the English department around me. Covert operations was, depending on how you looked at it, either all-too-familiar a topic to engage the interest of faculty themselves past masters at the academic variation, or simply didn't have the drawing power of the ancient and distinguished Bloomsburyan scheduled to give a lecture on the frantically unconventional Garnett family at the same time.

Promptly at three Bob Talbot came in accompanied by a tall and very thin man wearing an unobtrusively well-cut dark gray suit, off-white shirt, and crimson and dark blue lightning-bolt tie. He was shod comfortably in crepe-soled ankle boots of the kind my father used to call brothel creepers. Perhaps not so conventional himself.

Settled himself in the chair at the head of the long gleaming table, sipped appreciatively from his glass of sherry, laid an old gold watch on the table next to his sheaf of handwritten notes, patted his thin lips with a snowy handkerchief he drew from his cuff, and put on his tortoiseshell glasses. He peered round at the audience and blinked several times and then began to speak.

"Somewhat pretentiously, perhaps even defensively, I have entitled my talk today 'Sources for the History of British Secret Operations during World War II'. It is pretentiously entitled because as all of you in this room are aware, the Secret Operation Executive—SOE, to give it its more familiar name—had its origins under what seem to us today to be the most informal of circumstances. Its headquarters, fittingly enough, were situated in Baker Street and, because, as SOE's distinguished chronicler M R D Foot has pointed out, clearly, unless a secret service remains secret, it cannot do its work, there are"—very dry here—"few records: it was not, is not, in the best interests of a secret service to keep detailed records.

"My talk is defensively entitled because even today all the records which were kept have not been made public. Many of those who took part in the operations and many of the operations themselves are still veiled with a cloak of secrecy, now, nearly a half century afterward.

"So the best I can do is talk about what has been declassified, point to sources, and speculate." Gentle, self-deprecatory smile, and a throwaway line. "Historians make careers out of speculation.

"Thus what I have to say may prove pretty dull stuff." A donnish sniff. "For those of you desiring to know what it was really like to be an agent, I heartily recommend Bruce Marshall's grim account of Forest Frederic Yeo-Thomas's career with SOE called *The White Rabbit*; or Benjamin Cowburn's—Tinker's—*No Cloak, No Dagger*; and Gordon Young's *Cat With Two Faces*, the story of Victoire—Mme. Mathilde-Lily Carr's experience as a double agent."

Businesslike sip of sherry here, modest shooting of gold cufflinks.

"But to the matter at hand. Sources. To those of us who labour in the vineyards of the Public Records Office"—a nod to Bob here—"one of the thorny problems of research continues to be the uneven—if I can take refuge in that considerable understatement if not euphemism—release of so-called classified information.

"As you know"—apologetic glance—"the normal UK rule is accessibility to official papers after thirty years. I may say that it used to be fifty years until Harold Wilson overrode the civil servants in the mid-1960s. Therefore one might be led to expect that under normal circumstances Second World War materials classified under the Official Secrets Act would have been released in the early- to mid-1970s.

"But as many of us can attest with some asperity, there are plenty of exceptions to this rule. Mike Carver and Robert Blake have raised this very question of excessive delay with the Lord Chancellor who controls these matters. Mike Carver asked a question in the House. In his reply to Carver"—glasses whipped on here slightly askew, quick reference to notes—"Hansard House of Lords 28th January 1991 column 447"—glasses off more slowly—"the Lord Chancellor gave three reasons for making exceptions to the thirty-year rule: exceptional sensitivity and possible damage to the public interest; information supplied in confidence disclosure of which…might constitute a breach of good faith; and information which would cause distress and embarrassment to living persons or their immediate descendants.

"Therefore, it is by no means certain that all the government's files on secret operations in the Second World War have been made available in the PRO. Indeed, one may be sure that some have not, especially since the Lord Chancellor has reserved the right to postpone declassification of certain files for fifty or seventy-five years, or, in the case of the MI5 and MI6 files, to keep them closed forever.

"So you can see"—another quick glance around the table—"the vexations attendant upon the best efforts of serious researchers into the less well-known aspects of World War II secret strategy.

"That having been said and duly noted, it is well to point out that leaks *have* occurred. Details of secret operations which the Lord Chancellor and his Department would like to keep incommunicado continue to surface, granted in a very desultory fashion, for at least three reasons.

"Why? How has this come to happen? First, the files in the PRO have not always been efficiently weeded. There are sometimes references to secret matters in the files of the Foreign Office, the Treasury, and other departments which, by Whitehall criteria, ought to have been suppressed but, through carelessness or negligence, have not. Christopher Andrews and David Dilks discuss this in *The Missing Dimension* (1983),and so does Andrews in *Secret Service* (1985).

"Second, the existence, as Andrews and Dilks point out, of copies of governmental papers held in private archives. Officials and ministers were not supposed to keep such papers, but they often did, Winston Churchill being a prime offender. Researchers come across things… accidentally. For a number of reasons Whitehall usually does not claim its theoretical right to recover papers of this sort, even though it would never have allowed access to such papers if they had been in official custody. In any case the government authorities may well simply not know about the existence in private hands of papers of this nature.

"Third, papers of the sort which are kept out of public access in the UK not infrequently are available—or references to them are available—in Washington under the Freedom of Information Act. This was, in fact, how the Blunt affair burst upon the British scene."

Discreet, self-congratulatory murmur of recognition around the room: Sir Anthony Blunt, Surveyor of the Queen's Pictures, Apostles, Cambridge, Merchant & Ivory: in sepia distance, even divested of his title, very appealing.

"Just so. Now, to the American eye, if I may be permitted a wild and no doubt most unfair generalization, publication—the wider and noisier the better—hard upon the heels of discovery is pretty much taken for granted: What *can* the authorities be hiding? And sometimes as with Blunt, that has indeed occurred. Yes?"

It was Alexander Ashton, leaning forward. "But, Mr Speaker, have there been instances where researchers—historians—have found material which they have then decided, as it were, on their own motion to keep buried and out of sight of the public view?"

Mr Speaker toyed briefly with his papers, and then finished off what remained in his glass of sherry, neatly and quickly replenished from a cut glass decanter by my attentive friend Bob. "Your question presupposes"—dryly—"a modicum of morality among historians." Practiced housemaster's smile to rob the words of sting. "But I suppose so. I lie: Yes, there have been. Not all discoveries have resulted in publication. Occasionally a researcher may decide"—blandly—"to leave a find in decent, seemly obscurity. Not every researcher, I should point out, ought properly to stand charged with not having a sense of fitness or responsibility. Recall the third reason advanced to keep information classified which in the ordinary course of events would have been released: that is, information which would cause distress and embarrassment to living persons or their immediate descendants."

*   *   *   *

His gaze momentarily turned inward; the visitor took advantage of the rhetorical pause he'd created to polish off his second glass of sherry. "Let us say, to take a hypothetical example, that a young man, son of an American father and English mother—the mother herself with French antecedents and the young man fluent in French—travels in France just as war breaks out and through his mother's social contacts or through contacts made by himself while at university is taken on by SOE.

"He goes through training and is dropped—oh, near some little village in remote rural France not a score of miles, let's say, from Troyes, a place familiar to him from his prewar travels. He joins a group of Resistance fighters, one of whom he comes to suspect, wrongly, of being a German agent. This sort of thing happened all the time. He gets the man on his own away from the others and coshes him with a heavy spade or pitchfork—a useful weapon among the French peasantry.

"But it turns out that the man he kills is indeed a loyal member of the Resistance, though a Communist, as many were. The report on the episode acquits the agent, who is found to have acted honorably, though mistakenly.

"Now let's say the report on this tragic affair, which would normally have been released in 1975, was kept secret, because it was felt"—bland smile trotted out again—"its declassification could adversely affect both Anglo-Soviet and, the agent being an American, Anglo-American relations—"

Interruption from Alexander Ashton. "All well and good for your first and second reasons, Mr Speaker: 'exceptional sensitivity' and 'breach of faith', but what about the third reason, 'distress'?"

"Right." Tutor's nod of approbation. "Just so." He was choosing his words carefully. "Now, to take our hypothetical example one step further, let's say an allusion to this report has been come across"—urbanely—"either in an unweeded PRO file or in a private archive or in Washington. Our researcher does a little patient digging in one of the many open archives, and learns that soon after the incident the agent has asked and been allowed to resign from the service and return to his own country.

"And that, in the ordinary course of events, would be the end of that. So far as Great Britain is concerned, no medals, no bended knee before a grateful sovereign, no mention in the New Year's Honours List, no medal for desperately dangerous work performed past the limit of one's ability, no drinks party at the club afterwards. Indeed, the intrepid American would take nothing with him save for the satisfaction of having lived up to a particular ideal, plus a piece of paper stating he'd served his tour of duty with, say, a graves registration company in North Africa or a quartermaster unit supplying RAF comforts in East Anglia—not that our American would have expected more: SOE, as I have mentioned, was almost pathologically averse to self-promotion.

"It must be remembered, too, that in those unenlightened days there were not the support mechanisms and enlightened counseling services that are so much a part of today's de-mobbing protocol. One was expected simply to do the best one could and get on with the job. And our researcher determines that the young American has done just that, carved out for himself a perfectly respectable niche in a perfectly respectable profession.

"To make much of this tragic footnote to history would be, in our researcher's opinion, despicable…and he decides to leave these bones buried where they are.

"Does that answer your question?" Great show of looking at old gold watch. "Good Lord, look at the time!" A nod to Bob Talbot, an appreciative smile to acknowledge the audience's burst of applause. "I really must get to the airport."

* * * *

As people were getting to their feet and milling about prior to leaving the room, I was only dimly conscious of Alexander Ashton gently shaking my shoulder.

"Stephen. Here's someone who wants to talk to you." He stepped back out of the way.

"Coulter: Are you all right?" Genuine anxiety creased Tom Sturtevant's ruddy face as he bent concernedly over me. "Here, you look like you could use this." He hastily poured my glass full of sherry from the decanter. I nodded weakly. "I've been trying to get hold of you"—

"Yes, I know, I called you back a time or two and then left a message"—

"Right. Sometimes I'm hard to reach." He gave me a crooked, unexpectedly self-depreciating smile. "Well, this isn't the time to talk, but can you phone me in the morning?"

"Yes, sure. Just give me your number." I reached feebly for my pen.

Sturtevant was already jotting down numbers on the back of an old envelope.

*   *   *   *

"You've got powerful friends," Alexander Ashton observed as we left the building and walked across the plaza toward MacFarland Hall.

"What?" My thoughts were still in a turmoil. "Sorry, I wasn't listening."

"Sturtevant. Tom Sturtevant. If I may be so bold to ask, where do you know him from?"

"My friend the fashion plate?" I asked, thinking of the blue suit he'd worn that looked as if he'd bought it when he made his high school debating team. "Alex, I've only met the man twice—once to speak to—and that was back in September," I protested. "I really don't know him at all, certainly not well enough to call him a friend. Why do you ask?"

"Don't you ever look at a newspaper, Stephen?" I was silent. "For shame." He shook his head reprovingly. "Let me think where to begin. First off, the Sturtevants have been a force to be reckoned with in state politics for the last seventy years. His father was governor. He himself is an interesting bird. Went off to college—someplace like the University of Virginia, as I recall—inculcated with old Southern values and a respect for the liberal arts: not always the first virtues called to mind when you're thinking about the politically ambitious in Texas. Served in the military after graduation. As chairman of the senate finance committee he's a real power in this state. For another thing"—he glanced at me slyly—"his mother was old Simon Askew's daughter: newspapers, television stations, real estate consortia. So you could say you and I were there this afternoon"—Alex made a sweeping gesture to include the great gray building we were walking away from—"as the 'grace and favor' guests of your friend just-call-me-Tom and his family, since they're the ones who donated the money for SASAC. Heaven knows what connection the family may have had with old Hedrick Evers." Ashton broke off a self-derisory chuckle, and spoke with genuine concern. "Are you feeling all right, Stephen? You had me worried, you looked pretty peaked in there."

"I'm doing better now, thanks very much. I don't know what came over me." I looked at him. "You were very chatty at the meeting today, Alex, very much to the point."

"Was I? It's an interesting subject, I've always thought, and one in which, as time passes, fewer and fewer people seem to be interested— or knowledgeable about."

"I suppose you're right, I hadn't really thought about it that way. Look, Alex, you attend Commonwealth Studies meetings pretty regularly. Does Ed Vere come to them often? I really ought to see him."

"Ed? No, Ed's not what I'd call a regular. Nevertheless, it would not have surprised me to have seen him here today, except that I heard from Amanda Vennible that Priscilla's back in the hospital. Things have apparently taken a turn for the worse. I'm sure Ed's with her."

"Well, I guess it'll just have to wait," I said.

"That's right, you never did talk to him, did you? At least he never said anything to me about it."

No, I shook my head, I never had talked to Ed. Nor for that matter, I reflected guiltily, had I ever called Amanda about helping with his classes.

CHAPTER 21

▼

Saturday morning I called the home number Tom Sturtevant had given me. We arranged to meet for breakfast at Cisco's Bakery & Restaurant over on East Sixth Street, what I was to learn was a well-known gathering place for state and city power brokers.

When I got there Sturtevant was sitting in a booth in the back drinking a cup of coffee, munching on a bran muffin, and reading the City/State section of the newspaper.

I ordered coffee.

"Friend of yours?" He folded the newspaper open to the obit page and passed it across to me. Priscilla (Mrs Edward) Finch Vere had died, the notice said, "after a long illness, survived by her husband, Professor Edward Vere, and their son and daughter, Newbold and Jennifer Vere." Services were to be held at St Michael's on Tuesday, November 5th, at eleven o'clock.

"Jesus."

"I guess you knew her."

"Yeah. She was the wife of a colleague of mine. An older colleague." I handed the paper back to him.

"I figured you must've known her. Tough." He put the section with the rest of the paper, folded it, and placed it next to him on the banquette. "But thanks for coming. I'm glad you could make it."

"No problem. What's going on?"

"Listen, you know that stable where I met you, what do they call it, Gordonwood, back around Labor Day?"

"Right, that's the name. I remember."

"Well, some time ago I got this wild-hair notion I didn't have enough to do to fill up my time so I decided to buy a place where I could keep my horses and at least have a chance to ride during the week. That's what I was doing when we met that day, scouting around for a location close to town that already had some stables built on the place. Right now they're out at the ranch, which is about two hundred miles west of here, and I can't make it out there except maybe once or twice every six weeks or so—it's just too damned far. Right now I'm thinking of buying Gordonwood." He paused to drink his coffee, his eyes looking at me expectantly over the rim of the cup.

"Well, if you can afford what sounds like basically a private stable, it's a great idea," I said. "It's what everybody dreams of." At least for a while, I amended privately. "But wouldn't it be a hell of a lot easier as well as less expensive for you just to board your horses at some stable around here where you wouldn't have all the hassle of looking after them?" And it *was* a hassle: the continual problems of ordering grain, hay and bedding; scheduling vet appointments for shots and teeth floating; trying to court farriers to come out on a regular basis. Hiring—and keeping—stable help—"staff", as Serena used to say tongue-in-cheek, was another gnarly challenge. Added to these, of course, was the never-ending work to be done in keeping a place in decent repair, and looking after the accounts. Though with only one owner to report to and no bills to be sent out the situation would be greatly simplified.

"Well, yeah, what you say's true. I gave the matter a good deal of thought. Thing is, in what I do day-to-day with the legislature, I have to deal with so goddamned many people, I just can't face the thought of coming out to ride and being faced with other boarders, kids taking lessons, and so on, not to mention a bunch of pissant stable rules. The reason I've been trying to get in touch with you is, I wondered if you might be interested in running the barn for me. Strictly out of my own pocket for my own pleasure, no boarders, no fucking tax dodge, you know? You teach at The University—you're a lecturer, right?—but I don't think what I'm suggesting would be that much different from what you're already doing for Mrs Gordon, or cut into your time at The University more than what it does now."

"Mr Sturtevant, I really don't know what to say." Then I thought of K.C. and tried to keep my tone neutral. "Mrs Gordon told me that she was selling the place, and even though the buyer wanted his identity kept secret, she'd been offered the chance to keep her own horses there, at least until she made other plans." I hesitated. "She's done a lot for me."

"Yeah, that's right." He nodded in appreciation for what I was saying. "Truth is, I kind of admire her myself."

"She's a good person," I said. "I owe her a lot."

He acknowledged my concern. "She won't lose on the deal, I can promise you that."

"What kind of horses are you thinking of bringing over to Gordon-wood?"

He grinned. "Nothing very fancy, really. Well, out at the ranch we've got a pretty wide selection to pick from, from ranch stock to polo ponies. Right now I've got some half-breds I think might make good field hunters."

Field hunters?

"I wouldn't have thought there was much of a market for field hunters in Texas," I said slowly. "I mean, there isn't a lot of fox hunting around here, is there?"

"No, there isn't," he agreed.

Are you planning on showing? There's the Christmas show coming up we're about to send in entries for."

"And I'm not planning to get into selling horses. That'd be up to you. But there are a lot of other places to hunt besides Texas. So far's showing's concerned, I'm not wild about doing much of that, either, at least not at first."

"What about stable help?"

"So far's help's concerned, there are a couple of the younger men at the ranch—good workers—who wouldn't mind living near the big city for a couple months at a stretch. 'Course, now, you got to keep an eye on them." He chuckled, evidently savoring a memory of some juicy peccadillo he'd had to rescue them from. Nothing new there for me. I thought grimly of the night I'd been at Twenty-One celebrating a big win with Serena and gotten a call from Johnny Franzreb, the National's manager, who told me with ill-disguised glee that two of my men had gotten drunk and disorderly, pulled a gun on an undercover cop, and were at present languishing in the slammer. This would leave me to do all the grooming, feeding, braiding, and mucking out in time for the working hunter stake the next morning. "If you start now, Rusty," Franzreb confided sympathetically, "you ought to be right on time for the first class—if you don't go back to the hotel to change clothes first."

"Listen, Mr Sturtevant, there's something I think I ought to tell you—"

"Tom, please. And save it, we'll have a chance to talk later."

He paused. "Think it over, but don't take too long. I don't know what K.C.'s paying you, but I'll meet within reason whatever you think's fair. What's today, Saturday? What about getting back to me by the end of the week? Better yet, you got a pencil, piece of paper? Write this down: Chuckie Zimmerman, that's Miz, you can reach her same business number in San Antonio I gave you yesterday, I'm going to be out of pocket this week. I've spoken to her about you. You give Chuckie a call, work out the details. She knows I want to move on this, get things in place by the first of the year. Incidentally, I understand Mrs Gordon may have a few tax problems. I don't want her to get held up because of these, so I've told Chuckie to make my zen tax-meister, a guy name of Karl Kauffmann, available to give her a hand. Anything I can do—"

"That's very decent of you, Tom. Seeing that she had the advice of a good tax counsel would take a tremendous load off her mind."

"Karl's the best—"

"You seem to have thought of just about everything. Far as I'm concerned, Tom, I really don't know what to say." I said. "It's all pretty sudden, but I've got to confess it sounds pretty enticing. What about...riding?"

"Hell, yes, I want you riding, what d'you think? You forget, I've seen you ride. Work those horses, give me some lessons."

I grunted.

"You could even live there, in that little house, and I bet we could fix something up for the boys, kind of a bunkhouse, maybe, put in a bath and a kitchenette and an a.c. and some kind of septic."

Tom's energy was contagious, and I found myself swept along on the wave of his enthusiasm. Nevertheless, just as I remembered how, back in September, Sturtevant had sidestepped saying how good a friend he was of Art Simmons, I noted how he'd evaded saying anything very helpful about his horses. What were they really like, having been stuck out on a ranch in West Texas for God only knew how long? What would riding and training them involve?

For that matter, what kind of a rider was Sturtevant? I'd never seen him throw a leg over a horse. How long was he going to be in state government? What kind of operation did he want to run?

With Serena, I'd run my own sales and show barn, taking care of only two or three crack amateurs who'd bought horses from us—we very definitely called the shots. I really didn't have a feel for how well I'd do working for someone else whose dedication to the enterprise was an unknown—but then I reminded myself I'd been working for someone else now for the best part of a year and that experience really had been on balance a rewarding one.

Another thing I wondered was who else would be involved, besides
Tom Sturtevant, his woman of business Chuckie Zimmerman, and the
boys from the ranch who wouldn't mind getting close to the bright
lights for a month or two at a stretch?

It seemed as if the winkling process started by Melnick in the wake
of Roylett's death and nudged along by Huw with his scholarship committee and Sarah Jane with her plans for an honors course was going to
get a gigantic shot in the arm from the ebullient Tom Sturtevant.

*   *   *   *

On my way out to the stable I stopped at a Circle K where I bought
a pack of Camels, a newspaper, and a twenty-ounce Daybreaker coffee
refill.

At the desk in the stable office, I settled down with a fresh cigarette
and what was left of my coffee. I sorted through the pile of mail, and
saw that the premium list from the Christmas Show had arrived. Providing a top-class judge, serious prize money, and a bang-up exhibitors'
party, the show traditionally attracted a large number of exhibitors,
many from out of state. The organizers were offering a dressage division; working, amateur, junior and limit hunter divisions; and a couple
of jumper divisions. The Christmas Show had the reputation of being
an enjoyable show, fiercely and proudly local, but providing keen competition at every level, and I was sure our customers would want to participate. I scribbled a note to K.C., reminding her that paid entries and
stall fees were due by December first. Because this would probably be
her last horse show as owner of Gordonwood Stable, I knew she'd want
to make a special effort. Even though I'd been suspended from competition for several years now, I still felt a pang of regret as I realized that
I couldn't enter the ring.

Firmly putting aside such thoughts, I picked up the newspaper and
reread the notice of Priscilla Vere's death, counting back to when I'd

met her at Sebastian Roylett's memorial service. It had been a bit less than two months.

She could have been ill when I'd seen her, or right after. Two months should be plenty of time to qualify her illness as "long."

How many days, weeks, months did you have to lie there, anyway, old and frightened and awake, before the newspaper could say your illness was "long"?

I booted the mare up all 'round so she wouldn't hurt herself and took her hacking cross-country around K.C.'s acreage, doing a lot of trotting on a loose rein across the undulating terrain, and getting her to turn on my leg. I took my time doing her off afterward.

*   *   *   *

On Tuesday, for reasons I didn't try to analyse, I showed up for Mrs Vere's funeral. I sat in the back, to the side. St Michael's was pretty much empty except for a few rows up toward the front filled with older people, gray heads in the gray light, here and there roseate or pale mauve where the sunlight fell, diluted, through stained glass. The men wore blue suits that fit them loosely, the women, lightweight dresses in dark colors. Above the smell of incense I could smell that talcum powder peculiar to elderly ladies.

On the way out I met up with Alexander Ashton and we stopped to pay our respects to Ed Vere. He looked curiously shrunken.

"Professor Vere—Ed—is there anything I can do?" I asked awkwardly.

He stared at me.

"Do you have classes I could meet for you?"

"So kind, so kind," he murmured, seeming to stare right through me. "Amanda's arranged for Mike Byrd to take the Chaucer. The others...I don't know."

"I'll speak to Amanda," I promised him. Then I asked if I might call on him in a week or two if he felt up to it.

"Yes, two weeks. I should think that would be fine."

"Edward, are you all right?" Alex asked him solicitously. "Should you be alone?"

"I'm fine, thanks, Alex," Vere said with a faint smile. "Really. I just want to be by myself for a bit."

"Will I see you at mass on Sunday?"

"Perhaps. I don't know."

Alex nodded and we left the church, turning north along the Drag.

*   *   *   *

"Rusty Coulter?"

"This is…Rusty Coulter. Who's this?"

My pencil had been hovering over a phrase in a student paper describing Chaucer's life in London: "…and in the evening Geoffrey would go down from the tower and through the gate into the garden where he would take care of his ardor."

My thoughts came wrenching back to the telephone when my caller gave his name.

"Blair. Blair Foote. I ran into Serena over at Ann MacLeod's Saturday afternoon after the brush and timber races. She told me you were in Texas, gave me your number."

Blair Foote was an extremely knowledgeable horseman who traveled comfortably in two worlds. He raced a small but very successful string of Thoroughbreds at a few of the major tracks and he was also a well-respected trainer of hunters who managed to win consistently at the A circuit shows. Over the years I'd bought a few prospects from him and done well with them.

"Good to hear from you, Blair. What's going on?"

I wrote in the margin *What do you suppose Philippa thought about this?*

"Not a hell of a lot new, really, same-old same-old: getting the two-year-olds legged up, ready for the track, trying to spot a few good-looking ones with a case of the slows, start them over fences for the ring. But there is something causing me a bit of bother, and I thought maybe you could help me."

"Sure," I said. "If I can."

"There was this horse I showed last year at Devon and Upperville last two years, working hunter name of Signature, nice solid-looking brown sucker with white ankles and a bit of a blaze. 'Admit it, he wasn't any Lord of the Isles, I grant you, but he was a useful sort of horse nonetheless. I took out an ad for him and toward the end of the summer I got a call from your part of the country, young pro named Bobby Robberson—"

"I know Bobby," I said.

"A real charmboy, that blond hair, that smile. He said he wanted the horse for a kid rider he had in his barn. Make a long story short, he flew up, tried the horse out, liked it—"

"What happened, Blair, he stop payment on the check?"

"You know me better than that," he chuckled. "No way he was going to leave till I knew the check was good." Then his voice turned serious. "Wouldn't normally think anything about it, but looking through *The Chronicle* the other day I saw a picture of the horse winning at some big show in Dallas—they've given him a different name now, naturally. But the thing is, they're showing the horse in the green hunter division. And that's just not right."

"No, it isn't. Besides, it's against the rules, taking a made horse like you're talking about, and palming him off as a novice."

"Damn right it is," Blair said with feeling. "'I mean is, it's not just a matter of a rules violation, is it? 'Doesn't do me any good, does it, word gets around somebody's showing last year's reserve champion from Upperville first year green, and they bought it from me—he must've *known* I'd find out about it. It makes me look like I was part of the idea, like I'd been conniving with him. He had me fooled."

"That's rubbish, Blair," I told him. "Nobody who knows you would think anything of the kind"

"But the ones who don't know me—"

"That's something else, I agree. Why don't you speak to Bobby Robberson directly?"

"I thought of that. Bobby will tell me to go fly a kite. He'll flash that smile and say so far's what he knew from me, the horse *was* green. You, you're on the scene, Rusty; I'm fifteen hundred miles away, you see how it looks if it gets around: big Virginia trainer, covering his ass, coming down on a local boy, right? But even with you being set down, I know you haven't changed that much, you're a *presence*, whether you want to admit it or not. No, really. Talk to him."

"What else do I need to know?"

There was always something else.

"Nice horse like you've described," I said encouragingly, "why sell him all the way down here? If he's as good as you say, I should think there'd be plenty of buyers around Virginia couldn't wait to give him stall space."

Blair hesitated momentarily. "Okay, Rusty," he said, "I'll level with you. The truth is the horse is, as I explained very carefully to Bobby— but, naturally, with no evidence to support what I'm telling you—"

"Naturally."

"The horse has a small lameness problem. He's what you'd call very slightly second-hand. Enough to knock him out of contention on the big shows and indoor circuit. But look after him properly, don't hone on him—he doesn't need a lot of schooling—keep an eye on the way he's shod, he'll knock 'em dead in Texas. Bobby knew that, promised me he'd be real careful."

"Knock 'em dead in Texas" was the mantra of every Eastern pro selling a horse in Dallas, Houston, or San Antonio. Easier said than done, was my observation. Nevertheless, I knew in my bones that no matter what Bobby had promised he'd wring every last little effort out of a horse like the one Blair was talking about.

"Let me have your address, Rusty, and I'll send you a couple of photos and a copy of Signature's show record from the AHSF."

"Why don't you send me a copy of that *Chronicle* article, too," I said. "Along with the photo of him winning in Dallas. Then I'll see what I can do this end. No promises. Bobby and that barn of his are in the fast lane. I don't know if he'll listen to me, Blair. I keep a pretty low profile down here, especially since I'm set down."

For a long moment there was silence. "You been set down for years, Rusty," Blair said somberly. "That's something you decided. I won't pretend I ever figured out what went on with you and Serena and that Irish boy, or why you took off the way you did. None of my business. But I damn sure know you can't run away from what, who, you are. If you don't know who you are, what you are, I still do. Some things don't change. Give it your best shot is all I ask. The alternative is I'll have to complain to the association. Take steps. File charges. Hearings, all that sort of thing. Then this lameness thing comes up, get in a pissing match with a skunk, you see what I mean, Bobby denies what I told him. But I just can't stand by and do nothing, right?"

"Send me what you've got," I told him resignedly. "I'll see what I can do."

"Thanks, Rusty, I owe you one." He paused. "I have to tell you it hasn't really been the same around here since you left. You make it up this way, let me know, we'll go toss back a few at the old Moseley Inn, my treat."

"I'd like that," I said, and hung up, my mind occupied with what Blair had told me. My pencil added automatically in the margin, *"I think you want 'arbor,'* not *'ardor.'"*

CHAPTER 22

▼

As the semester once again tightened its grip, Blair Foote and his call, as well as my promise to talk with Ed Vere, almost immediately faded from the forefront of my mind.

By barely perceptible stages fall had finally arrived in Central Texas. Not the riotous autumn colors you found along the Eastern seaboard, with early morning ice skim on pond sedge, and a garish litter of scarlet and ochre leaves. A Texas fall was more subtle, an altogether gentler and sweetly melancholy affair, with the post oaks fading, the yellow wildflowers thinning, the ubiquitous cedars seeming to dissolve in hovering clouds of pollen, the hues of plants and trees muted like an ancient tartan uncovered on the site of some old battlefield. The dusty surface of the disused apartment pool was scattered with leaves. Lingering like a ghostly memory from childhood was the disheveled blonde standing on the blue lawn with tears streaming down her face and a champagne glass in her hand.

One morning I found myself reaching for an old tweed jacket. Despite the fact that K.C.'s horses spent most of their time in the semi-darkness of box stalls, their actinic nerves, responding to the shortening of the days, triggered a first growth of winter coat. Courting colds, students continued wearing shorts and T-shirts on campus, secure in the knowledge that The University would turn up classroom heat to a sauna-like 75 degrees.

The two weeks I'd allowed before speaking to Ed Vere came and passed and yet I found myself loath to intrude on Ed's grief not alone out of respect for the man but also from the realization that Roylett's death was, officially, a closed case. Besides, Alex told me, the Vere children had fought free of their various commitments Back East to make a short visit to their father and I had no desire to intrude on their privacy. I gathered from what Alex told me later that there was some at first delicate then distressingly blunt talk of nursing homes—neither Newbie nor Gwen, it seemed, felt in a position to take on their father as a longterm proposition upon retirement.

On the Tuesday and Wednesday before Thanksgiving, the 26th and 27th of November, my students were scheduled to hand in their long papers. There were a lot of students absent on Tuesday, and almost no one attended class on Wednesday, when I read Rochester's splendidly bawdy "To Phyllis" and I hoped made some modest headway in making once again fashionable the verb "to swive." Not many papers got turned in. Most students relied on the long weekend to finish writing them and gambling that I wouldn't invoke the draconian penalties set out for lateness in the policy statement. Predictably, no one came by during office hours and I spent the time answering mail.

Late that afternoon, after everyone had left the stable, I spent an hour muscling around jump standards and rails, building a little course of various types of low fences set at related distances from each other. Then I groomed the mare and walked and trotted her around the ring, weaving in and out of the jumps, circling them, and approaching them and stopping in front of them. The emphasis was on doing all this as precisely and in as relaxed a manner as possible. I insisted that the circles be circles, performed at a steady rhythm, and not ovals or ellipses at varying speeds. When I pulled her up in front of a jump, I pulled her up with her jaw and poll yielding and her hind legs under her, in a straight line perpendicular to the center of the jump, not at an angle. Afterward, now in the dark, I walked her on a loose rein.

On Thanksgiving morning I got to the stable early and while The Mare was eating I pulled a tape measure to double-check the distances between the jumps I'd set, making sure that if she trotted over the first element of a combination that she'd be able to canter naturally and comfortably out over the last. The moment she began to get quick I began the circling and stopping exercises until she gave up anticipating, and waited on me. All this I tried to do with as light a pressure on the reins as possible, sitting as quietly as I was able. The reward came when her ears snapped forward alertly as I presented her to a jump and she trotted confidently into it, set herself right and, extending her head and neck as she jumped it, made a neat bascule over it, knees snapped up to her chin, and landed softly, cantered on steadily without gaining speed, just feeling the bit, waiting for me to show her the next fence.

Afterward I did her off and put the jumps back where I found them. There was no sense in placing temptation in the way of the customers, or, as one old cavalryman of my acquaintance once remarked about draw reins, putting a razor in the hands of a monkey.

That afternoon I treated myself to a supermarket turkey roll and a bottle of Mouton Cadet which I took care of while I made a desultory hack at starting to grade the student papers that had come in. In the evening I listened to John Barry's film score for *Dances With Wolves*. I reflected that without the pressure of having to get ready for a show, my own riding was being geared to the learning curve of The Mare. I'd never really had that luxury before—always working under the gun of a sale or a show—and it was an irony that my pleasure came as a result of my suspension.

I figured The Mare had earned a day off, so I called the stable and fixed it with Joe to turn her out in one of the paddocks and keep an eye on her.

As the day wore on and the pile of student papers began to dwindle, my attention was drawn inevitably to the mass of Barrington material

cluttering up a shelf where I'd stuck it out of the way, but not, unfortunately, out of mind. Actually, I was approaching the end of my labors
with Barrington. I was up to the point where he'd been charged in Parliament with what the *Dictionary of National Biography* called "malver-
sation of funds." I saw he'd died at Versailles on April 8, 1834, aged
sixty-seven, a rogue, a crook, and a minor man of letters. If I contrived
to have my book accepted by a publisher—almost certainly an academic press; who else would want it? I doubted if the minute amount
of Barrington's unrepentant sense of mischief that I'd been at pains to
include would survive the editorial process. Mine would become just
another one of the thousands of books of scholarly criticism printed
yearly. It would almost instantly be remaindered, unconsulted save by
graduate students desperate to pad out a bibliography, unglanced at
except by harried members of recruitment or promotion committees.
It would fill, at most, a line of my vita. It would thus serve as a good
faith offering in a profession where more and more was being written,
often ingeniously if not bizarrely, about less and less.

*   *   *   *

Early Friday Alexander Ashton called to tell me that Ed Vere had
taken his own life. It was news for which I suppose I had been unconsciously waiting. Oddly I was not shocked so much by his death, as I
was made sensible that it signified a kind of caesura in the unremitting
succession of largely incomprehensible events that made up my life.

"The police are there now," Alex said, his voice carrying the merest
quaver of age. "They just now called me. One of the neighbors got
frightened when they heard a shot, called *them*. No note, per se, I
gather, but Ed'd given the neighbors my name and number in case of
emergency." He hesitated. "I wondered if you could lend me a hand,
Stephen, drive down there with me, sort things out?"

Clearly distraught over his wife's passing and coming back to an
empty house—that was the party line developed in the next few days—

Ed had, some time around midnight, blown his brains out with an old Webley Mark VI .455 service revolver, a real John Buchan cannon right in the grand tradition.

It made the hell of a bang down on Forest Glade, Joe Chavez told me later. Residents, who were pretty sophisticated about gunfire after dark, said they'd never heard anything quite like the Webley.

When I drove by to pick up Alex he was on the phone talking with the Vere children. After he hung up he gave me a pessimistic shake of the head and a faintly sour smile. In light of their recent visit after their mother's death, he told me, they didn't feel they could afford to make another trip to Texas again so soon. Was there any way Alex could arrange for the funeral? They'd be ever so grateful. Perhaps he could get in touch with Ed's bank and the utilities people, and ask the post office to forward his mail. While they'd been in Texas Ed'd given them his will and insurance policies. In due course they'd find a lawyer to put probate in motion and sell the house and car. They didn't expect there'd be a lot more to do; Ed didn't even have a credit card, let alone charge accounts, they said.

As I drove Alex south on MoPac, I reminded him that something was going to have to be done about Ed's classes. Not to worry, Alex told me, Ed would have left things in excellent shape. He knew for a fact that Ed had graded and returned all his classes' term papers. (I winced at this.) There would be, of course, the matter of Ed's final exams, but Alex felt that Huw would probably make these optional, and since I was responsible for teaching four sections—three preparations—he'd take on responsibility for turning Ed's grades in.

We arrived at the white frame house on Forest Glade to find that Ed's body had already been removed. For someone blowing his brains out with a baby howitzer there was remarkably little blood and spatter. I'd seen worse one Saturday night back at Benning when I'd been OG and a colonel's wife, adrift with painkillers and Johnny Walker red, plucked up her philandering husband's .45, placed it up under her crepy chin and squeezed off a round with her thumb on the trigger—

attentive army wife, she'd been and her other fingers curled around the safety in the rear of the butt.

Alex called a funeral home and I took care of calling the medical examiner's office. They said that it would be late Monday before they could release Ed's body. The funeral home agreed to take delivery and would send the bill to Newbie and Gwen.

Alex scheduled a rosary service at the funeral home for Tuesday evening.

"Open casket?"

"If at all possible. Then, I think, Stephen, graveside services at Memorial, where Priscilla is buried, perhaps late Wednesday morning—"

"Forgive me, Alex," I broke in, "I'm not really up on the fine points of Catholic doctrine here, but aren't RC graveside services supposed to be for those who don't die in a state of grace?"

Alex was imperturbable. "Once perhaps, but I don't think that distinction holds true any longer—no more, say, than that old business of not burying a suicide in consecrated ground." He smiled. "Perhaps when Ed's children get down here, that might be a good time to hold a memorial service. How does that sound?"

Fine, I told him, just don't count on me to be there. I'd go to the rosary service (well primed, I assured myself, with a generous dose of Wild Turkey), all right, but as far as the rest went, I'd had enough funeralizing to last me a lifetime.

Alex clucked disapprovingly but didn't try to talk me out of it.

Besides, I'd rather cherish the memory of Ed telling Adams and Bernstein that Kristeller Imperiale tasted like horse piss.

Out of the small selection in his closet—a trip down memory lane: behind the frayed blazer, seersucker, and tweed coats, Ed's working wardrobe, were a pair of polyester bellbottoms, a plaid jacket with broad lapels, a couple of daggercollared shirts and wide ties—Alex and I turned up an elderly blue suit, a vintage tie, and black shoes. While rummaging around in his dresser trying to find a clean white shirt, underwear, and socks, I came across a small box containing a medal in the shape of a Maltese Cross and crossed swords depending from a scarlet ribbon with narrow green stripes and a palm clasp. We decided to place the box in Ed's suit pocket when he was laid to rest in the casket.

If I'd known where to find a bottle of Salon de Mesnil, I'd have stashed that in the coffin alongside Ed, as well.

*   *   *   *

We settled down back in Alex's comfortable study over crystal tumblers of a single malt scotch whisky that Alex had brought back from his summer trip to the Highland distilleries and saved for special occasions.

I sipped it appreciatively, then took a good swallow.

"Okay, Alex," I said, "I think it's time you leveled with me about Ed Vere."

He looked at me appraisingly for a long moment.

"You're correct," he said finally. "There is a story."

He glanced at his watch; the day had flown by.

"Ed was a man who valued his privacy. And what I have to say I pieced together from what he said"—he shrugged—"and filled in the rest. As I expect you know from what I suppose that friend of yours, Lieutenant Melnick may have passed on to you, Ed grew up in Montana. He came from ranching stock. Jackson Vere, Ed's father, was the younger son who went off to college in Missoula, studied law, and then joined up with his older brother to go fight in France with the AEF during World War One. By June the elder brother was dead and Jackson Vere had half his left foot shot off—Château-Thierry or Belleau Wood, I can't recall which. While limping around Oxford on convalescent leave, Jackson Vere met, fell in love with, and, with help from his commanding officer and a sympathetic American Embassy—contrived to be discharged from the army and to marry a young student from the Ruskin Art School.

"Madeleine Vere, or Maddy as she was known, came from that upper middle-class guardian caste that England seems so off-handedly to produce. Effective and largely self-effacing, they were trained to serve, to get on with the job at hand and let others take the credit. Maddy's father was an Anglican clergyman, her uncle a genuine hero of the Boer War. On her mother's side, Maddy was half-French, something to do with the wine business and a dash of St Cyr cavalrymen thrown in for good measure. By the time she caught sight of tall, gaunt Jackson Vere limping along St Giles's with a guidebook in his musette bag and that big American smile on his face, almost every young man of Maddy's acquaintance had been killed.

"I daresay the thought of starting a new life as the mistress of a large ranch in Montana, surrounded by snow-capped mountains, grizzly bears, and Red Indians exercised an appeal on her artistic and no doubt romantic nature.

"Nothing worked out the way they'd planned.

"When the couple arrived in the United States they found his parents had died just a few days before, felled in the last of the epidemic of Spanish influenza that had swept the nation. Jackson Vere now found himself the sole owner of a large and, as it turned out, only marginally-profitable ranch. Dependent upon him were a middle-aged foreman and his wife, and a floating population of anywhere from three to five ranch-hands, some with families.

"It didn't take Jackson Vere long to decide he could make more money practicing law in Billings, the closest town of any real size, than he could ranching—indeed might provide him a way of holding on to the heavily-mortgaged ranch. The fact was that Jackson Vere had been educated with a career in law in mind; it had been his older brother who'd been the one singled out since childhood to run the ranch. Sure, he loved the old place with its many memories—he'd like to keep it— but the thought of ranching, with its few rewards and many rigors, attracted him not at all. Perhaps if his practice worked out, he could give a raise—or a percentage of profit (if any) as an incentive—to the foreman who'd carried on so capably while he'd been away. For additional consideration, the foreman's wife might be persuaded to help out at the big house, and continue cooking for the bachelor ranch-hands. After considering matters carefully, Jackson Vere traveled to Billings, introduced himself in the right quarters, and bought a small frame house on a side street. He turned the upstairs into a spacious apartment, the downstairs into a suite of offices, and hung out his shingle. So far as Maddy was concerned…

"So far as Maddy was concerned, she was proving uncharacteristically obdurate, loath to make the move to Billings, wholly indifferent to the attractions of town life. She had fallen in love with the country. She loved her husband, understood and approved what he was doing, missed him tremendously when he was gone, but found herself unwilling, unable to give up a wilderness solitude that oddly suited her.

CHAPTER 23

▼

"It was of course a compromise," said Alex, reaching to fill our glasses. "Implicit with calamity. In the event Jackson Vere came back to the ranch on the weekends, leaving Billings on Friday afternoons and driving several hours to get there in time for a candlelight dinner and, like John Churchill, to pleasure his wife while still in his jackboots, not necessarily in that order, I gather. He'd return to Billings crack of dawn Monday morning.

"Their only child, Ed was born in 1922, the product of one of those passionate weekend couplings.

"Maddy's life became centered around her son. There were other kids on the ranch—the foreman's and part of the floating hired hand population's—and it wasn't so bad when it was just grade school for him to attend in Hardin, the mothers could get them out to the highway for the bus or share driving duties.

"She used to read to him in the evenings, by gaslight, many of her own childhood favorites. Stories of the heroes from Bulfinch, Lamb's *Tales from Shakespeare*, King Arthur, Robin Hood, *Ivanhoe*, *The Talisman*, *Kim*, and the chronicles of Froissart. A little later she got him started on other books and stories by Kipling as well as dipping into the poetry of Keats, Sassoon, and Wilfred Owen, and Rupert Brooke, and, oh, I don't know who else. A mixed bag.

"Of course she taught him to speak faultless French.

"Then of course there was the history of the region where they lived steeped in glory and disaster. Ed told me that many times he and his mother frightened themselves silly as the gas lamps guttered, while out on the moonlit prairie the ghosts of the Sioux warriors and Seventh Cavalrymen went sliding by on the night wind.

"Ed was ready for high school at twelve, and even she could see that, like other ranching mothers, she'd simply have to move to town for the best part of the year. But where? By this time Jackson Vere had become involved in state politics and was having to spend a good bit of time in Helena, where he'd rented a house, two hundred miles farther from Billings—where she hadn't wanted to move to in the first place.

"Maddy reluctantly conceded that the best thing was for them to live in Helena while he went to school. Predictably, she hated Helena and what I'm sure she privately considered its pretentiousness; less predictably, Ed excelled in school and was very evidently happy to be with his father.

"Maddy had fallen in love with the ranch and the country roundabout; but as dreary month succeeded month in Helena, she realized it had been an affair of the heart, not a lifelong devotion; her roots were in England.

"The marriage had not so much foundered as drifted into an exquisite civility. When Ed was fourteen Maddy returned to England with a generous settlement from her husband, reconciled to leaving her very bright son to spend the remainder of his high school years living in town with his father.

"Back in England Maddy was welcomed by her old friends, in particular an old friend of hers, Helen Stirling, who was now married to a senior army officer in the War Office; the Stirlings made available for Maddy a cottage they owned but seldom found time to use in Devon.

"Maddy spent an idyllic two years down there, growing roses, painting watercolors, and, in general, finding her bearings again.

"Back in Helena, Ed Vere graduated at the top of his class. He was sixteen. Jackson Vere gave his blessing for Ed to go join his mother in England where he hoped to go to Oxford or Cambridge.

"Neither university was eager to take him; they felt he was too young. Ed decided to wander about a bit and acquaint himself with the French side of his family. For most of 1938 and a good bit of 1939 he travelled in France, making his main base with some of his mother's relatives in the champagne country north of Troyes—"

"'Horse piss,'" I muttered involuntarily.

Alex glanced at me perplexedly, shook his head, and continued.

"—becoming thoroughly conversant in French and getting to know France.

"He said he had a wonderful time. Vaguely aware of Chamberlain's visit, of course. Of the increasing momentum of the German war machine as days went by—much more aware. Made distinctly uneasy by the military side of his mother's family, two old dinosauric colonels maundering obliviously about the Maginot Line, while he wondered why the German army knowing of its location would then select that route of invasion.

"Ed returned to England in time to take up an invitation to shoot grouse in Scotland, but of course, bang! Hitler attacked Poland and a lot of grouse got a reprieve. Two days later France and Britain declared war.

"Ed told me that shortly after he returned to England he found out Oxford was now offering a shortened, two-year course. He applied, was accepted, and in the event received his BA. at twenty, immediately afterward going up to London to join his mother.

"Within a few days of war being declared Maddy had gone up to London and taken an intensive course in commercial drafting. Straightway afterward she applied for a job Colonel Stirling told her about in the tracing section of a new and very hush-hush War Office department—have you ever heard of something called 'Mulberry Harbours'?—where she appeared armed with high-powered references. I gather that shortly after she began work, the commanding officer of the new department picked her out to be his Personal Assistant.

"She ran the Operational Room, designed and constructed cardboard models to scale of the harbor walls, landing piers, and the unloading roadways to the beach; answered scrambled telephones, kept track of secret photographs, and charmingly conducted high-powered war chiefs around the blacked-out, high-security OR.

"It was in this position of considerable personal responsibility and friendship with high-ranking British officers that Ed Vere found his mother when he came down from Oxford. Determined himself to serve England, Ed Vere, who remember was, after all, half-British, was taken aboard in the Special Operations Executive."

Alex took a decidedly unprofessorial slug of his Glenmorangie.

"If you were to look at Ed's Vita, Stephen, I daresay that all it would say is simply that he had 'Military Service, 1943–1945,' without mentioning that he was serving England. You have read it, I daresay? Am I right?"

"Yes, I've read it, Alex, and you're quite right," I murmured.

"Ah, that fellow Melnick, I suppose?" He looked at me quizzically and when I didn't reply, he went on. "Ed's travels in France and his facility with the language recommended him for a particular mission.

"He was dropped by parachute somewhere in remote rural France. You know what happened. 'Honorably—though mistakenly', as our speaker put it the other day. Soon thereafter Edward, from what I've been able to make out, turned his back firmly on Froissart and Bulfinch, withdrew into himself, and finished his war out quietly. He embraced Roman Catholicism. He fled to a contemplative life, in his case the world of expiatory poetry of the fourteenth century. The fifteenth century—" He waved his hand dismissively.

"Now you know Ed's story, at least to the best of my knowledge."

"Thanks," I said, and meant it. "I feel in a strange way that I've earned it."

Alex favored me with his wintry glance. "I think you have."

I got to my feet. "I really have to go, there are some things I need to do."

"I appreciate your help, Stephen."

"Sure," I told him. "I'll be seeing you."

"I expect you will, at graduation. You're planning to go." It was a statement, not a question.

"I wasn't planning to, but I will."

"I'll miss you at Ed's funeral."

"Yes, well." I had no intention of giving in on that point.

He inclined his head.

Melnick would be there.

*   *   *   *

What I needed to do, first, was get out and ride, clear out the cobwebs.

I didn't hold with this New Age riding-as-therapy stuff, unless all you wanted to do was throw a leg over and slop around for an hour elevating your heart rate and concentrating on your deep breathing techniques. But if you were seriously interested in preparing for competition, then you'd best give the enterprise your full attention. This sometimes meant that you pulled back from making too many demands. Thanks to Joe, The Mare'd been turned out the day before. Reckoning that a bit of cosseting might help her to make a frictionless re-entry into the real world, I booted her up and worked her on the longe, letting her play and get the kinks out. Then I saddled and bridled her, and took her for a long hack along some of the dirt roads in the back of K.C.'s property. It did both of us good.

The second thing I needed to do was meet with K.C. about the Christmas show, now three weeks away and with all the paperwork due by Monday. The premium list made it clear that there would be no stalls assigned until entries had been made and—I winced—paid for. They'd settle for a blank signed check. For many small stables with kid riders, getting even a rough idea of who wanted to go to a show by the evening before constituted top-notch efficiency. So far as extracting entry and stall fees up front from kid riders' parents was concerned, that exercise ranked for difficulty right up there with drawing blood from a turnip.

I ran K.C. down in the indoor ring just as she was finishing a lesson and asked her to join me in the stable office.

"So we need to take the horses over to the exposition center sometime Friday, right?" I could tell from her tone of voice that she was getting excited now that the show was looming near.

"Yes. The best thing to do is to load everything we can up in the peak of the gooseneck—hay, hoses, shavings, grain, table, saddle and bridle racks, and so on—on Thursday afternoon." I made a note to myself. "Then fill the hay nets. Get the tack cleaned and packed in the tack trunks. Make sure all the horses have their fetlocks trimmed, and their ears and bridle-paths clipped. Then feed first thing Friday morning. Do them up, and then load them. Stow all the other stuff—don't forget plenty of clean towels—" for some reason you always needed lots of towels "—and head out of here as early as possible. That way we'll have a fighting chance to be ready for the customers when they start arriving at the show grounds to school that afternoon."

"You'll do the driving?" K.C.'s tone was plaintive, now that she was confronted with the logistical task of moving five horses and the considerable impedimenta that accompanied them—and taking responsibility for them and their riders in and out of the ring for the best part of three days. If she thought this scenario was stomach-churning to contemplate, I thought uncharitably, K.C. would have fainted dead away if she'd had to face showing at the Garden, which involved driving an eighteen-wheeler through tunnels or over bridges, negotiating the maniacal raceway of midtown New York traffic, offloading on the sidewalk under the attentive scrutiny of street people, and stabling your horses on the fifth floor of a high-rise. So far as warming up in a schooling area the size of an airplane lavatory—I chuckled involuntarily.

"Are you catching a cold, Stephen?" K.C. looked at me with alarm. And then when I said nothing, "Will you be finished in time at The University?"

"Yes," I said, immediately ashamed of my flight of fancy; I was really very fond of K.C. "I'm planning to be here that Thursday afternoon to help pack, and I'll drive them over on Friday," I said. "So far as The University goes, the semester ought to be pretty well wrapped up by then." I spoke with a good deal more confidence than I felt: there was still a lot of work to be done before I turned in final grades.

"And give me some help with the kids." The closer to the competition, the more nervous the kid.

"During the show, sure, K.C. But about Friday afternoon: my first obligation's to get the horses settled in comfortably and see that the tack stall's up. Which reminds me, have you spoken to Joe?"

She shifted her eyes. "Stephen, do you really think it's necessary for him to spend both nights out there?"

"Well, actually, K.C., I do," I said firmly. "I realize that there are a lot of stables, most of them, I daresay—Bobby's for example—that don't keep a man on duty at night, or even tip the security guard to look in while he's on his rounds. Nine times out of ten, no problem. But then there's the tenth: a fire breaks out—somebody's hot plate or heater, or a horse gets loose, or starts thrashing around with colic and gets cast in his stall, or somebody walks off with your tack. Having a man there at night's simply the prudent thing to do after you've made a tremendous investment in time and money in getting to the show. If you'd like, I'll talk to Joe myself. I'm sure he won't mind, you'll see. Which reminds me, what did you decide to charge for the daily show fee?"

Show fees, which could run anywhere from $25.00 to $200.00 a day, depending on what league you were playing in, were the daily surcharge that stable owners billed to customers to cover extra help, coaching, and other miscellaneous expenses while on the road. Before they took you on as a boarder, a lot of stables made you agree to go to a certain number of shows—so many show-days, really—per year, at a fixed price of so much a day for show fee, so much a mile for hauling. When you had a whole lot tied up in your extra help and transportation, if you didn't look after your interests, the customers could ruin you. ("Alicia didn't do well in school this last marking period, so we decided no more shows till she brings her grades up." "Freddy's decided he wants to go to Outward Bound this summer." "Melissa got tapped for Hyline.") One well-known pro of my acquaintance wouldn't let a customer's horse step on the van headed for the Arizona or Florida winter circuits without having ten thousand dollars in hand, cash or bank check.

People had a point who said the initial investment in a horse was nothing, it was the upkeep that killed you. But the bottom line was that, for a small stable, particularly one with no cushion of profit to draw on, show fees were an absolute necessity if you were to remain in business.

K.C. nodded no, tightly, she hadn't arrived at a show fee.

I was aghast.

"K.C. you've simply got to charge them. Otherwise you won't come anywhere close to covering your own out-of-pocket expenses, let alone remunerate you for coaching, or pay you lease-money for the horses during the show."

"I know," she said miserably. "But I feel so awful when I think of Mrs. Berry and her little daughter."

"Let me see if I can recall." I was merciless. "Wasn't she the one who came over to your house last holidays with the precious gift snapshot of little Pamela enclosed in her Christmas card, when she was four months behind on a nine-hundred-dollar board bill, which translates roughly, I'm guessing, into, what, about seven fifty out-of-pocket expenses, am I right?"

K.C. looked as if she might cry. "Okay," I told her, resigning myself to playing the heavy. "I'll try to figure it out for you, and give you a call this evening or first thing in the morning. Is that agreeable with you?"

"Oh, Stephen, would you?" Her face brightened.

"Yes," I said. "But one thing you've got to promise me."

"What's that?"

"You are going to have to tell them how much they're going to owe *before* they go to the show. That's the only fair way to do it."

She accepted this with only a murmur of discontent.

I sighed. "What divisions is the show offering?"

She gratefully riffled through the pages of the show's thick premium list. "Let's see, there's a jumper division, working hunter, amateur owner, green hunter—"

I was silent. We had nothing that stood even a remote chance of qualifying for those divisions even if we had a rider capable of piloting a horse around their courses. Those divisions were for dedicated point chasers intent upon winning annual awards.

"—junior jumper, junior hunter, green hunter—Stephen, don't we have *any* horses who can jump 3'6"?"

"On a good day, maybe, one or two, but the green hunter division is for horses 'in their first or second year of showing' in recognized shows. Take it from me, K.C., we don't have any green hunters."

Dispirited, she shrugged. "The ones I read out to you are all AHSF-recognized divisions, it says here in the prize list—" Her head ducked to the premium list again. "Here's adult hunter and pre-green—Claire Rodgers said she'd go in adult, what about pre-green for some of ours?"

Pre-green was what I'd entered The Mare in. "Every pro in this part of the country'll be in that," I told her. "Just like green hunter. And I can promise you, K.C., their horses will really be tuned up."

Enabling you to get some show experience over fences without losing your horse's eligibility as a first-year green hunter the following year, pre-green was a very popular division among professionals.

Pre-green fences were slightly under three feet, first-year green fences were three feet, and those for second-year green were three-six. Once you'd shown over three feet you were automatically second-year. The show world was littered with horses looking sensational over three feet who'd fallen to bits when faced with three-six. I aimed to see that The Mare would be able to start the new year as a squeaky clean first-year green prospect.

"And junior equitation—"

"No."

"How about children's hunter?

"What about *un*recognized divisions, K.C., are there any more listed than just the pre-green and adult?"

"Here. Novice hunter and limit hunter. Isn't that what we've been showing in, in the shows we've been going to? They're not AHSF-recognized. And there's novice and limit equitation classes, too—"

I took the premium list from her, and went over the division specifications. "The fence heights look okay," I said. "Acceptably within the potential of our stalwart crew. But the problem is…"

"Yes, Stephen?"

"I was going to say the problem is…how many kids you got going to the show, and what horses are we actually talking about?"

K.C. furrowed her brow. "Well, let's see, we've got I make it six lesson kids for our three horses, now that Linebacker's…gone." She shook her head at the painful memory. "But there's Harry—"

"Have you called Joan? She'll have to tell you what classes she wants to enter in the dressage division—" From what I'd noticed in recent weeks Joan was taking it a bit easier on the massive Warmblood, and he had been going more kindly for her.

"Okay, I'll see her when she comes out to ride tomorrow, and find out." She closed her eyes and concentrated. "Our three are Evening Shade, Far West, and Intrepid—"

Kevin, Warren, and Murray: the Geriatric Ward. I shook my head. "Who've you got riding?"

"We've got Catherine Epps, Anita Morales, Dorothy Winegard, Timothy Barber, Freddy Bullard, and Karen Clayton—"

"Six of them," I said. "You're sure all of them are novice or limit riders? None of them's won six blues, not even in little local shows? Is that right?"

She nodded.

"It's important, K.C. For two reasons. The first is, in hunter classes you're not allowed to enter the same horse more than once—the same's true for most all divisions: you get judged once per class. That means—"

"Only three of the kids can ride in each division."

"Right, so we better check and make sure, a, we've got three genuine limit riders—" Hearing my own words, I kept thought of that old Lone Ranger and Tonto joke: *What's this 'we' shit, white man?* I was really getting involved with this business.

"What are you laughing at, Stephen?"

"—and three novice riders. Nothing, really."

She frowned in concentration. "I believe so."

"—*And*, b, that there's no cross-entry rule prohibiting a horse from showing in both divisions." I thought for a moment. "But even if there is such a rule for this show, there may be another possibility. If it's an equitation over fences class, where the rider's being judged, not the horse, you might be able to get away with entering the same horse with more than one rider." I reached to look at the premium list again. Scanning it I didn't see any specific prohibition against the same horse being entered in novice and limit rider classes.

"Stephen, that's not all," K.C. said, beginning to glower defensively. "There's more. You know, when I give lessons there are these people who trailer over?"

Yes, I said, I'd noticed the trailers parked carelessly around the barn.

"Well, some of them want to come and stable with us. At the show."

"Oh?"

"Claire Rodgers is going to meet us at the show with that horse of hers, Flipper. She said that the little Maxwell girl who comes on Tuesdays and Fridays can ride Flipper, and we could charge the Maxwells for the use of him. Claire gave me her entries in the adult hunter over the phone; she wants us to pay her entry fees and show expenses out of what we take in from the Maxwells—"

"Claire Rodgers is a lovely woman, K.C., but she's got the soul of a Bengali bazaar merchant when it comes to negotiating business deals. If Savannah Maxwell's the only one Claire'll let ride Flipper, there's no way we can break even on the deal, not and pay Claire's way, too. She knows that perfectly well. Let Claire make her own entries and come to an arrangement with the Maxwells directly. According to the prize list, the show won't assign the horse a stall until its entries and stall fees are paid. So we bill the Maxwells like any other customer, up front: entry fees, stall fees, the whole thing, in your hand Sunday, with the rest. Let Claire do her own collecting. Okay?"

"Uh, Stephen, Mrs Maxwell's out of town and you know Mr Maxwell, he hates horses."

"Yeah, well. You'll just have to tell her that Savannah can't show with us unless she comes up with the money." I sighed again. "Is there anything else you need to tell me?"

"Mrs Ratliff called," K.C. added apologetically, "and she's got those two horses that she's been bringing over for the Stallings girls to ride. She wants Hilda to ride Honor Student in the limit division and the little one, Fran, to ride him in the novice, and—"

"Slow down to a trot, K.C.," I said. "This is the same problem we face with our own three. Let her sort it out with the secretary over the phone. The main thing is that, if she wants to stable with us, we have her entry and stall fees in time to hand in with all the rest on Sunday."

CHAPTER 24

▼

"There, that's settled," I said with a groan of relief, leaning back in my chair some forty-five minutes later, after sifting through the novice and limit business and deciding which kid would go with which horse in which class. Despite the satisfaction of coming up with a solution I felt a bit guilty, like a field marshal having committed his troops to what he knew would be a bloody enterprise—each of the three lesson horses was scheduled to make eight trips a day. K.C.'d better take care that no one got carried away during the Friday schooling sessions, and I'd keep a damned good eye peeled on the warm-up ring during the show— otherwise our nags would be dropping like flies by Saturday noon. Extra rations and an aggressive rubdown and bandage campaign were a must.

Another unwelcome thought occurred to me. "Are all the kids up-to-date members?" Some larger shows were not permitted to take your entries unless you were a member in good standing of both the AHSF or the state association. Strict secretaries insisted on being shown membership cards.

"Yes." Her hands twisted tightly together.

"I bet they told you that you could sign for them and say, yes, they were," I said, guessing. "And they're not. You know, K.C., if one of those kids should, by some weird chance, win, when they post the results back in New York, they're going to raise all sorts of Cain—"

"I know. I told them that. And they said—"

"And they said it didn't matter if they were suspended; that this was the only recognized show they were going to anyway, for the year; that they didn't care, even if they got fined for filing a false affidavit, this was their kid's last year of showing, anyway—"

K.C. shrugged helplessly, her eyes filling with tears not out of mortification that she was such an easy mark, but at the realization that it might not really matter. Now that she was selling her stable, it was likely to be her last show.

"K.C.," I said slowly, "do we have Cogginses on all these horses?" No recognized show would let you on the grounds without a valid Coggins test.

She looked at me blankly. "I think we have…some of them."

I made a note to check with the vet.

"What about The Mare, Stephen?" K.C. asked, eager to get away from the Cogginses and the ghastly business of show fees. "Are the Damons going to want to show?"

"I doubt it. The last time Janice Damon climbed on she took a hell of a spill." The truth was The Mare was just beginning to relax and trust me, and the last thing she needed was an unfamiliar rider plus the pressure of a show.

"The Mare's so pretty, I don't know why *you* don't ride her, you've been doing so well with her."

"Yeah, well, I tell you what I'll do," I said, trying to evade the issue. "I'll call the doctors Damon and let them know about the show—but my guess is that even as we speak they're probably getting ready to go hang-gliding over the South Pole or something. If they think of her at all it's doubtless with the idea of selling her."

"What a shame that would be," sighed K.C., clearly wanting stories to have happy endings. "Well, I guess my work's cut out for me. I'll get busy with the kids and talk to Joan—"

"And I'll call you as soon as I work up some figures to arrive at a show fee. We can meet here Sunday afternoon and I'll hand-carry the entries and checks over to the secretary's house."

*   *   *   *

That evening I made a start at arriving at a show fee, approximating where I could the costs for extra help and left a detailed message for K.C.

*   *   *   *

On Saturday I went over a few more student term papers and started in drafting the final exams. Late in the afternoon I took The Mare out on the longe and then worked her for forty-five minutes bending on my leg.

After Joe got finished feeding we inspected the truck and trailer, going over the hitch, checking the oil, batteries, transmission fluid, fan belts, brake hoses, tire pressure, and paying particular attention to the condition of the tires, and making sure the license, insurance, and inspection tags were current.

Joe agreed to work the weekend and stay nights out at the show grounds. His brother Pete would fill in doing the feeding and mucking out back at the stable.

When I finally tracked down the doctors Damon, my guess proved to be pretty much on target. They wanted to sell The Mare.

Classy Minx wasn't simply some ordinary Thoroughbred, they assured me proudly. Not only did she have Jockey Club papers, but she was by Sir Winterbourne, winner at two of the Saratoga Special; at three, the Dwyer; and, at four, the Brooklyn Handicap (not one of them a Grade I stake). If for some unforeseeable reason (I was at that moment recalling quite vividly the merest hint of white around her admittedly large and liquid eyes), she didn't prove out to be a champion grand prix jumper, she'd obviously make a nationally-ranked show hunter. (She stuck out at a bare sixteen one, too small by a couple of inches to fill a judge's eye.) Or a top-class child's hunter. Or, given that she'd finished in the money twice (out of twenty-one starts, I refrained from pointing out), they just knew she'd be a slam-dunk for eventing. And in any case, with her bloodlines ("Got the breeding of a field mouse," I could hear some of my old racetrack buddies scoffing), Texas bloodstock men would be falling all over themselves to buy her as a brood mare.

It was thus my unhappy duty to explain to them the Facts of Life.

"Yes," I told them, "she's pretty typy, all right, but she doesn't have the size or substance to travel in really good company as a hunter. So far as breeding goes, the truth of it is that there're a lot of people can get together enough money and have enough contacts to get their mare a service to a well-known stud, but that's just half, or less than half, of the equation. The mare's got to have what it takes. For preference she ought to be a stake winner herself, and come to the breeding shed with her own distinguished blood-line. Face it, neither Classy Minx's racing record nor her bloodlines recommend her as a brood mare. So far's making a jumper or event horse is concerned, it's too early to tell what kind of talent over fences she might have, though I'll be the first to grant you that a lot of pros would have found out what she was made of within two weeks. I just don't operate that way. I will say this: I think she's temperamentally unsuited to be a junior hunter—she's way too hot for most kids to handle."

All in all, they took it pretty well, even the part where I suggested that we get the mare out in front of some people at the Christmas show. The problem was of course who'd ride her. As I was under suspension—a circumstance which so far as I knew no one around had a clue about—I was ineligible. Janice Damon would take some very careful, not to say inspired, coaching if she were to navigate The Mare round a course without having a rail down, stopping out, or being thrown off. Bobby Robberson didn't have it all wrong, I thought: a good horse *is* sometimes too valuable to entrust to its owner. Instead of getting its mouth torn up, kidneys pounded, or crippled from being dropped into a jump by an owner on an ego trip, better by far the decorous once-a-week stroll on the end of the halter shank, chomping carrots and nibbling grass—and, for the owner, a genteel gin-and-tonic in the customers' lounge afterward, and discreet conversation about the indoor circuit.

*   *   *   *

The next day I started taking stock of what we'd need to pack for the Christmas show, one of the very few shows at which we stayed overnight.

Gordonwood wasn't anybody's idea of a show barn—not like Bobby's stalls where he set up a lounge, a tack stall, and a junk stall, the first two surrounded by Astroturf matting with potted palms inside a pristine white picket fence and Dom Perignon in the silver ice bucket in the lounge under the chandelier and the aisleway kept raked with colored sawdust. Everything, including the custom-built chrome and lacquered tack boxes, was color-coordinated in Bobby's stable colors, cerise and white, and meticulously monogrammed.

What Gordonwood had was largely and sometimes touchingly home-made. Instead of screw eyes and solid brass double-end snaps to fasten buckets in the stalls, I made shift with bailing wire. K.C. had managed to run up on her sewing machine a quite respectable set of home-made stall fronts and tack room drapes and stable banner in the stable colors. One of her friends had likewise manufactured some stall signs.

We needed to pack extension cords and a clamp light for the tack room, heavy-duty staplers and plenty of staples to put up the drapes, a couple of sheets of plywood to use for the floor of the tack room and the somewhat moth-eaten rugs to cover them, as well as the normal packing list for shows, like a tack hook pounded out by the farrier to hang in the aisle outside the tack room, a tool box, a seam ripper to take down the braided manes at the end of the show, a large soft drink cooler, buckets of various sizes and ages, hay nets, saddle stand, bridle brackets, saddle brackets, mirror, water heater, water hose complete with bracket hanger, washer, and nozzle.

Extra girths and bridles, grooming and tack cleaning supplies, bandages, bell boots, blankets, coolers, waffle anti-sweat sheet, an ancient rain sheet, clippers were contained in three old tack trunks that resided in the peak of trailer and stayed packed between shows. Filling out the load were hay and grain scoops, manure basket and aluminum muck scoop, grooming boxes redolent with the delightful aroma of Bigeloil and Absorbine and squished tubes of icthammol ointment, directors' chairs and card table (one always needed a place to sit down and something to lay things on), sacks of grain and hay and bran, and bags of compressed wood shavings for extra bedding. We also needed to have cash on hand to pay the braiders—an independent nocturnal crew who showed up usually about midnight and worked through the night, boom boxes blaring, then to disappear by light of dawn…

*   *   *   *

In the late afternoon, when I'd finished riding, I met with K.C. and picked up the paperwork and checks, and hand-delivered them to the show secretary who lived close to The University.

The final week of classes flashed by like a dream. I felt as if I were being scourged with a silk scarf that had thorns and cockleburs tangled in it.

I made it out to the stable only three times, making a conscious effort not to force upon The Mare my own anxieties and frustrations—rather, I fancied, as a lover might with a mistress he'd had to abandon momentarily and then return to, fearful of bringing muddy boots into the silken bedroom, wary of what mood she'd be in. My voice and hands and legs were full of murmured confidence and cosseting and sweet queries of what she'd been up to in my cruel absence. Wyatt could have written a sonnet about her.

I spent time with her on the longe, not simply letting her buck and play, as was my custom, but afterward knotting the reins underneath the tied-up irons, so that she bent at the poll, playing with the bit; and with the suggestion of the long whip behind her, she carried herself balanced squarely at the trot, striding out, ears alertly forward. Later I rode her at a walk, bending her on my leg, then trotted in and around the trees, until she waited, waited on me, then popped over the odd jump and cantered in smooth rhythm to the next. If she started to anticipate I pulled her up and made her stand foursquare and still.

Monday and Tuesday I forced myself to get up and run in the dark, hunched against the mist and chill, up and down the park trails along the creek.

On Wednesday I handed out evaluation forms to be filled in anonymously, assigning the teacher percentage grades under various headings such as *prepared for class, mastery of the material,* and *available during office hours.* Students were encouraged to write down personal individual comments. These evaluations were carefully considered when the time came to renew one's contract. Inevitably one's best students picked that class to skip; students who'd been absent for weeks invariably chose that class to attend. One of my spring semester's evaluations had gained some fame in the department, probably thanks to Huw. Printed laboriously in block letters, it said: MR COULTER ISNT FULL OF BULL SHIT LIKE THE REST OF THE ENGLISH DEP'T. Huw had said only half in jest, "A mighty responsibility, Stephen, to live up to! Now, if you'd only explicated the differences between closed and open compound words, and preached the capital virtue of the apostrophe, I'd bloody canonize you."

Final office hours for the semester fell on Wednesday afternoon and, by way of a treat, on my way back to campus after lunch I picked up some cider, doughnuts, and plastic cups, plates, and paper napkins in holiday colors. For a surprisingly large number of students I was the only teacher at The University with whom they had actually been able to talk face-to-face, a circumstance that they took advantage of shamelessly for (I suspected) whatever they might extract in the way of entertainment. Enlightenment on literary matters would be lagniappe. Several of my long-term waifs and strays bravely wanted to discuss what their grades might be likely to be, in consequence of their numerous absences from class ("not *four*, sir, there must be some mistake!") and, uh, late papers. Two offered top-of-the-line general confessions, a third presenting a quite moving theatrical presentation—all ultimately throwing themselves on my mercy. (Teacher: a child among men, a man among children, I reminded myself.) A few students dropped by or left notes to say how much they'd enjoyed the course. One solid B student came in with a gift-wrapped bottle of gin which I declined with genuine regret. For the life of me I couldn't always tell sincerity from the currying of favor. Maybe they didn't know, either. Others returned books I'd lent them.

On Thursday afternoon, I met my last class of sophomore literature. I read to them from William Faulkner's introduction to his collected stories where he speaks about how people write books to uplift men's hearts.

Perhaps a little bit of Faulkner might stick with them.

*   *   *   *

Before I said good-bye to my freshman English sections, I reviewed Sir Arthur Quiller-Couch's wonderful old essay "On Jargon," one of the lectures he delivered on writing at Cambridge in 1915. I recalled it as fitting for my final class meeting: "Perpend this, Gentlemen, and maybe you will not hereafter set it down to my reproach that I wasted an hour of a May morning in…exhorting you upon a technical matter at first sight so trivial as the choice between abstract and definite words…." But my heart sank as I glanced down the page to Q's peroration—"For the style is the man and where a man's treasure is there is his heart, and his brain, and his writing, will be also."

I pondered uneasily on how impossibly dated—not to mention irredeemably sexist—Quiller-Couch's diction must sound to my students' ears. With regret I put away the book.

CHAPTER 25

▼

"After summer was over, I never again saw Ed at Mass," Ashton confided to me at the dean's reception later that afternoon.

We were sitting comfortably in a corner, munching hors d'oeuvres and sipping an agreeable Llano Estacado Riesling. "So far as I know he didn't take communion after that time, at least not at St Michael's. He may have gone somewhere else, but I don't think so."

"Surely Ed must have known he was off the hook, and that the medical examiner had found the pre-existing condition..."

"What the hell did that matter?" Ashton spoke with uncharacteristic harshness. "Edward knew what he'd done. And it was something for which he was fully prepared to pay the price. It's something *they* would understand—" He nodded in the direction of some of the older faculty, most of them, I judged, retired, clustered near the well-stocked bar and table laden with appetizers.

As we watched, our host, the mad mullah dean, who had been talking animatedly—holding forth, actually—with a group of younger faculty, now synchromeshed silkily through his rhetorical gears and turned to address several of those older men and women. The dean was a pale-eyed man of middle height, lean and wiry, sparse hair cropped monkishly close to the skull. He wore a vividly checked shirt, corduroy trousers cinched round the waist by what appeared to be a British regimental tie striped in peculiarly repulsive hues, and burnished sandals with thick socks. He had about him the quietly confident air of a man recently returned from crossing "the Empty Quarter" alone, on foot.

"Stephen, were you paying attention to what I was saying?"

I shook my head in the direction of the dean. "As a friend of mine would put it, 'he's a real piece a work'."

"Our dean? The cant word is he's 'controversial'."

"Ah! Doesn't somehow come as a shock to me."

We both fell silent for a moment, then Alex plowed ahead. "'As the twig is bent, the tree's inclined.' Keep in mind that Ed was brought up to believe passionately in all those old romances; in the existence of right and wrong, good and evil; in the idea of personal responsibility—and, yes, honor, and even *patria* for good measure."

"Alex, how many people do you suppose knew or guessed that Ed...?"

"More I daresay than you'd think, particularly the ones close to his own age. One of their own, you know *they* weren't about to give anything away." He hesitated. "To paraphrase the rotund Chesterton in speaking of tradition—vile word these days!—in the democracy of the dead, a vote's given to those passed on before, and a refusal to bow under to those who merely happen to be walking around."

"Even so it struck me that they shut down the investigation pretty damn quick."

"'They'? Whom do you mean? Our administration? Now that's an interesting point. I expect they were probably more aware of what may actually have occurred than anyone was willing to give them credit for. When the prior existence of that potentially mortal illness Roylett suffered from was discovered in the autopsy"—he shrugged and lifted his hands, palms up—"it must've seemed a heaven-sent opportunity to shut the whole thing down. and at the same time to be seen honoring the legal necessities."

*   *   *   *

When I got back home I poured the first of several stiff drinks. Later that evening I placed a call to the old man. He seemed genuinely pleased to hear from me.

*   *   *   *

For the next few days I went out to run before dawn, finished up drafting examinations, and graded term papers. On the two afternoons I made it out to the stable to work The Mare, I kept hearing, oddly, in my mind's ear Louis Armstrong singing "We Have All the Time in the World" from the James Bond flick *On Her Majesty's Secret Service*. On Tuesday I went by the duplicating room and ran off copies of my exams.

On Wednesday and Thursday I gave my final examinations, managing to read through a good many of the first set as I sat invigilating the second class. Alex called me Thursday evening to tell me he'd turned in Ed's grades. On Friday I said to hell with it, and went out and rode; my final marks didn't have to be posted until the next week. I still kept hearing that song.

*   *   *   *

It was raining on Saturday afternoon as Alexander Ashton and I strode across campus to the Commencement exercises held in The University's immense performing arts center.

The wet streets and parking lot were jammed solid with cars, pickups, and RVs; people crowded out of the weather under the jutting marquee entrance.

At vast personal cost today's graduates had pinned their hopes to a symbolic walk across the stage and assigned a totemic value to the pieces of paper they'd receive in the mail, guarantees of their claim to a share in the American dream. We faculty, complicit in the construction of this chimera—through a highly-developed sense of self-preservation, through vanity—were on ritual annual display. Persons of authority and consequence, there we were, wrapped in our symbolic gowns, august and majestical. Would we lie?

Alex and I pressed though the throng, down the stairs to the robing room. Chromium garment racks were scattered about standing in a welter of dry-cleaners' plastic bags. A long table was set up in a corner with coffee and ice-water. End-of-term excitement, much covert sizing up of other people's gowns; discreet peering at unfamiliar doors along anonymous corridors in search of a bathroom.

From their familiar cocoons of earth-toned clothes faculty, by donning their robes, metamorphosed into tropical birds or iridescent fish. Black of egrets' plumes predominated, but there were blues ranging from shoalwater azure to Gulf Stream royal; scarlet, too; and dark burnt orange. Hoods cascaded down scholars' backs like the plumage of macaws, cockatiels, kingfishers, and cardinals. Full sleeves slashed with chevrons: the violet of architecture, white of arts and humanities, light blue of education, crimson of journalism, lemon of library science, pink of music, apricot of nursing, dark blue or black denoting philosophy, engineering's orange, the brown of fine arts, the purple majesty of law.

*   *   *   *

"Christ's teeth, girl, it's a bloody bird's nest on the ground."

Like many experienced teachers Huw had developed over the years a resonant kind of Royal Shakespeare Company—Albert Finney honk that now carried effortlessly through the room from where he, Joan Strossner-Boynton, and Carlotta du Plessis-Roylett were grouped in a corner.

Huw was swaggering just slightly in a tatty black gown, obviously the sherry-stained veteran of a thousand gory *viva voces*, whose meagre hood was trimmed with what appeared to be ancient rabbit. He was speaking intently with Joan, resplendent in her Yale blue, her black hair crisp and curly, eyes flashing, her hawklike features flushed and animated.

Carlotta was examining her image critically in one of the full-length wall mirrors. She adjusted her wide-sleeved gown of scarlet panama so that it hung open down the front, revealing a demure high-necked black dress which, when she turned away from the mirror, I saw was slit to the hipbone. She flashed me a brief, conspiratorial grin.

Huw said his editor was in town and Huw had been telling him about Joan's work. The editor was eager to meet her. The book she was writing would fit in nicely with a new series devoted to gender studies that his publishing house was just starting up. There had even been some talk of hiring a general academic editor and Huw had recommended Joan for the job.

"Get that under your belt, Joan," Huw promised, "and you'll get tenure, Bob's your uncle.

"My plans right now," Huw went on a bit grandly, "are a little up in the air—but you can always get in touch with me through Carlotta up at Cat Mountain—"

"Yes, of course, Huw," Joan said evenly. "I'll give him a call right away. And I *am* very grateful—"

Jesus wept! Rugger pissups and beer tins strewn among the copper pots!

"Mr Coulter." It was Amanda Vennible at my shoulder. "Do you need any safety pins?" Her eyes were steady on me and I flushed guiltily.

"Now, if we can just get through the next semester," Amanda breathed serenely.

*   *   *   *

Bob Talbot, wearing a brown suit and brown brogues with his crimson gown, was about to fly to England to take up a summer fellowship at St Antony's. At the end of term he'd once again experience the delights of doing research at the Public Records Office and returning at night to his bed-sitter in Earls Court and the bathroom he shared with three Sikh families.

After Alex and I had donned our robes we went out into the hall where the faculty were lining up for the procession. Through a nearby doorway marked "President's Party" I caught sight of Tom Sturtevant engaged in hearty conversation with various red-faced CEO types tussling with their robes.

Sturtevant looked up, smiled when he saw me, and came out to say hello. "What brings you here, Stephen?"

"Tom, this is Alex Ashton, also from English."

"Tom Sturtevant, Alex. Think we met briefly at Commonwealth Studies."

Alex nodded, yes.

"Same thing brings you, I guess, Tom. What university's that?" Looking at his robes.

"What?" For a moment he was nonplused. "Jesus, I don't know. I went to UVA. Hey, Bill"—Sturtevant turned and cried out across to the president—"where's this robe from?"

"We always keep a few on hand in the office, for the speakers," said the president with a straight face. "Not too many of them have—"

"No, goddamnit, Bill, what *college* is it from?"

"Columbia, goddamnit, I think, Tom."

"Columbia, Stephen, that's where I got my doctorate. Of course. For a moment I'd quite forgotten, would you believe it?"

From the auditorium we could hear The University band striking up William Walton's "Crown Imperial."

The faculty procession began to shuffle forward in a kind of lock-step.

"Let's get together afterward for a drink," Sturtevant suggested.

"Sounds good to me. Where d'you want to meet?"

"What d'you say to the Texas Chili Parlor?"

"Great. I'll see you there."

The grand chords crashed about us.

We processed toward the lighted stage. It was like a near death experience. Whitecaps on a turbulent sea, pale faces turned toward us and cameras flashed like strobe lights, memorializing the moment. From the anonymity afforded by the semidarkness there issued the odd ribald comment.

Surely those who kept the flame must have the answers.

Surely they must.

*   *   *   *

We stared past the footlights out into the vast auditorium.

Leading the president's party, The University marshal, Angelo Angelus, professor of classics, tall and grave, prowled up the aisle in a curiously atavistic shuffle, holding high before him The University's great mace with its brightly colored tassels, each denoting a college, swinging like scalps taken in barbaric combat.

Twenty-seven doctoral candidates were hooded in educational psychology, three in English, three in classics; two in history, one in philosophy.

Tom Sturtevant was the honored speaker. The message he sought to convey did not prove a popular one. "This university seeks to give tools to its graduates with which to seek work in the marketplace," he said. "It does *not* guarantee them jobs."

General stirring and discomfort with this unpopular notion.

The president played it safe: "We, the administration and faculty, would propose to honor, on our feet and with applause, the families of our graduates, in particular the mothers and fathers for whom this day has been a long-awaited and to-be-cherished event, the fruit of countless sacrifices and the repository of many hopes."

This was more like it: genial smiles, whistles, and widespread feelings of bonhomie.

Sarah Jane Collins, radiant in her scarlet robes with her blonde hair shining under her velvet Tudor cap, proclaimed the names of the new graduates, her impeccable mid-Atlantic accent booming out through the vast auditorium over the immensely powerful p.a. system.

Through some mechanical quirk of the single small speaker directed back toward those on stage, some of those names—so carefully prepared for and rehearsed by Sarah Jane—reached our ears invested with a refreshing exoticism: *Janette Frisby Croptop...Parchment Simoon Deckerfield...Chester Monet Diehard...Mary Catherine Del Nippling, with special honors in classes and vanities...Elizabeth Marie Fartkamp...Renée Marie Navel...Andrew Joshua Pimp...Gogol Swanna Punish...Twinkis Cuentes Strongyle.*

Catchlights sparkling in her aquamarine eyes, Sarah Jane seemed to me to have been quite transformed into Euterpe, the muse of poetry, speaking in tongues; or possibly because I had not quite given up thinking of her in other, less lofty terms, Erate, the muse of erotic poetry.

Bright lights shone on pony tails and through sheer black gowns as the candidates crossed the stage to receive their degrees. Then it was Melody's turn. She sauntered deliberately across the stage in a model's strut, her flowered panties and bra clearly visible through her backlit gown. Old faculty farts gave grim dry grins. As she passed in front of where Alex and I were sitting, she turned toward me, smiled widely, and stuck out her tongue. Ashton chuckled.

*   *   *   *

During the post-graduation concert on the tracker organ—something pyrotechnical, like Mulet or Widor, I thought—Sarah Jane provided the cynosure of a group of admiring students and their parents. She caught sight of me, broke off her conversation with a murmured apology, and extended a cool white hand.

She was very happy, she said. Huw, as acting chair—probably to be asked to serve as permanent chair—was solidly behind her proposal. Everyone, it seemed, was looking forward to getting the project off the ground.

She was earnest, and businesslike; she looked me in the eye.

Her face was once more exalted in that Candice Bergen-Joan of Arc way. I guessed I'd always fall for that kind of look.

No question about it, Sarah Jane Collins was definitely muse material. I was probably the kind of man who, in order to accomplish anything, requires a muse. Any woman who took me on would have to know that.

"Some of us are getting together, Stephen," she was saying, "and I wondered if you'd like to join us."

"There's nothing I'd rather do, Sarah Jane," I told her with genuine regret. "But I'm meeting some people myself, over at the Chili Parlor."

"Well, there will be time over the holidays," she said.

"Yes," I said. "I'd like that very much." I started to say I was looking forward to seeing her again, and soon; but by then, murmuring an apology to me and bestowing a rueful smile, she'd already turned away, back to her group of admirers.

*   *   *   *

"Dr. Coulter! Stephen!" With sparkling eyes, Melody ran toward me, breaking away from an older man with a camera, a stylishly dressed older woman, and a strapping young man whose arm she'd been cling-ing to, and looking up at adoringly. He was frowning.

She threw her arms around me and whispered into my ear. "Did you see me? Crossing the stage?"

"Of course I saw you," I murmured into her jasmine-scented hair. "So did the rest of the faculty. Shocking. Scandalous. Where's Henry?"

"Oh, God, I hoped I'd see you. I don't know where Henry is and I don't care if I never see him again. I wanted to thank you for your note. I hope you understand why I didn't answer. I felt so *ashamed*."

"No, no, you mustn't think that. Silly business. Here. I brought you a present." I extricated myself from her embrace, and handed her the small square package I'd had in my pocket. "Melody, don't you think you need to introduce me to…"

"A present? *Pour moi?* You shouldn't have." As she tore the wrap-pings off, I tried to summon up a reassuring smile to direct at her mother and father, obviously plucked from the comfortable rusticity of their retirement up on the Highland Lakes, set down in this academic Feast of Fools, and tilted off-balance by the warmth of their daughter's welcome to a middle-aged faculty member. The tall young man was definitely frowning now.

"Oh, Stephen! Ivor Novello! From *Perchance to Dream*. 'We'll Gather Lilacs in the Spring Again' and 'Love is my Reason': I just *love* them."

"It's a tape I made from some HMV 78s with Richard Tauber. On the other side you've got Noël Coward singing 'I'll See You Again,' 'Poor Little Rich Girl,' and 'A Room with a View'."

"Dad, Mom—and this is Mark, my friend from highschool: he owns the hardware store in Marble Falls now and is on the board of the bank—this is Stephen Coulter. *Doctor* Stephen Coulter." And then with a hint of the mischief I knew so well, but with genuine sincerity: "He's been a…mentor of mine." Her eyes were wet.

Fears at least partially dispelled, the parents murmured compliments for the help I'd given, and we shook hands. General Harker was a youthful-looking man with tanned unlined face and almost white hair; Mrs Harker was slim, dark, and petite. The young man had a grip like a blacksmith.

I couldn't help noticing that in the daylight Melody's robe was modestly opaque and gave no hint of how she'd strolled, a backlit force of life, across the stage and into my memory.

$$*\qquad*\qquad*\qquad*$$

Mentor. I experimented with the word, saying it aloud to myself as I started across campus to the parking lot near MacFarland Hall. It had rather a nice ring to it.

"Sorry, what did you say?" Henry Fishbach's voice came from behind me.

"What?"

"You were talking to yourself." Accusingly.

"I expect I was," I said. "Congratulations on earning your doctorate."

He jerked his head in ill-natured acknowledgment. "I wanted to have a word with you."

I stopped. "What's on your mind?" Having a word with Fishbach was not something I wanted to spend any more time on than I had to.

"I suppose I ought to thank you for helping out with my dissertation, Stephen," he said, at once taking advantage of that convention of the profession that puts new PhDs on a first-name basis with their committee members. "I know it really wasn't within your area of competence, but you obviously found my topic of some interest, so I guess we both profited from the exercise."

"I appreciate your kind words, Henry," I told him. "And I am certain that you will swiftly gain advancement in the profession." I wished desperately that I did not believe that part; the fact was, he *would* do well, learning more and more (and pontificating about) less and less, his writing comprehensible only to an anointed few.

Henry beamed.

CHAPTER 26

▼

There is a bittersweet melancholy that comes along with the end of a semester.

I felt like someone out of one of those old Michael Curtiz productions like *The Sea-Hawk*, with marvelously evocative background music by Erich Korngold.

Captain in a many-vesseled voyage of discovery, setting out in September to girdle the globe of English literature in sixteen weeks, I'd brought my ship back safe to port; my crew was dispersed. I was making my way to the admiralty, logbook tucked under my arm. Each crew member carried his own unique and imperishable recollections of the expedition.

Other crews' memories of the voyage and the ports of call would be vastly different. How they thought of those continents, archipelagos, and island chains whose ports of call we'd been ordered to fetch up at depended on the inclinations of their captains.

For the time being I'd have to put the props back in the box, though they were never far from my mind. Oak trees and laurel, pallets of straw, harps Germanic, Mediterranean, and Aeloian, rosebuds, lilies and rubies, sunsets, a collar set with diamonds, daggers both real and dreamt of, numerous birds, masses of ribbons, a spur, a pair of abhorred shears, lyres and dulcimers, a lute with a rift, one winged chariot, crowns, a set of mind-forged manacles, clouds of various shapes, a bunch of worms, the odd snail, lots of marble, a few monuments, a singing mermaid, writing pens, books, the drinking-skull from Newstead Abbey, and Shelley's scorched and shrunken heart pulled from the flames.

My God! There was enough for everyone: an inexhaustible embarrassment of riches for traditionalists, deconstructionists, postmodernists, practitioners of gender and minority studies, Marxists—The literature, I had faith, would survive the attempts of academics to explicate it.

None of them—even those young, brash, and brilliant, crowned by talent, haloed by promise—had *the* answer, no more than had those now-so-righteously despised academics of the past.

There was no single answer.

Time would winnow the wheat from the chaff. The university still represented the last best hope of civilization.

*   *   *   *

I found I was desperate to go out to the stable to ride; I had a hankering for fresh woods and pastures new.

*   *   *   *

Tom Sturtevant's choice of the Texas Chili Parlor as a meeting place didn't surprise me. The TCP was one of the last authentic bars, a stone's throw from the capitol and the congeries of state office buildings, down the street from a Christian Science reading room, and across from a bootmaker and saddle shop. It was a popular venue for state officials and power brokers, real estate entrepreneurs, office workers, failed poets, and bikers.

"Hey, Rusty!" Amid the dark-stained wood, deeply-carved tables, hinky signs ("Tipping is Not a Town in China"; "Don't Ask for any

Foo-Foo Drinks"), trophy heads, and beer spill, I was momentarily surprised to see Walter Melnick, dark suit, white shirt, and small-figured tie. Sitting next to him at a large table in the rear was a slim, dark, vivacious young woman in a sleeveless linen frock, laughing at something Walter had said, her head thrown back, her hand laid familiarly on his arm.

"Want you to meet someone." Melnick's natural ebullience was curiously reined in, as if he were just slightly anxious. "This is my daughter Paulina Eileen." He smiled proudly. "She just graduated today, found out she's been accepted in the graduate program. You might a seen Dr Coulter, Polly, from up on the stage?"

I had completely forgotten that Melnick's daughter was graduating.

"Hello," I said. "I'm Stephen Coulter. Congratulations. I know this is a big day for both of you."

"Thanks so much, Dr Coulter," she said. "I'm glad to meet you, my dad's told me a lot about you."

"I only wish Polly's mother could a been here," Walter Melnick said somberly.

✳   ✳   ✳   ✳

Tom Sturtevant's already ruddy face was flushed with what I guessed had been the regents' post-commencement sherry bash as he made his way to our table, accompanied by the striking woman who had been with him that first morning out at the stable. Her silver-threaded brown hair lay sleek to her head and was caught back in a neat chignon. She still had her glowing tan, set off by unfashionably pale lipstick. She had lovely eyes, and small laughter lines around them. She wore a smart navy blue Shantung silk suit, with an above-the-knee A-line skirt, short fitted jacket over an ivory silk shirt, navy hose, and plain court pumps. A black Hermès bag hung from her shoulder. A long pearl necklace played hide-and-seek along the mostly unbuttoned front of the shirt. She wore a bracelet of old gold coins.

Her hands were innocent of rings. She favored me with a direct look of amusement and challenge as she and Sturtevant sat down with the three of us.

"This is Lieutenant Walter Melnick and his daughter, Polly," I said. "Polly just graduated today. This is Senator Tom Sturtevant and—"

"And this is my sister, Mary Linscomb." Tom Sturtevant lit a cigarette. "Hello, Walter. Congratulations, Polly."

"Tom."

"A pleasure to meet you, senator."

"Your sister." I couldn't take my eyes off her.

"Half-sister, actually." He gave me a crooked smile. "Same father." And then, reprovingly: "She remembered *you*."

Mary Linscomb blushed.

"I can't think why. Have you stopped by the department today to check your mail?"

"What? No. Great speech." I was still looking at Mary Linscomb.

"Bullshit, great speech. Well, here." He took an envelope out of the breast pocket and held it out to me.

"What's this? You already know each other, obviously. You were expecting him, weren't you, Walter? How the hell did that happen?"

"Walter and I met some months ago," Sturtevant said.

A waitress took our orders.

"I expect that what Walter was doing was checking up on me. Am I right, Walter?"

"Of course. You were a suspect just like any a the rest. You said you had visitors out at the stable that morning. So I checked. Joe Chavez, that bingo crony a yours, he remembered the car and enough of that state official license plate for me to get a make on it. From then on it was easy."

Joe and his eidetic memory.

"So I called the senator, made an appointment, and paid a visit down the capitol." He smiled reminiscently.

"Amazing, really," said Tom to his sister, and including Polly with a civil nod. "Walter'd been with the NYPD Mounted Unit. We got to talking, about horses. He reached me just in time—"

Melnick nodded. "The senator was about to take off for two weeks in Ireland, that was what gave me the idea."

"Idea? What idea?"

"Just read the letter," Sturtevant advised me. They were all looking at me.

The waitress brought the drinks and I took a good slug out of mine.

The letter was written on AHSF letterhead and signed by the president, Carson Creswell. I scanned it. "Upon further evidence being received and examined, it is my distinct pleasure to inform you that, by unanimous motion of the Hearing Committee, you have been reinstated as a senior member of AHSF and are eligible to participate in AHSF-recognized competitions." At the foot of the letter, Carson had scrawled, "Congrats, Rusty, great see you again Devon and the Garden, lift a few. Get this way give a call lunch at club." Signed with a macho-cretinous captain-of-industry flourish in which the upper-case C was the only—barely—legible letter.

"The hell *is* this?"

"You see, the thing is, every fall I go over to hunt in Ireland," explained Sturtevant. "Papers've been on to it for years, very funny stuff, dressing up in a red coat and high-top boots chasing vermin over the bogs. Figure it's a very un-Texan thing to do, not manly sport like dynamiting fish, say, or putting out poison bait for coyotes."

"That was what gave me the idea," Walter said. "I figured as long's the senator was going over, he might look up that mick kid, that Jerry Fahey you had riding for you when you got set down moved back to Ireland."

"I didn't know anything about it until Walter told me. As a matter of fact, I never put you together with the Rusty Coulter used to ride hunters in the East. But because I'd just been informed that I'd been elected the new AHSF director from Texas, I thought I'd give it a shot, find out what I could. For the good of the sport."

It had been a long time since I'd heard those words.

"I finally found Fahey down in Tipperary, working for a race horse trainer near Cashel, mucking stalls. He looked like hell. When I got him talking after a few jars down the local after work, he got his tongue over the bit and admitted it'd been his idea to trank that horse in New York. Wanted to look good. Then, when the tests turned up positive, he got scared, decided to keep his mouth shut—and you got hung out to dry, twist slowly in the wind—"

Too tactful, I guessed, to comment more directly on the possibility of Serena's involvement, Tom shrugged. "When I got back and reported what I'd found to the AHSF, Creswell and the hearing committee reinstated you."

"I don't know what to say." I looked around. All of them were smiling broadly.

"You don't need to say anything, except maybe you could stand another drink. How about anyone else?" We gave our orders, Polly declining a second glass of white wine.

"That settled, Mrs Gordon's been telling me you've got a show coming up next weekend, and it strikes me there may be a class or two you might want to take that mare in, a good place to celebrate your reinstatement—"

"The Mare?"

"Yes, of course, the mare, the one you've been riding belongs those two bone doctors."

"Well I don't know if she's ready, I'd have to look at the premium list again."

Melnick made a rude noise.

I excused myself from the table. When I got back I told Melnick he'd been right. He smiled slightly and then he left the table.

Melnick was right, I did know. I knew The Mare was ready the same way I knew in my bones that the time had come to get Barrington off my back, in my mind's eye the sorry sonofabitch lounging around that sunlit quay in Calais sipping chocolate and laughing at his creditors and waiting for news from Ireland.

Mary and Polly were deep in conversation; they'd scarcely looked up when I'd returned.

"I take it you're going ahead with your plans to buy Gordonwood?"

Sturtevant nodded assent. "The papers are waiting for her to sign. Have you given any more thought to my offer?"

"Yes, I've thought about it a good deal. The first thing I wanted to make sure of was that K.C. came out right on the deal."

He gave me a faintly ironic grin. "Your concern does you credit. "Set your mind at rest, Mrs Gordon will be all right, no fancy pay-outs—unless she herself wants an exchange-of-property settlement plus cash to boot. And I've assured her that she's welcome to keep her own horses out there for the foreseeable future. On the side, I've also let her know that I'd see to it she got some help on her tax situation, not that it's a very serious one."

"She worries about it."

"Understood. What else is on your mind?"

"K.C.'s welfare is my first concern, and you've pretty well satisfied me on that score. But something else I need to get settled in my own mind before accepting your offer is if it will be possible for me to take a horse or two on for sales or training?"

"I don't have any problem with you taking on a couple of prospects for your own account, pro-rating expenses. Goes without saying, anything comes into the barn, I want right of first refusal. Your first loyalty's to me. What that means is that my horses get worked first, yours, if any, when convenient." He paused. "You're busy with The University and God knows I'm tied up down the legislature—so basically what it all boils down to is a question of goodwill."

I told him that sounded fair. Fair but tough, I amended privately: it did boil down to goodwill in the end.

Mary Linscomb turned away from her conversation with Polly Melnick, and laid a hand on her brother's arm. "Tom, I hate to interrupt." She favored us with a dazzling smile. "But if we're to get over to Bill's before the reception's over we really ought to be on our way."

She gave me a straight glance. "I look forward to seeing you next weekend, Stephen," she said. "Tom's promised to take me to the show."

"Rusty," I said. "Call me Rusty."

*   *   *   *

Melnick had settled the bill unobtrusively on his trip to the gents, and departed for the Omni with Polly, on foot; they'd been invited out to dinner by the family of one of her classmates.

Mary and I stood on the sidewalk outside the Chili Parlor while Tom went round the corner for the car.

"I thought."

"Yes," Mary said. "I can imagine. My brother's good at letting people imagine things." She smiled. "You'll need to watch him. He can be tricky."

"The schoolboy suit and frayed ties, you mean?"

"That and—did that nice policeman end up paying for the drinks? Never mind."

"Are you...? I know it's none of my business—"

"No," she said giving me a frank, level stare. "It isn't yet, anyway. But the answer is no. I'm not married. Was once."

"I too. Am still, in a way: we've been separated for years."

"I can imagine that too."

There was a pause.

"No significant other?"

"Absolutely no entanglements..."

Tom had pulled up and was holding the door open.

"Good bye."

"See you next weekend."

"At the show. Yes. The eclipsed knight returns to the lists." She kissed me on the cheek. I helped her into the car and shut the door, and then I was standing alone in the street.

*   *   *   *

Back in the apartment, I stared at the pile of Barrington manuscript. For the life of me I couldn't begin to fathom why I had devoted such a great amount of time to such a marginal figure—except that, of course, thinking about it with a stiff drink in my fist, I admitted to myself that perhaps it was because Barrington *was* marginal, and had therefore little written about him, that my heart had gone out to him. No better reason than that. No scholarly reason at all.

I had several more stiff drinks. Then several more, one right after the other. Then I lost count, and after a while it didn't matter. The ice cubes didn't matter, the mixer didn't matter, and finally drinking out of a glass didn't matter. Nothing mattered, except preserving what remained of the precious warmth I'd taken away with me from the festive conviviality of the Chili Parlor. But that warmth was fast fading in the presence of the ambient chill I seemed to carry with me in my bones, my heart. Mad fellow out on the headland, bellowing other men's words into the wind, no thoughts, no feelings of his own. I knew on some very elemental level that it wasn't just my disappointment with Barrington that caused me to drink. The truth was that the impulse to drink to oblivion struck me without evident rhyme or reason, at any time.

Perhaps it was the bittersweetness of the end of the semester and the sundering of relationships established over sixteen weeks. Perhaps it was the ache of physical frustration I could no longer ignore. Perhaps it was the isolation and affectlessness of one left always on the shore.

A genuine display of affection, Melody's impulsive, innocent embrace had provided a leaping spark surging for connection. I could still feel against me the searing imprint of her vibrant body clinging to mine, her small breasts flattening against my chest, her pelvis grinding momentarily against my groin. Emotionally I was dry charged tinder primed for the flame. My natural instinctive response had been abandoned automatically, but with a natural reluctance. To indulge my inclination would be, first of all (and quite literally) criminal behavior; it was also expressly forbidden, an obvious abuse of trust, of authority. I had drawn back from that which I wanted—lusted after—promising myself—what?—that the old words, what I taught in class—what I told myself I believed in—had bedrock value. That had all been decided one winter on the Jersey Shore.

Perhaps it was just that I was facing another lonely Christmas in Texas drinking too much and working in desultory bursts on preparing lesson plans for a spring semester that seemed to stretch away in infinity.

But now I reminded myself that there would be horses to ride in the winter sunshine, and the possibility of a straightforward relationship with no entanglements, no commitments. Honest. Mary and I would be using each other, true enough, but answering needs—hurting no one but perhaps ourselves—and what was the harm in that?

Yes, I felt lonely, but I mean so what?

CHAPTER 27

▼

I slept a good part of Sunday and barely managed to get out to ride in the afternoon. It was still raining off and on, and the footing was too slick to jump. Monday I pushed myself to finish grading finals. Monday night I turned my attention to the sizable, still unread stack of term papers, some of which hadn't been turned in until the day of the examination. Tuesday I got around to the tedious task of weighting the various requirements for the course as set out in my policy statements—it seemed an age at least since that Labor Day night when I'd drafted those!—and tempering justice with mercy (recalling less than creditable parts of my own undergraduate years) assigned final grades. Late Tuesday night I went out and bought a string of little red jalapeno pepper lights and a tiny Christmas tree. After I set them up, I made a gift list. The apartment complex and the streets near The University were all but deserted; most people had gone home for the holidays.

Wednesday morning I stopped by the office to turn in final grades. Afterward I went by the mail room, where Huw was puffing cheerfully on a cigar, and going through letters and packages that hadn't been sorted.

"Hello, Stephen," he said. "Season's greetings."

"Merry Christmas to you, too, Huw." We both laughed. In my box were a couple of Christmas cards, two computerized spring semester renewal notices for books I'd checked out in the fall, various university notices dealing with holiday work schedules, an invitation to a Commonwealth Studies party, and two missing term papers from students for whom I'd just finished turning in failing grades.

"Amanda's off today, and I thought I'd see what came in…" Huw's voice trailed off. "God *damn*. Will you look at this."

He held out a library faculty book renewal notice, computer-addressed to Professor S. Roylett, Department of English.

"Take the staple out, open it up."

The notice was similar to the ones I'd received, and asked politely if Professor Roylett wished to renew the book originally checked out to him in March, renewed in May, and again in August, for the upcoming spring semester. If so, would he please mark the appropriate boxes and return to the library. The book in question was identified as *The Winchester Malory*, published by the Early English Text Society.

"Fuck me blind," breathed Huw reverently. "What the hell did Roylett want with Malory?"

"Sheer meanness, I expect," I said. "It's too late to do anything now."

"You're right. But another thing." Giving me a flash of those terrible white teeth. "About that business with Oscar Wilde—"

I looked blank.

"What I said to you, leaving here on the way to the police station."

"Yes?"

"Easy enough to tell, looking at you, you had an acquaintance with wild regrets and bloody sweats—but that's not exactly uncommon with the goliard lecturers, am I right?"

"Oh, right."

"But the part had my knickers in a twist was the part that you finished off—"

"'For he who lives more lives than one,/More deaths than one must die'?"

:"That's the very one. You said that to me the first day, finished off the tag. I was wrong. You weren't...*aren't*...that way, and I need to apologize—"

"Huw, for Christ's sake. None needed. Really."

"No, I do," he said doggedly. "It seemed to me that you were a cannon about to go off in some weird direction. Never really fitting into things, possibly pursuing some private agenda, don't you know? But no. Now you've seeped into the fabric of things—"

"Well, thanks."

"Another thing. Saturday in the robing room you were practically falling over your ears there when I was talking with Joan."

"And Carlotta," I said.

"Yes, and Carlotta. I expect it seemed a bit..."

"No, no, not at all."

"Bizarre. But the truth is—"

"The truth is, I suspect, Huw—incidentally I read and thoroughly enjoyed that long poem of yours—that you really are deeply in love with Mrs du Plessis Roylett, and she with you. I wish you well. The rest—Joan—will all fall into place."

I was shocked to see that Huw's eyes were moist with deep feeling.

*   *   *   *

It was a winy clear afternoon, crisp and cool. The tackroom had a cheerful, bustling, holiday atmosphere. People were scurrying about with bits of sponge and saddle soap. Carols on the radio. Soft drinks, a cooler full of white wine and beer. Hot cider in a thermos flask brought by Joan. Cake and somebody'd put up a Christmas tree. There was the usual last-minute rush to get off, turning the tackroom upside down in a frantic effort to find the least disreputable halters and lead shanks, and something to use for a mounting block. I laid the presents for Joe and K.C. and Joan at the foot of the tree.

"How'd she go?"

"Just swell." In fact especially taking into account that she hadn't had much real work in the last week, she'd gone splendidly.

"Saw you out there with a tape measure wrestling around with those jumps."

"*Always* got a tape measure."

"When're you taking them over?"

"Friday as early as I can get off."

"K.C. gave us a school yesterday."

"Going to braid?"

"Of course I'm going to braid.".

"I'm so happy you decided to ride, Stephen"—the ins-and-outs of why exactly I hadn't been competing in shows escaped K.C.—"but are you sure you're going to have enough time to help me with the children?"

*   *   *   *

By seven-thirty everybody had left. I fixed a cup of instant coffee and thought over what I needed to do. The Coggins tests were on K.C.'s desk and I stuck them in the envelope I took to the shows, along with a package of safety pins and assorted hairnets I'd picked up earlier: there was always a screaming need for these when the kids' classes got started. Then I inspected the oil level, batteries, and brake fluid in K.C.'s pickup, started it up, hooked it up to the six-horse, and checked the transmission fluid level, the braking system, the clearance and brake lights, and the turn signals, and drove to an all-night filling station out on the highway where I filled up both tanks and cleaned the windshield.

Back at the stable I went over what Joe and I had already packed and dragged out what we'd need to load in the morning. Then I parked the truck and trailer in a good place to load from, where the morning sun would illuminate the interior of the trailer, and lowered the ramps.

Afterwards I filled the haynets and went home, rustled up a sandwich, threw some clothes in a suitcase, and grabbed a few hours' sleep.

Friday passed in a predictable blur. I fed just as the sun was coming up red, and I'd started to knock the worst off the skins we were taking to the show; dandy brushes and rub rags could wait until the afternoon: the horses were going to get dusty traveling, anyway. Afterward I ran on the cottons and shipping bandages and the odd tail wrap for the ones who liked to sit back during a trip.

They loaded with no problem. The trip out in the country east to the state park where the exposition center was located took just under an hour. The complex was sited on high ground and had stabling for, I guessed, more than five hundred horses, two dressage rings, two warm-up rings, a novice ring, and the main ring in the coliseum itself. It was obviously a popular venue for horse shows: vast manure piles from recent events loomed in the rear of the property down near the winding creek bottom separating the grounds from the state park and highway beyond.

I checked in at the secretary's office and received our numbers and stall assignments. In observance of the season, the show's organizers had gone to a lot of trouble to decorate the premises. Somebody must've talked a couple of big nurseries into donating shrubs and plants to fill out around the in- and out-gates and in front of the judge's stands. The rings themselves were draped lavishly with yards of red and green fabric swagged at intervals with huge tartan bows and clusters of pine cones. It even smelled like Christmas; the air was redolent of pine and spruce. Trucks with unsold Douglas firs were offloading to use as filler in the newly painted jumps. Holiday songs blared over the public address system. Altogether, it made for a cheerful, festive sight, and brought home to me the realization of just how long it had been since I'd really felt a part of something that had meant so much to me.

Unsurprisingly, because we were a small stable, we had been assigned stalls in the farthest barn. Unsurprisingly, because The Mare had been a late entry, we were using what had been our junk stall as a stall for her. Even though K.C. showed up around noon, bringing sandwiches and coffee and moral support, it took me until the middle of the afternoon to finish unloading the trailer, hanging haynets and buckets, and settling the horses in their stalls. For a while I entertained the hope that it would be possible to work The Mare before the hordes of Genghis Khan descended after school, but it was not to be.

Heralded by high-pitched chatter, the children appeared *en masse*, just as I was putting the finishing touches on our tackroom, and I quickly revised my schedule. Very probably I wouldn't have a chance to ride until after they were gone that evening, if the rings were even open for schooling then. More probably I'd have to make a push to pop over a few fences very early in the morning before the show got underway. I never liked that last-minute business much: if something went wrong it usually stayed wrong all day long, whereas if there was a problem when you schooled the afternoon before, both rider and horse had a chance to regroup mentally before going in the ring to be judged.

K.C. and I helped the children groom, saddle up, and get on their horses. Checking that they hadn't forgotten their hard hats, we walked up with them to the mêlée of the warm-up ring. After they'd had a chance to walk, trot, and canter both ways of the ring—I resolutely turned a blind eye to whether they stumbled into the correct lead or not: there was no sense in tempting fate—we took them over to the novice and limit ring where a low course of jumps had been set up and a rough kind of follow-the-leader rota was in effect, with what amounted to an instructor or two standing by each fence. This was where a lot could go wrong; timid riders or horses could easily get hurt and lose their confidence for an entire show. Good pros tended to be very careful not only with their own kids, but kept a weather eye out for those belonging to others as well. A really good riding master of the old school taught a hell of a lot more than how to post at the trot: he or she taught good manners and decency to others. Unfortunately there weren't that many good pros around, or coming up through the ranks.

Bare civility let alone common courtesy was on the decline in the show world as everywhere. The macho pro with something to prove, and the odd bumptious parent—never a good idea, that, schooling one's own kids!—could pose a real menace by tying up a jump or letting one kid cut in front of another coming into a fence or just by being generally bloody-minded.

Our kids and riders got through their school reasonably well. I only saw one cold-jawed runaway (Honor Student, with one of the Stallings twins), three or four runouts or refusals, and only a bare dozen or so knockdowns, necessitating some fast footwork to get the fences back up before the next kid came banging down the line. Now, so far as form was concerned, either kids' or horses', that was another story…

By the time that the horses were done off, tack cleaned and put away, and I'd finished sweeping the aisleway, everybody'd left, and my watch said it was after seven. Schooling hours were over, the ring crew had removed the jumps from the rings, and all the lights had been lowered. I consoled myself with the fact that if I wasn't going to have a chance to get on The Mare, at least I wouldn't be running the risk of getting her banged up in the mêlée I'd observed that afternoon.

The peacefulness of the huge barn was punctuated by fitful stamping and the occasional snort and tiny explosions as horses broke wind. In the distance I could hear a vague clatter from the direction of the concession stand, and salsa blaring from a tack room radio. Exhibitors had gone home or out to an early dinner, wanting to get a good night's sleep. The auto parts store where Joe worked didn't shut until seven on Fridays. If he stopped by his house to change clothes and get some dinner before driving out to the show grounds, he wouldn't be likely to arrive much before nine or nine-thirty. The braiders, those mysterious nocturnal creatures, weren't likely to put in an appearance for several hours after that.

I pushed the large double barn doors ajar and went outside for a cigarette.

The wind had started blowing in from the north. By the weak light of a sickle moon, I could see dark cloud wrack scudding across the sky. The temperature was dropping fast. I went back inside, making sure to close the big doors behind me.

If I couldn't ride The Mare, I told myself as I picked up a halter shank and went along to her stall, I could at least walk her around to get used to the place and stretch out a few kinks. By the time I put her back in her stall a half-hour later, after having led her up and down the deserted aisleways and over to the rings, I could feel the cold biting through my barn jacket. Blanket time.

Before ransacking the tack trunks, I paused to run my eye down our stalls.

Nobody'd be likely to confuse us with Bobby's Hickory Creek, much less one of the well-known show barns in the East, like Cismont Manor or Hunterdon, but I nevertheless felt a surge of quiet pride in contemplating the neat and workmanlike appearance of our stalls. Bandages and cottons had been rolled and put away, the aisleway was swept bone clean, the hose was coiled and hung on a bracket, and the stall signs were lined up like wine glasses at a formal dinner.

For all the world reminding me of a veteran repertory troupe called up from resting to take a new play on a tour of the provinces, the Gordonwood horses had decided to make the best of things. They actually looked presentable, reveling in the rare luxury of standing ankle deep in fresh shavings, snatching bites of coastal from the filled, slung nets, waiting impatiently for their evening feed. They'd been groomed to a fare-thee-well, and the trouble I'd taken clipping their bridle paths and muzzles gave their heads some real distinction. Even after the pandemonium of the afternoon's schooling, they appeared cheerful at the prospect of spending most of the next two days hauling little kids around a multitude of low courses.

I snorted. Romantic bullshit.

I peered at Murray a bit more closely. He was shifting his weight from foot to foot, like a man whose shoes are uncomfortable. While I watched he swung his head back to nip at his flank, as if something had pricked or stung him. Signs of intestinal trouble? Perhaps. On the other hand, maybe he *had* been bitten by something. I couldn't detect any localized swelling, but on the other hand there weren't any droppings in his stall, either. If it was a stomach problem, it was still a long way from a full-blown attack of colic. I decided to fix him a bran mash to see if it wouldn't ease things a bit; if he didn't improve I'd leave word for the show vet.

I set a half-full bucket of water out in the middle of the aisleway. At the bottom of a grooming box I found a stick heater and extension cord. I plugged the heater into one end of the extension cord, stood the heater up in the bucket, and inserted the other end of the cord into a hot flanged wall receptacle.

Then I picked up another bucket, turned up the collar of my canvas coat, and went outside.

The wind was raw and cutting as I trudged down the long dark hill to the trailer where I'd left the bran and other items which under ordinary circumstances would have been stored in the junk stall now occupied by The Mare.

There they were as I went around the end of the trailer: two men, one kneeling next to one of the trailer tires, working something shiny with his hands; the other, standing, with his mouth open in a wide "O" of surprise at my unexpected appearance, the slim beam from the flashlight he held jerking up to my face. I started toward them, and that was the last thing I remember except a feral smell of musk. There were three of them, and the third had come up silently behind me.

Light as gossamer his hands clamped down momentarily on my carotid arteries and I immediately felt light-headed, and then dizzy and buckled at the knees.

Then his hands commenced a wicked cruel dance. Steel-talon fingers probed deep into my right trapezius, right at the juncture of neck and shoulder, paused, shifted, then unhesitatingly pierced needle-like into the deltoid and triceps muscles in my upper arms, lingered, and hooked confidently into the upper lateral cutaneous and median nerves. Explosions of white and yellow seared my eyeballs. My whole upper body was now in helpless agony, vulnerable to his assault, while his fingers rioted self-assuredly among the carpal bones and ligaments in my wrists. Pain blossomed, searing through muscle, cartilage, and into the very center of my joints. I could not move and still the cruel dance continued.

Then darkness, blessed darkness.

CHAPTER 28

▼

When I came to, Melnick was kneeling over me, silhouetted against
the sky. My head was stuffed full of crisped short-circuited wiring.
Once in a while there'd be a hallucinatory burst of pure ozone.

"Rusty," Walter's voice was pleading, "are you all right?"

"I can't…seem to…move." I tried to laugh.

"Just take it easy for a minute."

"No problem…doing that." The cloud wrack was clearing. I could
see the Milky Way coming out of Melnick's ears. "Did you catch a
look at them?"

I hesitated. "Never seen them…before."

"Figures." And he swore a great oath.

"How long…have I been here?"

"Five minutes maybe. You still weren't down, that one hadn't finished with you. They must've seen my flashlight. Ran." He pointed the
beam of his flashlight down the hill to where the wooded creek bottom
meandered between the fields out to a culvert and overpass on the
highway. "I tried to follow them. I couldn't catch them. Did hear,
what, sound of one a those big motorcycles…"

"Hogs, fat boys, probably on their way to Montana by now—"
Something I recalled from my trip to Bobby's back in September: tall,
thin, helmeted figure.

"What were there, three of them?"

"Yes, I think so. I'd just come down to fetch some bran—" Suddenly I remembered the stick heater in the aisleway. "Walter, I left—"

"The bucket heating up? Relax, I pulled the plug. That's how I knew you'd be down here. Bran mash, right?"

"Bran mash. Murray looked like he might be getting…a bit colicky."

"Fuck Murray," said Melnick. "At least for right now. You just take it easy."

I laid back and tried to not to think what had been done to me.

"I'd just come around…the back of the trailer. There were two of them, crouching there near the wheels. The third—" That smell of rotting musk, cheap gigolo cologne from singles bars. "The third came up behind me."

"And you don't…"

"No, not a thing." I was very definite and if Melnick heard anything disingenuous in my voice he was too much of a gentleman to show his doubts.

"You just stay there a minute, I'll take a look at the trailer." He wadded up his jacket and placed it carefully under my head. Then he got to his feet, momentarily blocked out the starry sky, and disappeared from view.

A few minutes later he was back. "Mischief, looks like. Bled the brake lines, took off a bunch a lug nuts. No attempt to hide anything, fluid's leaked all over. Pain in the ass, but that's all." He dusted his hands. "Think you can get up?"

"Give it a try, you give me a hand."

With Melnick shouldering my weight I tried to get up off the ground. My legs seemed relatively undamaged save for a place on one thigh where I'd been kicked hard, but my torso and arms were useless. My head felt propped up on an armature of burnt-out wires, my eyes melted in their sockets like weirdly runny pearls.

"Jesus, Rusty, what the hell did that guy do to you?"

"I...don't know," I told him between gritted teeth. But I did. That dance of hands, swift as lightning. Steely probing fingers. Intimately knowledgeable, almost...affectionate.

I closed my eyes against the waves of pain as Melnick tried to drape my arm over him and then I was retching into the grass, leaning over against the pressure of his arm. I hoped it didn't get on his shoes.

"Rest a minute."

"I'm okay."

"Sure you are."

I rested, utterly drained of strength, my entire upper body a battlefield of outraged tissue.

"We need to get you back to the barn," Melnick said, taking hold of my right arm again, once more setting off a pyrotechnical display all the way from my shoulder joint down through my strained hands and fingers.

"Jesus, Walter, I don't know. I don't think..."

"You'll be all right. We'll just take it slow."

We took it slow, a walk I'd never forget.

A figure stood in the light streaming down from the barn's open door. It was Joe Chavez and when he recognized me he ran to help Melnick. The two of them carried me up the hill to the barn, depositing me gently in one of the directors' chairs outside the tack room. I slumped back, my body a shrieking mass of pain.

Melnick looked at me carefully. "You're sure you didn't—"

I shook my head feebly, no. I figured I owed Beddington one for sucker-punching him at Rhonda's place. Happy Trails, amigo!

"What a piece a work," Melnick said, not totally without admiration. "Fucking John Wayne, you are."

"'Man's gotta do...'"

"Yeah, yeah, I saw that one, too." He hesitated. "Nerve damage, reminds me of that Icelandic spear-chucker. Same sort of deal."

I swiveled my eyes agonizingly toward Joe. "Murray," I said. "Bran mash. The water ought to be hot."

Joe went down the aisleway.

"Tough guy. You think you'll be able to ride?"

"Sure."

He looked at me skeptically. "I saw that stick heater in the bucket bubbling away and the buckets set out with the bran and I knew you couldn't be far away. No bran in the tack room, I figured I'd take a look where the trailer was parked. I'll go out and see if that concession stand guy's still there, got any aspirin." He looked at me closely. "You want me to run you in to the hospital?"

I shook my head again and wished I hadn't. "See if there's a vet on the grounds, take a look at Murray, maybe score me some bute. Too damn long, drive in to cooler. Get cold, stiffen up. Awkward, anyway: questions."

Melnick went on his way as soon as Joe got back from feeding the horses and giving Murray his long-postponed bran mash. The two of us sat there, oddly peaceful. After a while Joe asked if he ought to blanket the horses and I said yes, please.

"Got it," Melnick said, reappearing with a huge white 1000-milligram tablet of Butazolidin. In his other hand he was carrying a styrofoam cup of water which he put down on a tack trunk. He placed the pill on the tack trunk and split it with the blade of his pocketknife. Then he chopped a half into very small pieces. "Here, swallow this," he ordered, feeding me bits of pill interspersed with driblets of water. "Does you any good, take the other half tonight." He chuckled. "Told the vet I had a horse fell through a fence, talked him out a this. Said he'd be over to take a look at Murray soon's he gets through with another colic he's working on."

I finally got the bute down; it was like trying to swallow rocks.

"How you doing?"

"Fine," I said. "Just great."

I still couldn't move my arms and every time I tried to change position and find a less agonizing place to slump, shards of rusty steel pierced my joints. "See if you can find a shovel around here some place."

Melnick looked at me quizzically, then went back to find a shovel, one of those big aluminum muck scoops. "Smaller one, too," I told him. "And ask Joe what we did with that old rain sheet we packed."

"Rain sheet?"

"And bring a chair, one of those folding kind."

"You give a lot a orders, guy's practically a vegetable."

"One more thing. You see one of those braiders, tell them I need to get The Mare braided for the stake—you can get the money out of my wallet."

"You are too fucking much, you are, you know that?"

Then he went on his way, returning after a while with Joe, the rubber rain sheet, the extra shovel, and a metal chair he'd rustled up from somewhere.

"Wrap the rain sheet around me," I instructed them. "Then pick up the chair, carry me outside."

"Outside?" Melnick was aghast. "It's fucking freezing out there."

"Yeah, I fucking know," I said, too tired to explain what I had in mind.

"You got a plan?" Melnick asked. "You know where we're going?"

"Down back. All the way in the back."

They started carrying me, setting the chair down every hundred feet or so. It was a long haul but they were very gentle and they never complained.

"There," I said weakly. "Dig there."

In front of us was one of those vast manure piles I'd spotted driving in.

Melnick shrugged and then he and Joe started digging. After a while we could see steam rising in the cold air from the pit they'd dug. "Keep digging. Make it big enough for the chair and cover me up to the chin. And put something on my head."

Melnick started giggling uncontrollably and after a while Joe favored us with his Indian smile. But they kept on digging.

*   *   *   *

"Up to my neck in shit."
"Yes. But you have the soldier's eye."
"If I may say so, sir, *you* have the soldier's eye," I told Melnick.
"No game for knights."
"No game for knights, indeed."
"Very nice," Walter said. "A little Chandler to begin with. General Sternwood steeped in horse manure. But now let's skip the preliminaries: how did you know, really know, it was Vere?"

*   *   *   *

It was late by then. Melnick had given Joe the keys to his car and Joe had come back with a couple of chairs and the car and reported that the vet was looking at Murray. He'd built a little fire in a feed tub which he fed with dead wood he'd gathered from along the creek bottom. Before he'd gone back to the tack room to catch a few hours sleep, he left a pile of brush to replenish the fire with.

Melnick had draped a blanket over his shoulders and was pouring himself a stiff drink from a bottle of Black Jack he'd rummaged out of the trunk.

"How hot you reckon it is in there?"

I shrugged and although the pain lanced through my shoulders and arms I thought perhaps it wasn't quite so bad as it had been. And my thinking was clearer and I was able to talk. I turned down the offer of a slug of bourbon much as the occasion invited it; the one thing I liked better than booze was horses and I'd never showed tight. Melnick placed a cigarette between my lips from time to time—when I had smoked it down I'd spit it out, and smoldering stubs littered the dung piled up around me—and fixed up a cup and straw I could sip hot coffee from. "I dunno."

"Where the hell you get that idea, anyway?"

"Old-timey," I said. "Very old-fashioned idea. Jockeys used to make their weight like this a hundred years ago."

"Jesus, they must've been a sweet-smelling lot. *You're* going to be smelling sweet, too…"

*   *   *   *

"You're asking me how I knew it was Vere? By process of elimination, mostly. They *all* had motive, means, opportunity and, as it turned out, the capability of committing murder. Even Vere had motive, as I learnt from Amanda Vennible: he'd been victimized for years by Roylett. But for the life of me I couldn't see him having the capability of actually bludgeoning somebody to death.

"As it turned out, though, the only one who had actually done somebody in, in hot blood, was good old Ed Vere.

"It all began to come into focus when I went to Roylett's memorial service and Mrs Vere spilt out the contents of her purse and began chattering at me. Usually you see someone *or* you hear them—I'm not much good at putting the two together—but this time in some curious way what she was saying meshed with what I was seeing…"

"I don't get it."

"Well, there she was, somehow animated and eyes…shining. Which for someone as ill as she was said to be, was a bit odd. That is, till her purse spilt. There were dozens of pill bottles in that purse, Walter, including, I saw, some high-grade tranquilizers and sleeping remedies. Stuff everybody knows about: Valium, Equanil, Halcion…

"At the same time as we were scrabbling around on the floor for the contents of her purse she was prattling on about how everyone always remembers where he was the day Kennedy was assassinated—or used to, at least—and how she wondered what she was doing when Sebastian Roylett was killed. 'There he was being killed,' she told me, while she was getting herself organized. Among other things, she said she was doing that morning, such as making tea and watching a television preacher, she brought in the paper.

"Seeing those pills and hearing about how she brought the paper in struck a chord with me. I recalled that on the morning of the murder I'd dropped by a convenience store to pick up a paper after jogging and there was a man there complaining that the newspapers don't make home delivery until six. It's true. There weren't any on my run. But if Vere was indeed the creature of habit everybody said he was, and he was off as was his wont to eight o'clock mass, he'd have had plenty of time to bring in the paper before he left home to go to church. How easy it would have been, my dirty little mind was wondering, for Vere to double up his wife's medications the night before along with the cocoa—thinking sleeping pills here, or tranquilizers—take your pick, plenty of both in that purse—then get up an hour earlier, put the clocks back an hour, and leave the house not at seven but a bit before six—clocks saying seven—but early enough so that the paper hadn't yet been delivered. The poor old gal'd give him a cast-iron alibi: he'd gone to eight o'clock service at St Michael's—where he'd been seen—and then, after church, he'd walked over to see Huw at the English department. Then home and some clever footwork when she napped to set the clocks forward to the correct time—my dear the afternoon went so quickly—hoping to Christ she wasn't watching some television show she knew what time it came on. Well, they say everything has its risks.

"But if he'd left an hour earlier, why then he'd have been able to have gotten over to MacFarland Hall and waited for Roylett—whom he knew to have an early morning appointment with Huw Rhys-Davies. Then slip over to St Michael's, then back again to see Huw."

"Vere's being able to be placed on the scene to kill Roylett didn't really put me a whole lot further in the picture, because *everybody* had an opportunity to do him in: Carlotta and Joan by, as it turned out, both coming back home early on separate flights, Melody and Fishbach's absences from their house, Huw's unsupported papergrading after his rugby bash...

"Same held true for capability: little by little, we learned that each of the people could physically have done him in; that is, all but Vere, which was not in itself enough to make me suspicious of him. In addition, until Amanda spilled her guts over Roylett's treatment of Vere, I'd had no real idea that he even had a motive.

"But something Vere said had been nagging away at me since Monday morning. I almost started to tell you about it, but then it seemed so stupid, really. I was in the duplicating room when, quite unusually for him, I thought, Ed flared out at two assistant profs in the department who were nattering on about some champagne they'd had the night before at a wine-tasting and Vere called it horse piss and praised some bubbly I'd never heard of by the name of Salon le Mesnil. Odd name. When I went by the library the other day to check on Huw's poetry and look into the Malory facsimile, I slipped down to the map room, and looked the place up: there it was, in the champagne country between Epernay and Vertus, south of Rheims, north of Troyes. Very specific, very small. And I might add, very expensive. Betokening a knowledge of that particular area that Vere would have had. And it happened, I suddenly recalled, to have been the same kind of wine my father'd sent me when my wife and I had married. Ironic.

"All very interesting but not making a lot of sense to me until I went to a talk at Commonwealth Studies the other day on the history of the British Special Operations Executive—the SOE—in World War II and the speaker got queried about declassifying information and used as an example the story of a young American whose history, really, bore remarkable resemblances to what I'd figured out about Vere's own war record: father American, mother English, travel in France in 1939, and so on. I knew from reading his dossier that Vere'd received a degree from Oxford in 1942 and had served in the military.

"That it was the British military he'd served in and not the American I arrived at when I heard that he'd been unable to get a loan on his house a few years ago—if he'd really served in the American forces, he'd have been eligible for a VA loan—and nothing like that was ever mentioned."

"But *why?*"

"Why? Because…sight of the book probably helped him to make his mind up as well as gave him a weapon. Malory. It was very fitting.

"The motivation wasn't going to be something relatively simple and straightforward, like not getting tenure; or greed; or even, as in Huw's case, frustration at being kept in the dark about his future.

"The motivation was supplied by the collision of what Vere had been brought up to believe in and what he had acted upon and what he'd tried to be: decent, hardworking, traditional—and romantic: coming up against, what? A smug supercilious intellectuality, a self-satisfied tolerance for any views so long as they were your own? Opportunism, an easy kind of relativism…

"It was all, finally, too much for Vere and the sight of that book which he'd been trying to get his hands on for weeks, in Roylett's uncaring hands, the book coincidentally of a bad man who'd realized his failure from the ideals he believed in and yet had written one of the chief glories of the English language, *Le Morte Darthur*. In addition, he'd named his children Thomas Newbold—Malory'd lived at a place called Newbold Revel—and Jennifer whom he called Gwen—short for Guenevere—another pretty clear lead.

"My guess is that Vere turned to the expiatory stuff of Piers Plowman afterwards but always had that vagrant love for the sheer unabashed romanticism of Malory, Malory, who was, after all, hardheaded and a pragmatist, but who nevertheless tried to fit the romanticism he so passionately believed in, into the framework of his—to him—debased age. Malory proved in the event too much. Vere picked up the book and hit Roylett over the head with it.

"As the Kikuyu proverb went that Ruark used, don't screw around with somebody's system of beliefs unless you have something of value to replace it with.

"They met in the mailroom. And that's when Vere killed him. A true crime of passion. I don't suppose he'd even decided on a weapon. After all, this is a man who'd clubbed a man to death with a spade or grubhoe, and I expect he'd be prepared to do in Roylett with a rolled up copy of the *Chronicle of Higher Education*, or whatever. But there was Roylett and there was the book. We'll never know if Roylett came strolling in there fortuitously Malory in hand maybe having decided to hand it over. Now we'll never know. But bad luck if Vere had any second thoughts. Unlikely, I should think: the sight of that particular book was enough to, as they say, harden his resolve and that was that. Vere's strength was as the strength of ten, or twelve—and there was Roylett lying on the floor in his raw silk jacket with blood leaking out of his ears, and Vere on his way to early mass. And no, he didn't take communion.

"Odd deal. Roylett was, as it happened, only a heartbeat away from death in any case, what with the Sturge-Weber syndrome he suffered from…." I shrugged and we stared at the fire. After a while Melnick got up and broke off a few branches from the pile of brushwood Joe had left. He stuffed them in the bucket and the yellow flames crackled and seethed.

CHAPTER 29

▼

"You asked me one time about Devers."

"So I did."

"It was after I'd gotten back from Thailand. I'd been assigned to an élite unit, the First Special Warfare Training Battalion at Fort Bragg, for training in North Carolina. This was the summer of 1976, the Bicentennial year. A group of us got orders to take part in a big public relations hoo-haw in Massachusetts.

"Naturally, of course, now that the war was over, military funding was at an all-time low. Congress was axing the defense budget. Soldiers returning from the East were being spat on in airports. It was an election year. Washington decided that stunts such as this one were a way to refurbish the army's image.

"They dressed us up in these fancy Revolutionary War uniforms, knee breeches, wigs, muskets, fifes and drums, the whole thing. While you were probably chilling out with a gin-and-tonic catching the Tall Ships in New York harbor on t.v.—we were doing close-order drill all over New England.

"It turned out, naturally, to be a fucking disaster. We got trash thrown at us and shouted at...How are we doing for cigarettes?"

Melnick fixed me another smoke.

"You've heard the phrase, 'something snapped'? Well, something snapped. Drunk and disorderly, conduct unbecoming…and so on. Not to mention damage to private property, and a couple of personal injury lawsuits. The long and the short of it is that I just missed getting court-martialed…They sent me to Walter Reed and then on convalescent leave near Hot Springs.

"My mother died just about then. That made it easy to let me out of the service."

"I see. That makes things a bit clearer."

"Sorry?"

"Never mind," said Melnick. "Here, let me get some more coffee, see if they got any cigarettes."

"Non-filter." Very gingerly I tried to shrug my shoulders.

"Sure."

The generalized agony was subsiding slightly. Feeling and with it excruciating pain were centering in the joints in my shoulders, arms, wrists, and fingers, and in the muscles in my neck and across my back. The one place on my thigh throbbed insistently.

*   *   *   *

A few minutes shy of midnight, a tall middleaged man stepped into the small circle of firelight. He wore his thinning hair long, and his gray beard came halfway down his chest. He was wearing jeans that had seen better days, runover boots, and a beat up Carhartt coat over an expensive checked flannel shirt. His gray eyes were very clear.

Melnick got to his feet. "Hey, doc, good to see you. Rusty, this is Dr Eliot. Dr Eliot, Rusty Coulter.

The man nodded at me. "Tim Eliot."

"How about a drink, drive off the chill?" Melnick held out the bottle.

"Don't mind if I do." He passed a hand over his face, then took a long drink from the bottle. "Long day." He handed the bottle back and turned his attention to what was showing of me above the muck heap. "I guess this is the horse you were telling me about fell through a fence."

Melnick nodded. "Yeah."

"Well, well," he murmured. "Can't say I recall ever seeing anything like this before." He fished out of a jacket pocket a thermometer attached to a long piece of twine. "You mind?" He burrowed into the loose manure by my side and buried the thermometer deep in the pile, paying out the twine so the loose end lay visible on the surface.

He pulled out an old silver hunting-case watch, checked it, and sipped absent-mindedly at his drink.

"Who knows, could be an article for me in here somewhere. Whole new approach. New Age stuff, holistics. Very big these days."

"Dr Eliot's the show vet," Melnick said.

"Oh, really?" I tried to summon up interest.

"And also the vet for Hickory Creek."

Dr Eliot's lucent gray eyes suddenly locked on mine. "*Was* the vet. You know Bobby Robberson?"

Yes, I said, I knew Bobby. Why "was"?

He smiled. "Don't mind doing a favor for a friend when I can, now and then. You know what I mean? Man comes to me, I'm working, busy, he tells me he's got a horse…got hurt, have I got something? Seems like a good sort, responsible, you know, I might just part with the odd…anti-inflammatory…pill. Shoot, they got too many damn laws these days, anyway. It's got so a man can't even fight chickens legal, anymore, you know that? What's the world coming to?

"But getting back to 'was.' Hickory Creek, that Bobby Robberson, he's gotten I guess you could say a little exotic. Sophisticated, anyway. In his demands. And I thank you two gentlemen, it's been a pleasure. Hope you get to feeling better. Oh, your old horse I looked at seems fine, ought to be okay to show this morning. A little gas was all. Let's see what this thing says."

He dropped to his heels and pulled up the string til he held the thermometer in his hands. He turned it carefully to the light, and whistled. "Well," he said, "you couldn't exactly boil coffee with what that temperature is down there, but it's better than half way."

*   *   *   *

"No breach of professional ethics there."

"No, that's right, but it sure sounded like Bobby's been after him to bend a few rules here and there."

"Unsurprising."

"You still can't remember who it might a been?"

"No. I can't remember a thing."

*   *   *   *

"We had this guy with the mounted unit you would have liked, Gino Martini, a guinea from Queens. You know you got to serve X years on patrol, hold the rank of detective before they let you join the troop?"

"No kidding."

"Yeah. Anyway, something about his name. Why not Giovanni Martini, I said to him once. That'd be John Martin in American. You know what he said?"

"No, Walter, what did he say?"

"He looked me straight in the eye and he said, 'Bring pacs, be quick.'"

"What's that suppose' to mean?"

"'Bring pacs, be quick.' You don't know what that means? That's the last words came back from Custer. Sent by a trumpeter, Giovanni Martini, John Martin, depends which source you read."

"Very interesting."

"Point is, that Gino, he knew about the Custer story."

"So?"

"That's why I'm here, Rusty. Goddamn, I'm tired a people who got no sense a history." He paused. "Anyway, I always wondered what happened to John Martin, Giovanni Martini, whatever. He got back alive, ended up his days in the Big Apple, what, probably down on Mott Street somewhere, big Italian section."

"And?"

"And so did Custer's wife. She lived on Fifth Avenue. She didn't die till the early thirties. You reckon they ever met?"

"Enough, General Sternwood, enough. What happened to your guinea friend, the historian?"

"Gino? Got shot, retired upstate. Eight-year-old girl with a zip gun, do you every time."

*　　*　　*　　*

Dawn came with clouds of dirty pewter. Joe and Melnick assisted me out of the muck heap. Even though I was creaky as an old man, I could feel that the overnight heat treatment had done some good, or the bute had, one, or probably both. My legs, except for that one place on my thigh, seemed okay, but above the waist I was still hurting. The pain had now localized in my neck, shoulders, and wrists. I stripped down in the tack room and toweled off clean as best I could. Walter brought me some clean clothes from the suitcase I'd packed. Then I borrowed a razor and soap from Joe and made a feeble attempt to shave. I finally settled for bracing my upper arm against my body and, without bending my neck, trying to get my face in range of the razor.

As soon as the concession stand opened for breakfast Walter went up to grab the three of us a couple of tacos and coffee. No sooner had he gotten there, he told us later, than he was treated to the sight of Bobby bursting out of the secretary's office, cursing blue murder at the top of his lungs. "'Sonofabitch,' he was yelling," Walter said, laughing at the memory. "'Why'nt somebody *do* something, for Christ's sake?

Where the hell's the fucking security, anyway?' At that point the secretary came out of his office and told Bobby to watch his language, he'd have him thrown off the grounds. Rich, that was. He went back inside, somebody asked him, 'What's the problem, Bobby?' 'Problem, I'll tell you what the fucking problem is—" he's speaking a little quieter now—"three of those lowlife scumbags I got working for me ran off last night.' 'You want me to call the sheriff?' the other guy asks. 'What did they leave with?' And Bobby tells him, 'The bastards didn't leave *with* anything, they left *without*—without feeding, watering, mucking out or grooming.'" At which point Bobby gave a highly-colored description of the three, one of whom could well have been the ubiquitous Beddington. "When I left he was holding out a fifty-dollar bill trying to get someone to pitch in and help him."

"Couldn't happen to a nicer guy."

"'Goes around, comes around."

"Slick, though, you've got to admit that. Washed his hands of them."

"Indeed he did."

*   *   *   *

I was sitting on a hay bale watching the last of the vampires braiding The Mare when Audrey Simmons came back to see me. She was wearing jeans and a T-shirt, her hair in pigtails, her face fresh-washed, and her eyes clear.

"What's the matter with your fingers, you're not braiding her yourself?"

"I caught them in the trailer door, Audrey. How's that nice big brown horse of yours?"

"Oh, okay, I guess. I haven't been riding him much, he's been lame the last couple of weeks.

"Bobby's got me back riding Linebacker." She didn't sound disappointed. "I really love that old horse, you know what I mean, Mr

Coulter? And Bobby's been looking after him better the last couple of months, you ought to see him."

"Good, Audrey. I'm glad to hear it."

"The thing is, I've won out of the limit division—"

"Yes?"

"And"—the words cascaded, like a shameful confession—"I don't know if I really want to show anymore, anyway, even if it didn't mean graduating to the junior division. I'd just like to, you know, *ride*. Ride, like, Linebacker. I guess that sounds pretty weird."

"Not at all, Audrey. Some people who ride, they may even love horses, who knows?—the two aren't always the same—shouldn't show them: they may lack the talent or the temperament, or have a wholly commendable sense of self-preservation. Instead of it being the celebration of a certain kind of communion, it too often becomes a single-character, ego-driven play, motivation supplied by others…outside. So if you love it, ride. Forget the showing. No one who counts will ever think the less of you."

Silence while she digested this speech.

"That's thirty-five. How many are you going to do?"

"Ninety-two."

The braider looked over his shoulder, consternation on his face, but then saw I was kidding.

"You're funny, you know that Mr Coulter?"

How's that, I asked her.

"You don't get all upset all the time. You laugh a lot."

"I do?" I thought for a moment. "Maybe because it's supposed to be fun, Audrey. It can get to be a lot of other things, too, but it ought to be fun. When it quits being fun, then it's no good."

"Yeah, well, Bobby's not that way. He's always laughing, but it's more like he's, you know, sniggering, all the time being sarcastic about somebody—"

"Well, now, maybe you shouldn't be so critical. Bobby's a fine rider. Your mother and father like him…"

"Not now, my father doesn't. You ought to hear him. He says Bobby's a bloodsucking slimeball who's going to force him to take Chapter Eleven, talking him into buying that brown horse and having to pay two commissions, and then interest on top of that—"

"…and he's got a dickens of a big barn, goes to all the shows, lots of nice kids—"

"Nice, schmice. Bunch of stuck-up snots is what they are. Who's got the most money, most expensive horse. And that isn't all. My *mother* says," said Audrey looking at me from under her lashes, "that she doesn't like the way Bobby looks at me."

"You're getting to be a big girl now, Audrey," I said.

"It isn't that I *mind* sticking my tits out," said Audrey thoughtfully. "But Bobby had me wearing this bra…"

"I think you're a lovely young lady right this minute," I told her hastily, "and you're going to be a Class A Number One Knock-out…and I think your chest looks just fine as it is."

"That'd be a great name for a horse," Audrey mused.

"What would?"

"Number One Knockout."

*   *   *   *

"Hi Mr Coulter."

"Hello, Stephen."

"Hi, Savannah, Claire. Hi, ladies."

The customers—mainly little girls—arrived in a wave, and instantly the neat aisleway and tack room were littered with diet soft drink cans, sugarless gum wrappers, whips, gloves, coats, numbers, hard hats, boot jacks, bags of carrots, and Coach handbags full of Clinique lipstick—"that's the only kind won't give you zits"—and small mirrors with pink plastic frames. There was a lot of chatter: "Oh, please, do my hair now" and "But Mr Coulter said he was going to buy hairnets" and "Yes"—whispered fiercely—"I know, but he always gets the wrong kind, with big holes" and "Nobody wears pins with their chokers any-more, I don't care if your grandmother did give it to you, it's so last year" and "I seriously think I'm going to be sick" and "I know I'll never remember the course" and "Did you see the syrup Freddy put on his hot cakes at breakfast—it was disgusting." Gloriously replete and unre-pentant, Freddy and his equally unregenerate sidekick, Tim Barber, in ready-tied ties and new, too-big shirts, stumped around chewing on toothpicks, looking red-faced and proud. Joe Chavez, aghast, mum-bled something unintelligible and fled in the direction of the restrooms.

"Is it true what Mr Sturtevant is saying, that you were champion at the Garden?" It was K.C., showing up just in the nick of time.

I assured her that there was nothing much to tell; it had all been years ago.

"You never said anything..." she continued doubtfully. Then, tak-ing a closer look at me, "Are you all right, Stephen? You look kind of peaked."

I promised her that there was nothing to worry about, I probably just had a touch of the flu. Fueled by the confidence-building exhilara-tion of actually being at the show and sparked by a fugitive bit of mis-placed maternal instinct, K.C. informed me that if I didn't feel up to it, please not to worry, she was perfectly capable of schooling the kids. After all, she pointed out, my class wasn't til the end of the afternoon and I might as well catch some rest if I had the chance.

Mrs Ratliff and the Stallings girls arrived with Honor Student, and started getting ready for the novice classes. Honor Student, I noted dourly, was sporting a large red ribbon tied in his tail: the warning that he was a kicker. Great. Just what was needed in the stable area.

K.C. and I gathered the kids for a pep talk outside the tackroom. I emphasized to those riding the three old veterans—Catherine Epps, Anita Morales, Dorothy Winegard, Timothy Barber, Freddy Bullard, and Karen Clayton—that they had an obligation to those grand old gents to take it easy on them in the warm-up, and not get carried away with excitement. Their eyes glazed over when I mentioned "duty" and "responsibility," but they were not bad kids and perhaps something would stick. I could but try.

*   *   *   *

I spent most of the morning dozing in the back of the six-horse, stirring from time to time to drink some water and pop a handful of aspirin.

Showing The Mare was so damned stupid, really. It wasn't as though she had a great bloodline, or blinding talent, or this was Devon, or I had something to prove. Lord of the Isles had been bred in the purple, welcomed by champagne in a comfortable foaling stall in Kentucky, sired by a Triple Crown winner undefeated in sixteen straight races, one over two miles, carrying top weight; his dam a stakes' winning mare by an imported winner of the St Leger. Unless I missed my guess Bitch Kitty'd first seen the light of day out in a West Texas pasture with her mother standing guard against wild dogs or the odd wild cat, sired by a tough fifteen-hand Texas-bred stallion whoop-and-a-holler over 300 yards, praise-the-Lord and pass the peach cordial, don't mind if I do, fire up the pickup, trailer to Ruidoso in the morning.

It wasn't as though she were some great established talent. Sure, I'd liked what I saw of her and felt over a fence, but I wasn't at all certain that wasn't because I hadn't seen or ridden anything really good to compare her with in a long time. Only memories of good horses, and a gut instinct telling me that this flighty, elegant creature might just have it in her to nail down eight fences solidly and look stylish while she was doing it. So far as showing went—producing a winning round on the right day at the right time and in the right place—she was a blank.

It wasn't as if this were some great show, either; it wasn't. No Michael Carney or Meyer Davis orchestra playing "New York, New York" and the tailcoats and evening gowns and drinks all night at

Twenty-One and your picture and a write up in *The Chronicle* or *Spur*, high point champion of the year. This was just another "B" show being held, so far as the horse world was concerned, in the middle of nowhere. Nothing that went on here would be likely to exert the slightest impact on the sports horse industry. Nationally, the most it would be remembered for would be the dressage judge homing in on a likely prospect for a customer Back East or the hunter judge telling the story of how he got indigestion from a Mexican dinner he'd insisted his hosts take him to. That was all.

Nor was it as though I had something to prove—but here I was lying. I did have something to prove. Not to others: I'd ridden on the "A" circuit and won. But to myself. More than anything, I realized, I wanted never to return to what I'd been at the end of summer, before the day I'd come across Roylett's body. A creature at pains to conceal himself and his feelings, keeping always a wary distance from others, reveling in an intellectual self-pity, rusting unburnished.

Showing The Mare was for me, not who I'd been. I would just have to trust her to look after me, the shape I was in.

I made an effort to relax joint by joint, limb by limb, muscle by muscle, and took stock of myself. My legs and lower trunk seemed to have suffered little or no damage: serviceably sound, as the rules had it. If I could just get a leg on each side, I reckoned I could sit her. Ah, but the rest! My neck was terminally stiff. It was a good thing I'd memorized the simple courses, for I'd never manage turning my head to look for the next jump. My shoulders and my arms were, despite the improvement wrought by the heat and bute, still excruciating and my hands and fingers were badly strained. If The Mare pulled one of her Bitch Kitty hissy-fits, sticking her head down like a toilet plunger and scampering off with the bit between her teeth, there was absolutely nothing I could do about it—I simply lacked the strength to do more than barely grasp the reins.

I'd known I was stretching things the day before when I got involved with the kids and been done out of a proper schooling session.

That would have been dicey enough, getting her out at the crack of dawn and praying nothing would go wrong to unsettle her for the rest of the day. But now that I was hurt I knew damned well that it was long odds against me making it around a course without a wreck, let alone a putting in a decent round. I'd have to take my chances warming up, pop over a practice jump, and go straight into the ring to be judged. The best I could hope for was to interfere with her balance minimally, and try to make it look as if it were all her own idea.

Showing The Mare was stupid.

CHAPTER 30

▼

Shortly before noon I pulled myself together and made my way up to the novice and limit ring to watch the Geriatric Ward in action. On the way I caught sight of Joan trotting out Harry across the diagonal of the dressage ring, a broad smile on Joan's face and Harry pumped up mightily and showing a lot of extension.

I arrived at the kids' ring just in time to see Kevin and Murray coming through with a third and a fourth for Anita and Tommy in the limit over fences. Karen, riding Warren, choked and lost her course, taking the little oxer backward and dissolving into tears as she was blown out of the ring. In novice equitation Catherine and Dorothy came in second and third. Pam Berry and the Stallings twins received two fifths and a sixth. All told, we had only two refusals, one of them, Murray with Freddy Bullard up, infusing the proceedings with a moment of high drama. When Murray stopped at the chicken coop, the red-faced Freddy, with murder in his heart, flourished his whip and shrilled out "motherfucker." This earned him not only a well-deserved tongue-lashing from the gray-haired lady judge, but guaranteed him instant celebrity among his pre-teen peers, a number of whom were clamoring for his autograph as he reached the out-gate.

None of the kids fell off, and I was heartened to see that, after they'd seen to their horses, most of them returned to the stands to cheer on their friends from the stable.

During lunch break, while I was tacking up The Mare to longe, Joan returned from her first dressage class. "I don't suppose you had a chance to see—"

"As a matter of fact, I did," I said. "But only for a moment, across a diagonal at an extended trot. You both looked great, the two of you. Were you pleased?"

"Very much so. He didn't pin his ears or switch his tail once. For the first time…"

"You look really happy, Joan."

"I am," she said. "I *am* happy." She blushed, color mantling her hawk's face. "I guess I've been pretty difficult during the last few months—"

"Not at all," I assured her. "You've got nothing to apologize for."

"Oh, yes I do," she said evenly. "One of the things is that I feel so foolish, all this time with you here, and I never realized"—she found blessed sanctuary in the academic phrase—"what your credentials were."

Rubbish, I told her. Absolute balderdash.

That elicited a smile. "And another thing." Her blush deepened. "You've probably heard. Huw's taken an interest in my book and it looks as though he's found me a publisher."

"And that means you'll get tenure. That's great, Joan. My congratulations."

"*If* I decide to stay; there's an opening at Wisconsin I'm looking into."

I murmured approvingly.

"They say my book can travel with me. And I hear there are some good stables near Madison. Perhaps you can help me."

"Of course," I said. "Be delighted."

"And," Joan looked me in the eye, "Carlotta and I are still friends."

*   *   *   *

I found a relatively flat piece of terrain down near the creek bottom where I could longe The Mare. As I let her out on the line, I noticed how she filled my eye: the fine head, with not a hint of coarseness at the throat-latch, broad chest, short, strong back, low-set hocks and high-set tail. She shook her head a time or two, but without putting pressure on the longe line. Then on her own volition she started out counterclockwise in a strong, well-balanced trot, feet two and two— near fore-off hind, off fore-near hind—evenly striking the ground, and for an instant between, she seemed suspended in the air, spurning the earth altogether. She made a very picture of feminine elegance and grace. I hoped fervently she'd stay that way, since I doubted if I could muster the strength necessary to hold her if she decided to come unglued and run off.

For the life of me I couldn't get a handle on how she'd be likely to act in the ring, with the unfamiliar fences, and the announcer, and the crowd. Once again I felt pretty stupid about deciding to show her.

*   *   *   *

Melnick turned up to watch. During the morning he'd found time to drive home and shower and change clothes. He was wearing dark gray trousers, a blue oxford shirt with small-figured tie, and a good-looking black-and-white herringbone sports coat. He was standing in the aisleway as I came out of the tackroom after putting on my breeches. "What's the matter?"

"I can't get my boots on. My hands are too sore to pull on the boot-hooks."

"Try these," Walter said, and held out a can of baby powder and a pair of nylon stockings he'd borrowed from his daughter.

*   *   *   *

When we heard my class being called over the public address system, the kids' classes were still going on, and our aisleway was deserted. Joe slipped back from his duties with K.C. up in the warm-up ring to lend me a hand saddling up.

Although the pain in my neck, shoulders, and arms was still intense, it was fractionally less than it had been, and sensation was seeping back into my fingers, putting me in mind of a time I'd been recovering from a near miss with frostbite, when it felt as though someone was holding the blue cone of an acetylene torch an inch from my ears.

I asked Walter to tie the reins in a kind of jockey's knot so that even if The Mare dropped her head through the floor they wouldn't rip right through my useless fingers and dangle dangerously to trip over. Climbing on proved to be a real production, with Melnick giving me a leg up and Joe standing by on the off side to catch me if I started to topple over.

What help I could give The Mare was limited to my seat and my legs. The best thing I could do was to try to sit still, advice I was in the habit of freely giving and which I realized anew was desperately difficult to put into action.

*   *   *   *

With twelve in my class, the hunter warm-up ring was crowded and I was apprehensive lest we be jostled and The Mare blow sky-high, so I stuck to the rail, well out of the way of Bobby Robberson hand-galloping a tall, rangy chestnut with a flashy stripe and white socks. I was about halfway down the order of start and finally Melnick was able to set a small fence which I trotted over a couple of times without incident.

Then the paddock master called our number and it was time for us to go in the ring.

*   *   *   *

To my astonishment The Mare evinced none of her usual ditzy Bitch Kitty tricks. She struck off into a balanced canter and made her circle to the first jump as if she were on tracks, heeding the pressure of my calf. We met the first fence with plenty of impulsion and proceeded smoothly down the outside. Responsive to my leg, she came out of the corner with her hocks under her and galloped steadily down to the fences on the diagonal, meeting them crisply, extending through the double and neatly changing hand in the corner before going down the other side. Her stride length couldn't have varied three inches coming down the second diagonal to the last fence—a single toward the out-gate—which she took off a booming solid stride. She came back to me immediately on landing and made a decorous circle before dropping back to a walk, stretching out her neck, and leaving the ring on a loose rein. There was an almost palpable buffet of applause from the packed stands.

Once in a long while you were given to, not taken from, and this was one of those times.

Generous-spirited, The Mare had baby sat me throughout the round while my contribution had been to sit still and not interfere. To the unknowledgeable onlooker, there should have been nothing remarkable about the round. Certainly nothing noticeable about the rider. Anyone could have done that, should have been the thought. The word *sprezzatura* came to mind, the art that concealed art: that's what you aimed for. It happened rarely—but it happened, even in Texas, in a relatively small show that would never get reported in *The Chronicle of the Horse*, and it was what made you love the sport.

*   *   *   *

"Nice round, Coulter," said Bobby Robberson, lying through his capped teeth as I left the ring. I patted The Mare's neck, slid off her, ran up the irons and loosened the girth, then handed her reins over to Joe who walked her around while we waited for the callback.

"Thanks, Bobby," I said. "You had a good round, too." What I'd seen of it, anyway. If you liked that kind of slightly jumpy handridden style he was so effective with. But you had to give him credit, he'd nailed down eight fences almost precisely alike.

*   *   *   *

The Mare got called back first to jog for soundness and Bobby's face, already suffused with blood, darkened even more as I took The Mare from Joe and managed to shuffle into a jog in front of the judge. Once I'd passed where he was standing I pulled out of the way of the others and stood The Mare up foursquare, neck extended, in a fashion that Kenny Wheeler or Sallie Sexton or Paul Fout, the best in the business, wouldn't have been ashamed of. Thanks to Joe's ministrations, her coat gleamed, her hoofs sparkled, her eye was bright: she looked enchanting.

The callback for soundness stood and the judge signed the card. As the ringmaster pinned The Mare's blue he told me to stay in the ring to have a picture taken while the trophy was being presented. I caught sight of the doctors Damon, standing ringside, attired in matching track suits and grinning idiotically. I signaled them to come in the ring, and the three of us stood together as a pretty girl held out the trophy. I wondered briefly if the Damons might have a change of heart about selling The Mare. As we walked toward the out-gate, the ringmaster called out after me, "Judge said tell you he's coming back to see you after the last class." Bobby, standing nearby explaining his loss to one of his sleek owners, cheered up visibly at hearing this, thinking perhaps that I was in for a tongue-lashing for some hitherto undiscovered offense.

*   *   *   *

A broadly smiling Joe awaited me at the out-gate, holding the stable's one respectable wool cooler. I handed Joe the reins, undid the girth, and took off the saddle, while Joe carefully arranged the cooler over the mare's back and loins.

One of the other grooms sidled up to him, said something, and stuck a bill in Joe's shirt pocket.

He laughed.

"Jesus, Joe, I think you had money riding on me."

Joe shook his head, still grinning.

I felt good for the first time that day, my aches and pains beginning to fade.

Melnick appeared, holding out a coffee cup. "Here, Rusty, you're through for the day, you could use this." I took a gulp and came up spluttering for air. Melnick looked hurt and clapped me on the back. "Damn, I thought you liked Wild Turkey."

*   *   *   *

"Neat round, Mr Coulter…"

Everybody was in a holiday mood back at the stalls, and an impromptu party was going full blast. Somebody had set up a boom box. Melnick showed up with a large picnic cooler full of iced beer and a bottle of Wild Turkey. A number of parents had brought soft drinks and various munchies, and Mary Linscomb and Tom Sturtevant had hauled in two ancient wicker hampers packed with sandwiches and white wine. Joan came in bearing a home-made chocolate cake and a Mason jar of pear cordial her mother had sent her.

Joe Chavez saw to it that The Mare's blue ribbon got pride of place up on the tackroom stable banner next to the other ribbons won during the day. I had to promise to return it to the Damons after the show. I noticed with amusement that they were still clutching the silver trophy possessively, and clearly apprehensive about letting the blue out of their sight; perhaps they weren't quite ready to sell The Mare.

We toasted the kids and The Mare and the future of Gordonwood.

K. C. was looking tremendously relieved, now that the kids—and horses—had got through the day and nobody hurt.

It was about then that I glanced down the aisleway and saw the judge—Harry Fitzgerald, a veteran pro I'd known for twenty-five years—at about the same time he caught sight of me. Harry, I recalled, was a bit on the deaf end, and when he spoke his words seemed to reverberate through the barn.

"Jesus, Rusty, it's good to see you, fella. Heard somewhere you'd gone to Texas, but, hell, didn't really hold out a lot of hope. Say, saw where that business at the Garden finally got straightened out. About time." He reached out to give me a hearty handshake, but I involuntarily backed away.

"Good to see you, Harry." I lifted my hands, palms out. "Got a little banged up."

His eyes narrowed in comprehension.

"What'd you have, a bit of a wreck? 'Fact, wasn't sure at first that was you riding, all hunched over, but I've got to say one thing, you sure-God left that mare alone, let her pick her own way. Came back to ask you, you free for dinner tomorrow night?"

"Nothing I'd rather do," I assured him. "Get a chance to visit, talk over old times. Listen, I've got some friends I'd like you to meet." I shepherded him around, introducing him to the group from the stable.

"Get yourself a drink, make yourself at home. I'll be right back, there's something I've got to do."

I left Harry contentedly recounting old and discreditable stories while Walter made sure that his glass remained full to the brim.

*   *   *   *

Bobby was at the concession stand buying a beer.

"Hey, Bobby, you got a minute? I need to talk to you."

He picked up his change and reluctantly turned to face me.

"Let's step over here." We walked ringside and sat in the empty stands, watching them drag the dirt and haul in jumps for the next day.

"Bobby, this might come as a shock to you, but you're going to have to return that Linebacker horse to K.C. Incidentally I want to thank you for doing exactly as I said; he's looking a hell of a lot better. And I must say, it was a good idea of yours, drop that lawsuit. What happened, couldn't get the vet to swear to the x-rays? Who was your attorney, anyway, some customer owed on a board bill, throw a scare into Mrs Gordon?"

"I...*what?*

"You're going to give Linebacker back to K.C. Otherwise I'm going to get you set down. You know what that means, getting set down by AHSF? No? Let me tell you."

Which I proceeded to do.

"You might want to how I'm going to get you set down.

"Two weeks ago, I got a call from Blair Foote. You know him. He told me there was this horse he'd had, showed working hunter last two years at Devon and Upperville. Not maybe a world-beater, but a pretty useful sort of horse. Come to find out he didn't quite have the tread depth on his Pirellis you need for the "A" circuit so Blair said he decided to sell him out of state. He'd make a great kids' or ami hunter, if whatever pro handled the deal saw to it he didn't take a pounding. 'Said you answered an ad he placed in *The Chronicle*, flew up, took a look, bought him. He explained it all to you, he said."

Bobby was contemptuous, amused. "Yeah, so what? I buy lots of horses."

"So what is, Blair says looking through *The Chronicle* the other day he saw his horse's picture winning up at the Dallas international—in the green hunter division. And that's against the rules, palming off a made horse as a greenie. Blair's mighty pissed off. Somebody starts complaining, puts him in a bad light."

"You're threatening to blackmail me—" Bobby was beginning to see that cloud no bigger than a man's hand on his clear horizon.

"Well, yes, I suppose you could say that."

"You're fucking nuts, is what I think, you know that?"

"'Thing is, Blair said he liked you. Instead of writing to the federation and getting mixed up in a pissing match, hearing committees and lawyers and depositions, he asked would I talk with you; he's going to send me a copy of the horse's show record, and the article and photo were in *The Chronicle*—"

"Bull*shit*. I ain't going to listen to this—"

"It's a real pity," I told him. "With what you enjoy the most—a tremendous amount of God-given talent—you're contented least. Listen to me, Bobby. I know professionals back East would give their right arm they had an eye for distances the way you do, how you can set a horse up coming into a fence without messing him up, your position over a fence.

"But that's not enough, is it, Bobby? Say this: right now you've still got all the talent in the world, but that talent of yours, that timing, they're not going to last forever. Do you ever think about that?"

He tried to laugh, but it was a bit uncertain.

"Those pros running show barns back East, they know talent's cheap. Riders are a dime a dozen, maybe not so talented as you, but some of them pretty damn good. You used to see them in their Gucci loafers coming around after the indoor circuit looking for a place to spend the winter before Palm Beach and the Arizona shows start up. But you hire them, next thing is you find them back of the barn with one of the customers packing nose candy. Thing is, *you can always find another rider*.

"You want to run a barn, a real show barn, you've got to have discipline. And that's what I don't know about you." I hesitated. "It's your call, Bobby, you can do anything you want."

He looked at me sullenly.

*   *   *   *

When I returned to the tack room I found that Art and Terri Simmons had joined the party. Terri looked very much in a holiday mood, wearing a scarlet, snugly-fitting, mostly unbuttoned knit shirt under an open waistcoat shimmering with sequined reindeer, Christmas trees, and glass ornaments. Art, in green suede blazer and check shirt, was listening open-mouthed to Harry Ferguson, while Terri talked animatedly with Tom Sturtevant.

I guessed word had spread that Tom was the new owner of Gordonwood. That one of the Gordonwood horses had won the pre-green and that the judge was rumored to be favoring the stable party with his presence had probably hastened their steps along to our stalls.

"You were just great, Stephen," Terri effervesced, briefly leaning forward and treating me to a glimpse of her exquisite bosom. "That was so exciting!" In her manner there was absolutely none of the antagonism she'd exhibited when I'd last seen her at Bobby's or when I'd called asking after Audrey. "Did you hear, we're thinking of moving from Hickory Creek?"

"Are you?" I asked politely. "No, I hadn't heard."

Walter was at my shoulder. "Rusty."

One of Bobby's grooms was leading a gray horse up the aisleway towards us.

"That looks like Linebacker," said Terri, surprised.

"Mrs. Gordon?"

"I'm...Mrs Gordon," said K.C., breaking off her conversation with one of the mothers.

"Mr Robberson say bring him to you, where you want me to put him?"

"Stick him in the next to last stall," I said. "Claire's gone on home with Flipper: he threw a shoe and tore up his foot, so she scratched him out of his other classes."

"Stephen. I don't understand."

"Here," I told K.C., handing her Linebacker's halter shank, "take him, he's yours. Thanks, Pete, and, say, tell Mr Robberson thanks, too."

"But I don't understand—"

"I'll explain it later. Just take him."

I looked at K.C. walking the old horse to his stall. On her face was the expression of an awestruck child vouchsafed a sight of Santa Claus.

"Say, isn't that the horse Audrey's been riding?" asked Art. "What's it doing here?"

"Bobby sent him over," Terri said. "He's K.C.'s." Then, to me: "Bobby was going to sell him to us."

"After we got squared away with the brown horse," Art put in.

"I thought you'd bought the brown horse," I said.

"Well, we did. We just hadn't finished paying for him—"

—at what astronomical sum I could only guess at—

—"and then he—"

"You see, there is this small problem with the brown horse," Terri admitted. Lameness, I expected. "and we didn't see why we ought to pay for damaged goods."

"And we were talking to Bobby about working a deal out with Line-backer—"

"Well, now you'll have to talk to K.C. about that," I said. "She's the new owner."

"But that's just wonderful, Art, don't you see?" You really had to hand it to Terri. She gave me her earnest slightly-furrowed brow look, made sure she had my attention, and leaned forward again. "The thing we really want to do is to come back to Gordonwood or whatever Tom

is going to call it, if he'll have us. Having learned our lesson. But everything we did was in Audrey's best interest, isn't that right?"

"Absolutely," said Art.

"And I know you're fond of Audrey, right? And so…no hard feelings?"

"It's Rusty's call," deadpanned Tom Sturtevant. They were the first
words he'd spoken.

"I'd love to have Audrey back," I said. "Just keep in mind that as a
boarder you've got two privileges: to do what I say, and to pay your
bills on time. Remember one thing. If by chance Audrey wants to
show, and I'm not at all sure she does, and you come to the show, I
don't want to see you in the stable area or the warm-up ring before a
class. She's a daughter anybody'd be proud to have, and this is her
thing, not yours. Understood?" Terri dropped her glance and Art
flushed.

"Okay," he said, finally. "I guess we can live with that."

"I think," Tom Sturtevant said judiciously, looking at his watch,
"it's about time for me to get back to town." He turned to go, trying to
hide a smile. "Are you coming, Sis?"

"No, I think I'll stay around here for a while." Mary looked at me.
"Perhaps Mr. Coulter can give me a ride home."

*   *   *   *

"…Zürs? It's not too late, darling." Seductive late-night transatlan-
tic blackcord fever. Serena and her friends, Concorde flights and champagne, chasing the sun and the snow and the hunting seasons.

Serena: chiseled profile and windflushed cheeks and sparkling hazel
eyes, the mass of platinum hair caught back artlessly, the old red Irish
gold and the emerald ring. The scent of Van Cleef & Arples's First.
These were all accessories, though fondly remembered, not a real person. Looking back on it, I knew we'd never had much more in common than the horses—God bless 'em!—and dogs and a certain kind of

life I thought I wanted. It had all been enough for me once, but no longer.

That's really very kind of you, I told Serena, but I'll think I'll stay here. I have holiday plans.

The little Christmas tree lights burned brightly.

Mary sitting on my ratty sofa smiled drowsily. Long legs curled under her, froth of slip riding up, strap fallen off one shoulder, loose cloud of brown silver-threaded hair and those lovely brown eyes. "What are you staring at?"

"At you."

"You, you're all over bruises, scars."

"New bruises, old scars...do you still have that watermelon silk blouse?"

"The one I wore the day we met? Of course I do. Say, did you ever hear that old song of Kurt Weill's from *Knickerbocker Holiday*: 'When lovely Venus lies beside/Her lord and master Mars/They mutually profit/By their scars'?"

The End

0-595-26455-7

.

Printed in the United States
21602LVS00002B/38